PRAISE FOR JAMES LEE BURKE

"James Lee Burke is the reigning champ of nostalgia noir."
—*The New York Times Book Review*

"A gorgeous prose stylist."

—Stephen King

"James Lee Burke is the heavyweight champ, a great American novelist whose work, taken individually or as a whole, is unsurpassed."
—Michael Connelly

"Burke's evocative prose remains a thing of reliably fierce wonder."
—*Entertainment Weekly*

"America's best novelist."

—*The Denver Post*

"Burke can touch you in ways few writers can."
—*The Washington Post*

"For five decades, Burke has created memorable novels that weave exquisite language, unforgettable characters, and social commentary into written tapestries that mirror the contemporary scene. His work transcends genre classification."
—*The Philadelphia Inquirer*

"Burke's writing [is] Faulkner-esque in its beauty, its feel on the ear like a southern breeze blowing through magnolia blossoms and oil fields."
—*Missoulian*

ALSO BY JAMES LEE BURKE

DAVE ROBICHEAUX NOVELS

Robicheaux
Light of the World
Creole Belle
The Glass Rainbow
Swan Peak
The Tin Roof Blowdown
Pegasus Descending
Crusader's Cross
Last Car to Elysian Fields
Jolie Blon's Bounce
Purple Cane Road
Sunset Limited
Burning Angel
Dixie City Jam
In the Electric Mist with Confederate Dead
A Stained White Radiance
A Morning for Flamingos
Black Cherry Blues
Heaven's Prisoners
The Neon Rain

HACKBERRY HOLLAND NOVELS

House of the Rising Sun
Wayfaring Stranger
Feast Day of Fools
Rain Gods
Lay Down My Sword and Shield

BILLY BOB HOLLAND NOVELS

In the Moon of Red Ponies
Bitterroot
Heartwood
Cimarron Rose

OTHER FICTION

The Jealous Kind
Jesus Out to Sea
White Doves at Morning
The Lost Get-Back Boogie
The Convict and Other Stories
Two for Texas
To the Bright and Shining Sun
Half of Paradise

Cadillac Jukebox

A NOVEL

James Lee Burke

Simon & Schuster Paperbacks
New York   London   Toronto   Sydney   New Delhi

Simon & Schuster Paperbacks
An Imprint of Simon & Schuster, Inc.
1230 Avenue of the Americas
New York, NY 10020

This Simon & Schuster trade paperback edition November 2018

SIMON & SCHUSTER PAPERBACKS and colophon are registered trademarks of Simon & Schuster, Inc.

For information about special discounts for bulk purchases, please contact Simon & Schuster Special Sales at 1-866-506-1949 or business@simonandschuster.com.

The Simon & Schuster Speakers Bureau can bring authors to your live event. For more information or to book an event, contact the Simon & Schuster Speakers Bureau at 1-866-248-3049 or visit our website at www.simonspeakers.com.

Manufactured in the United States of America

3 5 7 9 10 8 6 4 2

Library of Congress Control Number: 95050045

ISBN 978-1-9821-0032-2
ISBN 978-1-5011-2213-2 (ebook)

For Russ and Jayne Piazza

Chapter 1

Aaron Crown should not have come back into our lives. After all, he had never really been one of us anyway, had he? His family, shiftless timber people, had come from north Louisiana, and when they arrived in Iberia Parish, they brought their ways with them, occasionally stealing livestock along river bottoms, poaching deer, perhaps, some said, practicing incest.

I first saw Aaron Crown thirty-five years ago when, for a brief time, he tried to sell strawberries and rattlesnake watermelons out on the highway, out of the same truck he hauled cow manure in.

He seemed to walk sideways, like a crab, and wore bib overalls even in summertime and paid a dollar to have his head lathered and shaved in the barber shop every Saturday morning. His thick, hair-covered body gave off an odor like sour milk, and the barber would open the front and back doors and turn on the fans when Aaron was in the chair.

If there was a violent portent in his behavior, no one ever saw it. The Negroes who worked for him looked upon him indifferently, as a white man who was neither good nor bad, whose moods and elliptical peckerwood speech and peculiar green eyes were governed by thoughts and explanations known only to himself. To entertain the Negroes who hung around the shoeshine stand in front of the old Frederick Hotel on Saturday mornings, he'd scratch matches alight

1

on his clenched teeth, let a pool of paraffin burn to a waxy scorch in the center of his palm, flip a knife into the toe of his work boot.

But no one who looked into Aaron Crown's eyes ever quite forgot them. They flared with a wary light for no reason, looked back at you with a reptilian, lidless hunger that made you feel a sense of sexual ill ease, regardless of your gender.

Some said he'd once been a member of the Ku Klux Klan, expelled from it for fighting inside a Baptist church, swinging a wood bench into the faces of his adversaries.

But that was the stuff of poor-white piney woods folklore, as remote from our French-Catholic community as tales of lynchings and church bombings in Mississippi.

How could we know that underneath a live oak tree hung with moss and spiderwebs of blue moonlight, Aaron Crown would sight down the barrel of a sporterized Mauser rifle, his body splayed out comfortably like an infantry marksman's, the leather sling wrapped tightly around his left forearm, his loins tingling against the earth, and drill a solitary round through a plate glass window into the head of the most famous NAACP leader in Louisiana?

It took twenty-eight years to nail him, to assemble a jury that belonged sufficiently to a younger generation that had no need to defend men like Aaron Crown.

Everyone had always been sure of his guilt. He had never denied it, had he? Besides, he had never been one of us.

IT WAS EARLY fall, an election year, and each morning after the sun rose out of the swamp and burned the fog away from the flooded cypress trees across the bayou from my bait shop and boat-rental business, the sky would harden to such a deep, heart-drenching blue that you felt you could reach up and fill your hand with it like bolls of stained cotton. The air was dry and cool, too, and the dust along the dirt road by the bayou seemed to rise into gold columns of smoke and light through the canopy of oaks overhead. So when I glanced up from sanding the planks on my dock on a Saturday morning and saw Buford LaRose and his wife, Karyn, jogging through the long tunnel of trees toward me, they seemed like part of a photograph in a health magazine, part of an idealized moment caught by a creative photographer in a depiction of what is called the New South, rather than an oddity far removed from the refurbished plantation home in which they lived twenty-five miles away.

I convinced myself they had not come to see me, that forcing them to stop their run out of reasons of politeness would be ungenerous on my part, and I set down my sanding machine and walked toward the bait shop.

"Hello!" I heard Buford call.

Your past comes back in different ways. In this case, it was in the form of Karyn LaRose, her platinum hair sweat-soaked and piled on her head, her running shorts and purple-and-gold Mike the Tiger T-shirt glued to her body like wet Kleenex.

"How y'all doin'?" I replied, my smile as stiff as ceramic.

"Aaron Crown called you yet?" Buford asked, resting one hand on the dock railing, pulling one ankle up toward his muscular thigh with the other.

"How'd you know?" I said.

"He's looking for soft-hearted guys to listen to his story." Buford grinned, then winked with all the confidence of the eighty-yard passing quarterback he'd been at L.S.U. twenty years earlier. He was still lean-stomached and narrow-waisted, his chest flat like a prizefighter's, his smooth, wide shoulders olive with tan, his curly brown hair bleached on the tips by the sun. He pulled his other ankle up behind him, squinting at me through the sweat in his eyebrows.

"Aaron's decided he's an innocent man," he said. "He's got a movie company listening to him. Starting to see the big picture?"

"He gets a dumb cop to plead his cause?" I said.

"I said 'soft-hearted,'" he said, his face beaming now.

"Why don't you come see us more often, Dave?" Karyn asked.

"That sounds good," I said, nodding, my eyes wandering out over the water.

She raised her chin, wiped the sweat off the back of her neck, looked at the sun with her eyelids closed, and pursed her lips and breathed through them as though the air were cold. Then she opened her eyes again and smiled good-naturedly, leaning with both arms on the rail and stretching her legs one at a time.

"Y'all want to come in for something to drink?" I asked.

"Don't let this guy jerk you around, Dave," Buford said.

"Why should I?"

"Why should he call you in the first place?"

"Who told you this?" I asked.

"His lawyer."

"Sounds like shaky legal ethics to me," I said.

"Give me a break, Dave," he replied. "If Aaron Crown ever gets out of Angola, the first person he's going to kill is his lawyer. That's after he shoots the judge. How do we know all this? Aaron called up the judge, collect, mind you, and told him so."

They said good-bye and resumed their jog, running side by side past the sprinklers spinning among the tree trunks in my front yard. I watched them grow smaller in the distance, all the while feeling that somehow something inappropriate, if not unseemly, had just occurred.

I got in my pickup truck and caught up with them a quarter mile down the road. They never broke stride.

"This bothers me, Buford," I said out the window. "You wrote a book about Aaron Crown. It might make you our next governor. Now you want to control access to the guy?"

"Bothers you, huh?" he said, his air-cushioned running shoes thudding rhythmically in the dirt.

"It's not an unreasonable attitude," I said.

Karyn leaned her face past him and grinned at me. Her mouth was bright red, her brown eyes happy and charged with energy from her run.

"You'll be bothered a lot worse if you help these right-wing cretins take over Louisiana in November. See you around, buddy," he said, then gave me the thumbs-up sign just before he and his wife poured it on and cut across a shady grove of pecan trees.

* * *

SHE CALLED ME that evening, not at the house but at the bait shop. Through the screen I could see the lighted gallery and windows in my house, across the dirt road, up the slope through the darkening trees.

"Are you upset with Buford?" she said.

"No."

"He just doesn't want to see you used, that's all."

"I appreciate his concern."

"Should I have not been there?"

"I'm happy y'all came by."

"Neither of us was married at the time, Dave. Why does seeing me make you uncomfortable?"

"This isn't turning into a good conversation," I said.

"I'm not big on guilt. It's too bad you are," she replied, and quietly hung up.

The price of a velvet black sky bursting with stars and too much champagne, a grassy levee blown with buttercups and a warm breeze off the water, I thought. Celibacy was not an easy virtue to take into the nocturnal hours.

But guilt over an impulsive erotic moment wasn't the problem. Karyn LaRose was a woman you kept out of your thoughts if you were a married man.

AARON CROWN WAS dressed in wash-faded denims that were too tight for him when he was escorted in leg and waist chains from the lock-down unit into the interview room.

He had to take mincing steps, and because both wrists were cuffed to the chain just below his rib cage he had the bent appearance of an apelike creature trussed with baling wire.

"I don't want to talk to Aaron like this. How about it, Cap?" I said to the gunbull, who had been shepherding Angola convicts under a double-barrel twelve gauge for fifty-five years.

The gunbull's eyes were narrow and valuative, like a man constantly measuring the potential of his adversaries, the corners webbed with wrinkles, his skin wizened and dark as a mulatto's, as if it had been smoked in a fire. He removed his briar pipe from his belt, stuck it in his mouth, clicking it dryly against his molars. He never spoke while he unlocked the net of chains from Aaron Crown's body and let them collapse around his ankles like a useless garment. Instead, he simply pointed one rigid callus-sheathed index finger into Aaron's face, then unlocked the side door to a razor-wire enclosed dirt yard with a solitary weeping willow that had gone yellow with the season.

I sat on a weight lifter's bench while Aaron Crown squatted on his haunches against the fence and rolled a cigarette out of a small leather pouch that contained pipe tobacco. His fingernails were the thickness and mottled color of tortoiseshell. Gray hair grew out of his ears and nose; his shoulders and upper chest were braided with knots of veins and muscles. When he popped a lucifer match on his thumbnail and cupped it in the wind, he inhaled the sulfur and glue and smoke all in one breath.

"I ain't did it," he said.

"You pleaded nolo contendere, partner."

"The shithog got appointed my case done that. He said it was worked out." He drew in on his hand-rolled cigarette, tapped the ashes off into the wind.

When I didn't reply, he said, "They give me forty years. I was sixty-eight yestiday."

"You should have pleaded out with the feds. You'd have gotten an easier bounce under a civil rights conviction," I said.

"You go federal, you got to cell with colored men." His eyes lifted into mine. "They'll cut a man in his sleep. I seen it happen."

In the distance I could see the levee along the Mississippi River and trees that were puffing with wind against a vermilion sky.

"Why'd you choose me to call?" I asked.

"You was the one gone after my little girl when she got lost in Henderson Swamp."

"I see . . . I don't know what I can do, Aaron. That was your rifle they found at the murder scene, wasn't it? It had only one set of prints on it, too—yours."

"It was stole, and it didn't have no *set* of prints on it. There was one thumbprint on the stock. Why would a white man kill a nigger in the middle of the night and leave his own gun for other people to find? Why would he wipe off the trigger and not the stock?"

"You thought you'd never be convicted in the state of Louisiana."

He sucked on a tooth, ground out the ash of his cigarette on the tip of his work boot, field-stripped the paper and let it all blow away in the wind.

"I ain't did it," he said.

"I can't help you."

He raised himself to his feet, his knees popping, and walked toward the lockdown unit, the silver hair on his arms glowing like a monkey's against the sunset.

Chapter
2

THE FLOODED CYPRESS and willow trees were gray-green smudges in the early morning mist at Henderson Swamp. My adopted daughter, Alafair, sat on the bow of the outboard as I swung it between two floating islands of hyacinths and gave it the gas into the bay. The air was moist and cool and smelled of schooled-up *sac-a-lait*, or crappie, and gas flares burning in the dampness. When Alafair turned her face into the wind, her long Indian-black hair whipped behind her in a rope. She was fourteen now, but looked older, and oftentimes grown men turned and stared at her when she walked by, before their own self-consciousness corrected them.

We traversed a long, flat bay filled with stumps and abandoned oil platforms, then Alafair pointed at a row of wood pilings that glistened blackly in the mist. I cut the engine and let the boat float forward on its wake while Alafair slipped the anchor, a one-foot chunk of railroad track, over the gunwale until it bit into the silt and the bow swung around against the rope. The water in the minnow bucket was cold and dancing with shiners when I dipped my hand in to bait our lines.

"Can you smell the *sac-a-lait*? There must be thousands in here," she said.

"You bet."

"This is the best place in the whole bay, isn't it?"

"I don't know of a better one," I said, and handed her a sandwich after she had cast her bobber among the pilings.

It had been almost nine years since I had pulled her from the submerged and flooded wreckage of a plane that had been carrying Salvadoran war refugees. Sometimes in my sleep I would relive that moment when I found her struggling for breath inside the inverted cabin, her face turned upward like a guppy's into the wobbling and diminishing bubble of air above her head, her legs scissoring frantically above her mother's drowned form.

But time has its way with all of us, and today I didn't brood upon water as the conduit into the world of the dead. The spirits of villagers, their mouths wide with the concussion of airbursts, no longer whispered to me from under the brown currents of the Mekong, either, nor did the specter of my murdered wife Annie, who used to call me up long-distance from her home under the sea and speak to me through the rain.

Now water was simply a wide, alluvial flood plain in the Atchafalaya Basin of south Louisiana that smelled of humus and wood smoke, where mallards rose in squadrons above the willows and trailed in long black lines across a sun that was as yellow as egg yoke.

"You really went to see that man Aaron Crown at Angola, Dave?" Alafair asked.

"Sure did."

"My teacher said he's a racist. He assassinated a black man in Baton Rouge."

"Aaron Crown's an ignorant and physically ugly man. He's the kind of person people like to hate. I'm not sure he's a killer, though, Alf."

"Why not?"

"I wish I knew."

Which was not only an inadequate but a disturbing answer.

Why? Because Aaron Crown didn't fit the profile. If he was a racist, he didn't burn with it, as most of them did. He wasn't political, either, at least not to my knowledge. So what was the motivation, I asked myself. In homicide cases, it's almost always money, sex, or power. Which applied in the case of Aaron Crown?

"Whatcha thinking about, Dave?" Alafair asked.

"When I was a young cop in New Orleans, I was home on vacation and Aaron Crown came to the house and said his daughter was lost out here in a boat. Nobody would go after her because she was fourteen and had a reputation for running off and smoking dope and doing other kinds of things, you with me?"

She looked at her bobber floating between the pilings.

"So I found her. She wasn't lost, though. She was in a houseboat, right across the bay there, with a couple of men. I never told Aaron what she had been doing. But I think he knew."

"You believe he's innocent?"

"Probably not. It's just one of those strange deals, Alf. The guy loved his daughter, which means he has emotions and affections like the rest of us. That's something we don't like to think about when we assign a person the role of assassin and community geek."

She thought the word *geek* was funny and snorted through her nose.

It started to sprinkle, and we hung raincoats over our heads like cloistered monks and pulled *sac-a-lait* out of the pilings until mid-morning, then layered them with crushed ice in the cooler and headed for home just as a squall churned out of the south like smoke twisting inside a bottle.

WE GUTTED AND half-mooned the fish at the gills and scaled them with spoons under the canvas tarp on the dock. Batist, the black man who worked for me, came out of the bait shop with an unlit cigar stuck in his jaw. He let the screen slam behind him. He was bald and wore bell-bottomed blue jeans and a white T-shirt that looked like rotted cheesecloth on his barrel chest.

"There's a guard from the prison farm inside," he said.

"What's he want?" I said.

"I ain't axed. Whatever it is, it don't have nothing to do with spending money. Dave, we got to have these kind in our shop?"

Oh boy, I thought.

I went inside and saw the old-time gunbull from the lockdown unit I had visited at Angola just yesterday. He was seated at a back table by the lunch meat cooler, his back stiff, his profile carved out of teak. He wore a fresh khaki shirt and trousers, a hand-tooled belt, a white straw hat slanted over his forehead. His walking cane, whose point was sheathed in a six-inch steel tube, the kind road gang hacks used to carry, was hooked by the handle over the back of his chair. He had purchased a fifty-cent can of soda to drink with the brown paper bag of ginger snaps he had brought with him.

"How's it goin', Cap?" I said.

"Need your opinion on something," he replied. His accent was north Louisiana hill country, the vowels phlegmy and round and deep in the throat, like speech lifted out of the nineteenth century.

His hands, which were dotted with liver spots, shook slightly with palsy. His career reached back into an era when Angola convicts were beaten with the black Betty, stretched out on anthills, locked down in sweatboxes on Camp A, sometimes even murdered by guards on a whim and buried in the Mississippi levee. In the years I had known him I had never seen him smile or heard him mention any form of personal life outside the penitentiary.

"Some movie people is offered me five thousand dollars for a interview about Crown. What do you reckon I ought to do?" he said.

"Take it. What's the harm?"

He bit the edge off a ginger snap.

"I got the feeling they want me to say he don't belong up there on the farm, that maybe the wrong man's in prison."

"I see."

"Something's wrong, ain't it?"

"Sir?"

"White man kills a black man down South, them Hollywood people don't come looking to get the white man off."

"I don't have an answer for you, Cap. Just tell them what you think and forget about it." I looked at the electric clock on the wall above the counter.

"What I think is the sonofabitch's about half-human." My eyes met his. "He's got a stink on him don't wash off. If he ain't killed the NAACP nigger, he done it to somebody else."

He chewed a ginger snap dryly in his jaw, then swallowed it with a small sip of soda, the leathery skin of his face cobwebbed with lines in the gloom.

WORD TRAVELS FAST among the denizens of the nether regions.

On Tuesday morning Helen Soileau came into my office at the Iberia Parish Sheriff's Department and said we had to pick up and hold a New Orleans hoodlum named Mingo Bloomberg, who was wanted as a material witness in the killing of a police officer in the French Quarter.

"You know him?" she asked. She wore a starched white shirt and blue slacks and her badge on her gunbelt. She was a blonde, muscular woman whose posture and bold stare always seemed to anticipate, even relish, challenge or insult.

"He's a button man for the Giacano family," I said.

"We don't have that."

"Bad communications with NOPD, then. Mingo's specialty is disappearing his victims. He's big on fish chum."

"That's terrific. Expidee Chatlin is baby-sitting him for us."

We checked out a cruiser and drove into the south part of the parish on back roads that were lined with sugarcane wagons on their way to the mill. Then we followed a levee through a partially cleared field to a tin-roofed fish camp set back in a grove of persimmon and pecan trees. A cruiser was parked in front of the screened-in gallery, the front doors opened, the radio turned off.

Expidee Chatlin had spent most of his law-enforcement career as a crossing guard or escorting drunks from the jail to guilty-court. He had narrow shoulders and wide hips, a tube of fat around his waist, and a thin mustache that looked like grease pencil. He and another uniformed deputy were eating sandwiches with Mingo Bloomberg at a plank table on the gallery.

"What do you think you're doing, Expidee?" Helen asked.

"Waiting on y'all. What's it look like?" he replied.

"How's it hanging, Robicheaux?" Mingo Bloomberg said.

"No haps, Mingo."

He emptied his beer can and put an unlit cigarette in his mouth. He was a handsome man and wore beltless gray slacks and loafers and a long-sleeved shirt printed with flowers. His hair was copper-colored and combed straight back on his scalp, his eyes ice blue, as invasive as a dirty finger when they locked on yours.

He opened his lighter and began to flick the flint dryly, as though we were not there.

"Get out of that chair and lean against the wall," Helen said.

He lowered the lighter, his mouth screwed into a smile around his cigarette. She pulled the cigarette out of his mouth, threw it over her shoulder, and aimed her nine millimeter into the middle of his face.

"Say something wise, you fuck. Go ahead. I want you to," she said.

I pulled him to his feet, pushed him against the wall, and kicked his ankles apart. When I shook him down I tapped a hard, square object in his left pocket. I removed a .25 caliber automatic, dropped the magazine, pulled the slide back on the empty chamber, then tossed the pistol into Expidee's lap.

"Nobody told me. I thought the guy was suppose to be a witness or something," he said.

Helen cuffed Mingo's wrists behind him and shoved him toward the screen door.

"Hey, Robicheaux, you and the lady take your grits off the stove," he said.

"It's up to you, Mingo," I said.

We were out front now, under a gray sky, in the wind, in leaves that toppled out of the trees on the edge of the clearing. Mingo rolled his eyes. "Up to me? You ought to put a cash register on top of y'all's cruiser," he said.

"You want to explain that?" I said.

He looked at Helen, then back at me.

"Give us a minute," I said to her.

I walked him to the far side of our cruiser, opened the back door, and sat him down behind the wire-mesh screen. I leaned one arm on the roof and looked down into his face. An oiled, coppery strand of hair fell down across his eyes.

"You did the right thing with this guy Crown. You do the right thing, you get taken care of. Something wrong with that?" he said.

"Yeah. I'm not getting taken care of."

"Then that's your fucking problem."

"When you get back to the Big Sleazy, stay there, Mingo," I said, and closed the car door.

"I got a permit for the piece you took off me. I want it back," he said through the open window.

I waited for Helen to get behind the wheel, drumming my fingers on the cruiser's roof, trying to conceal the disjointed expression on my face.

IF YOU SERIOUSLY commit yourself to alcohol, I mean full-bore, the way you take up a new religion, and join that great host of revelers who sing and lock arms as they bid farewell to all innocence in their lives, you quickly learn the rules of behavior in this exclusive fellowship whose dues are the most expensive in the world. You drink down. That means you cannot drink in well-lighted places with ordinary people because the psychological insanity in your face makes you a pariah among them. So you find other drunks whose condition is as bad as your own, or preferably even worse.

But time passes and you run out of geography and people who are in some cosmetic way less than yourself and bars where the only admission fee is the price of a 6 A.M. short-dog.

That's when you come to places like Sabelle Crown's at the Underpass in Lafayette.

The Underpass area had once been home to a dingy brick hotel and row of low-rent bars run by a notorious family of Syrian criminals. Now the old bars and brick hotel had been bulldozed into rubble, and all that remained of the city's last skid-row refuge was Sabelle's, a dark, two-story clapboard building that loomed above the Underpass like a solitary tooth.

It had no mirrors, and the only light inside came from the juke-box and the beer signs over the bar. It was a place where the paper Christmas decorations stayed up year-round and you never had to see your reflection or make an unfavorable comparison between yourself and others. Not unless you counted Sabelle, who had been a twenty-dollar whore in New Orleans before she disappeared up north for several years. She was middle-aged now, with flecks of gray in her auburn hair, but she looked good in her blue jeans and V-necked beige sweater, and her face retained a kind of hard beauty that gave fantasies to men who drank late and still believed the darkness of a bar could resurrect opportunities from their youth.

She opened a bottle of 7-Up and set it in front of me with a glass of ice.

"You doin' all right, Streak?" she said.

"Not bad. How about you, Sabelle?"

"I hope you're not here for anything stronger than Seven-Up."

I smiled and didn't reply. The surface of the bar stuck to my wrists. "Why would a New Orleans gumball named Mingo Bloomberg have an interest in your father?" I said.

"You got me."

"I went over everything I could find on Aaron's case this afternoon. I think he could have beat it if he'd had a good lawyer," I said.

She studied my face curiously. The beer sign on the wall made tiny red lights, like sparks, in her hair.

"The big problem was Aaron told some other people he did it," I said.

She put out her cigarette in the ashtray, then set a shot glass and a bottle of cream sherry by my elbow and walked down the duck-boards and around the end of the bar and sat down next to me, her legs hooked in the stool's rungs.

"You still married?" she said.

"Sure."

She didn't finish her thought. She poured sherry into her shot glass and drank it. "Daddy went to the third grade. He hauled manure for a living. Rich people on East Main made him go around to their back doors."

I continued to look into her face.

"Look, when this black civil rights guy got killed with Daddy's rifle, he started making up stories. People talked about him. He got to be a big man for a while," she said.

"He lied about a murder?"

"How'd you like to be known as white trash in a town like New Iberia?"

"Big trade-off," I said.

"What isn't?"

She gestured to the bartender, pointed to a shoebox under the cash register. He handed it to her and walked away. She lifted off the top.

"You were in the army. See what you recognize in there. I don't know one medal from another," she said.

It was heavy and filled with watches, rings, pocketknives, and military decorations. Some of the latter were Purple Hearts; at least two were Silver Stars. It also contained a .32 revolver with electrician's tape wrapped on the grips.

"If the medal's got a felt-lined box, I give a three-drink credit," she said.

"Thanks for your time," I said.

"You want to find out about my father, talk to Buford LaRose. His book sent Daddy to prison."

"I might do that."

"When you see Buford, tell him—" But she shook her head and didn't finish. She pursed her lips slightly and kissed the air.

I WENT HOME FOR lunch the next day, and as I came around the curve on the bayou I saw Karyn LaRose's blue Mazda convertible back out of my drive and come toward me on the dirt road. She stopped abreast of me and removed her sunglasses. Her teeth were white when she smiled, her tanned skin and platinum hair dappled with sunlight that fell through the oak trees.

"What's up, Karyn?"

"I thought this would be a grand time to have y'all out."

"I beg your pardon?"

"Oh, stop all this silliness, Dave."

"Listen, Karyn—"

"See you, kiddo," she said, shifted into first, and disappeared in my rearview mirror, her hair whipping in the wind.

I PULLED INTO OUR dirt drive and parked by the side of the house, which had been built out of notched and pegged cypress during the Depression by my father, a huge, grinning, hard-drinking Cajun who was killed on the salt in an oil well blowout. Over the years the tin roof on the gallery had turned purple with rust and the wood planks in the walls had darkened and hardened with rain and dust storms and smoke from stubble fires. My wife, Bootsie, and I had hung baskets of impatiens from the gallery, put flower boxes in the windows, and planted the beds with roses, hibiscus, and hydrangeas, but in the almost year-round shade of the live oaks and pecan trees, the house had a dark quality that seemed straight out of the year 1930, as though my father still held claim to it.

Bootsie had fixed ham and onion sandwiches and iced tea and potato salad for lunch, and we set the kitchen table together and sat down to eat. I kept waiting for her to mention Karyn's visit. But she didn't.

"I saw Karyn LaRose out on the road," I said.

"Oh, yes, I forgot. Tomorrow evening, she wants us to come to a dinner and lawn party."

"What did you tell her?"

"I didn't think we had anything planned. But I said I'd ask you." She had stopped eating. I felt her eyes on my face. "You don't want to go?"

"Not really."

"Do you have a reason? Or do we just tell people to drop dead arbitrarily?"

"Buford's too slick for me."

"He's a therapist and a university professor. Maybe the state will finally have a governor with more than two brain cells."

"Fine, let's go. It's not a problem," I said.

"*Dave . . .*"

"I'm looking forward to it."

Finally her exasperation gave way to a smile, then to a laugh.

"You're too much, Streak," she said.

I wiped at my mouth with my napkin, then walked around behind her chair, put my arms on her shoulders, and kissed her hair. It was the color of dark honey and she brushed it in thick swirls on her head, and it always smelled like strawberry shampoo. I kissed her along the cheek and touched her breasts.

"You doin' anything?" I said.

"You have to go back to work."

"The perps will understand."

She reached behind the chair and fitted her hand around the back of my thigh.

The curtains in the bedroom, which were white and gauzy and printed with tiny flowers, puffed and twisted in the wind that blew through the trees in the yard. When Bootsie undressed, her body seemed sculpted, glowing with light against the window. She had the most beautiful complexion of any woman I ever knew; when she made love it flushed with heat, as though she had a fever, and took on the hue of a new rose petal. I kissed her breasts and took her nipples in my mouth and traced my fingers down the flatness of her stomach, then I felt her reach down and take me in her palm.

When I entered her she hooked her legs in mine and laced the fingers of one hand in my hair and placed the other hand hard in the small of my back. I could feel her breath against the side of my face, the perspiration on her stomach and inside her thighs, then her tongue on my neck, the wetness of her mouth near my ear. I wanted to hold it, to give more satisfaction than I received, but that terrible moment of male pleasure and solitary indulgence had its way.

"Boots—" I said hoarsely.

"It's all right, Dave. Go ahead," she whispered.

She ran both palms down my lower back and pushed me deeper inside, then something broke like a dam and melted in my loins and I closed my eyes and saw a sailfish rise from a cresting wave, its mouth torn with a hook, its skin blue and hard, its gills strung with pink foam. Then it disappeared into the wave again, and the groundswells were suddenly flat and empty, dented with rain, sliding across the fire coral down below.

IT SHOULD HAVE been a perfect afternoon. But on my way out Bootsie asked, almost as an afterthought, "Was there any other reason you didn't want to go to the LaRoses'?"

"No, of course not."

I tried to avert my eyes, but it was too late. I saw the recognition in her face, like a sharp and unexpected slap.

"It was a long time ago, Boots. Before we were married."

She nodded, her thoughts concealed. Then she said, her voice flat, "We're all modern people these days. Like you say, Streak, no problem."

She walked down to the pond at the back of our property by herself, with a bag of bread crusts, to feed the ducks.

Chapter
3

AT SUNRISE THE next day, while I was helping Batist open up the bait shop before I went to work, the old-time gunbull called me long-distance from Angola.

"You remember I told you about them movie people come see me? There's one ain't gonna be around no more," he said.

"What happened, Cap?"

"My nephew's a uniform at NOPD in the First District. They thought it was just a white man interested in the wrong piece of jelly roll. That's till they found the camera," he said.

After I hung up the phone I filled minnow buckets for two fishermen, put a rental outboard in the water, and pulled the tarp on guy wires over the spool tables on the dock in case it rained. Batist was sprinkling hickory chips on the coals in the barbecue pit, which we had fashioned from a split oil drum to cook chickens and links of sausage for our midday customers.

"That was that old man from up at the prison farm?" he asked.

"I'm afraid so."

"I ain't going to say it but once, no. It don't matter what that kind of man bring into your life, it ain't no good."

"I'm a police officer, podna. I can't always be selective about the people I talk to."

He cut his head and walked away.

21

I left a message for the nephew at NOPD and drove to the office just as it started to mist. He returned my call two hours later, then turned over the telephone to a Homicide detective. This is how I've reconstructed the story that was told to me.

VICE HAD IDENTIFIED the hooker as Brandy Grissum, a black twenty-five-year-old heroin addict who had done a one-bit in the St. John the Baptist jail for sale and possession.

She worked with three or four pimps and Murphy artists out of the Quarter. The pimps were there for the long-term regular trade. The Murphy artists took down the tourists, particularly those who were drunk, married, respectable, in town on conventions, scared of cops and their employers.

It was an easy scam. Brandy would walk into a bar, well dressed, perhaps wearing a suit, sit at the end of the counter, or by herself in a booth, glance once into the john's face, her eyes shy, her hands folded demurely in front of her, then wait quietly while her partner cut the deal.

This is the shuck: "My lady over there ain't a reg'lar, know what I'm sayin'? Kind of like a schoolgirl just out on the town." Here he smiles. "She need somebody take her 'round the world, know what I'm sayin'? I need sixty dollars to cover the room, we'll all walk down to it, I ain't goin' nowhere on you. Then you want to give her a present or something, that's between y'all."

The difference in the scenario this time was the john had his own room as well as agenda.

His name was Dwayne Parsons, an Academy Award nominee and two-time Emmy winner for his documentary scripts. But Dwayne Parsons had another creative passion, too, one that was unknown to the hooker and the Murphy artist and a second black man who was about to appear soon—a video camera set up on a tripod in his closet, the lens pointed through a crack in the door at the waterbed in his leased efficiency apartment a block off Bourbon.

Parsons and the woman were undressed, on top of black satin

sheets, when the hard, insistent knock came at the door. The man's head jerked up from the pillow, his face at first startled, then simply disconcerted and annoyed.

"They'll go away," he said.

He tried to hold her arms, hold her in place on top of him, but she slid her body off his.

"It's my boyfriend. He don't let me alone. He's gonna break down the do'," she said. She began to gather her clothes in front of her breasts and stomach.

"Hey, I look like a total schmuck to you?" Parsons said. "Don't open that door . . . Did you hear me . . . Listen, you fucking nigger, you're not hustling me."

She slid back the deadbolt on the door, and suddenly the back and conked and side-shaved head of a gargantuan black man were in the lens. Whoever he was, he was not the man Brandy Grissum had expected. She swallowed as though she had a razor blade in her throat.

But Dwayne Parsons was still not with the script.

"You want to rob me, motherfucker, just take the money off the dresser. You get the gun at the Screen Actors Guild?" he said.

The black man with the gun did not speak. But the terror in the woman's face left no doubt about the decision she saw taking place in his.

"I ain't seen you befo', bitch. You trying to work independent?" he said.

"No . . . I mean yes, I don't know nobody here. I ain't from New Orleans." She pressed her clothes against her breasts and genitalia. Her mouth was trembling.

One block away, a brass street band was playing on Bourbon. The man thought some more, then jerked the barrel of his automatic toward the door. She slipped her skirt and blouse on, wadded up her undergarments and shoes and purse, and almost flew out the door.

Dwayne Parsons's face had drained. He started to get up from the bed.

"No, no, my man," the black man said, approaching him, blocking off the camera's view of Parsons's face. "Hey, it comes to everybody.

You got it on with the sister. It could be worse. I said don't move, man. It's all gonna come out the same way. They ain't no need for suffering."

He picked up a pillow, pressed it down in front of him, his upper arm swelling to the diameter and hardness of a fireplug while Dwayne Parsons's body flopped like a fish's. The man with the gun stepped back quickly and fired two shots into the pillow—*pop, pop*—and then went past the camera's lens, one grizzled Cro-Magnon jaw and gold tooth flashing by like a shark's profile in a zoo tank.

In the distance the street band thundered out "Fire House Blues." Dwayne Parsons's body, the head still covered by the pillow, looked like a broken white worm in the middle of the sheet.

THE LAROSE PLANTATION was far out in the parish, almost to St. Martinville. The main house had been built in 1857 and was the dusty color of oyster shells, its wide, columned front porch scrolled by live oak trees that grew to the third floor. A row of shacks in back that had once been slave quarters was now stacked with baled hay, and the old brick smithy had been converted into a riding stable, the arched windows sealed by the original iron shutters, which leaked orange rust as though from a wound.

Bootsie and I drove past the LaRose company store, with its oxidized, cracked front windows and tin-roofed gallery, where barrels of pecans sat by the double screen doors through which thousands of indebted tenants had passed until the civil rights era of the 1960s brought an end to five-dollar-a-day farm labor; then we turned into a white-fenced driveway that led to the rear of the home and the lawn party that was already in progress against a backdrop of live oaks and Spanish moss and an autumnal rose-stippled sky that seemed to reassure us all that the Indian summer of our lives would never end.

While the buffet was being laid out on a row of picnic tables, Buford organized a touch football game and prevailed even upon the most reluctant guests to put down their drinks and join one team or another. Some were from the university in Lafayette but most were people well known in the deceptively lighthearted and carnivallike atmosphere of Louisiana politics. Unlike their counterparts from the piney woods parishes to the north, they were bright, educated, openly hedonistic, always convivial, more concerned about violations of protocol than ideology.

They were fun to be with; they were giddy with alcohol and the exertion of the game, their laughter tinkling through the trees each time the ball was snapped and there was a thumping of feet across the sod and a loud pat of hands on the rump.

Then a white-jacketed black man dinged a metal triangle and everyone filed happily back toward the serving tables.

"Run out, Dave! Let me throw you a serious one!" Buford hollered, the football poised in his palm. He wore tennis shoes, pleated white slacks, the arms of his plum-colored sweater tied around his neck.

"That's enough for me," I said.

"Don't give me that 'old man' act," he said and cocked his arm to fire a bullet, then smiled and lofted an easy, arching pass that dropped into my hands as though he had plopped it into a basket.

He caught up to me and put his hand on my shoulder.

"Wow, you feel like a bag of rocks. How much iron do you pump?" he said.

"Just enough to keep from falling apart."

He slipped the football out of my hands, flipped it toward the stable. He watched it bounce and roll away in the dusk, as though he were looking at an unformed thought in the center of his mind.

"Dave, I think we're going to win next month," he said.

"That's good."

"You think you could live in Baton Rouge?"

"I've never thought about it."

Someone turned on the Japanese lanterns in the trees. The air smelled of pecan husks and smoke from a barbecue pit dug in the earth. Buford paused.

"How'd you like to be head of the state police?" he asked.

"I was never much of an administrator, Buford."

"I had a feeling you'd say something like that."

"Oh?"

"Dave, why do you think we've always had the worst state government in the union? It's because good people don't want to serve in it. Is the irony lost on you?"

"I appreciate the offer."

"You want to think it over?"

"Sure, why not?"

"That's the way," he said, and then was gone among his other guests, his handsome face glowing with the perfection of the evening and the portent it seemed to represent.

Karyn walked among the tree trunks toward me, a paper plate filled with roast duck and venison and dirty rice in one hand, a Corona bottle and cone-shaped glass with a lime slice inserted on the rim gripped awkwardly in the other. My eyes searched the crowd for Bootsie.

"I took the liberty," Karyn said, and set the plate and glass and beer bottle down on a table for me.

"Thank you. Where'd Boots go?"

"I think she's in the house."

She sat backward on the plank bench, her legs crossed. She had tied her hair up with a red bandanna and had tucked her embroidered denim shirt tightly into her blue jeans. Her face was warm, still flushed from the touch football game. I moved the Corona bottle and glass toward her.

"You don't drink at all anymore?" she said.

"Nope."

"You want a Coke?"

"I'm fine, Karyn."

"Did Buford talk to you about the state police job?"

"He sure did."

"Gee, Dave, you're a regular blabbermouth, aren't you?"

I took a bite of the dressing, then rolled a strip of duck meat inside a piece of French bread and ate it.

Her eyes dilated. "Did he offend you?" she said.

"Here's the lay of the land, Karyn. A hit man for the New Orleans mob, a genuine sociopath by the name of Mingo Bloomberg, told me I did the right thing by not getting involved with Aaron Crown. He said I'd get taken care of. Now I'm offered a job."

"I don't believe you."

"Believe what?"

"*You*. Your fucking presumption and self-righteousness."

"What I told you is what happened. You can make of it what you want."

She walked away through the shadows, across the leaves and molded pecan husks to where her husband was talking to a group of people. I saw them move off together, her hands gesturing while she spoke, then his face turning toward me.

A moment later he was standing next to me, his wrists hanging loosely at his sides.

"I'm at a loss, Dave. I have a hard time believing what you told Karyn," he said.

I laid my fork in my plate, wadded up my paper napkin and dropped it on the table.

"Maybe I'd better go," I said.

"You've seriously upset her. I don't think it's enough just to say you'll go."

"Then I apologize."

"I know about your and Karyn's history. Is that the cause of our problem here? Because I don't bear a resentment about it."

I could feel a heat source inside me, like someone cracking open the door on a woodstove.

"Listen, partner, a guy like Mingo Bloomberg isn't an abstraction. Neither is a documentary screenwriter who just got whacked in the Quarter," I said.

His expression was bemused, almost doleful, as though he were looking down at an impaired person.

"Good night to you, Dave. I believe you mean no harm," he said, and walked back among his guests.

I stared at the red sun above the sugarcane fields, my face burning with embarrassment.

Chapter
4

IT WAS RAINING hard and the traffic was heavy in New Orleans when I parked off St. Charles and ran for the colonnade in front of the Pearl. The window was steamed from the warmth inside, but I could see Clete Purcel at the counter, a basket of breadsticks and a whiskey glass and a schooner of beer in front of him, reading the front page of the *Times-Picayune*.

"Hey, big mon," he said, folding his paper, grinning broadly when I came through the door. His face was round and Irish, scarred across the nose and through one eyebrow. His seersucker suit and blue pork-pie hat looked absurd on his massive body. Under his coat I could see his nylon shoulder holster and blue-black .38 revolver. "Mitch, give Dave a dozen," he said to the waiter behind the counter, then turned back to me. "Hang on a second." He knocked back the whiskey glass and chased it with beer, blew out his breath, and widened his eyes. He took off his hat and mopped his forehead on his coat sleeve.

"You must have had a rocky morning," I said.

"I helped repossess a car because the guy didn't pay the vig on his bond. His wife went nuts, said he wouldn't be able to get to work, his kids were crying in the front yard. It really gives you a sense of purpose. Tonight I got to pick up a skip in the Iberville Project. I've got another one hiding out in the Desire. You want to hear some more?"

The waiter set a round, metal tray of raw oysters in front of me.

The shells were cold and slick with ice. I squeezed a lemon on each oyster and dotted it with Tabasco. Outside, the green-painted iron streetcar clanged on its tracks around the corner of Canal and headed up the avenue toward Lee Circle.

"Anyway, run all this Mingo Bloomberg stuff by me again," Clete said.

I told him the story from the beginning. At least most of it.

"What stake would Bloomberg have in a guy like Aaron Crown?" I said.

He scratched his cheek with four fingers. "I don't get it, either. Mingo's a made-guy. He's been mobbed-up since he went in the reformatory. The greaseballs don't have an interest in pecker-woods, and they think the blacks are cannibals. I don't know, Streak."

"What's your take on the murdered scriptwriter?"

"Maybe wrong place, wrong time."

"Why'd the shooter let the girl slide?" I said.

"Maybe he didn't want to snuff a sister."

"Come on, Clete."

"He knew she couldn't turn tricks in the Quarter without permission of the Giacano family. Which means she was producing a weekly minimum for guys you don't mess with."

"Which means the guy's a pro," I said.

He raised his eyebrows and lit a cigarette. "That might be, noble mon, but it all sounds like a pile of shit you don't need," he said. When I didn't answer, he said, "So why are you putting your hand in it?"

"I don't like being the subject of Mingo Bloomberg's conversation."

His green eyes wandered over my face.

"Buford LaRose made you mad by offering you a job?" he asked.

"I didn't say that."

"I get the feeling there's something you're not telling me. What was that about his wife?" His eyes continued to search my face, a grin tugging at the corner of his mouth.

"Will you stop that?"

"I'm getting strange signals here, big mon. Are we talking about memories of past boom-boom?"

I put an oyster in my mouth and tried to keep my face empty. But it was no use. Even his worst detractors admitted that Clete Purcel was one of the best investigative cops NOPD ever had, until his career went sour with pills and booze and he had to flee to Central America on a homicide warrant.

"So now she's trying to work your crank?" he said.

"Do you have to put it that way? . . . Yeah, okay, maybe she is."

"What for? . . . Did you know your hair's sweating?"

"It's the Tabasco. Clete, would you ease up, please?"

"Look, Dave, this is the basic lesson here—don't get mixed up with rich people. One way or another, they'll hurt you. The same goes for this civil rights stuff. It's a dead issue, leave it alone."

"Do you want to go out and talk to Jimmy Ray Dixon or not?" I said.

"You've never met him?"

"No."

"Jimmy Ray is a special kind of guy. You meet him once and you never quite forget the experience."

I waited for him to finish but he didn't.

"What do I know?" he said, flipped his breadstick into the straw basket, and began putting on his raincoat. "There's nothing wrong with the guy a tube of roach paste couldn't cure."

WE DROVE THROUGH the Garden District, past Tulane and Loyola universities and Audubon Park and rows of columned antebellum homes whose yards were filled with trees and flowers. The mist swirled out of the canopy of oak limbs above St. Charles, and the neon tubing scrolled on corner restaurants and the empty outdoor cafes looked like colored smoke in the rain.

"Was he in Vietnam?" I asked.

"Yeah. So were you and I. You ever see his sheet?" Clete said.

I shook my head.

"He was a pimp in Chicago. He went down for assault and battery and carrying a concealed weapon. He even brags on it. Now you hear him talking on the radio about how he got reborn. The guy's a shithead, Dave."

Jimmy Ray Dixon owned a shopping center, named for his assassinated brother, out by Chalmette. He also owned apartment buildings, a nightclub in the Quarter, and a five-bedroom suburban home. But he did business in a small unpainted 1890s cottage hung with flower baskets in the Carrollton district, down by the Mississippi levee, at the end of St. Charles where the streetcar turned around. It was a neighborhood of palm trees and green neutral grounds, small restaurants, university students, art galleries, and bookstores. It was a part of New Orleans unmarked by spray cans and broken glass in the gutters. In five minutes you had the sense Jimmy Ray had chosen the role of the thumb in your eye.

"You're here to ask me about the cracker that killed my brother? You're kidding, right?"

He chewed and snapped his gum. He wore a long-sleeved blue-striped shirt, which hid the apparatus that attached the metal hook to the stump of his left wrist. His teeth were gold-filled, his head mahogany-colored, round and light-reflective as a waxed bowling ball. He never invited us to sit down, and seemed to make a point of swiveling his chair around to talk to his employees, all of whom were black, in the middle of a question.

"Some people think he might be an innocent man," I said.

"You one of them?" He grinned.

"Your humor's lost on me, sir."

"It took almost thirty years to put him in Angola. He should have got the needle. Now the white folks is worried about injustice."

"A kid in my platoon waited two days at a stream crossing to take out a VC who killed his friend. He used a blooker to do it. Splattered him all over the trees," I said.

"Something I ain't picking up on?"

"You have to dedicate yourself to hating somebody before you can lay in wait for him. I just never made Aaron Crown for that kind of guy," I said.

"Let me tell you what I think of Vietnam and memory lane, Jack.

I got this"—he tapped his hook on his desk blotter—"clearing toe-poppers from a rice paddy six klicks out of Pinkville. You want to tell war stories, the DAV's downtown. You want to spring that cracker, that's your bidness. Just don't come around here to do it. You with me on this?"

Clete looked at me, then lit a cigarette.

"Hey, don't smoke in here, man," Jimmy Ray said.

"*Adios,*" Clete said to me and went out the door and closed it behind him.

"Have any of these documentary movie people been to see you?" I asked.

"Yeah, I told them the right man's in jail. I told them that was his rifle lying out under the tree. I told them Crown was in the KKK. They turned the camera off while I was still talking." He glanced at the dial on his watch, which was turned around on the bottom of his wrist. "I don't mean you no rudeness, but I got a bidness to run."

"Thanks for your help."

"I ain't give you no help. Hey, man, me and my brother Ely wasn't nothing alike. He believed in y'all. Thought a great day was coming. You know what make us all equal?" He pulled his wallet out of his back pocket, splayed it open with his thumb, and picked a fifty-dollar bill out of it with his metal hook. "Right here, man," he said, wagging the bill on the desk blotter.

LATE THE NEXT day, after we ate supper, I helped Bootsie wash and put away the dishes. The sun had burned into a red ember inside a bank of maroon-colored clouds above the treeline that bordered my neighbor's cane field, and through the screen I could smell rain and ozone in the south. Alafair called from the bait shop, where she was helping Batist close up.

"Dave, there's a man in a boat who keeps coming back by the dock," she said.

"What's he doing?"

"It's like he's trying to see through the windows."

"Is Batist there?"

"Yes."

"Put him on, would you?"

When Batist came on the line, I said, "Who's the man in the boat?"

"A guy puts earrings."

As was Batist's way, he translated French literally into English, in this case using the word *put* for *wear.*

"Is he bothering y'all?" I said.

"He ain't gonna bother *me*. I'm fixing to lock up."

"What's the problem, then?"

"They ain't one, long as he's gone when I go out the do'."

"I'll be down."

The air was heavy and wet-smelling and crisscrossed with birds when I walked down the slope toward the dock, the sky over the swamp the color of scorched tin. Batist and Alafair had collapsed the Cinzano umbrellas set in the center of the spool tables and turned on the string of overhead lights. The surface of the bayou was ruffling in the wind, and against the cypress and willows on the far side I could see a man sitting in an outboard, dressed in a dark blue shirt and a white straw hat.

I walked to the end of the dock and leaned against the railing.

"Can I help you with something?" I asked.

He didn't reply. His face was shadowed, but I could see the glint of his gold earrings in the light from the dock. I went inside the bait shop.

"Turn on the flood lamps, Alf," I said.

When she hit the toggle switch, the light bloomed across the water with the brilliance of a pistol flare. That's when I saw his eyes.

"Go on up to the house, Alafair," I said.

"You know him?" she said.

"No, but we're going to send him on his way just the same. Now, do what I ask you, okay?"

"I don't see why I—"

"Come on, Alf."

She lifted her face, her best pout in place, and went out the screen door and let it slam behind her.

Batist was heating a pot of coffee on the small butane stove behind the counter. He bent down and looked out the window at the bayou again, a cigar in the center of his mouth.

"What you want to do with that fella, Dave?" he said.

"See who he is."

I went outside again and propped my hands on the dock railing. The flood lamps mounted on the roof of the bait shop burned away the shadows from around the man in the boat. His hair was long, like a nineteenth-century Indian's, his cheeks unshaved, the skin dark and grained as though it had been rubbed with black pepper. His arms were wrapped with scarlet tattoos, but like none I had ever seen before. Unlike jailhouse art, the ink ran in strings down the arms, webbed in bright fantails, as though all of his veins had been superimposed on the skin's surface.

But it was the eyes that caught and impaled you. They were hunter's eyes, chemical green, rimmed with a quivering energy, as though he heard the sounds of hidden adversaries in the wind.

"What's your business here, podna?" I asked.

He seemed to think on it. One hand opened and closed on an oar.

"I ain't eat today," he said. The accent was vaguely Spanish, the tone flat, disconnected from the primitive set of the jaw.

Batist joined me at the rail with a cup of coffee in his hand.

"Come inside," I said.

Batist's eyes fixed on mine.

The man didn't start his engine. Instead, he used one oar to row across the bayou to the concrete ramp. He stepped into the water, ankle-deep, lifted the bow with one hand, and pulled the boat up until it was snug on the ramp. Then he reached behind him and lifted out a stiff bedroll that was tied tightly with leather thongs.

His work boots were loud on the dock as he walked toward us, his Levi's high on his hips, notched under his rib cage with a wide leather belt and brass buckle.

"You oughtn't to ax him in, Dave. This is our place," Batist said.

"It's all right."

"No, it surely ain't."

The man let his eyes slide over our faces as he entered the bait shop. I followed him inside and for the first time smelled his odor, like charcoal, and kerosene, unwashed hair, mud gone sour with stagnant water. He waited expectantly at the counter, his bedroll tucked under his arm. His back was as straight as a sword.

I fixed him two chili dogs on a paper plate and set them in front of him with a glass of water. He sat on the stool and ate with a spoon, gripping the handle with his fist, mopping the beans and sauce and ground meat with a slice of bread. Batist came inside and began loading the beer cooler behind the counter.

"Where you from?" I said.

"El Paso."

"Where'd you get the boat?"

He thought about it. "I found it two weeks back. It was sunk. I cleaned it up pretty good." He stopped eating and watched me.

"It's a nice boat," I said.

His face twitched and his eyes were empty again, the jawbones chewing.

"You got a rest room?" he asked.

"It's in the back, behind those empty pop cases."

"How much your razor blades?" he said to Batist.

"This ain't no drug sto'. What you after, man?" Batist said.

The man wiped his mouth with the flats of his fingers. The lines around his eyes were stretched flat.

Batist leaned on his arms, his biceps flexing like rolls of metal washers.

"Don't be giving me no truck," he said.

I eased along the counter until the man's eyes left Batist and fixed on me.

"I'm a police officer. Do you need directions to get somewhere?" I said.

"I got a camp out there. That's where I come from. I can find it even in the dark," he said.

With one hand he clenched his bedroll, which seemed to have tent sticks inside it, and walked past the lunch meat coolers to the small rest room in back.

"Dave, let me ax you somet'ing. You got to bring a 'gator in your hog lot to learn 'gators eat pigs?" Batist said.

Ten minutes passed. I could hear the man splashing water behind the rest room door. Batist had gone back out on the dock and was chaining up the rental boats for the night. I walked past the cooler and tapped with one knuckle on the bolted door.

"We're closing up, podna. You have to come out," I said.

He jerked open the door, his face streaming water. His dark blue shirt was unbuttoned, and on his chest I could see the same scarlet network of lines that was tattooed on his arms. The pupils in his eyes looked broken, like India ink dropped on green silk.

"I'd appreciate your cleaning up the water and paper towels you've left on the floor. Then I'd like to have a talk with you," I said.

He didn't answer. I turned and walked back up front.

I went behind the counter and started to stock the candy shelves for tomorrow, then I stopped and called the dispatcher at the department.

"I think I've got a meltdown in the shop. He might have a stolen boat, too," I said.

"The governor in town?"

"Lose the routine, Wally."

"You hurt my feelings . . . You want a cruiser, Dave?"

I didn't have the chance to answer. The man in the white straw hat came from behind me, his hand inserted in the end of his bedroll. I looked at his face and dropped the phone and fell clattering against the shelves and butane stove as he flung the bedroll and the sheath loose from the machete and ripped it through the air, an inch from my chest.

The honed blade sliced through the telephone cord and sank into the counter's hardwood edge. He leaned over and swung again, the blade whanging off the shelves, dissecting cartons of worms and dirt, exploding a jar of pickled sausage.

Batist's coffee pot was scorched black and boiling on the butane fire. The handle felt like a heated wire across my bare palm. I threw the coffee, the top, and the grinds in the man's face, saw the shock in his eyes, his mouth drop open, the pain rise out of his throat like a broken bubble.

Then I grabbed the tattooed wrist that held the machete and pressed the bottom of the pot down on his forearm.

He flung the machete from his hand as though the injury had come from it rather than the coffee pot. I thought I was home free. I wasn't.

He hit me harder than I'd ever been struck by a fist in my life, the kind of blow that fills your nose with needles, drives the eye deep into the socket.

I got to my feet and tried to follow him out on the dock. One side of my face was already numb and throbbing, as though someone had held dry ice against it. The man in the white straw hat had leaped off the dock onto the concrete ramp and mounted the bow of his boat with one knee and was pushing it out into the current, his body haloed with humidity and electric light.

Batist came out of the tin shed in the willows where we stored our outboard motors, looked up at me, then at the fleeing man.

"Batist, no!" I said.

Batist and I both stood motionless while the man jerked the engine into a roar with one flick of the forearm, then furrowed a long yellow trough around the bend into the darkness.

I used the phone at the house to call the department again, then walked back down to the dock. The moon was veiled over the swamp; lightning forked out of a black sky in the south.

"How come you ain't want me to stop him, Dave?" Batist said.

"He's deranged. I think it's PCP," I said. But he didn't understand. "It's called angel dust. People get high on it and bust up brick walls with their bare hands."

"He knowed who you was, Dave. He didn't have no interest in coming in till he seen you . . . This started wit' that old man from the penitentiary."

"What are you talking about?"

"That guard, the one you call Cap'n, the one probably been killing niggers up at that prison farm for fifty years. I tole you not to have his kind in our shop. You let his grief get on your front porch, it don't stop there, no. It's gonna come in your house. But you don't never listen."

He pulled his folded cap out of his back pocket, popped it open, and fitted it on his head. He walked down the dock to his truck without saying good night. The tin roof on the bait shop creaked and pinged against the joists in the wind gusting out of the south.

Chapter
5

MONDAY MORNING THE sky was blue, the breeze warm off the Gulf when I drove to the University of Southwestern Louisiana campus in Lafayette to talk with Buford LaRose. Classes had just let out for the noon hour, and the pale green quadrangle and colonnaded brick walkways were filled with students on their way to lunch. But Buford LaRose was not in his office in the English department, nor in the glassed-in campus restaurant that was built above a cypress lake behind old Burke Hall.

I called his office at the Oil Center, where he kept a part-time therapy practice, and was told by the receptionist I could find him at Red Lerille's Health and Racquet Club off Johnson Street.

"Are you sure? We were supposed to go to lunch," I said.

"Dr. LaRose always goes to the gym on Mondays," she answered.

Red's was a city-block-long complex of heated swimming pools, racquet ball and clay tennis courts, boxing and basketball gyms, indoor and outdoor running tracks, and cavernous air-conditioned rooms filled with hundreds of dumbbells and weight benches and exercise machines.

I looked for Buford a half hour before I glanced through the narrow glass window in the door of the men's steam room and saw him reading a soggy newspaper, naked, on the yellow tile stoop.

I borrowed a lock from the pro shop, undressed, and walked into the steam room and sat beside him.

His face jerked when he looked up from his paper. Then he smiled, almost fondly.

"You have a funny way of keeping appointments," I said.

"You didn't get my message?"

"No."

"I waited for you. I didn't think you were coming," he said.

"That's peculiar. I was on time."

"Not by my watch," he said, and smiled again.

"I wanted to tell you again I was sorry for my remarks at your party."

"You went to a lot of trouble to do something that's unnecessary."

The thermostat kicked on and filled the air with fresh clouds of steam. I could feel the heat in the tiles climb through my thighs and back. I wiped the sweat out of my eyes with my hand.

"Your jaw's bruised," he said.

"We had a visitor at the bait shop this weekend. NOPD thinks he's a Mexican carnival worker who got loose from a detox center."

He nodded, gazed without interest at the tile wall in front of us, pushed down on the stoop with the heels of his hands, and worked the muscles in his back, his brown, hard body leaking sweat at every pore. I watched the side of his face, the handsome profile, the intelligent eyes that seemed never to cloud with passion.

"You have Ph.D. degrees in both English and psychology, Buford?" I said.

"I received double credits in some areas, so it's not such a big deal."

"It's impressive."

"Why are you here, Dave?"

"I have a feeling I may have stuck my arm in the garbage grinder. You know how it is, you stick one finger in, then you're up to your elbow in the pipe."

"We're back to our same subject, I see," he said.

Other men walked back and forth in the steam, swinging their arms, breathing deeply.

"How do you know Aaron Crown's daughter?" I asked.

"Who says I do?"

"She does."

"She grew up in New Iberia. If she says she knows me, fine . . . Dave, you have no idea what you're tampering with, how you may be used to undo everything you believe in."

"Why don't you explain it to me?"

"This is hardly the place, sir."

We showered, then went into an enclosed, empty area off to one side of the main locker room to dress. He dried himself with a towel, put on a pair of black nylon bikini underwear and flipflops, and began combing his hair in the mirror. The muscles in his back and sides looked like tea-colored water rippling over stone.

"I've got some serious trouble, Dave. These New York film people want to make a case for Aaron Crown's innocence. They can blow my candidacy right into the toilet," he said.

"You think they have a vested interest?"

"Yeah, making money . . . Wake up, buddy. The whole goddamn country is bashing liberals. These guys ride the tide. A white man unjustly convicted of killing a black civil rights leader? A story like that is made in heaven."

I put on my shirt and tucked it in my slacks, then sat on the bench and slipped on my loafers.

"Nothing to say?" Buford asked.

"Your explanations are too simple. The name Mingo Bloomberg keeps surfacing in the middle of my mind."

"This New Orleans mobster?"

"That's the one."

"I've got a fund-raiser in Shreveport at six. Come on the plane with me," he said.

"What for?"

"Take leave from your department. Work for me."

"Not interested."

"Dave, I'm running for governor while I teach school. I have no machine and little money. The other side does. Now these sonsofbitches from New York come down here and try to cripple the one chance we've had for decent government in decades. What in God's name is wrong with you, man?"

MAYBE BUFORD WAS right, I thought as I drove down the old highway through Broussard into New Iberia. I sometimes saw design where there was none, and I had maintained a long and profound distrust of all forms of authority, even the one I served, and the LaRose family had been vested with wealth and power since antebellum days.

But maybe it was also time to have another talk with Mingo Bloomberg, provided I could find him.

As irony would have it, I found a message from Mingo's lawyer in my mailbox when I got back to the department. Mingo would not be hard to find after all. He was in New Orleans City Prison and wanted to see me.

LATE TUESDAY MORNING I was at the barred entrance to a long corridor of individual cells where snitches and the violent and the incorrigible were kept in twenty-three-hour lockdown. The turnkey opened Mingo's cell, cuffed him to a waist chain, and led him down the corridor toward me. While a second turnkey worked the levers to slide back the door on the lockdown area, I could see handheld mirrors extended from bars all the way down the series of cells, each reflecting a set of disembodied eyes.

Both turnkeys escorted us into a bare-walled interview room that contained a scarred wood table and three folding chairs. They were powerful, heavyset men with the top-heavy torsos of weight lifters.

"Thanks," I said.

But they remained where they were.

"I want to be alone with him. I'd appreciate your unhooking him, too," I said.

The turnkeys looked at each other. Then the older one used his key on each of the cuffs and said, "Suit yourself. Bang on the door when you're finished. We won't be far."

After they went out, I could still see them through the elongated, reinforced viewing glass in the door.

"It looks like they're coming down pretty hard on you, Mingo. I thought you'd be sprung by now," I said.

"They say I'm a flight risk."

He was clean-shaven, his jailhouse denims pressed neatly, his copper hair combed back on his scalp like a 1930s leading man's. But his eyes looked wired, and a dry, unwashed odor like sweat baked on the skin by a radiator rose from his body.

"I don't get it. Your people don't protect cop killers," I said.

He propped one elbow on the table and bit his thumbnail.

"It's the other way around. At least that's what the prosecutor's office thinks. That's what those clowns you used to work with at First District think," he said.

"You've lost me."

"You remember the narc who got capped in the Quarter last year? I was in the cage at First District when the cops brought in the boon who did it. Somebody, and I said *somebody*, stomped the living shit out of him. They cracked his skull open on a cement floor and crushed his, what do you call it, his thorax. At least that's what people say. I don't know, because I didn't see it. But the dead boon's family is making a big stink and suing the city of New Orleans for fifty million dollars. Some cops might end up at Angola, too. You ever see a cop do time? Think about the possibilities for his food before he puts a fork in it."

I kept my eyes flat, waited a moment, removed my sunglasses from their case and clicked them in my palm.

"What are you trying to trade?" I asked.

"I want out of here."

"I don't have that kind of juice."

"I want out of lockdown."

"Main pop may not be a good place for you, Mingo."

"You live on Mars? I'm safe in main pop. I got problems when I'm in lockdown and cops with blood on their shoes think I'm gonna rat 'em out."

"You're a material witness. There's no way you're going into the main population, Mingo."

The skin along his hairline was shiny with perspiration. He screwed a cigarette into his mouth but didn't light it. His blue eyes were filled with light when they stared into mine.

"You worked with those guys. You get word to them, I didn't see anything happen to the boon. I'll go down on a perjury beef if I have to," he said.

I let my eyes wander over his face. There were tiny black specks in the blueness of his eyes, like pieces of dead flies, like microscopic traces of events that never quite rinse out of the soul. "How many people have you pushed the button on?" I asked.

"What? Why you ask a question like that?"

"No reason, really."

He tried to reconcentrate his thoughts. "A Mexican guy was at your place, right? A guy with fried mush. It wasn't an accident he was there."

"Go on."

"He was muleing tar for the projects. They call him Araña, that means 'Spider' in Spanish. He's from a village in Mexico that's got a church with a famous statue in it. I know that because he was always talking about it."

"That sure narrows it down. Who sent him to my bait shop?"

"What do I get?"

"We can talk about federal custody."

"That's worse. People start thinking Witness Protection Program."

"That's all I've got."

He tore a match from a book and struck it, held the flame to his cigarette, never blinking in the smoke and heat that rose into his handsome face.

"There's stuff going on that's new, that's a big move for certain people. You stumbled into it with that peckerwood, the one who killed Jimmy Ray Dixon's brother."

"What stuff?"

He tipped his ashes in a small tin tray, his gaze focused on nothing.

His cheeks were pooled with color, the fingers of his right hand laced with smoke from the cigarette.

"I don't think you've got a lot to trade, Mingo. Otherwise, you would have already done it."

"I laid it out for you. You don't want to pick up on it . . ." He worked the burning end of the cigarette loose in the ashtray and placed the unsmoked stub in the package. "You asked me a personal question a minute ago. Just for fun, it don't mean anything, understand, I'll give you a number. Eleven. None of them ever saw it coming. The guy with the fried head at your place probably wasn't a serious effort.

"I say 'probably.' I'm half-Jewish, half-Irish, I don't eat in Italian restaurants. I'm outside the window looking in a lot of the time. Hey, you're a bright guy, I know you can connect on this."

"Enjoy it, Mingo," I said, and hit on the door with the flat of my fist for the turnkey to open up.

LATER THAT SAME day, just before I was to sign out of the office, the phone on my desk rang.

It was like hearing the voice of a person who you knew would not go away, who would always be hovering around you like a bad memory, waiting to pull you back into the past.

"How's life, Karyn?" I said.

"Buford will be in Baton Rouge till late tonight. You and I need to talk some things out."

"I don't think so."

"You want me to come to your office? Or out to your house? I will, if that's what it takes."

I left the office and drove south of New Iberia toward my home. I tried to concentrate on the traffic, the red sky in the west, the egrets perched on the backs of cattle in the fields, the cane wagons being towed to the sugar mill. I wasn't going to give power to Karyn LaRose, I told myself. I owed her nothing. I was sure of that.

I was still trying to convince myself of my freedom from the past when I made an illegal U-turn in the middle of the road and drove to the LaRose plantation.

SHE WORE A yellow sundress, with her platinum hair braided up on her head, a Victorian sapphire brooch on a gold chain around her neck.

"Why'd you park in back?" she said when she opened the door.

"I didn't give it much thought," I said.

"I bet."

"Let's hear what you have to say, Karyn. I need to get home."

She smiled with her eyes, turned, and walked away without speaking. When I didn't immediately follow, she paused and looked back at me expectantly. I followed her through the kitchen, a den filled with books and glass gun cases and soft leather chairs, down a darkened cypress-floored hallway hung with oil paintings of Buford's ancestors, into a sitting room whose windows and French doors reached to the ceiling.

She pulled the velvet curtains on the front windows.

"It's a little dark, isn't it?" I said. I stood by the mantel, next to a bright window that gave onto a cleared cane field and a stricken oak tree that stood against the sky like a clutch of broken fingers.

"There's a horrid glare off the road this time of day," she said. She put ice and soda in two glasses at a small bar inset in one wall and uncorked a bottle of Scotch with a thick, red wax seal embossed on it.

"I don't care for anything, thanks," I said.

"There's no whiskey in yours."

"I said I don't want anything."

The phone rang in another room.

"Goddamn it," she said, set down her glass, and went into a bedroom.

I looked at my watch. I had already been there ten minutes and had accomplished nothing. On the mantel piece was a photograph of a U.S. Army Air Corps aviator who was sitting inside the splintered Plexiglas nose of a Flying Fortress. The photo must have been taken at high altitude, because the fur collar on his jacket was frozen with his sweat, like a huge glass necklace. His face was exhausted, and except for the area around his eyes where his goggles had been, his skin was black with the smoke of *ack-ack* bursts.

I could hear Karyn's voice rising in the next room: "I won't sit still for this again. You rent a car if you have to . . . I'm not listening to that same lie . . . You're not going to ruin this, Buford . . . You listen . . . No . . . No . . . No, you listen . . ."

Then she pushed the door shut.

When she came out of the room her eyes were electric with anger, the tops of her breasts rising against her sundress. She went to the bar and drank off her Scotch and soda and poured another one. I looked away from her face.

"Admiring the photo of Buford's father?" she said. "He was one of the bombardiers who incinerated Dresden. You see the dead oak tree out by the field? Some of Buford's other family members, gentlemen in the Knights of the White Camellia, hanged a Negro and a white carpetbagger there in 1867. If you live with Buford, you get to hear about this sort of thing every day of your life."

She drank three fingers of Scotch on ice, her throat swallowing methodically, her mouth wet and cold-looking on the edge of the glass.

"I'd better get going, Karyn. I shouldn't have bothered you," I said.

"Don't be disingenuous. I brought you here, Dave. Sometimes I wonder how I ever got mixed up with you."

"You're not mixed up with me."

"Your memory is selective."

"I'm sorry it happened, Karyn. I've tried to indicate that to you. It's you and your husband who keep trying to resurrect the past or bring me into your lives."

"You say 'it.' What do you mean by 'it'?"

"That night by the bayou. I'm sorry. I don't know what else to say."

"You don't remember coming to my house two weeks later?"

"No."

"Dave?" Her eyes clouded, then looked into mine, as though she were searching for a lie. "You have no memory of that afternoon, or the next?"

I felt myself swallow. "No, I don't. I don't think I saw you again for a year," I said.

She shook her head, sat in a deep leather chair that looked out onto the dead tree.

"That's hard to believe. I never blamed you for the worry and anxiety and pain I had to go through later, because I didn't make you take precautions. But when you tell me—"

Unconsciously I touched my brow.

"I had blackouts back then, Karyn. I lost whole days. If you say something happened, then—"

"Blackouts?"

"I'd get loaded at night on Beam and try to sober up in the morning with vodka."

"How lovely. What if I told you I had an abortion?"

The skin of my face flexed against the bone. I could feel a weakness, a sinking in my chest, as though weevil worms were feeding at my heart.

"I didn't. I was just late. But no thanks to you, you bastard . . . Don't just look at me," she said.

"I'm going now."

"Oh no you're not." She rose from the chair and stood in front of me. "My husband has some peculiar flaws, but he's still the best chance this state has and I'm not letting you destroy it."

"Somebody tried to open me up with a machete. I think it had to do with Aaron Crown. I think I don't want to ever see you again, Karyn."

"Is that right?" she said. The tops of her breasts were swollen and hard, veined with blue lines. I could smell whiskey on her breath, perfume from behind her ears, the heat she seemed to excrete from her sun-browned skin. She struck me full across the face with the flat of her hand.

I touched my cheek, felt a smear of blood where her fingernail had torn the skin.

"I apologize again for having come to your home," I said.

I walked stiffly through the house, through the kitchen to the back-yard and my parked pickup truck. When I turned the ignition, I looked through the windshield and saw her watching me through the back screen, biting the corner of her lip as though her next option was just now presenting itself.

Chapter
6

It RAINED ALL that night. At false dawn a white ground fog rolled out of the swamp, and the cypress trees on the far bank of the bayou looked as black and hard as carved stone. Deep inside the fog you could hear bass flopping back in the bays. When the sun broke above the horizon, like a red diamond splintering apart between the tree trunks, Batist and I were still bailing out the rental boats with coffee cans. Then we heard a car on the road, and when we looked up we saw a purple Lincoln Continental, with Sabelle Crown in the passenger's seat, stop and back up by our concrete boat ramp.

It wasn't hard to figure out which American industry the driver served. He seemed to consciously dress and look the part—elk hide halftop boots, pleated khakis, a baggy cotton shirt that was probably tailored on Rodeo Drive, tinted rimless glasses, his brown hair tied in a ponytail.

As he walked down the ramp toward me, the windburned face, the cleft chin, the Roman profile, became more familiar, like images rising from the pages of *People* or *Newsweek* magazine or any number of television programs that featured film celebrities.

His forearms and wrists were thick and corded with veins, the handshake disarmingly gentle.

"My name's Lonnie Felton, Mr. Robicheaux," he said.

"You're a movie director."

"That's right."

"How you do, sir?"

"I wonder if we could go inside and talk a few minutes."

"I'm afraid I have another job to go to when I finish this one."

Sabelle stood by the fender of the Lincoln, brushing her hair, putting on makeup from her purse.

"Some people are giving Aaron Crown a rough time up at the pen," he said.

"It's a bad place. It was designed as one."

"You know what the BGLA is?"

"The Black Guerrilla Liberation Army?"

"Crown's an innocent man. I think Ely Dixon was assassinated by a couple of Mississippi Klansmen. Maybe one of them was a Mississippi highway patrolman."

"You ought to tell this to the FBI."

"I got *this* from the FBI. I have testimony from two ex-field-agents."

"It seems the big word in this kind of instance is always 'ex,' Mr. Felton," I said.

He coughed out a laugh. "You're a hard-nose sonofabitch, aren't you?" he said.

I stood erect in the boat where I'd been bailing, poured the water out of the can into the bayou, idly flicked the last drops onto the boat's bow.

"I don't particularly care what you think of me, sir, but I'd appreciate your not using profanity around my home," I said.

He looked off into the distance, suppressing a smile, watching a blue heron lift from an inlet and disappear into the fog.

"We had a writer murdered in the Quarter," he said. "The guy was a little weird, but he didn't deserve to get killed. That's not an unreasonable position for me to take, is it?"

"I'll be at the sheriff's department by eight. If you want to give us some information, you're welcome to come in."

"Sabelle told me you were an intelligent man. Who do you think broke the big stories of our time? My Lai, Watergate, CIA dope smuggling, Reagan's gun deals in Nicaragua? It was always the media, not the government, not the cops. Why not lose the 'plain folks' attitude?"

I stepped out of the boat into the shallows and felt the coldness through my rubber boots. I set the bailing can down on the ramp, wrapped the bow chain in my palm and snugged the boat's keel against the waving moss at the base of the concrete pad, and cleared an obstruction from my throat.

He slipped his glasses off his face, dropped them loosely in the pocket of his baggy shirt, smiling all the while.

"Thanks for coming by," I said.

I walked up the ramp, then climbed the set of side stairs onto the dock. I saw him walk toward his car and shake his head at Sabelle.

A moment later she came quickly down the dock toward me. She wore old jeans, a flannel shirt, pink tennis shoes, and walked splay-footed like a teenage girl.

"I look like hell. He came by my place at five this morning," she said.

"You look good, Sabelle. You always do," I said.

"They've moved Daddy into a cellhouse full of blacks."

"That doesn't sound right. He can request isolation."

"He'll die before he'll let anybody think he's scared. In the meantime they steal his cigarettes, spit in his food, throw pig shit in his hair, and nobody does anything about it." Her eyes began to film.

"I'll call this gunbull I know."

"They're going to kill him, Dave. I know it. It's a matter of time."

Out on the road, Lonnie Felton waited behind the steering wheel of his Lincoln.

"Don't let this guy Felton use you," I said.

"*Use* me? Who else cares about us?" Even with makeup, her face looked stark, as shiny as ceramic, in the lacy veil of sunlight through the cypress trees. She turned and walked back up the dock, her pink underwear winking through a small thread-worn hole in the rump of her jeans.

* * *

The sheriff was turned sideways in his swivel chair, his bifocals mounted on his nose, twisting strips of pink and white crepe paper into the shape of camellias. On his windowsill was a row of potted plants, which he watered daily from a hand-painted tea kettle. He looked like an aging greengrocer more than a law officer, and in fact had run a dry cleaning business before his election to office, but he had been humble enough to listen to advice, and over the years we had all come to respect his judgment and integrity.

Only one door in his life had remained closed to us, his time with the First Marine Division at the Chosin Reservoir during the Korean War, until last year, when he suffered a heart attack and told me from a bed in Iberia General, his breath as stale as withered flowers, of bugles echoing off frozen hills and wounds that looked like roses frozen in snow.

I sat down across from him. His desk blotter was covered with crepe paper camellias.

"I volunteered to help decorate the stage for my granddaughter's school play. You any good at this?" he said.

"No, not really. A movie director, a fellow named Lonnie Felton, was out at my place with Sabelle Crown this morning. They say some blacks are trying to re-create the Garden of Gethsemane for Aaron Crown. I called Angola, but I didn't get any help."

"Don't look for any. We made him the stink on shit."

"I beg your pardon?"

"A lot of us, not everybody, but a lot of us, treated people of color pretty badly. Aaron represents everything that's vile in the white race. So he's doing our time."

"You think these movie guys are right, he's innocent?"

"I didn't say that. Look, human beings do bad things sometimes, particularly in groups. Then we start to forget about it. But there's always one guy hanging around to remind us of what we did or what we used to be. That's Aaron. He's the toilet that won't flush . . . Did I say something funny?"

"No, sir."

"Good, because what I've got on my mind isn't funny. Karyn LaRose and her attorney were in here earlier this morning." He set his elbows on his desk blotter, flipped an unfinished paper flower to the side. "Guess what she had to tell me about your visit last night at her house?"

"I won't even try to."

"They're not calling it rape, if that makes you feel any better." He opened his desk drawer and read silently from a clipboard. "The words are 'lascivious intention,' 'attempted sexual battery,' and 'indecent liberties.' What do you have to say?" His gaze moved away from my face, then came back and stayed there.

"Nothing. It's a lie."

"I wish the court would just accept my word on the perps. I wish I didn't have to offer any evidence. Boy, that'd be great."

I told him what had happened, felt the heat climbing into my voice, wiped the film of perspiration off my palms onto my slacks.

His eyes lingered on the scratch Karyn had put on my cheek.

"I think it's a lie, too," he said. He dropped the clipboard inside the drawer and closed it. "But I have to conduct an internal investigation just the same."

"I go on the desk?"

"No. I'm not going to have my department manipulated for someone's political interests, and that's what this is about. You're getting too close to something in this Aaron Crown business. But you stay away from her."

I still had my morning mail in my hand. On the top was a pink memo slip with a message from Bootsie, asking me to meet her for lunch.

"How public is this going to get?" I asked.

"My feeling is she doesn't intend it to be public. Aside from the fact I know you, that was the main reason I didn't believe her. Her whole account is calculated to be vague. Her charges don't require her to offer physical evidence—vaginal smears, pubic hair, that kind of stuff. This is meant as a warning from the LaRose family. If I have to, I'll carry this back to them on a dung fork, podna."

He folded his hands on the desk, his face suffused with the ruddy glow of his hypertension.

Way to go, skipper, I thought.

MOST PEOPLE IN prison deserve to be there. Old-time recidivists who are down on a bad beef will usually admit they're guilty of other crimes, perhaps much worse ones than the crimes they're down for.

There're exceptions, but not many. So their burden is of their own creation. But it is never an easy one, no matter how modern the facility or how vituperative the rhetoric about country club jails.

You're a nineteen-year-old fish, uneducated, frightened, with an IQ of around 100. At the reception center you rebuff a trusty wolf who works in records and wants to introduce you to jailhouse romance, so the trusty makes sure you go up the road with a bad jacket (the word is out, you snitched off a solid con and caused him to lose his goodtime).

You just hit main pop and you're already jammed up, worried about the shank in the chow line, the Molotov cocktail shattered inside your cell, the whispered threat in the soybean field about the experience awaiting you in the shower that night.

So you make a conscious choice to survive and find a benefactor, "an old man," and become a full-time punk, one step above the yard bitches. You mule blues, prune-o, and Afghan skunk for the big stripes; inside a metal toolshed that aches with heat, you participate in the savaging of another fish, who for just a moment reminds you of someone you used to know.

Then a day comes when you think you can get free. You're mainline now, two years down with a jacket full of goodtime. You hear morning birdsong that you didn't notice before; you allow your mind to linger on the outside, the face of a girl in a small town, a job in a piney woods timber mill that smells of rosin and hot oil on a ripsaw, an ordinary day not governed by fear.

That's when you tell your benefactor thanks for all his help. He'll understand. Your next time up before the board, you've got a real chance of entering the world again. Why blow it now?

That night you walk into the shower by yourself. A man who had never even glanced at you before, a big stripe, hare-lipped, flat-nosed, his naked torso rife with a raw smell like a freshly uprooted cypress, clenches your skull in his fingers, draws you into his breath, squeezes until the cracking sound stops, and you hear the words that he utters with a lover's trembling fondness an inch from your mouth: *I'm gonna take your eyes out with a spoon.*

It was late afternoon when the gunbull drove me in his pickup down to the Mississippi levee, where Aaron Crown, his face as heated as a baked apple under a snap-brim cap, was harrowing an open field, the tractor's engine running full bore, grinding the sun-hardened rows into loam, twisting the tractor's wheel back through the haze of cinnamon-colored dust, reslicing the already churned soil as though his work were an excuse to avenge himself and his kind upon the earth.

At the edge of the field, by a grove of willows, four black inmates, stripped to the waist, were heaping dead tree branches on a fire.

"Y'all ought to have Aaron in isolation, Cap," I said.

He cut the ignition and spit tobacco juice out the window.

"When he asks," he replied.

"He won't."

"Then that's his goddamn ass."

The captain walked partway out in the field on his cane and raised the hook and held it motionless in the air. Aaron squinted out of the dust and heat and exhaust fumes, then eased the throttle back without killing the engine, as though he could not will himself to separate entirely from the mechanical power that had throbbed between his thighs all day.

Aaron walked toward us, wiping his face with a dirty handkerchief, past the group of blacks burning field trash. Their eyes never saw him; their closed circle of conversation never missed a beat.

He stood by the truck, his body framed by the sun that hung in a liquid yellow orb over the Mississippi levee.

"Yes, sir?" he said to the captain.

"Water it and piss it, Crown," the captain said. He limped on his cane to the shade of a gum tree and lit his pipe, turned his face into the breeze off the river.

"I understand you're having some trouble," I said.

"You ain't heered me say it."

He walked back to the watercooler belted with bungee cord to the wall of the pickup bed. He filled a paper cup from the cooler and drank it, his gaze fixed on the field, the dust devils swirling in the wind.

"Is it the BGLA?" I asked.

"I don't keep up with colored men's organizations."

"I don't know if you're innocent or guilty, Aaron. But up there at Point Lookout, the prison cemetery is full of men who had your kind of attitude."

"That levee yonder's got dead men in it, too. It's the way it is." He wadded up the paper cup by his side, kneaded it in his hand, a piece of cartilage working against his jawbone.

"I'm going to talk to a civil rights lawyer I know in Baton Rouge. He's a black man, though. Is that going to be a problem?"

"I don't give a shit what he is. I done tole you, I got no complaint, long as I ain't got to cell with one of them."

"They'll eat you alive, partner."

He stepped toward me, his wrists seeming to strain against invisible wires at his sides.

"A man's got his own rules. I ain't ask for nothing except out . . . Goddamn it, you tell my daughter she ain't to worry," he said, his eyes rimming with water. The top of his denim shirt was splayed tightly against his chest. He breathed through his mouth, his fists gathered into impotent rocks, his face dilated with the words his throat couldn't form.

I got back home at dark, then I had to go out again, this time with Helen Soileau to a clapboard nightclub on a back road to investigate a missing person's report.

"Sorry to drag you out, Dave, but the grandmother has been yelling at me over the phone all day," Helen said. "I made a couple of calls, and it looks like she's telling the truth. The girl's not the kind to take off and not tell anybody."

A black waitress had left the club with a white man the night before; she never returned home, nor did she report to work the next day. The grandmother worked as a cook in the club's kitchen and lived in a small frame house a hundred yards down the road. She was a plump, gray-haired woman with a strange skin disease that had eaten white and pink discolorations in her hands, and she was virtually hysterical with anger and grief.

"We'll find her. I promise you," Helen said as we stood in the woman's dirt yard, looking up at her on her tiny, lighted gallery.

"Then why ain't you looking right now? How come it takes all day to get y'all out here?" she said.

"Tell me what the man looked like one more time," I said.

"Got a brand-new Lincoln car. Got a pink face shaped like an egg. Got hair that ain't blond or red, somewhere in between, and he comb it straight back."

"Why did she go off with him?" I asked.

" 'Cause she's seventeen years old and don't listen. 'Cause she got this on her hands, just like me, and reg'lar mens don't pay her no mind. That answer your question?"

Helen drove us back down the dirt road through the fields to the state highway. The night was humid, layered with smoke from stubble fires, and the stars looked blurred with mist in the sky. We passed the LaRose company store, then the plantation itself. All three floors of the house were lighted, the columned porch decorated with pumpkins and scarecrows fashioned from cane stalks and straw hats. In a back pasture, behind a railed fence, horses were running in the moonlight, as though spooked by an impending storm or the rattle of dry poppy husks in the wind.

"What's on your mind?" Helen asked.

"The description of the white man sounds like Mingo Bloomberg."

"I thought he was in City Prison in New Orleans."

"He is. Or at least he was."

"What would he be doing back around here?"

"Who knows why these guys do anything, Helen? I'll get on it in the morning."

I looked back over my shoulder at the LaRose house, the glitter of a chandelier through velvet curtains, a floodlighted gazebo hooded with Confederate jasmine and orange trumpet vine.

"Forget those people. They wouldn't spit on either one of us unless we had something they wanted. Hey, you listening to me, Streak?" Helen said, and hit me hard on the arm with the back of her hand.

I GOT UP EARLY the next morning, left a message on Clete Purcel's answering machine, then drove back to the grandmother's house by the nightclub. The girl, whose name was Barbara Lavey, had still not returned home. I sat in my truck by the front of the grandmother's house and looked at the notes in my notebook. For some reason I drew a circle around the girl's name. I had a feeling I would see it on a case file for a long time.

The grandmother had gone back inside and I had forgotten her. Suddenly she was at the passenger door window. Her glasses fell down on her nose when she leaned inside.

"I'm sorry I was unpolite yestiday. I know you working on it. Here's somet'ing for you and the lady," she said. She placed a brown paper bag swollen with pecans in my hand.

THE SUN WAS still low in the eastern sky when I approached the LaRose plantation. I saw Buford, naked to the waist, in a railed lot by the barn, with a half dozen dark-skinned men who were dressed in straw hats coned on the brims and neckerchiefs and cowboy boots and jeans molded to their buttocks and thighs.

I knew I should keep going, not put my hand again into whatever it was that drove Karyn and Buford's ambitions, not fuel their anger, not give them a handle on an Internal Affairs investigation, but I was never good at taking my own counsel and I could feel the lie she had told turning in my chest like a worm.

I turned into the drive, passed a row of blue-green poplars on the side of the house, and parked by the back lot. A balmy wind, smelling of rain, was blowing hard across the cane acreage, and a dozen roan horses with brands burned deep into the hair were running in the lot, turning against one another, rattling against the railed fence, their manes twisted with fire in the red sunrise.

When I stepped out of the truck, Buford was smiling at me. His skin-tight white polo pants were flecked with mud and tucked inside his polished riding boots. His eyes looked serene, his face pleasant and cool with the freshness of the morning.

I almost extended my hand.

He looked at the sunrise over my shoulder.

"'Red sky at dawn, sailor be forewarned,'" he said. But he was smiling when he said it.

"I shouldn't be here, but I needed to tell you to your face the charges your wife made are fabricated. That's as kind as I can say it."

"Oh, that stuff. She's dropping it, Dave. Let's put that behind us."

"Excuse me?"

"It's over. Come take a look at my horses."

I looked at him incredulously.

"She slandered someone's name," I said.

He blew out his breath. "You and my wife were intimate. She probably still bears you a degree of resentment. The god Eros was never a rational influence, Dave. At the same time she doesn't want to see my campaign compromised because you've developed this crazy notion about Aaron Crown being railroaded. So she let both her imagination and her impetuosity cause her to do something foolish. We're sorry for whatever harm we've done you."

I cupped my hand on a fence rail, felt the hardness of the wood in my palm, tried to see my thoughts in my head before I spoke.

"I get the notion I'm in a therapy session," I said.

"If you were, you'd get a bill."

The back door of the house opened, and a slender, white-haired man with a pixie face, one wrinkled with the parchment lines of a chronic cigarette smoker, stepped out into the wind and waved at Buford. He wore a navy blue sports jacket with brass buttons and a champagne-colored silk scarf. I knew the face but I couldn't remember from where.

"I'll be just a minute, Clay," Buford called. Then to me, "Would you like to join us for breakfast?"

"No, thanks."

"How about a handshake, then?"

Two of the wranglers were yelling at each other in Spanish as the horses swirled around them in the lot. One had worked a hackamore over a mare's head and the other was trying to fling a blanket and saddle on her back.

"No? Stay and watch me get my butt thrown, then," Buford said.

"You were born for it."

"I beg your pardon?"

"The political life. You've got ice water in your veins," I said.

"You see that dead oak yonder? Two men were lynched there by my ancestors. When I went after Aaron Crown, I hoped maybe I could atone a little for what happened under that tree."

"It makes a great story."

"You're a classic passive-aggressive, Dave, no offense meant. You feign the role of liberal and humanist, but Bubba and Joe Bob own your heart."

"So long, Buford," I said, and walked back to my truck. The wind splayed and flattened the poplar trees against Buford's house. When I looked back over my shoulder, he was mounted on the mare's back, one hand twisted in the mane, the hackamore sawed back in the other, his olive-tan torso anointed with the sun's cool light, sculpted with the promise of perfection that only Greek gods know.

LATER, CLETE PURCEL returned my call and told me Mingo Bloomberg had been sprung from City Prison three days ago by attorneys who worked for Jerry Joe Plumb, also known as Short Boy Jerry, Jerry Ace, and Jerry the Glide.

But even as I held the receiver in my hand, I couldn't concentrate on Clete's words about Mingo's relationship to a peculiar player in the New Orleans underworld. The dispatcher had just walked through my open door and handed me a memo slip with the simple message written on it: *Call the Cap up at the zoo re: Crown. He says urgent.*

It took twenty minutes to get him on the phone.

"You was right. I should have listened to you. A bunch of the black boys caught him in the tool shack this morning," the captain said.

He'd had to walk from the field and he breathed hard into the telephone.

"Is he dead?" I asked.

"You got it turned around. He killed two of them sonsofbitches with his bare hands and liked to got a third with a cane knife. That old man's a real shit storm, ain't he?"

Chapter 7

Bootsie, Alafair, and I were eating supper in the kitchen that evening when the phone rang on the counter. Bootsie got up to answer it. Outside, the clouds in the west were purple and strung with curtains of rain.

Then I heard her say, "Before I give the phone to Dave, could you put Karyn on? I left her a couple of messages, but she probably didn't have time to call . . . I see . . . When will she be back? . . . Could you ask her to call me, Buford? I've really wanted to talk with her . . . Oh, you know, those things she said about Dave to the sheriff . . . Hang on now, here's Dave."

She handed me the phone.

"Buford?" I said.

"Yes." His voice sounded as though someone had just wrapped a strand of piano wire around his throat.

"You all right?" I said.

"Yes, I'm fine, thanks . . . You heard about Crown?" he said.

"A guard at the prison told me."

"Does this give you some idea of his potential?"

"I hear they were cruising for it."

"He broke one guy's neck. He drowned the other one in a barrel of tractor oil," he said.

"I couldn't place your friend this morning. He's Clay Mason, isn't he? What are you doing with him, partner?"

"None of your business."

"That guy was the P. T. Barnum of the acid culture."

"As usual, your conclusions are as wrong as your information."

He hung up the phone. I sat back down at the table.

"You really called Karyn LaRose?" I asked.

"Why? Do you object?" she said.

"No."

She put a piece of chicken in her mouth and looked at me while she chewed. My stare broke.

"I wish I hadn't gone out to see her, Boots."

"He's mixed up with that guru from the sixties?" she said.

"Who knows? The real problem is one nobody cares about."

She waited.

"Aaron Crown had no motivation to kill Ely Dixon. I'm more and more convinced the wrong man's in prison," I said.

"He was in the Klan, Dave."

"They kicked him out. He busted up a couple of them with a wood bench inside a Baptist church."

But why, I thought.

It was a question that only a few people in the Louisiana of the 1990s could answer.

HIS NAME WAS Billy Odom and he ran a junkyard on a stretch of state highway west of Lafayette. Surrounded by a floodplain of emerald green rice fields, the junkyard seemed an almost deliberate eyesore that Billy had lovingly constructed over the decades from rusted and crushed car bodies, mountains of bald tires, and outbuildings festooned with silver hubcaps.

Like Aaron Crown, he was a north Louisiana transplant, surrounded by papists, blacks who could speak French, and a historical momentum that he had not been able to shape or influence or dent in any fashion. His face was as round as a moonpie under his cork sun helmet, split with an incongruous smile that allowed him to hide his thoughts while he probed for the secret meaning that lay in the speech of others. A Confederate flag, almost black with dirt, was nailed among the yellowed calendars on the wall of the shed where he kept his office. He kept licking his lips, leaning forward in his chair, his eyes squinting as though he were staring through smoke.

"A fight in a church? I don't call it to mind," he said.

"You and Aaron were in the same klavern, weren't you?"

His eyes shifted off my face, studied the motes of dust spinning in a shaft of sunlight. He cocked his head philosophically but said nothing.

"Why'd y'all run him off?" I asked.

" 'Cause the man don't have the sense God give an earthworm."

"Come on, Billy."

"He used to make whiskey and put fertilizer in the mash. That's where I think he got that stink at. His old woman left him for a one-legged blind man."

"You want to help him, Billy, or see him hung out to dry at Angola?"

His hands draped over his thighs. He studied the backs of them.

"It was 'cause of the girl. His daughter, what's her name, Sabelle, the one runs the bar down at the Underpass."

"I don't follow you."

"The meeting was at a church house. She wasn't but a girl then, waiting outside in the pickup truck. Two men was looking out the window at her. They didn't know Crown was sitting right behind them.

"One goes, 'I hear that's prime.'

"The other one goes, 'It ain't bad. But you best carry a ball of string to find your way back out.'

"That's when Crown put the wood to them. Then he tore into them with his boots. It taken four of us to hold him down."

"You kicked him out of the Klan for defending his daughter?" I said.

Billy Odom pried a pale splinter out of his grease-darkened desk and scratched lines in his skin with it.

"When they're young and cain't keep their panties on, the old man's in it somewhere," he said.

"*What?*"

"Everybody had suspicioned it. Then a woman from the welfare caught him at it and told the whole goddamn town. That's how come Crown moved down here."

"Aaron and his daughter?" I said.

THE MAN WHO had seen the accident did not report it for almost three days, not until his wife was overcome with guilt herself and went to a priest and then with her husband to the St. Martin Parish sheriff's office.

Helen Soileau and I stood on the levee by a canal that rimmed Henderson Swamp and watched a diver in a wetsuit pull the steel hook and cable off the back of a wrecker, wade out into the water by a row of bridge pilings, sinking deeper into a balloon of silt, then disappear beneath the surface. The sky was blue overhead, the moss on the dead cypress lifting in the breeze, the sun dancing on the sandbars and the deep green of the willow islands. When a uniformed sheriff's deputy kicked the winch into gear and the cable clanged tight on the car's frame, a gray cloud of mud churned to the surface like a fat man's fist.

Helen walked up on the wood bridge that spanned the canal, rubbed her shoe on one unrailed edge, and walked back down on the levee again. The front tires of the submerged car, which lay upside down, broke through a tangle of dead hyacinths.

The man who had seen the accident sat on the levee with his wife at his side. He wore a greasy cap, with the bill pulled low over his eyes.

"Go through it again," I said.

He had to crane his head upward, into the sunlight, when he spoke.

"It was dark. I was walking back to the camp from that landing yonder. There wasn't no moon. I didn't see everything real good," he replied. His wife looked at the steel cable straining against the automobile's weight, her face vaguely ashamed, the muscles collapsed.

"Yes, you did," I said.

"He fishtailed off the levee when he hit the bridge, and the car went in. The headlights was on, way down at the bottom of the canal."

"Then what happened?" I asked.

He flexed his lips back on his teeth, as though he were dealing with a profound idea.

"The man floated up in the headlights. Then he come up the levee, right up to the hard road where I was at. He was all wet and walking fast." He turned his face out of the sunlight again, retreated back into the shade of his cap.

I tapped the edge of my shoe against his buttock.

"You didn't report an accident. If we find anything in that car we shouldn't, you'd better be in our good graces. You with me on this?" I said.

His wife, who wore a print-cotton dress that bagged on her wide shoulders, whispered close to his face while her hand tried to find his.

"He tole me to forget what I seen," the man said. "He put his mout' right up against mine when he said it. He grabbed me. In a private place, real hard." The flush on the back of his neck spread into his hairline.

"What did he look like?" Helen said.

"He was a white man, that's all I know. He'd been drinking whiskey. I could smell it on his mout'. I ain't seen him good 'cause the moon was down."

"You see that power pole there? There's a light on it. It comes on every night," I said.

The diver walked out of the shallows next to the overturned Lincoln as the winch slid it up on the mudbank. All the windows were closed, and the interior was filled from the roof to the floor with brown water. Then, through the passenger's side, we saw a brief pink-white flash against the glass, like a molting fish brushing against the side of a dirty aquarium.

The diver tried to open the door, but it was wedged into the mud. He got a two-handed ball peen hammer, with a head the size of a brick, and smashed in the passenger window.

The water burst through the folded glass, peppering the levee with crawfish, leeches, a nest of ribbon-thin cottonmouths that danced in the grass as though their backs were broken. But those were not the images that defined the moment.

A woman's hand, then arm, extended itself in the rushing stream, as though the person belted to the seat inside were pointing casually to an object in the grass. The fingers were ringed with costume jewelry, the nails painted with purple-polish, the skin eaten by a disease that had robbed the tissue of its color.

I squatted down next to the man who had seen the accident and extended my business card on two fingers.

"He didn't try to pull her out. He didn't call for help. He let her drown, alone in the darkness. Don't let him get away with this, podna," I said.

CLETE CALLED THE bait shop Saturday morning, just as I was laying out a tray of chickens and links on the pit for our midday fishermen.

"You got a boat for rent?" he asked.

"Sure."

"Can you rent the guy with me some gear?"

"I have a rod he can borrow."

"It's a fine day for it, all right."

"Where are you?"

"Right up the road at the little grocery store. The guy's sitting out in my car. But he doesn't like to go where he's not invited, know what I'm saying, Dave? You want Mingo? Anytime I got to run down a skip, all I got to do is talk to the guy in my car. In this case, he feels a personal responsibility. Plus, y'all go back, right?"

"Clete, you didn't bring Jerry Joe Plumb here?" I said.

HE WAS NOTORIOUS by the time he was expelled from high school his senior year—a kid who'd grin just before he hit you, a bouree player who won high stakes from grown men at the saloon downtown, the best dancer in three parishes, the hustler who cast aluminum replicas of brass knuckles in the metal shop foundry and sold them for one dollar apiece with the ragged edges unbuffed so they could stencil daisy chains of red flowers on an adversary's face.

But all that happened after Jerry Joe's mother died his sophomore year. My memory was of a different boy, from a different, earlier time.

In elementary school we heard his father had been killed at Wake Island, but no one was really sure. Jerry Joe was one of those boys who came to town and left, entered and withdrew from school as his mother found work wherever she could. They used to live in a shack on the edge of a brickyard in Lafayette, then for several years in a trailer behind a welding shop south of New Iberia. On Sundays and the first Fridays of the month we would see him and his mother walking long distances to church, in both freezing weather and on one-hundred-degree afternoons. She was a pale woman, with a pinched and fearful light in her face, and she made him walk on the inside, as though the passing traffic were about to bolt across the curb and kill them both.

For a time his mother and mine worked together in a laundry, and Jerry Joe would come home from school with me and play until my mother and his came down the dirt road in my father's lopsided pickup. We owned a hand-crank phonograph, and Jerry Joe would root in a dusty pile of 78's and pull out the old scratched recordings of the Hackberry Ramblers and Iry LeJeune and listen to them over and over again, dancing with himself, smiling elfishly, his shoulders and arms cocked like a miniature prizefighter's.

One day after New Year's my father came back unexpectedly from offshore, where he worked as a derrick man, up on the monkey board, high above the drilling platform and the long roll of the Gulf. He'd been fired after arguing with the driller, and as he always did when he lost his job, he'd spent his drag-up check on presents for us and whiskey at Provost's Bar, as though new opportunity and prosperity were just around the corner.

But Jerry Joe had never seen my father before and wasn't ready for him. My father stood silhouetted in the doorway, huge, grinning, irreverent, a man who fought in bars for fun, the black hair on his chest bursting out of the two flannel shirts he wore.

"You dance pretty good. But you too skinny, you. We gone have to fatten you up. Y'all come see what I brung," he said.

At the kitchen table, he began unloading a canvas drawstring bag that was filled with smoked ducks, pickled okra and green tomatoes, a fruit cake, strawberry preserves, a jar of cracklings, and bottle after long-necked bottle of Jax beer.

"Your mama work at that laundry, too? . . . Then that's why you ain't eating right. You tell your mama like I tell his, the man own that place so tight he squeak when he walk," my father said. "Don't be looking at me like that, Davie. That man don't hire white people lessen he can treat them just like he do his colored."

Jerry Joe went back in the living room and sat in a stuffed chair by himself for a long time. The pecan trees by the house clattered with ice in the failing light. Then he came back in the kitchen and told us he was sick. My father put a jar of preserves and two smoked ducks in a paper bag for him and stuck it under his arm and we drove him home in the dark.

That night I couldn't find the hand crank to the phonograph, but I thought Jerry Joe had simply misplaced it. The next day I had an early lesson about the nature of buried anger and hurt pride in a child who had no one in whom he could confide. When the school bus stopped on the rock road where Jerry Joe lived, I saw a torn paper bag by the ditch, the dog-chewed remains of the smoked ducks, the strawberry preserves congealed on the edges of the shattered mason jar.

He never asked to come to our house again, and whenever I saw him he always conveyed the feeling I had stolen something valuable from him rather than he from us.

CLETE PARKED HIS dinged, chartreuse Cadillac convertible by the boat ramp and walked down the dock with Jerry Joe toward the bait shop. Jerry Joe was ebullient, enthused by the morning and the personal control he brought to it. His taut body looked made of whipcord, his hair thick and blond and wavy, combed in faint ducktails in back. He wore oxblood tasseled loafers, beige slacks, a loose-fitting navy blue sports shirt with silver thread in it. I said he walked down the dock. That's not true. Jerry Joe rolled, a Panama hat spinning on his finger, his thighs flexing against his slacks, change and keys ringing in his pockets, the muscles in his shoulders as pronounced as oiled rope.

"*Comment la vie*, Dave? You still sell those ham-and-egg sandwiches?" he said, and went through the screen door without waiting for an answer.

"Why'd you do this, Clete?" I said.

"There're worse guys in the life," he replied.

"Which ones?"

Jerry Joe bought a can of beer and a paper plate of sliced white boudin at the counter and sat at a table in back.

"You're sure full of sunshine, Dave," he said.

"I'm off the clock. If this is about Mingo, you should take it to the office," I said.

He studied me. At the corner of his right eye was a coiled white scar. He speared a piece of boudin with a toothpick and put it in his mouth.

"I'm bad for business here, I'm some kind of offensive presence?" he asked.

"We're way down different roads, Jerry Joe."

"Pull my jacket. Five busts, two convictions, both for operating illegal gambling equipment. This in a state that allows cock fighting . . . You got a jukebox here?"

"No."

"I heard about the drowned black girl. Mingo's dirty on this?"

"That's the name on the warrant."

"He says his car got boosted."

"We've got two witnesses who can put him together with the car and the girl."

"They gotta stand up, though. Right?" he asked.

"Nobody had better give them reason not to."

He pushed his plate away with the heel of his hand, leaned forward on his elbows, rolling the toothpick across his teeth. Under the bronze hair of his right forearm was a tattoo of a red parachute and the words *101st Airborne*.

"I hire guys like Mingo to avoid trouble, not to have it. But to give up one of my own people, even though maybe he's a piece of shit, I got to have . . . what's the term for it . . . compelling reasons, yeah, that's it," he said.

"How does aiding and abetting sound, or conspiracy after the fact?"

He scratched his face and glanced around the bait shop. His eyes crinkled at the corners. "You like my tattoo? Same outfit as Jimi Hendrix," he said.

I pushed a napkin and a pencil stub toward him. "Write down an address, Jerry Joe. NOPD will pick him up. You won't be connected with it."

"Why don't you get a jukebox? I'll have one of my vendors come by and put one in. You don't need no red quarters. You keep a hundred percent," he said. "Hey, Dave, it's all gonna work out. It's a new day. I guarantee it. Don't get tied up with this Aaron Crown stuff."

"What?"

But he drank his beer, winked at me as he fitted on his Panama hat, then walked out to the Cadillac to wait for Clete.

Chapter
8

Monday morning, when I went into work, I walked past Karyn LaRose's blue Mazda convertible in the parking lot. She sat behind the wheel, in dark glasses with a white scarf tied around her hair. When I glanced in her direction, she picked up a magazine from the seat and began reading it, a pout on her mouth.

"There's a guy talks like a college professor waiting to see you, Dave," Wally, the dispatcher, said. His great weight caused a perpetual flush in his neck and cheeks, as though he had just labored up a flight of stairs, and whenever he laughed, usually at his own jokes, his breath wheezed deep in his chest.

I looked through the doorway of the waiting room, then pointed my finger at the back of a white-haired man.

"That gentleman there?" I asked Wally.

"Let's see, we got two winos out there, a bondsman, a woman says UFOs is sending electrical signals through her hair curlers, the black guy cleans the johns, and the professor. Let me know which one you t'ink, Dave." His face beamed at his own humor.

Clay Mason, wearing a brown narrow-çut western coat with gold and green brocade on it, a snap-button turquoise shirt, striped vaquero pants, and yellow cowboy boots on his tiny feet, sat in a folding chair with a high-domed pearl Stetson on his crossed knee.

I was prepared to dislike him, to dismiss him as the Pied Piper of hallucinogens, an irresponsible anachronism who refused to die with the 1960s. But I was to learn that psychedelic harlequins don't survive by just being psychedelic harlequins.

"Could I help you, sir?" I asked.

"Yes, thank you. I just need a few minutes," he said, turning to look up at me, his thought processes broken. He started to rise, then faltered. I placed my hand under his elbow, and was struck by his fragility, the lightness of his bones.

A moment later I closed my office door behind us. His hair was as fine as white cornsilk, his lined mouth and purple lips like those of an old woman. When he sat down in front of my desk his attention seemed to become preoccupied with two black trusties mowing the lawn.

"Yes, sir?" I said.

"I've interposed myself in your situation. I hope you won't take offense," he said.

"Are we talking about the LaRoses?" I tried to smile when I said it.

"She's contrite about her behavior, even though I think she needs her rear end paddled. In lieu of that, however, I'm passing on an apology for her." The accent was soft, deep in the throat, west Texas perhaps. Then I remembered the biographical sketches, the pioneer family background, the inherited oil fortune, the academic scandals that he carried with him like tattered black flags.

"Karyn lied, Dr. Mason. With forethought and malicious intent. You don't get absolution by sending a surrogate to confession."

"That's damn well put. Will you walk with me into the parking lot?"

"No."

"Your feelings are your feelings, sir. I wouldn't intrude upon them." His gaze went out the window. He flipped the back of his hand at the air. "It never really changes, does it?"

"Sir?"

"The black men in prison clothes. Still working off their indenture to the white race."

"One of those guys molested his niece. The other one cut his wife's face with a string knife."

"Then they're a rough pair and probably got what's coming to them," he said, and rose from his chair by holding on to the edge of my desk.

I walked him to the back door of the building. When I opened the door the air was cool, and dust and paper were blowing in the parking lot. Karyn looked at us through the windshield of her car, her features muted inside her scarf and dark glasses. Clay Mason waved his Stetson at the clouds, the leaves spinning in the wind.

"Listen to it rumble, by God. It's a magic land. There's a thunder of calvary in every electric storm," he said.

I asked a deputy to walk Clay Mason the rest of the way.

"Don't be too hard on the LaRoses," Mason said as the deputy took his arm. "They put me in mind of Eurydice and Orpheus trying to flee the kingdom of the dead. Believe me, son, they could use a little compassion."

Keep your eye on this one, I thought.

Karyn leaned forward and started her car engine, wetting her mouth as she might a ripe cherry.

HELEN SOILEAU WALKED into my office that afternoon, anger in her eyes.

"Pick up on my extension," she said.

"What's going on?"

"Mingo Bloomberg. Wally put him through to me by mistake."

I punched the lighted button and placed the receiver to my ear. "Where are you, Mingo?" I said.

"You got Short Boy Jerry to jam me up," he said.

"Wrong."

"Don't tell me that. The bondsman pulled my bail. I got that material witness beef in my face again." A streetcar clanged in the background, vibrated and squealed on the tracks.

"What do you want?" I said.

"Something to come in."

"Sorry."

"I don't like being made everybody's fuck."

"You let that girl drown. You're calling the wrong people for sympathy."

"She wanted some ribs. I went inside this colored joint in St. Martinville. I come back out and the car's gone."

I could hear him breathing in the silence.

"I delivered money to Buford LaRose's house," he said.

"How much?"

"How do I know? It was locked in a satchel. It was heavy, like it was full of phone books."

"If that's all you're offering, you're up Shit's Creek."

"The guy gonna be governor is taking juice from Jerry Ace, that don't make your berries tingle?"

"We don't monitor campaign contributions, Mingo. Call us when you're serious. Right now I'm busy," I said. I eased the receiver down in the cradle and looked at Helen, who was sitting with one haunch on the corner of my desk.

"You going to leave him out there?" she said.

"It's us or City Prison in New Orleans. I think he'll turn himself in to us, then try to get to our witnesses."

"I hope so. Yes, indeedy."

"What'd he say to you?"

"Oh, he and I will have a talk about it sometime." She opened a book that was on my desk. "Why you reading Greek mythology?"

"That fellow Clay Mason compared the LaRoses to Orpheus and Eurydice . . . They're characters out of Greek legend," I said. She flipped through several pages in the book, then looked at me again. "Orpheus went down into the Underworld to free his dead wife. But he couldn't pull it off. Hades got both of them."

"Interesting stuff," she said. She popped the book closed, stood up, and tucked her short-sleeved white shirt into her gunbelt with her thumbs. "Bloomberg goes down for manslaughter, Dave, leaving the scene of a fatal accident, abduction, anything we can hang on him. No deals, no slack. He gets max time on this one."

"Why would it be otherwise?"

She leaned on the desk and stared directly into my face. Her upper arms were round and hard against the cuffs of her sleeves.

"Because you've got a board up your ass about Karyn LaRose," she said.

THAT NIGHT, IN my dreams, Victor Charles crawled his way once again through a moonlit rice field, his black pajamas glued to his body, his triangular face as bony and hard as a serpent's. But even though he himself was covered with mud and human feces from the water, the lenses on the scope of his French rifle were capped and dry, the bolt action and breech oiled and wiped clean, the muzzle of the barrel wrapped with a condom taken off a dead GI. He was a very old soldier who had fought the Japanese, the British, German-speaking French Legionnaires, and now a new and improbable breed of neo-colonials, blue-collar kids drafted out of slums and rural shitholes that Victor Charles would not be able to identify with his conception of America.

He knew how to turn into a stick when flares popped over his head, snip through wire hung with tin cans that rang like cowbells, position himself deep in foliage to hide the muzzle flash, count the voices inside the stacked sandbags, wait for either the black or white face that flared wetly in a cigarette lighter's flame.

With luck he would always get at least two, perhaps three, before he withdrew backward into the brush, back along the same watery route that had brought him into our midst, like the serpent constricting its body back into its hole while its enemies thundered past it.

That's the way it went down, too. Victor Charles punched our ticket and disappeared across the rice field, which was now sliced by tracers and geysered by grenades. But in the morning we found his scoped, bolt-action rifle, with leather sling and cloth bandoliers, propped in the wire like a monument to his own denouement.

Even in my sleep I knew the dream was not about Vietnam.

* * *

THE NEXT DAY I called Angola and talked to an assistant warden. Aaron Crown was in an isolation unit, under twenty-three-hour lockdown. He had just been arraigned on two counts of murder.

"You're talking about first-degree murder? The man was attacked," I said.

"Stuffing somebody upside down in a barrel full of oil and clamping down the top isn't exactly the system's idea of self-defense," he replied.

I called Buford LaRose's campaign office in New Iberia and was told he was giving a speech to a convention of land developers in Baton Rouge at noon.

I took the four-lane into Lafayette, then caught I-10 across the Atchafalaya swamp. The cypress and willows were thick and pale green on each side of the elevated highway, the bays wrinkled with wind in the sunlight. Then the highway crossed through meadowland and woods full of palmettos, and up ahead I saw the Mississippi bridge and the outline of the capitol building and the adjacent hotel where Buford was speaking.

He knew his audience. He was genteel and erudite, but he was clearly one of them, respectful of the meretricious enterprises they served and the illusions that brought them together. They shook his hand after his speech and touched him warmly on the shoulders, as if they drew power from his legendary football career, the radiant health and good looks that seemed to define his future.

At the head table, behind a crystal bowl filled with floating camellias, I saw Karyn LaRose watching me.

The dining room was almost empty when Buford chose to recognize me.

"Am I under arrest?"

"Just one question: Why did Crown leave his rifle behind?"

"A half dozen reasons."

"I've been through your book with a garden rake. You never deal with it."

"Try he panicked and ran."

"It was the middle of the night. No one else was around."

"People tend to do irrational things when they're killing other people."

The waiters were clearing the tables and the last emissary from the world of Walmart had said his farewell and gone out the door.

"Take a ride up to Angola with me and confront Crown," I said.

He surprised me. I saw him actually think about it. Then the moment went out of his eyes. Karyn got up from her chair and came around the table. She wore a pink suit with a corsage pinned above the breast.

"Crown might get a death sentence for killing those two inmates," I said, looking back at Buford.

"Anything's possible," he replied.

"That's it? A guy you helped put in prison, maybe unjustly, ends up injected, that's just the breaks?"

"Maybe he's a violent, hateful man who's getting just what he deserves."

I started to walk away. Then I turned.

"I'm going to scramble your eggs," I said.

I was so angry I walked the wrong way in the corridor and went outside into the wrong parking lot. When I realized my mistake I went back through the corridor toward the lobby. I passed the dining room, then a short hallway that led back to a service elevator. Buford was leaning against the wall by the elevator door, his face ashen, his wife supporting him by one arm.

"What happened?" I said.

The elevator door opened.

"Help me get him up to our room," Karyn said.

"I think he needs an ambulance."

"No! We have our own physician here. Dave, help me, *please*. I can't hold him up."

I took his other arm and we entered the elevator. Buford propped the heel of his hand against the support rail on the back wall, pulled his collar loose with his fingers, and took a deep breath.

"I did a five-minute mile this morning. How about that?" he said, a smile breaking on his mouth.

"You better ease up, partner," I said.

"I just need to lie down. One hour's sleep and I'm fine."

I looked at Karyn's face. It was composed now, the agenda, whatever it was, temporarily back in place.

We walked Buford down to a suite on the top floor and put him in bed and closed the door behind us.

"He's talking to a state police convention tonight," Karyn said, as though offering an explanation for the last few minutes. Through the full-glass windows in the living room you could see the capitol building, the parks and boulevards and trees in the center of the city, the wide sweep of the Mississippi River, the wetlands to the west, all the lovely urban and rural ambience that came with political power in Louisiana.

"Is Buford on uppers?" I asked.

"No. It's . . . He has a prescription. He gets overwrought sometimes."

"You'd better get him some help, Karyn."

I walked through the foyer to the door.

"You're going?" she said.

She stood inches from me, her face turned up into mine. The exertion of getting Buford into the room had caused her to perspire, and her platinum hair and tanned skin took on a dull sheen in the overhead light. I could smell her perfume in the enclosure, the heat from her body. She leaned her forehead into my chest and placed her hands lightly on my arms.

"Dave, it wasn't just the alcohol, was it? You liked me, didn't you?"

She tapped my hips with her small fists, twisted her forehead back and forth on my chest as though an unspoken conclusion about her life were trying to break from her throat.

I put one hand on her arm, then felt behind me for the elongated door handle. It was locked in place, rigid across the sweating cup of my palm.

Chapter
9

A DAY LATER CLETE Purcel's chartreuse Cadillac convertible, the top down, pulled up in front of the sheriff's department with Mingo Bloomberg in the passenger's seat. Clete and Mingo came up the walk, through the waiting room, and into my office. Mingo stood in front of my desk in white slacks and a lemon yellow shirt with French cuffs. He rotated his neck, as though his collar were too tight, then put a breath mint in his mouth.

"My lawyer's getting me early arraignment and recognizance. I'm here as a friend of the court, so you got questions, let's do it now, okay?" he said. He snapped the mint in his molars.

"Mingo, I don't think that's the way to start out the day here," Clete said.

"What's going on, Clete?" I said.

Clete stepped out into the hall and waited for me. I closed the door behind me.

"Short Boy Jerry gave me two hundred bucks to deliver the freight. Don't let Mingo take you over the hurdles. Jerry Joe and NOPD both got their foot on his chain," he said.

I opened the door and went back in.

"How you feel, Mingo?" I said.

"My car was boosted. I didn't drown a black girl. So I feel okay."

"You a stand-up guy?" I said.

"What's that mean?"

"Jerry Ace is giving us an anchovy so we don't come back for the main meal. You comfortable with that, Mingo? You like being an hors d'oeuvre?" I said.

"What I don't like is being in New Orleans with a target painted on my back. I'm talking about the cops in the First District who maybe stomped a guy's hair all over the cement . . . I got to use the john. Purcel wouldn't stop the car."

He looked out the glass partition, then saw the face looking back at him.

"Hey, keep her away from me," he said.

"You don't like Detective Soileau?" I said.

"She's a muff-diver. I told her over the phone, she ought to get herself a rubber schlong so she can whip it around and spray trees or whatever she wants till she gets it out of her system."

Helen was coming through the door now. I put my hand on her shoulder and walked her back into the corridor.

"Jerry Joe Plumb made him surrender," I said.

"Why?" she said, her eyes still fastened on Mingo.

"He's tied up somehow with Buford LaRose and doesn't want us in his face. Mingo says he's getting out on his own recognizance. I think he's going to head for our witnesses."

"Like hell he is. Has he been Mirandized?"

"Not yet."

She opened the door so abruptly the glass rattled in the frame.

A HALF HOUR LATER she called me from the jail.

"Guess what? Shithead attacked me. I'll have the paperwork ready for the court in the morning," she said.

"Where is he?"

"Iberia General. He fell down a stairs. He also needed twelve stitches where I hit him with a baton. Forget recognizance, baby cakes. He's going to be with us awhile."

"Helen?"

"The paperwork is going to look fine. I went to Catholic school. I have beautiful penmanship."

CLETE AND I ATE lunch at an outdoor barbecue stand run by a black man in a grove of oak trees. The plank table felt cool in the shade, and you could smell the wet odor of green cordwood stacked under a tarp next to the stand.

"Because I was up early anyway, I happened to turn on the TV and catch *Breakfast Edition*, you know, the local morning show in New Orleans," he said. His eyes stayed on my face. "What the hell you doing, Streak?"

"Aaron Crown bothers me."

"You went on television, Dave, with this Hollywood character, what's-his-name, Felton, whatever."

"I was taped here while he interviewed me on the phone, then it was spliced into the show."

"Forget the technical tour. Why don't you resign your job while you're at it? What's your boss have to say?"

"I don't think he's heard about it yet."

"You don't take police business to civilians, big mon. To begin with, they don't care about it. They'll leave you hanging in the breeze, then your own people rat-fuck you as a snitch."

"Maybe that's the way it's supposed to shake out," I said.

He drank from a bottle of Dixie beer, one eye squinting over the bottle at me. "Something else is involved here, mon," he said.

"Don't make it a big deal, Clete."

"It's the broad, isn't it?" he said.

"No."

"You got into the horizontal bop once with her and you're worried you're going to do it again. So you got rid of temptation with a baseball bat. In the meantime maybe you just splashed your career into the bowl . . . Wait a minute, you didn't pork her again, did you?"

"No . . . Will you stop talking like that?"

"Dave, rich guys don't marry mud women from New Guinea. She's one hot-ass piece of work. We all got human weaknesses, noble mon. All I got to do is see her on TV and my Johnson starts barking."

"You were a fugitive on a homicide warrant," I said. "The victim was a psychopath, and his death was a mistake, but the point is you killed him. What if you hadn't beat it? What if you were put away for life unjustly?"

He wiped a smear of barbecue sauce off his palm with a napkin, looked out at the sunlight on the street.

"This guy Crown must mean a lot to you . . . I think I'm going to Red's in Lafayette, take a steam, start the day over again," he said.

AN HOUR LATER the sheriff buzzed my extension and asked me to walk down to his office. By now I was sure he had heard about my appearance on *Morning Edition*, and all the way down the corridor I tried to construct a defense for conduct that, in police work, was traditionally considered indefensible. When I opened the door he was staring at a sheet of lined notebook paper in his hand, rubbing his temple with one finger. His Venetian blinds were closed, and his windowsill was green with plants.

"Why is everything around here hard? Why can't we just take care of the problems in Iberia Parish? Can you explain that to me?" he said.

"If you're talking about my being on *Morning Edition*, I stand behind what I said, Sheriff. Aaron Crown didn't have motivation. I think Buford LaRose is building a political career on another man's broken back."

"You were on *Morning Edition*?"

The room was silent. He opened the blinds, and an eye-watering light fell through the window.

"Maybe I should explain," I said.

"I'd appreciate that."

When I finished he picked up the sheet of notebook paper and looked at it again.

"I wish you hadn't done that," he said.

"I'm sorry you feel that way."

"You don't understand. I wanted to believe the Mexican with the machete was simply a deranged man, not an assassin. I wanted to believe he had no connection with the Crown business."

"I'm not with you."

"I don't want to see you at risk, for God's sake. We got two calls from Mexico this morning, one from a priest in some shithole down in the interior, the other from a Mexican drug agent who says he's worked with the DEA in El Paso . . . The guy with the spiderweb tattoos, the lunatic, some *rurales* popped holes all over him. He's dying and he says you will, too . . . He says 'for the *bugarron*.' What's a *bugarron*?"

"I don't know."

"There's a storm down there. I got cut off before I could make sense out of this drug agent . . . Get a flight this afternoon. Take Helen with you. Americans with no backup tend to have problems down there."

"We have money for this?"

"Bring me a sombrero."

Chapter 10

W<small>E FLEW INTO</small> El Paso late that night. By dawn of the next day we were on a shuttle flight to a windswept dusty airport set among brown hills five hundred miles into Mexico. The Mexican drug agent who met us wore boots and jeans, a badge on his belt and a pistol and a sports coat over a wash-faded blue golf shirt. His name was Heriberto, and he was unshaved and had been up all night.

"The guy try to kill you, huh?" he said, as he unlocked the doors to the Cherokee in the parking lot.

"That's right," I said.

"I wouldn't want a guy like that after me. *Es Indio*, man, know what I mean? Guy like that will cook your heart over a fire," he said. He looked at Helen. "*Gringuita*, you want to use the rest room? Where we going, there ain't any bushes along the road."

He looked indolently at the flat stare in her face.

"What did you call her?" I asked.

"Maybe you all didn't get no sleep last night," he said. "You can sleep while I drive. I never had a accident on this road. Last night, with no moon, I come down with one headlight."

The sun rose in an orange haze above hills that looked made of slag, with cactus and burnt mesquite and chaparral on the sides. The dirt road twisted through a series of arroyos where the sandstone walls were scorched by grass fires, then we forded a river that splayed like coffee-stained milk over a broken wood dam and overflowed the banks into willows and rain trees and a roofless mud brick train station by tracks that seemed to disappear into a hillside.

"You looking at where those tracks go?" Heriberto said. "The mine company had a tunnel there. The train's still inside."

"Inside?" I said.

"Pancho Villa blew the mountain down on the tunnel. When a train full of Huerta's jackals was coming through. They're still in there, man. They ain't coming out."

I took my notebook out of my shirt pocket and opened it.

"What's *bugarron* mean?" I asked.

Helen had fallen asleep in back, her head on her chest.

"It's like *maricon*, except the *bugarron* considers himself the guy."

"You're talking about homosexuals? I don't get it."

"He's *adicto*, man. Guy's got meth and lab shit in his head. Those double-ought buckshots in him don't help his thinking too good, either."

"What lab shit?"

He concentrated on the road, ignoring my question, and swerved around an emaciated dog.

"Why'd you bring us down here?" I said, trying to keep the frustration out of my voice.

"The priest is my wife's cousin. He says you're in danger. Except what he knows he knows from the confession. That means he can't tell it himself. You want to go back to the airport, man, tell me now."

The sun rose higher in an empty cobalt sky. We crossed a flat plain with sloughs and reeds by the roadside and stone mountains razored against the horizon and Indian families who seemed to have walked enormous distances from no visible site in order to beg by the road. Then the road began to climb and the air grew cooler. We passed an abandoned ironworks dotted with broken windows, and went through villages where the streets were no more than crushed rock and the doors to all the houses were painted either green or blue. The mountains above the villages were gray and bare and the wind swept down the sheer sides and blew dust out of the streets.

"It's all Indians here. They think you paint the door a certain color, evil spirits can't walk inside," Heriberto said.

Helen was awake now and looking out the window.

"This is what hell must look like," she said.

"I grew up here. I tell you something, we don't got guys like Araña here. He's from Jalisco. I tell you something else, they don't even got guys like Araña *there*. Guys like him got to go to the United States to get like that, you understand what I'm saying?"

"No," she answered, looking at the back of his neck.

"My English ain't too good. It's a big problem I got," he said.

We pulled into a village that was wedged like a toothache in a steep-sided, narrow canyon strewn with the tailings from a deserted open-pit mine on the mountain above. Some of the houses had no outbuildings, only a piece of concrete sewer pipe inserted vertically into the dirt yard for a community toilet. Next to the cantina was the police station, a squat, whitewashed building with green shutters that were latched shut on the windows. A jeep carrying three *rurales* and a civilian with a bloody ear and hair like a lion's mane came up the road in a flume of dust from the direction of the mine and parked in front. The three *rurales* wore dirty brown uniforms and caps with lacquered brims and World War I thumb-buster U.S. Army .45 revolvers. The civilian's clothes were in rags and his hands were roped behind him. The *rurales* took him inside the building and closed the door.

"Are these the guys who popped Araña?" I asked.

"Yeah, man, but you don't want to be asking them no questions about it, know what I'm saying?" Heriberto said.

"No, I don't."

He scratched his nose, then told me a story.

The village had been visited by a carnival that featured a pedal-operated Ferris wheel, a donkey with a fifth leg that grew like a soft carrot out of its side, a concessionaire who sold hand-corked bottles of mescal that swam with thread worms, and Araña, the Spider, a magical man who swallowed flame and blew it like a red handkerchief into the air, whose scarlet, webbed tattoos, Indian-length hair, blackened mouth, and chemical green eyes could charm mountain women from their marital beds. His sexual energies were legendary.

"Araña was in the sack with the wrong man's wife?" I said.

"They gonna tell you that. You go away with that, take that story back home, everything's gonna be fine. You don't, you keep asking questions, maybe we got a problem. You see that guy they just took in? You don't want to go in there today."

"What'd he do?" Helen asked.

"Two children went in those empty buildings up at the mines and didn't come back. See, where all those pieces of tin are flapping in the wind. He lives in there by himself, he don't ever take a bath, comes down at night and steals food from people."

"Why'd they shoot Araña?" I said.

"Look, man, how I'm gonna tell you? This ain't no *marijuanista* we're talking about. This guy takes high-powered stuff into the States sometimes. These local guys know that. It's called *la mordita*, you got to pay the bite, man, or maybe you have a shitload of trouble. Like the guy behind those green shutters now. He don't want to see nobody light a cigar."

The infirmary had been built by an American mining company in the oblong shape of a barracks on a bench above the main street of the village. The lumber had warped the nails out of the joists, and the windows were covered with ragged plastic sheets that popped in the wind. In back, a gasoline-powered generator throbbed next to a water well that had been dug in the middle of a chicken yard.

Inside, the beds were in rows, squared away, either a slop jar or spittoon under each one, the steel-gray blankets taut with a military tuck. The woodstove was unlighted, the open door congealed with dead ash. The bare walls and floors seemed enameled with cold.

But the man named Araña needed no heat source other than his own.

He lay on top of the sheet, naked except for a towel across his loins, the scarlet tattoos on his skin emblazoned with sweat. His chest was peppered with wounds that had been dressed with squares of gauze and tape and a yellow salve that smelled like an engine lubricant. But that was not where the offensive odor came from. His right thigh was twice the size it should have been, the shiny reddish black color of an eggplant.

The priest who had called the sheriff brought us chairs to sit by the bed. He was a thin, pale man, dressed in a windbreaker, flannel shirt, khaki pants, and work boots that were too big for his ankles, his black hair probably scissor-cropped at home. He put his hand on my arm and turned me aside before I sat down. His breath was like a feather that had been dipped in brandy.

"Araña has absolution but no rest. He believes he served evil people who are going to hurt you," he said. "But I'm not sure of anything he says now."

"What's he told you?"

"Many things. Few of them good."

"Father, I'm not asking you to violate the seal of the confessional."

"He's made himself insane with injections. He talks of his fears for young people. It's very confusing."

I waited. There was a pained glimmer in the priest's eyes. "Sir?" I said.

"The man some think killed children up at the mines is his relative," the priest said. "Or maybe he was talking about what he calls the *bugarron*. I don't know."

Helen and I sat down next to the bed. Helen took a tape recorder out of her purse and clicked it on. The man who was named Araña let his eyes wander onto my face.

"You know me, partner?" I said.

He tilted his chin so he could see me better, breathed hard through his nostrils. Then he spoke in a language I didn't recognize.

"It's an Indian dialect," the priest said. "No one speaks it here, except his relative, the crazy one who lives inside the mines."

"Who sent you to New Iberia, Araña?" I said.

But my best attempts at reaching inside his delirium seemed to be of no avail. I tried for a half hour, then felt my own attention start to wander. The priest left and came back. Helen yawned and straightened her back. "Sorry," she said. She took one cartridge out of the recorder and put in another.

Then, as though Araña had seen me for the first time, his hand cupped around my wrist and squeezed it like a vise.

"The *bugarron* ride a saddle with flowers cut in it. I seen him at the ranch. You messing everything up for them. They gonna kill you, man," he said.

"Who's this guy?"

"He ain't got no name. He got a red horse and a silver saddle. He like Indian boys."

Inadvertently, his hand drew mine against his gangrenous thigh. I saw the pain jump in his face, then anger replace the recognition that had been in his eyes.

"What's this man look like?" I said.

But I had become someone else now, perhaps an old enemy who had come aborning with the carrion birds.

Helen and I walked outside with the priest. The sunlight was cold inside the canyon. Heriberto waited for us in the Cherokee.

"I have no authority here, Father. But I'm worried about the fate of the man from the mines, the one inside the police station," I said.

"Why?"

"Heriberto says the *rurales* are serious men."

"Heriberto is corrupt. He takes money from drug smugglers. The *rurales* are Indians. It's against their way to deliberately injure an insane person."

"I see. Thank you for your goodwill, Father."

That night Helen and I boarded a four-engine plane for the connection flight back to El Paso. She looked out the window as we taxied onto the runway. Heriberto was standing by a hangar, one hand lifted in farewell.

"How do you read all that?" she said, nodding toward the glass.

"What?"

"Everything that happened today."

"It's an outdoor mental asylum," I said.

Later, she fell asleep with her head on my shoulder. I watched the clouds blowing through the propellers, then the sky was clear again and far below I saw the lights of a city spread through a long valley and the Rio Grande glowing under the moon.

Chapter 11

MONDAY MORNING KARYN LaRose walked through the department's waiting room and paused in front of the dispatcher's office. She didn't need to speak. Wally took one look at her and, without thinking, rose to his feet (and later could not explain to himself or anyone else why he did).

"Yes, ma'am?" he said.

She wore a snug, tailored white suit, white hose, and a wide-brim straw hat with a yellow band.

"Can Dave see me?" she asked.

"Sure, Ms. LaRose. You bet. I'll call him and tell him you're on your way."

He leaned out his door and watched her all the way down the hall.

When I opened the door for her I could feel a flush of color, like windburn, in my throat. Two deputies passing in the hall glanced at us, then one said something to the other and looked back over his shoulder again.

"You look flustered," she said.

"How you doin', Karyn?" I said.

She sat down in front of my desk. Her hat and face were slatted with sunlight.

"Clay said I have to do this. I mean apologize . . . here . . . in your office. To the sheriff, too. Otherwise, he says I'll have no serenity," she said. She smiled. Her platinum hair was tucked inside her hat. She looked absolutely beautiful.

"Why are you hanging around with Clay Mason?" I said.

"He was a guest of the university. He's a brilliant man. He's a very good poet, too."

"I heard he blew his wife's head off at a party in Mexico."

"It was an accident," she said.

I let my eyes drop to my watch.

"I'm sorry that I wronged you, Dave. I don't know what else to say." She took a breath. "Why do you have to treat me with fear and guilt? Is it because of the moment there in the hotel room? Did you think I wanted to seduce you with my husband sleeping a few feet away, for God's sake?"

"There's only one issue here, Karyn. Buford's not the man people think he is. He's taking money from Jerry Joe Plumb. The guy who delivered it to y'all's house was Mingo Bloomberg."

"Who?"

"He kills people. Right now he's in custody for leaving a black girl to drown in a submerged automobile in Henderson Swamp."

"I never heard of him. I doubt if Buford has, either."

"Jerry Joe's mobbed-up. Why do mobbed-up guys want your husband in Baton Rouge?"

"I can't understand you. What are you trying to do to us? Buford's opponents are the same people who supported David Duke."

"So what? Y'all have made a scapegoat out of Aaron Crown."

"Dave, you've let yourself become the advocate of a misanthropic degenerate who molested his daughter and murdered the bravest civil rights leader in Louisiana."

"How do you know he molested Sabelle?"

"I'm sorry, I'm not going to discuss a man like that."

I looked out the window, fiddled with a paper clip on my blotter.

"You're committed to lost and hopeless causes," she said. "I don't think it's because you're an idealist, either. It's pride. You get to be the iconoclast among the Philistines."

"I used to buy into psychobabble myself, Karyn. It's a lot of fun."

"I guess there's not much point in any of this, is there?" she said. Her skirt was tight against her body when she gathered up her purse and rose from her chair. "I wish it had been different, Dave. I wish the grog hadn't gotten you. I wish I'd been able to help. I can't say for sure I loved you, but I loved being with you. Be good to yourself, kiddo."

With that, she went out the door. I could hear my ears ring in the silence.

JUST BEFORE LUNCH the sheriff came into my office.

"This morning I've had a call from the mayor's office, one from the chamber of commerce, and one from the New Iberia Historical Preservation Society," he said. "Did you know Jerry Joe Plumb just bought an acre lot right down from the Shadows?"

"No."

"He also bought a bunch of rural property south of the city limits. How well do you get along with him?"

"All right."

"Find out what he's up to. I don't want any more phone calls."

"Where is he?"

"Watching a bulldozer level the house that's on the lot by the Shadows."

I drove down East Main under the arched live oaks that spanned the street, toward the Shadows, a red brick and white-columned antebellum home built in 1831 on Bayou Teche. The acre Jerry Joe had purchased was located between two Victorian homes and went all the way back to the bayou and was shaded by oaks that were over one hundred years old. I drove through the piked gate and parked next to a salvage truck and an earth grader, where a group of workmen were eating lunch. Down by the bayou was a huge pile of splintered cypress boards, twisted pipe, crushed plaster powdering in the wind, and a flattened gazebo with the passion vine still clinging to the lattice work.

"Y'all couldn't move it instead?" I said.

"The termites was too heavy to get on the truck. That's a pure fact," a man in a yellow hardhat with a jaw full of bread and Vienna sausage said. He and his friends laughed.

"Where's Jerry Joe? I'll tell him how effective you are at doing PR with the sheriff's department."

It was a short drive to Mulate's in Breaux Bridge. As soon as I stepped through the door I heard Clifton Chenier's "Hey Tite Fille" on the jukebox and saw Jerry Joe out on the polished wood floor, dancing with a waitress. His elbows were tucked close to his ribs, his fingers pointed at angles like a 1940s jitterbugger, his oxblood loafers glinting. His whole body seemed animated with rhythm. His shoulders tilted and vibrated; he jiggled and bopped and created an incredible sense of energy and movement without ever stepping out of a twelve-inch radius, and all the while his face beamed at the waitress with genuine pleasure and affection.

I ordered a 7-Up at the bar and waited for him to sit down. When he finished dancing he squeezed the waitress's hand, walked past me, his eyes fixed on the black barman, and said, "Bring my friend the same order I got."

"Don't do that, Jerry Joe," I said to his back.

He pulled out a chair at a table covered with a red-and-white-checkered cloth. "You got it whether you want it or not . . . Catfish filet with étouffée on the top. This is food you expect only in the afterlife," he said. He twisted another chair out. "What's the haps?"

"Some people want to know why you just bulldozed down a house that George Washington Cable once lived in."

"Who?"

"A famous writer."

"Because it had an asbestos roof, because the floors were like walking on wet cardboard, because there were vampire bats in the drainpipes."

"Why not work with people, Jerry Joe, explain that to them, instead of giving them heart failure?"

"Because the problem is not what I'm tearing down, it's what they think I'm going to build. Like maybe a pink elephant in the middle

of the historical district." He put a stuffed mushroom in his mouth.
"*What?* Oh, I get it. They got reason to have those kind of concerns?"

"I didn't say that."

"What are we talking about, then? I got it. It's not the house, it's me."

"No one can accuse you of being a Rotarian."

"I told you, my sheet's an embarrassment. I'm on a level with un-
licensed church bingo."

"You and some others guys hit a fur truck. You also stuffed a building contractor into a cement mixer."

"He was taking scabs through our picket. Besides, I pulled him back
out."

"Why are you buying property south of town?"

He patted his palm on top of his forearm, glanced toward the
sound of someone dropping coins inside the jukebox. "Maybe I want
out. Maybe I'm tired of New Orleans, being in the life, all that jazz.
So maybe I got a chance and I'm taking it."

"I'm not with you."

"Buford LaRose is good for business . . . Turn on your brain for
a minute, Dave . . . What if these peckerwoods get in Baton Rouge?
New Orleans will be a worst toilet than it already is."

"A Mexican guy tried to take me out. Your man Mingo says it was
a hit. Why do mobbed-up people in New Orleans care about a cop
in Iberia Parish?"

Jerry Joe scratched the red tattoo of a parachute on his forearm.

"Number one, Mingo's not my man. Number two, times are changing, Dave. Dope's gonna be out one day. The smart money is looking
for a new home . . . Listen to that . . . 'La Jolie Blon' . . . Boy, I love
that song. My mom taught me to dance to it."

"Where'd the hit come from?"

"I don't know. That's the honest-to-God truth. Just leave this civil
rights garbage alone and watch yourself with Karyn LaRose."

"How did you—"

"You want to ask me where she's got a certain birthmark?" He
pressed his hands flat on the tablecloth and looked at them. "Try a
little humility, Dave. I hate to tell you this, but some broads ain't any

different from men. They like to screw down and marry up. She ever talk about marriage to you?"

He raised his eyes and started to grin. Then his face became embarrassed and he grimaced and looked around the room. The coiled white scar at the corner of his eye was bunched in a knot.

"You want a breadstick?" he asked.

OUR JAILER, KELSO Andrepont, was a three-hundred-pound bisexual black man who pushed his way through life with the calm, inert certitude of a glacier sliding downhill. The furrows in his neck gave off an oily shine and were dotted with moles that looked like raisins pasted on his skin, and his glasses magnified his eyes into luminous orbs the size of oysters.

He stared up at me from his cluttered desk.

"So why are we holding the guy here if he's got a negligent homicide beef in St. Martin Parish?"

"We're treating the case as an abduction. The abduction happened inside Iberia Parish," I said. "We're working with St. Martin on the other charge."

"Yeah, shit rolls downhill, too. And I'm always downhill from you, Robicheaux."

"I'm sorry to hear you take that attitude."

"This guy was born for Camp J. He don't belong here. I got enough racial problems as it is."

"How about starting over, Kelso?"

"He complains he's being discriminated against, get this, because he's Jewish and we're making him eat pork. So he throws his tray in a trusty's face. Then he says he wants isolation because maybe there's a black guy coming in here to whack him out.

"I go, 'What black guy?'

"He goes, 'How the fuck should I know? Maybe the guy I just threw the food at.'

"I go, 'Your brain's been doing too many pushups, Bloomberg. You ought to give it a rest.'

"He goes, 'I come in here on my own and a dyke blindsides me with a baton and charges me with assault. No wonder you got a jail ninety percent cannibal. No one else would live in a shithole like this.' "

"You've got him in isolation now?" I asked.

"A guy who uses words like *cannibal* to a black man? No, I got him out there in the yard, teaching aerobics to the brothers. This job would drive me to suicide if it wasn't for guys like you, Robicheaux."

Five minutes later I checked my weapon with a guard who sat inside a steel-mesh cage, and a second guard unlocked a cell at the end of a sunlit corridor that rang with all the sounds of a jailhouse—clanging doors and mop buckets, a dozen radios tuned to a half dozen stations, shouted voices echoing along the ceilings. Mingo Bloomberg sat in his boxer undershorts on a bunk that was suspended from the wall with chains. His body was pink, hairless, without either fat or definition, as though it had been synthetically manufactured. The stitches above his ear looked like a fine strand of black barbed wire embedded in his scalp.

"Kelso says you're being a pain in the ass," I said.

He let a towel dangle between his legs and bounced it idly on top of his bare toes.

"Did your lawyer tell you our witnesses are going to stand up?" I said.

I expected anger, another run at manipulation. Instead, he was morose, his attention fixed on the sounds out in the corridor, as though they held meaning that he had never quite understood before.

"Did you hear me?" I said.

"I talked to my cousin last night. The wrong people think you got dials on me. There's a black guy, out of Miami, a freelance 'cause Miami's an open city. He's supposed to look like a six-and-a-half-foot stack of apeshit. The word is, maybe he's the guy did this screenwriter in the Quarter. My cousin says the Miami guy's got the whack and is gonna piece it off to some boons inside the jail."

"You're the hit?"

He stared at the floor, put his little finger in his ear as though there were water in it.

"I never broke no rules. It feels funny," he said.

"Who's setting it up, Mingo?"

"How many guys could I put inside? You figure it out."

"You ever hear of a *bugarron*?" I asked.

"No . . . Don't ask me about crazy stuff I don't know anything about. I'm not up for it." His shoulders were rounded, his chest caved-in. "You've read a lot, haven't you, I mean books in college, stuff like that?"

"Some."

"I read something once, in the public library, up on St. Charles. It said . . . in your life you end up back where you started, maybe way back when you were little. The difference is you understand it the second time around. But it don't do you no good."

"Yes?"

"That never made sense to me before."

THAT NIGHT A GUARD escorted Mingo Bloomberg down to the shower in his flipflops and skivvies. The guard ate a sandwich and read a magazine on a wood bench outside the shower wall. The steam billowed out on the concrete, then the sound of the water became steady and uninterrupted on the shower floor. The guard put down his magazine and peered around the opening in the wall. He looked at Mingo's face and the rivulets of water running down it, dropped the sandwich, and ran back down the corridor to get the count man from the cage.

Chapter
12

It was sunrise when I turned into Buford LaRose's house the next morning. I saw him at the back of his property, inside a widely spaced stand of pine trees, a gray English riding cap on his head, walking with a hackamore in his hand toward a dozen horses that were bolting and turning in the trees. The temperature had dropped during the night, and their backs steamed like smoke in the early light. I drove my truck along the edge of a cleared cane field and climbed through the railed fence and walked across the pine needles into the shade that smelled of churned sod and fresh horse droppings.

I didn't wait for him to greet me. I took a photograph from my shirt pocket and showed it to him.

"You recognize this man?" I asked.

"No. Who is he, a convict?"

"Mingo Bloomberg. He told me he delivered money to your house for Jerry Joe Plumb."

"Sorry. I don't know him."

I took a second photograph from my pocket, a Polaroid, and held it out in my palm.

"That was taken last night," I said. "We had him in lockup for his own protection. But he hanged himself with a towel in the shower."

"You really know how to get a jump start on the day, Dave. Look, Jerry Joe's connected to a number of labor unions. If I refuse his contribution, maybe I lose several thousand union votes in Jefferson and Orleans parishes."

"It sure sounds innocent enough."

"I'm sorry it doesn't fit into your moral perspective . . . Don't go yet. I want to show you something."

He walked deeper into the trees. Even though there had been frost on the cane stubble that morning, he wore only a T-shirt with his khakis and half-topped boots and riding cap. His triceps looked thick and hard and were ridged with flaking skin from his early fall redfishing trips out on West Cote Blanche Bay. He turned and waited for me.

"Come on, Dave. You made a point of bringing your photographic horror show to my house. You can give me five more minutes of your time," he said.

The land sloped down through persimmon trees and palmettos and a dry coulee bed that was choked with leaves. I could hear the horses nickering behind us, their hooves thudding on the sod. Ahead, I could see the sunlight on the bayou and the silhouette of a black marble crypt surrounded by headstones and a carpet of mushrooms and a broken iron fence. The headstones were green with moss, the chiseled French inscriptions worn into faint tracings.

Buford pushed open the iron gate and waited for me to step inside.

"My great-grandparents are in that crypt," he said. He rubbed his hand along the smooth stone, let it stop at a circular pinkish white inlay that was cracked across the center. "Can you recognize the flower? My great-grandfather and both his brothers rode with the Knights of the White Camellia."

"Your wife told me."

"They weren't ashamed of it. They were fine men, even though some of the things they did were wrong."

"What's the point?"

"I believe it's never too late to atone. I believe we can correct the past, make it right in some way."

"You're going to do this for the Knights of the White Camellia?"

"I'm doing it for my family. Is there something wrong with that?" he said. He continued to look at my face. The water was low and slow moving in the bayou and wood ducks were swimming along the edge of the dead hyacinths. "Dave?"

"I'd better be going," I said.

He touched the front of my windbreaker with his fingers. But I said nothing.

"I was speaking to you about a subject that's very personal with me. You presume a great deal," he said. I looked away from the bead of light in his eyes. "Are you hard of hearing?" He touched my chest again, this time harder.

"Don't do that," I said.

"Then answer me."

"I don't think they were fine men."

"Sir?"

"Shakespeare says it in *King Lear*. The Prince of Darkness is a gentleman. They terrorized and murdered people of color. Cut the bullshit, Buford."

I walked out the gate and back through the trees. I heard his feet in the leaves behind me. He grabbed my arm and spun me around.

"That's the last time you'll turn your back on me, sir," he said.

"Go to hell."

His hands closed and opened at his sides, as though they were kneading invisible rubber balls. His forearms looked swollen, webbed with veins.

"You fucked my wife and dumped her. You accuse me of persecuting an innocent man. You insult my family. I don't know why I ever let a piece of shit like you on my property. But it won't happen again. I guarantee you that, Dave."

He was breathing hard. A thought, like a dark bird with a hooked beak, had come into his eyes, stayed a moment, then left. He slipped his hands stiffly into his back pockets.

The skin of my face felt tight, suddenly cold in the wind off the bayou. I could feel a dryness, a constriction in my throat, like a stick turned sideways. I tried to swallow, to reach for an adequate response. The leaves and desiccated twigs under my feet crunched like tiny pieces of glass.

"You catch me off the clock and repeat what you just said . . ." I began.

"You're a violent, predictable man, the perfect advocate for Aaron Crown," he said, and walked through the pines toward the house. He flung the hackamore into a tree trunk.

THAT NIGHT I LAY in the dark and looked at the ceiling, then sat on the side of the bed, my thoughts like spiders crawling out of a paper bag I didn't know how to get rid of. A thick, low fog covered the swamp, and under the moon the dead cypress protruded like rotted pilings out of a white ocean.

"What is it?" Bootsie said.

"Buford LaRose."

"This morning?"

"I want to tear him up. I don't think I've ever felt like that toward anyone."

"You've got to let it go, Dave."

I rubbed my palms on my knees and let out my breath.

"Why does he bother you so much?" she asked.

"Because you never let another man talk to you like that."

"People have said worse to you." She lay her hand on my arm. "Put the covers over you. It's cold."

"I'm going to fix something to eat."

"Is it because of his background?"

"I don't know."

She was quiet for a long time.

"Say it, Boots."

"Or is it Karyn?" she asked.

I went into the kitchen by myself, poured a glass of milk, and stared out the window at my neighbor's pasture, where one of his mares was running full-out along the fence line, her breath blowing, her muscles working rhythmically, as though she were building a secret pleasure inside herself that was about to climax and burst.

*   *   *

THE NEXT MORNING I parked my truck on Decatur Street, on the edge of the French Quarter, and walked through Jackson Square, past St. Louis Cathedral, and on up St. Ann to the tan stucco building with the arched entrance and brick courtyard where Clete Purcel kept his office. It had rained before dawn, and the air was cool and bright, and bougainvillea hung through the grillwork on the balcony upstairs. I looked through his window and saw him reading from a manila folder on top of his desk, his shirt stretched tight across his back, his glasses as small as bifocals on his big face.

I opened the door and stuck my head inside.

"You still mad?" I said.

"Hey, what's goin' on, big mon?"

"I'll buy you a beignet," I said.

He thought about it, made a rolling, popping motion with his fingers and hands, then followed me outside.

"Just don't talk to me about Aaron Crown and Buford LaRose," he said.

"I won't."

"What are you doing in New Orleans?"

"I need to check out Jimmy Ray Dixon again. His office says he's at his pool hall out by the Desire."

He tilted his porkpie hat on his head, squinted at the sun above the rooftops.

"Did you ever spit on baseballs when you pitched American Legion?" he said.

We had beignets and coffee with hot milk at an outdoor table in the Cafe du Monde. Across the street, sidewalk artists were painting on easels by the iron fence that bordered the park, and you could hear boat horns out on the river, just the other side of the levee. I told him about Mingo Bloomberg's death.

"It doesn't surprise me. I think it's what they all look for," he said.

"What?"

"The Big Exit. If they can't get somebody to do it for them, they do it themselves. Most of them would have been better off if their mothers had thrown them away and raised the afterbirth."

"You want to take a ride?"

"That neighborhood's a free-fire zone, Streak. Let Jimmy Ray slide. He's a walking ad for enlistment in the Klan."

"See you later, then."

"Oh, your ass," he said, and caught up with me on the sidewalk, pulling on his sports coat, a powdered beignet in his mouth.

The poolroom was six blocks from the Desire welfare project. The windows were barred, the walls built of cinder blocks and scrolled with spray-painted graffiti. I parked by the curb and stepped up on the sidewalk, unconsciously looked up and down the street.

"We're way up the Mekong, Dave. Hang your buzzer out," Clete said.

I took out my badge holder and hooked it through the front of my belt, listened to somebody shatter a tight rack and slam the cue stick down on the table's edge, then walked through the entrance into the darkness inside.

The low ceiling seemed to crush down on the pool shooters like a fist. The bar and the pool tables ran the length of the building, a tin-hooded lamp creating a pyramid of smoky light over each felt rectangle. No one looked directly at us; instead, our presence was noted almost by osmosis, the way schooled fish register and adjust to the proximity of a predator, except for one man, who came out of the rest room raking at his hair with a steel comb, glanced toward the front, then slammed out of a firedoor.

Jimmy Ray Dixon was at a card table in back, by himself, a ledger book, calculator, a filter-tipped cigar inside an ashtray, and a stack of receipts in front of him. He wore a blue suit and starched pink shirt with a high collar, a brown knit tie and gold tie pin with a red stone in it.

"I seen you on TV, still frontin' points for the man killed my brother," he said, without looking up from his work. He picked up a receipt with his steel hook and set it down again.

"I need your help," I said. I waited but he went on with his work. "Sir?" I said.

"What?"

"Can we sit down?"

"Do what you want, man."

Clete went to the bar and got a shot and a beer, then twisted a chair around and sat down next to me.

"Somebody put a hit on Mingo Bloomberg," I said.

"I heard he hung himself from a water pipe in y'all's jail," Jimmy Ray said.

"Word gets around fast."

"A dude like that catch the bus, people have parades."

"He told me a black guy out of Miami had a contract on him. He said a guy who looks like a six-and-a-half-foot stack of apeshit."

Clete scraped a handful of peanuts from a bowl on the next table, his eyes drifting down the bar.

"Maybe you ought to give some thought to where you're at," Jimmy Ray said.

"You heard about a mechanic out of Miami?" I said.

"I tell you how I read this sit'ation. You put a snitch jacket on a guy and jammed him up so he didn't have no place to run. So maybe somebody's conscience bothering him, know what I mean?" he said.

"I think the same hitter popped Lonnie Felton's scriptwriter."

"Could be. But ain't my bidness."

"What is your business?"

"Look, man, this is what it is. A smart man got his finger in lots of pies. Don't mean none of them bad. 'Cause this guy's a brother, you ax me if I know him. I don't like to give you a short answer, but you got a problem with the way you think. It ain't much different than that cracker up at Angola."

Clete leaned forward in his chair, cracked the shell off a peanut, and threw the peanut in his mouth.

"You still pimp, Jimmy Ray?" he asked, his eyes looking at nothing.

"You starting to burn your ticket, Chuck."

"I count eight bail skips in here. I count three who aren't paying the vig to the Shylock who lent them the bail. The guy who went out the door with his hair on fire snuffed one of Dock Green's hookers in Algiers," Clete said.

"You want to use the phone, it's a quarter," Jimmy Ray said.

"No black hitter works the town without permission. Why let him get the rhythm while you got the blues?" Clete said.

"All my blues is on the jukebox, provided to me by Mr. Jerry Joe Plumb, boy you grew up with," Jimmy Ray said to me.

"Crown has to stay down for Buford LaRose to go to Baton Rouge. Tell me you're not part of this, Jimmy Ray," I said.

He looked up at the clock over the bar. "The school kids gonna be out on the street. Y'all got anything in your car you want to keep? . . . Excuse me, I got to see how much collards I can buy tonight."

He began tapping figures off a receipt onto his calculator.

THAT EVENING, UNDER a gray sky, Alafair and I raked out the shed and railed horse lot where she kept her Appaloosa. Then we piled the straw and dried-out green manure in a wheelbarrow and buried it in the compost pile by our vegetable garden. The air was cool, flecked with rain, and smelled like gas and chrysanthemums.

"Who's that man down on the dock, Dave?" Alafair said.

He was squatted down on his haunches, with his back to us. He wore a fedora, dark brown slacks, and a scuffed leather jacket. He was carving a stalk of sugarcane, notching thick plugs out of the stalk between his thumb and the knife blade, feeding them off the blade into his mouth.

"He was in the shop this afternoon. He has a red parachute tattooed on his arm," she said.

I propped my foot on the shovel's blade and rested my arm across the end of the shaft. "Jerry Joe Plumb," I said.

"Is he a bad man?"

"I was never sure, Alf. Tell Bootsie I'll be along in a minute."

I walked down to the end of the dock and leaned my palms on the rail. Jerry Joe continued to look out at the brown current from under the brim of his fedora. He folded his pocketknife against the heel of his hand. The blade was the dull color of an old nickel.

"You figure I owe you?"

"What for?"

"I took something out of your house a long time ago."

"I don't remember it."

"Yeah, you do. I resented you for it."

"What's up, partner?"

The scar at the corner of his eye looked like bunched white string.

"My mom used to clean house for Buford LaRose's parents . . . The old man could be a rotten bastard, but he gave me a job roughnecking in West Texas when I was just seventeen and later on got me into the airborne. It was the way the old man treated Buford that always bothered me, maybe because I was part responsible for it. You think they won't take you off at the neck because they're rich? It's not enough they win; somebody's got to lose. What I'm saying is, everybody's shit flushes. You're no exception, Dave."

"You're not making any sense."

"They'll grind you up."

What follows is my best reconstruction of Jerry Joe's words.

Chapter
13

BY SAN ANTONE I'd run out of bus and food money as well as confidence in dealing with the Texas highway patrol, who believed patching tar on a country road was a cure for almost anything. So I walked five miles of railroad track before I heard a doubleheader coming up the line and took off running along the gravel next to a string of empty flat wheelers, that's boxcars with no springs, my duffle bag banging me in the back, the cars wobbling across the switches and a passenger train on the next track coming up fast, but I worked the door loose, running full-out, flung my duffle on the floor, and crawled up inside the warm smell of grain sacks and straw blowing in the wind and the whistle screaming down the line.

It was near dawn when I woke up, and I knew we were on a trestle because all you could hear was the wheels pinching and squealing on the rails and there wasn't any echo off the ground or the hillsides. The air was cold and smelled like mesquite and blackjack and sage when it's wet, like no one had ever been there before, no gas-driven machines, no drovers fording the river down below, not even Indians in the gorges that snaked down to the bottoms like broken fingers and were cluttered with yellow rocks as big as cars.

There were sand flats in the middle of the river, with pools of water in them that were as red as blood, and dead deer that turkey buzzards had eaten from the topside down so that the skeletons stuck out of the hides and the buzzards used the ribs for a perch. Then we were on a long plateau, inside an electric storm, and I began to see cattle pens and loading chutes and busted windmills that were wrapped with tumbleweed, adobe houses with collapsed walls way off in the lightning, a single-track dirt road and wood bridge and a state sign that marked the Pecos, where the bottom was nothing but baked clay that would crack and spiderweb under your boots.

The old man, Jude LaRose, told me the name of the town but not how to get to it. That was his way. He drew lines in the dirt, and if you fit between them, he might be generous to you. Otherwise, you didn't exist. The problem was you never knew where the lines were.

I hadn't realized I'd climbed aboard a hotshot, a straight-through that doesn't stop till it reaches its destination. I dropped off on an upgrade, just before another trestle, hit running, and slid all the way down a hill into a wet sand flat flanged with willows that had once been a riverbed and was pocked with horses' hooves and deer tracks that were full of rainwater. I walked all day in the rain, crossed fences with warning signs on them in Spanish and English, saw wild horses flowing like shadows down the face of a ridge, worked my way bare-foot across a green river with a soap-rock bottom and came out on a dirt road just as a flatbed truck boomed down with drill pipe and loaded with Mexicans sleeping under a tarp ground through a flooded dip in the road and stopped so the man leaning against the top of the cab with an M-l carbine could say, "Where you think you goin', man?"

I guess I looked like a drowned cat. I hadn't eaten in two days, and my boots were laced around my neck and the knees were tore out of my britches. He had on a blue raincoat and a straw hat, with water sluicing off the brim, and his beard was silky and black and pointed like a Chinaman's.

"Jude LaRose's place. It's somewhere around here, ain't it?" I said.

"You on it now, man."

"Where's he live at?"

"Why you want to know that?"

"I'm a friend of his. He told me to come out."

He leaned down to the window of the cab and said to the Mexicans inside, *"Dice que es amigo del Señor LaRose."* They laughed. The ones in back had the tarp pushed up over their heads so they could see me, and two of them were eating refried beans and tortillas they had folded into big squares between their fingers. But they were a different sort, not the kind to laugh at other people.

"You know where his house is at?" I said.

He'd already lost interest. He hit on the roof with his fist, and they drove off in the rain, with the drill pipe flopping off the back of the bed and the Mexicans in back looking out at me from under the tarp.

I found Jude LaRose's town that evening. It was nothing more than a dirt crossroads set in a cup of hills that had gone purple and red in the sunset. It had a shutdown auction barn and slaughterhouse, a dried-out hog feeder lot next to a railroad bed with no track and a wood water tank that had rotted down on itself, and a shingle-front two-story saloon and cafe, where a little black girl was laying out steaks on a mesquite fire in back. The sidewalk was almost higher than the pickups and horses in front of it, iron-stained with the rusted cusps of tethering rings and pooled with the blood of a cougar someone had shot that day and had hung with wire around the neck from the stanchion of an electric Carta Blanca sign that was the same blue as the glow above the hills.

The inside of the saloon had a stamped tin ceiling, card and domino tables in back, a long bar with old-time towel rings and a wall mirror and brass rail and spittoons, and antlers nailed all over the support posts. A dozen cowboys and oil field roughnecks were playing five-card stud and sipping shots with *Pearl* and *Grand Prize* on the side.

The menu was on a chalkboard over the bar. The bartender wore a red chin beard, and his eyes were hollowed deep in his face and his arms were as thick as hams. A fat black woman set a platter of barbecue sandwiches in the service window and rang a bell. The bread was gold and brown with butter and grill marks and soft in the center from the barbecue sauce that had soaked through. The bartender put four bottles of Pearl on the tray and carried it to the card table.

"How much is just the lima bean soup without the sandwich?"

I asked. I had to keep my hands flat on the bar when I said it, too, because there was a wood bowl full of crackers and pickles right at the end of my fingers.

"Twenty cents," he said.

"How much for just a cup?"

"Where you from, boy?"

"Louisiana."

"Go around back and I'll tell the nigger to fix you something."

"I ain't ask for a handout."

He pulled up his apron, took a lighter out of his blue jeans, and lit a cigarette. He smoked it and spit a piece of tobacco off the tip of his tongue. He picked up the bowl of crackers and pickles and set it on the counter behind him with the bottles of whiskey and rum and tequila.

"You cain't hang around here," he said.

It had started to rain again, and I could see the water dripping off the Carta Blanca sign on the face of the dead cougar. Its eyes were seamed shut, like it had gone to sleep. A man opened the front door and the rain blew across the floor.

"How far is it to the LaRose house?" I said.

"What you want out there?"

"Mr. LaRose told me to come out."

The cigarette smoke trailed out of the side of his mouth. A shadow had come into his face, like a man who's caught between fear and suspicion and anger at himself and an even greater fear you'll see all these things going on inside him.

He walked down the duckboards and used the phone on the counter. When he put the receiver back down his eyes wouldn't stay fixed on mine.

"Mr. LaRose says for you to order up. He'll be along when it quits raining," he said. He set the bowl of pickles and crackers back in front of me, then pried off the top of a Barge's root beer on a wall opener and set it next to the bowl.

"How about a steak and eggs and those stewed tomatoes?" I said.

"Anything else?"

"How about some fried potatoes?"

"What else?"

"How come a Mexican would carry a M-l carbine on a pipe truck?" I asked.

He leaned on the bar. I could smell soap and sweat in his clothes. "Where you seen it?" he asked.

"Coming north of the river."

"You ever heard of no God or law west of the Pecos?"

"No."

"It means you see wets, you forget it."

"I don't understand."

"It's a subject you'd best carry on the end of a shit fork," he said.

An hour later the sky was empty and dry and pale behind the hills and you could see the sage for miles when Jude LaRose pulled up next to the sidewalk in a wood-paneled Ford station wagon, leaned over, and popped open the passenger door and looked at me from under the brim of his Stetson with those blue eyes you didn't ever forget. He was a handsome man in every respect—tall, with a flat stomach, his gray hair cropped GI, his skin sun-browned the shade of a cured tobacco leaf—but I never saw beautiful eyes like that on a man before or since. They were the dark blue you see in patches of water down in the Keys, when the day's hot and bright before a storm and a cloud of perfect blue darkness floats across the reef, and you almost think you can dip your hand into the color and rub it on your skin, like you would ink, but for some reason, down below that perfect piece of color, down in those coral canyons, you know a school of hammerheads are shredding the bonito into pink thread.

I sat down next to him, with my duffle between my legs, and closed the door. The seats were made from rolled yellow leather, and the light from the mahogany dashboard shone on the leather and reflected up in Jude's face.

"They want you?" he asked.

"Sir?"

"You know what I mean."

"There're ain't any warrant."

"What was it?"

"A man whipped me with his belt behind Provost's saloon. Another man held me while he done it."

"What else?"

"I caught him later that night. When he was by himself. It worked out different this time."

He unsnapped the button on his shirt pocket and took a Camel out and fitted it in his mouth without ever letting go of my eyes.

"You're not lying about the warrant, are you?" he said.

"I wouldn't lie about something like that."

"What would you lie about?"

"Sir?"

When we drove away I saw the little black girl who had been laying steaks on the mesquite fire run out from the side of the building and wave at the station wagon.

That night I slept on a bare mattress on the floor of a stucco cottage full of garden tools behind the main house. I dreamed I was on a flat-wheeler freight, high up on a trestle above a canyon, and the trestle's supports were folding under the train's weight and the wheels were squealing on the rail as they gushed sparks and fought to gain traction.

THE MAIN HOUSE was three-story purple brick, with white balconies and widow's walks and poplar trees planted as windbreaks around the yard. There was a bunkhouse with a tar paper roof for the field-hands, rows of feeder lots and corrugated water tanks and windmills for the livestock, a red barn full of baled hay you could stuff a blimp in, a green pasture with hot fences for Jude's thoroughbreds, a scrap yard that was a museum of steam tractors and Model T flatbed trucks, a hundred irrigated acres set aside for vegetables and melons and cantaloupes, and through a long, sloping valley that fanned into a bluff above the river, deer and Spanish bulls mixed in together, belly-deep in grass.

Every fence had a posted sign on it, and for those who couldn't read, animals and stray wetbacks, Jude's foreman had nailed dead crows or gutted and salted coyotes to the cedar posts.

The lights in the main house went on at 4 A.M., when Mrs. LaRose, a black-haired German lady with red cheeks and big arms Jude had brought back from the war, read her Book of Mormon at the kitchen table, then walked down to the open-air shed by the bunkhouse and fired the wood cook stove.

By 7 A.M. my first day I was wearing bradded work gloves and a hard hat and steel-toe boots and wrestling the drill bit on the floor of an oil rig right above the Rio Grande, the drill motor roaring, tongs clanging, the chain whipping on the pipe, and drilling mud and salt water flooding out of the hole like we'd punched into an underground lake.

After a week Jude walked down to my cottage and stood in the doorway with Buford, who was just seven years old then and the miniature of his daddy in short pants.

"You got any questions about how things run?" he said.

"No, sir."

He nodded. "You sure about that?"

"I'm getting along real fine. I like it here."

"That's good." He turned and looked off at the sun on the hills. His eyes were close-set, almost violet, like they were painted with eye shadow.

"Sometimes the Mexican boys talk. They forget what it was like down in the bean field in Chihuahua."

"I don't pay it no mind."

"Pay what no mind?"

"They talk in Spanish. So I don't waste my time listening."

"I see." He cupped his hand on Buford's head. "I want you to take him to work in the tomato field tomorrow."

"I'm supposed to be on the rig."

"I want Buford to start learning work habits. Come up to the house and get him at six."

"Yes, sir, if that's what you want."

"My foreman said you asked about the wages the Mexican boys were making."

"I guess I don't recall it," I said.

He studied the side of my face, all the time his fingers rubbing a little circle in Buford's hair.

"Next time you bring your questions to me," he said.

I looked at the floor and tried not to let him see the swallow in my throat.

YOU DIDN'T HAVE to roughneck long in Jude's oil patch to find out what was going on. You could hear the trucks at night, grinding across the riverbed. Jude's foreman had moved all the cattle to the upper pasture and dropped the fences along the riverbank so the trucks could cross when the moon was down and catch the dirt road that wound into the ranch next door, where another oil man, a bigger one than Jude, was running the same kind of economics.

A white man got two dollars an hour on the floor of a rig and two twenty-seven up on the monkey board. Wetbacks would do it for four bits and their beans. They'd drill into pay sands with no blowout preventers on the wellhead; work on doodlebug crews in an electric storm, out on a bald prairie, with dynamite and primers and nitro caps in the truck, all those boys strung out along a three-hundred-foot steel tape, handling steel chaining pins and a range pole that might as well have been a lightning rod. I had a suspicion it made for a religious moment.

I saw boys on the rig pinch their fingers off with pipe chains, get their forearms snapped like sticks by the tongs, and find out they weren't taking anything back to Mexico for it but a handshake.

The ranch next door was even worse. I heard a perforating gun blew up and killed a wet on the rig floor. A deputy sheriff helped bury him in a mesquite grove, and an hour later the floor was hosed down and pipe was singing down the hole.

That's not all of it, either. Jude and some of his friends had a special crew of higher-paid wets and white boys who'd been in Huntsville and on the pea farm at Sugarland that were slant drilling, which is when you drill at an angle into somebody else's pool or maybe a company storage sand and you pay off whoever is supposed to be watching the pressure gauges. They'd siphon it out like soda through a straw, cap the well, call it a duster, and be down in Saucillo, drinking Dos X's and mescal before the Texaco Company knew they'd been robbed blind.

I had no complaint, though. Jude paid me a white person's wage, whether I was clanging pipe or watching over Buford in the field. He was a cute little guy in his short pants and cowboy hat. We'd hitch a mule to the tomato sled, set four baskets on it, and pick down one row and up the other, and I'd always let him drive the mule and see how far he could fling the tomatoes that had gotten soft.

The second month I was there, Buford and me started pulling melons at the back end of the field, where a black family lived in a shack by a grove of dried-up mesquite trees. Jude rode his horse out in the field and stretched in the saddle and leaned his arms on the pommel and pushed his hat up on his brow with his thumb. Buford was slapping the reins on the mule's butt and gee-hawing him in a circle at the end of the row.

"How's he doing?" Jude said.

"He's a worker," I said.

"That's good." He looked over at the black family's shack. A little girl was playing with a doll on the gallery. "Y'all been working straight through?"

"Yes, sir, haven't missed a beat," I said.

"I don't want him playing with anybody back here."

I tried to keep my focus on Buford and the sled at the end of the row, let the words pass, like it wasn't really important I hear them.

"You understand what I'm saying?" Jude said.

"Yes, sir. You're pretty clear."

"You bothered by what I'm telling you?"

"That's the little girl who works with her mom at the cafe, ain't it?"

"Don't look at something else when you talk to me, Jerry Joe."

I raised my eyes up to his. He looked cut out of black cloth against the sun. My eyes burned in the heat and dust.

"It's time the boy learns the difference, that's all," he said.

"I'm not here to argue, Mr. Jude."

"You may intend to be polite, Jerry Joe. But don't ever address a white man as a person of color would."

Jude knew how to take your skin off with an emery wheel.

I LIKED MRS. LAROSE. She cooked big breakfasts of eggs and smoke-house ham and refried beans and grits for all the hands and was always baking pies for the evening meal. But she seemed to have a blind spot when it came to Jude. Maybe it was because he was a war hero and her father died in one of Hitler's ovens and Jude brought her here from a displaced persons camp in Cyprus. What I mean is, he wasn't above a Saturday night trip down into Mexico with his foreman, a man who'd been accused of stealing thoroughbred semen from a ranch he worked over in Presidio. One Sunday morning, when the foreman was still drunk from the night before and we were driving out to the rig, he said, "Y'all sure must grow 'em randy where you're from."

"Beg your pardon?" I said.

"Bringing back a German heifer ain't kept Jude from milking a couple at a time through the fence."

Later, he caught me alone in the pipe yard. He was quiet a long time, cleaning his nails with a penknife, still breathing a fog of tequila and nicotine. Then he told me I'd better get a whole lot of gone be-tween me and the ranch if I ever repeated what he'd said.

Don't misunderstand, I looked up to Jude in lots of ways. He told me how scared he'd been when they flew into German *ack-ack*. He said it was like a big box of torn black cotton, and there was no way to fly over or around or under it. They'd just have to sit there with their sweat freezing in their hair while the plane shook and bounced like it was breaking up on a rock road. Right after Dresden a piece of shrapnel the size and shape of a twisted teaspoon sliced through his flight jacket and rib cage so he could actually put his hand inside and touch the bones.

I blame myself for what happened next.

Buford and me were hoeing weeds in the string beans at the end of the field, when this old Mexican hooked one wheel of the pump truck off the edge of the irrigation ditch and dropped the whole thing down on the axle. I left Buford alone and got the jack and some boards out of the cab, and the old man and me snugged them under the frame and started jacking the wheel up till we could rock it forward and get all four wheels on dirt again. Then I looked through the square of light under the truck and saw Buford across the field, playing under a shade tree with the little black girl just as Jude came down the road in his station wagon.

I felt foolish, maybe cowardly, too, for a reason I couldn't explain, lying on my belly, half under the truck, while Jude got out of his station wagon and walked toward his son with a look that made Buford's face go white.

He pulled Buford by his hand up on the black family's gallery, went right through their door with no more thought than he would in kicking open a gate on a hog lot, and a minute later came back outside with one of the little girl's dresses wadded up in his hand.

First, he whipped Buford's bare legs with a switch, then pulled the dress down over his head and made him stand on a grapefruit crate out in the middle of the field, with all the Mexicans bent down in the rows, pretending they didn't see it.

I knew I was next.

He drove out to where the pump truck was still hanging on the jack, and stared out the car window at me like I was some dumb animal he knew would never measure up.

"You didn't mind your priorities. What you see yonder is the cost of it," he said.

"Then you should have took it out on me."

"Don't be a hypocrite on top of it. If you had any guts, you'd have spoken up before I whipped him."

I could feel my eyes watering, the words quivering in my mouth. "I think you're a sonofabitch, Jude."

"He's a LaRose. That's something you won't ever understand, Jerry Joe. You come from white trash, so it's not your fault. But you've got a chance to change your life here. Don't waste it."

He dropped the transmission in first gear, his face as empty of feeling as a skillet, and left me standing in the weeds, the dust from his tires pluming in a big cinnamon cloud behind his car.

I'D LIKE TO tell you I drug up that night, but I didn't. Jude's words burned in my cheeks just like a slap, like only he knew, of all the people in the world, who I really was.

It's funny how you can become the reflection you see in the eyes of a man you admire and hate at the same time. The family went back to Louisiana in the fall, and I stayed on and slant drilled, brought wets across the river, killed wild horses for a dog food company, and fell in love every Saturday night down in Chihuahua. Those boys from Huntsville pen and the pea farm at Sugarland didn't have anything on me.

When he died of lung cancer ten years later, I thought I'd go to the funeral and finally make my peace with him. I made it as far as the door, where two guys told me Mr. LaRose had left instructions the service was to be attended only by family members.

Ole Jude really knew how to do it.

Chapter
14

IT WAS DARK now and rain was falling on the bayou and the tin roof of the bait shop. Jerry Joe drank out of a thick white coffee cup across the table from me. A bare electric light bulb hung over our heads, and his face was shadowed by his fedora.

"What's the point?" I said.

"You're a parish cop in a small town, Dave. When's the last time you turned the key on a rich guy?"

"A DWI about twenty years ago."

"So am I getting through here?"

"It doesn't change anything."

"I saw Buford pitch in a college game once. A kid slung the bat at him on a scratch single. The kid's next time up, Buford hit him in the back with a forkball. He acted sorry as hell about it while the kid was writhing around in the dirt, but after the game I heard him tell his catcher, 'Looks like we made a Christian today.'"

"Buford's not my idea of a dangerous man."

"It's a way of mind. They don't do things to people, they let them happen. Their hands always stay clean."

"If you're letting the LaRoses use you, that's your problem, Jerry Joe."

"Damn, you make me mad," he said. He clicked his spoon on the handle of his cup and looked out at the rain falling through the glare of the flood lamps. His leather jacket was creased and pale with wear, and I wondered how many years ago he had bought it to emulate the man who had helped incinerate the Florence of northern Europe.

"Take care of what you got, Dave. Maybe deep-six the job, I'll get you on with the union. It's easy. You get a pocketful of ballpoint pens and a clipboard and you can play it till you drop," he said.

"You want to come up and eat with us?"

"That's sounds nice . . ." His face looked melancholy under his fedora. "Another time, though. I've got a gal waiting for me over in Lafayette. I was never good at staying married, know what I mean? . . . Dave, the black hooker who saw the screenwriter popped, you still want to find her, she works for Dock Green . . . Hey, tomorrow I'm sending you a jukebox. It's loaded, podna—Lloyd Price, Jimmy Clanton, Warren Storm, Dale and Grace Broussard, Iry LeJeune . . . Don't argue."

And he went out the screen door into the rain. The string of electric bulbs overhead made a pool of yellow light around his double shadow, like that of a man divided against himself at the bottom of a well.

DOCK GREEN WAS an agitated, driven, occasionally vicious, ex-heavy-equipment operator, who claimed to have been kidnapped from a construction site near Hue by the Viet Cong and buried alive on the banks of the Perfume River. His face was hard-edged, as though it had been layered from putty that had dried unevenly. It twitched constantly, and his eyes had the lidless intensity of a bird's, focusing frenetically upon you, or the person behind you, or the inanimate object next to you, all with the same degree of wariness.

He owned a construction company, a restaurant, and half of a floating casino, but Dock's early money had come from prostitution. Whether out of an avaricious fear that his legitimate businesses would dry up, or the satisfaction he took in controlling the lives of others, he had never let go of the girls and pimps who worked the New Orleans convention trade and kicked back 40 percent to him.

He had married into the Giacano family but soon became an embarrassment to them. Without warning, in a restaurant or in an elevator, Dock's voice would bind in his throat, then squeeze into a higher register, like a man on the edge of an uncontrollable rage. During these moments, his words would be both incoherent and obscene, hurled in the faces of anyone who tried to console or comfort him.

He had a camp and acreage off of old Highway 190 between Opelousas and Baton Rouge, right by the levee and the wooded mud-flats that fronted the Atchafalaya River. His metallic gray frame house, with tin roof and screened gallery, was surrounded by palm and banana trees, and palmettos grew in the yard and out in his pasture, where his horses had snubbed the winter grass down to the dirt. Clete and I drove down the service road in Clete's convertible and stopped at the cattleguard. The gate was chain-locked to the post.

A man in khakis and a long-sleeved white shirt with roses printed on it was flinging corncobs out of a bucket into a chicken yard. He stopped and stared at us. Clete blew the horn.

"What are you doing?" I said.

"He's crazy. Give him something to work with."

"How about waiting here, Clete?"

"The guy's got syphilis of the brain. I wouldn't go in his house unless I put Kleenex boxes over my shoes first."

"It's Tourette's syndrome."

"Sure, that's why half of his broads are registered at the VD clinic."

I climbed through the barbed wire fence next to the cattleguard. Dock Green was motionless, the bale of the bucket hooked across his palm as if it had been hung from stone. His thin brown hair was cut short and was wet and freshly combed. I saw the recognition come into his eyes, a tic jump in his face.

But the problem in dealing with Dock Green was not his tormented and neurotic personality. It was his intuitive and uncannily accurate sense about other people's underlying motivations, perhaps even their thoughts.

"Who told you I was here?" he said.

"You've got a lot of respect around here, Dock. The St. Landry sheriff's office likes to know when you're in town."

"Who's in the shit machine?"

"Clete Purcel."

He put down the bucket, cupped one hand to his mouth, the other to his genitalia, and shouted, "Hey, Purcel, I got your corndog hanging!"

"Dock, I'm looking for a black hooker by the name of Brandy Grissum."

"An addict, the one saw the screenwriter get capped?"

"That's right."

"I don't know anything about her. Why's he parked out there?"

"You just said—"

"NOPD already talked to me. That's how I know." The skin under his eye puckered, like paint wrinkling in a bucket. "Short Boy Jerry put you here?"

"Why would he do that?" I smiled and tried to keep my eyes flat.

"Y'all went to school together. Now he's moving back to New Iberia. Now you're standing on my property. It don't take a big brain to figure it out."

"Give me the girl, Dock. I'll owe you one."

"You looking for a black whore or a black hit man, you should be talking to Jimmy Ray Dixon."

"I'm firing in the well, huh?" I said. The wind puffed the willow trees that grew on the far side of the levee. "You've got a nice place here."

"Don't give me that laid-back act, Robicheaux. I'll tell you what this is about. Short Boy Jerry thought he could throw up some pickets on my jobs and run me under. It didn't work. So now he's using you to put some boards in my head. I think he dimed me with NOPD, too."

"You're pretty fast, Dock."

His eyes focused on the front gate.

"I can't believe it. Purcel's taking a leak in my cattleguard. I got neighbors here," Dock said.

"You and the Giacanos aren't backing Buford LaRose, are you?" I asked.

For the first time he smiled, thin-lipped, his eyes slitted inside the hard cast of his face.

"I never bet on anything human," he said. "Come inside. I got to get a Pepto or something. Purcel's making me sick."

The pine walls of his front room were hung with the stuffed heads of antelope and deer. A marlin was mounted above the fireplace, its lacquered skin synthetic-looking and filmed with dust. On a long bookshelf was a line of jars filled with the pickled, yellowed bodies of rattlesnakes and cottonmouth moccasins, a hairless possum, box turtles, baby alligators, a nutria with its paddlelike feet webbed against the glass.

Dock went into the kitchen and came back with a beer in his hand. He offered me nothing. Behind him I saw his wife, one of the Giacano women, staring at me, hollow-eyed, her raven hair pulled back in a knot, her skin as white as bread flour.

"Purcel gets under my skin," Dock said.

"Why?"

"Same reason you do."

"Excuse me?"

"You make a guy for crazy, you think you can drop some coins in his slot, turn him into a monkey on a wire. The truth is, I've been down in a place where your eye sockets and your ears and your mouth are stuffed with mud, where there ain't any sound except the voices of dead people inside your head . . . You learn secrets down there you don't ever forget."

"I was over there, too, Dock. You don't have a franchise on the experience."

"Not like I was. Not even in your nightmares." He drank from his beer can, wiped his mouth on the inside of his wrist. His eyes seemed to lose interest in me, then his face flexed with an idle thought, as though a troublesome moth had swum into his vision.

"Why don't you leave me alone and go after that Klansman before he gets the boons stoked up again. At least if he ain't drowned. We got enough race trouble in New Orleans as it is," he said.

"Who are you talking about?"

He looked at me for a long moment, his face a bemused psycho-drama, like a metamorphic jigsaw puzzle forming and re-forming itself.

"That guy Crown, the one you were defending on TV, he jumped into the Mississippi this morning," he said. "Your shit machine don't have a radio?"

He drank from his beer can and looked at me blankly over the top of it.

Chapter
15

IT WAS RAINING and dark the next morning when Clete let me off in front of the Iberia Parish Sheriff's Department, then made an illegal U-turn into the barbecue stand across the street. Lightning had hit the department's building earlier, knocking out all the electricity except the emergency lights. When I went into the sheriff's office, he was standing at his window, in the gloom, with a cup of coffee in his hand, looking across the street.

"Why's Purcel in town?" he asked.

"A couple of days' fishing."

"So he drives you to work?"

"My truck's in the shop."

"He's a rogue cop, Dave."

"Too harsh, skipper."

"He has a way of writing his name with a baseball bat. That's not going to happen here, my friend."

"You made your point, sir," I said.

"Good."

Then he told me about yesterday's events at Angola and later at a sweet potato farm north of Morganza.

Aaron Crown had vomited in his cell, gone into spasms on the floor, like an epileptic during a seizure or a man trying to pass gallstones. He was put in handcuffs and leg chains and placed in the front seat of a van, rather than in the back, a plastic sick bag in his lap, and sent on his way to the infirmary, with a young white guard driving.

The guard paid little attention, perhaps even averted his eyes, when Aaron doubled over with another coughing spasm, never seeing the bobby pin that Aaron had hidden in his mouth and that he used to pick one manacle loose from his left wrist, never even thinking of Aaron as an escape risk within the rural immensity of the farm, nor as an inmate whose hostility and violence would ever become directed at a white man.

Not until they rounded a curve by the river and Aaron's left arm wrapped around the guard's neck and Aaron's right fist, the loose handcuff whipping from the wrist, smashed into the guard's face and splintered his jawbone.

Then he was hobbling through gum trees and a soybean field, over the levee, down into the willows along the mudflat, where he waded out through the backwater and the reeds and cattails and plunged into the current, his ankles raw and bleeding and still chained together.

By all odds he should have drowned, but later a group of West Feliciana sheriff's deputies with dogs would find a beached tangle of uprooted trees downstream, with a piece of denim speared on a root, and conclude that Aaron had not only grabbed on to the floating island of river trash but had wedged himself inside its branches like a muskrat and ridden the heart of the river seven miles without being seen before the half-submerged trees bumped gently onto a sandspit on the far side and let Aaron disembark into the free people's world as though he had been delivered by a specially chartered ferry.

Then he was back into the piney woods, hard-shell fundamentalist country in which he had been raised, that he took for granted would never change, where a white man's guarantees were understood, so much so that when he entered the barn of a black farmer that night and began clattering through the row of picks and mattocks and scythes and axes and malls hung on the wall to find a tool sharp and heavy enough to cut the chain on his ankles, he never expected to be challenged, much less threatened at gunpoint.

The black man was old, barefoot, shirtless, wearing only the overalls he had pulled on when he had heard Aaron break into his barn.

"What you doin', old man?" he said, and leveled the dogleg twenty gauge at Aaron's chest.

"It's fixing to storm. I come out of it." Aaron held his right wrist, with the manacle dangling from it, behind his back.

The lightning outside shook like candle flame through the cracks in the wall.

"You got a chain on your feet," the black man said.

"Cut it for me."

"Where you got out of?"

"They had me for something I ain't did. Cut the chain. I'll come back and give you some money."

"You the one they looking for, the one that killed that NAACP man, ain't you?"

"It's a goddamn lie they ruint my life over."

"Now, I ain't wanting to harm you . . . You stand back, I said you—"

Aaron tore the shotgun from the black man's hand and clutched his throat and squeezed until the black man's knees collapsed, then he wrapped him to a post with baling wire, tore the inside of his house apart, and looted his kitchen.

Five minutes later Aaron Crown disappeared into the howling storm in the black man's pickup truck, the shotgun and a cigar box filled with pennies and a bag of groceries on the seat beside him.

"WHERE YOU THINK he's headed?" I said.

"He got rid of the pickup in Baton Rouge late last night. A block away a Honda was stolen out of a filling station. Guess what? Crown's lawyer, the one who pled him guilty, has decided to go to Europe for a few weeks."

"How about the judge who sent him up?"

"The state police are guarding his house." He watched my face. "What's on your mind?"

"If I were Aaron Crown, my anger would be directed at somebody closer to home."

"I guess you picked my brain, Dave."

"I don't like the drift here, Sheriff."

"The next governor is not going to get murdered in our jurisdiction."

"Not me. No, sir."

"If you don't want to be around the LaRoses personally, that's your choice. But you're going to have to coordinate the surveillance on their house . . . Look, the election's Tuesday. Then the sonofabitch will probably be governor. That's the way we've always gotten rid of people we don't like—we elect them to public office. Go with the flow."

"Wrong man."

"Karyn LaRose doesn't think so. She called last night and asked for you specifically . . . Could you be a little more detailed on y'all's history?"

"It all seems kind of distant, for some reason."

"I see . . ." He sucked a tooth. "Okay, one other thing . . . Lafayette PD called a little earlier. Somebody broke into a pawnshop about five this morning. He took only one item—a scoped .303 Enfield rifle with a sling. You ever hear of a perp breaking into a pawnshop and stealing only one item? . . . I saw British snipers use those in Korea. They could bust a silhouette on a ridge from five hundred yards . . . Don't treat this as a nuisance assignment, Dave."

LONNIE FELTON'S PURPLE Lincoln Continental was parked under a dripping oak in my drive when Clete dropped me off from work that evening. I ran through the rain puddles in the yard, onto the gallery, and smelled the cigarette smoke drifting through the screen.

He sat on the divan, tipping his ashes in a glass candy dish. Even relaxed, his body had the muscular definition of a gymnast, and with his cleft chin and Roman profile and brown ponytail that was shot with gray, he could have been either a first-rate charismatic confidence man, second-story man, or the celebrity that he actually was.

"How you do, sir," I said.

"I feel old enough without the 'sir,' " he said. His teeth were capped and white, and, like most entertainment people I had met, he didn't allow his eyes to blink, so that they gave no indication of either a hidden insecurity or the presence or absence of an agenda.

"I'm trying to get Mr. Felton to stay for dinner," Bootsie said.

I took off my raincoat and hat and put them on the rack in the hall. "Sure, why don't you do that?" I said.

"Thanks, another night. I'll be around town a week or so."

"Oh?"

"I want to use Aaron Crown's old place, you know, that Montgomery Ward brick shack on the coulee, and juxtapose it with the LaRose plantation."

"It seems like you'd have done that early on," I said, and sat down on the stuffed chair at the end of the coffee table.

His eyes looked amused. The *Daily Iberian* was folded across the middle on top of the table. I flipped it open so he could see the front page. A three-column headline read: LOCAL MAN ESCAPES ANGOLA.

"The end of your documentary might get written in New Iberia," I said.

"How's that?"

"You tell me," I said.

"I have a hard time following your logic. You think the presence of a news camera caused Jack Ruby to kill Lee Harvey Oswald?"

Bootsie got up quietly and went into the kitchen and began fixing coffee on a tray. His eyes stayed on her as she left the room, dropping for a split second to her hips.

"What do you want from me, sir?" I asked.

"You're an interesting man. You had the courage to speak out on Crown's behalf. I'd like for you to narrate two or three closing scenes. I'd like to be with you during the surveillance of LaRose's house."

"I think you want gunfire on tape, sir."

He put on his glasses and craned his head around so he could see the wall area next to the window behind him.

"Is that where the bullet holes were?" he asked.

"*What?*"

"I did some deep background on you. This is where your wife killed another woman, isn't it? You didn't have media all over you after she splattered somebody's brains on your wallpaper?"

"My wife saved my life. And you get out of our house, Mr. Felton."

Bootsie stood framed in the kitchen doorway, frozen, the tray motionless between her hands.

Felton put out his cigarette in the candy dish and got to his feet slowly, unruffled, indifferent.

"If I were you, I'd spike Buford LaRose's cannon while I had the chance. I think he's a believer in payback," he said. He turned toward Bootsie. "I'm sorry for any inconvenience, Ms. Robicheaux."

"If my husband told you to get out, he meant it, bubba," she said.

A YEAR AGO I had stripped the paper from the wall next to the window, put liquid wood filler in the two bullet holes there, then sanded them over and repapered the cypress planks. But sometimes in an idle moment, when my gaze lingered too long on the wall, I remembered the afternoon that an assassin had pointed a .22-caliber Ruger at the side of my face, when I knew that for me all clocks everywhere were about to stop and I could do nothing about it but cross my arms over my eyes, and Bootsie, who had never harmed anyone in her life, had stepped out into the kitchen hallway and fired twice with a nine-millimeter Beretta.

Lonnie Felton backed his Lincoln into the road, then drove toward the drawbridge through the mist puffing out of the tree trunks along the bayou's edge.

"There goes your Hollywood career, Streak," Bootsie said.

"Somehow I don't feel the less for it."

"You think Aaron Crown is back?"

"It's too bad if he is. Say, you really shook up Felton's cookie bag."

"You like that hard gal stuff, huh? Too bad for whom?"

"I think Buford's hooked up with some New Orleans wiseguys. Maybe Aaron won't make the jail . . . Come on, forget this stuff. Let's take the boat down the bayou this evening."

"In the rain?"

"Why not?"

"What's bothering you, Dave?"

"I have to baby-sit Buford. His plane comes back in from Monroe at ten."

"I see."

"It'll be over Tuesday."

"No it won't," she said.

"Don't be that way," I said, and put my hands on her shoulders.

"Which way is that?" Then her eyes grew bright and she said it again, "Which way is that, Dave?"

LATER THAT NIGHT Helen Soileau and I met Buford's private plane at the Lafayette airport and followed him back to the LaRose plantation in a cruiser. Then we parked by his drive in the dark and waited for the midnight watch to come on. The grounds around the house, the slave quarters now filled with baled hay, the brick, iron-shuttered riding stable, were iridescent in the humidity and glare of the security flood lamps that burned as brightly as phosphorous flares. One by one the lights went off inside the house.

"Can you tell me why an assignment like this makes me feel like a peon with a badge?" Helen said.

"Search me," I said.

"If you were Crown and you wanted to take him out, where would you be?"

"Inside that treeline, with the sun rising behind me in the morning."

"You want to check it out?"

"It's not morning."

"Casual attitude."

"Maybe Buford should have the opportunity to face his sins."

"I'll forget you said that."

The next morning, Saturday, just before sunrise, I dressed in the cold, with Bootsie still asleep, and drove back to the LaRose plantation and walked the treeline from the road back to the bayou. In truth,

I expected to find nothing. Aaron had no military background, was impetuous, did not follow patterns, and drew on a hill-country frame of reference that was as rational as a man stringing a crowning forest fire around his log house.

However, I had forgotten that Aaron was a lifetime hunter, not for sport or even for personal dominion over the land but as one who viewed armadillos and deer, possums and ducks, squirrels and robins, even gars that could be shot from a boat, as food for his table, adversaries that he slew in order to live, none any better or worse or more desirable than another, and he went about it as thoroughly and dispassionately as he would butcher chickens and hogs on a block.

On second consideration, I thought the best trained military sniper could probably take a lesson from Aaron Crown.

One hundred yards from Buford's backyard, with a clear view of the converted carriage house, the driveway, the parked automobiles, I saw the broken gray leaves, the knee and boot marks in the soft ground behind a persimmon tree, an empty Vienna sausage can, crumbs from saltine crackers, the detritus of field-stripped hand-rolled cigarettes.

Then I thought I heard feet running, a shadow flowing between trees, dipping down into a dry coulee bed, racing past the black marble crypt in the center of the LaRose cemetery. But in the muted pink softness of the morning, in the rain that continued to tumble like crystal needles out of the sunlight, I looked again and saw only red horses turning among the tree trunks, divots of impacted layered leaves exploding from their hooves, their backs auraed with vapor from their bodies.

I took a Ziploc bag from my coat pocket and began picking up the torn cigarette papers and the Vienna sausage can with the tip of a ball-point pen just as Buford came out his back door, dressed in jeans, cowboy boots, charcoal suede jacket, and gray Stetson hat, his face raised toward the dawn and the special portent that it seemed to contain.

I wondered if he had ever envisioned his face locked down inside a telescopic sight, just before a toppling .303 round was about to scissor a keyhole through the middle of it.

Maybe he had. Or maybe my fantasy indicated a level of abiding resentment that I did not want to recognize.

THAT AFTERNOON CLETE parked his Cadillac by the boat ramp and walked down the dock and into the bait shop, where I was stacking the chairs and mopping the floor. He poured a cup of coffee for himself at the counter and drank it.

"You looked like you got rained on today," I said.

"I did."

"You catch anything?"

"Nope. The water's getting too cool. I found Brandy Grissum, though."

I fitted a chair upside down on a table and put down my mop.

"My main meal ticket is still running down bail skips for Nig Rosewater and Wee Willie Bimstine," he said. "So I checked in with Nig this afternoon to see if he had anything for me, and out of nowhere he tells me a black broad named Brandy Grissum skipped on a prostitution charge and left Nig and Willie holding the bond. But because most of the lowlifes consider Nig a fairly decent guy for a bondsman, Brandy calls him up from a halfway house in Morgan City and says she's scared shitless to come back to New Orleans, and can Nig square her beef with the court and renew her bond.

"Can you imagine the faith these people put in a bondsman? I used to miss my shield. Now I think I'll get me one of those little cinder block offices with a neon sign down by the City Prison."

"She's in a halfway house?" I said.

"Not for long. She's about to get kicked out. Y'all got a snitch fund?"

"We're lucky to pay the light bill."

"I wouldn't put that on the top of the discussion."

THE TWO-STORY HALFWAY house was painted canary yellow and decorated with flower boxes on a shell road that paralleled a canal lined with banana trees and wild elephant ears. The leaves of the elephant ears were withered and streaked white from the water splashed out of potholes by passing automobiles. A rotted-out shrimp boat was half submerged on the far side of the canal, and gars were feeding on something dead that streamed off one of the scuppers. The gallery of the halfway house was cluttered with green plants and straight-back wood chairs, on which both black and white people sat, most of them in mismatched clothes, and smoked cigarettes and looked at nothing or at their shoes or watched the passing of an automobile, until it finally turned onto the highway that led back into Morgan City, which seemed painted with an electric glow against the evening sky.

Brandy Grissum sat with us at a picnic table strewn with children's toys under a Chinaberry tree. She wore lip gloss and rouge high on her cheekbones and a hair net with sequins in it, and jeans and purple cloth slippers and a long-sleeved denim shirt with lace sewn on the cuffs. The whites of her eyes were threaded with blood vessels.

"You can get me some money?" she said.

"Depends on what you've got, Brandy," I said.

"They gonna put me out tomorrow. I ain't got nowhere to go. He know where my family's at."

"The shooter?" I said.

"He found me twice. He took me out in the woods . . . he made me do things in the back of his car." Her eyes flicked away from my face.

"Who's the guy, Brandy?" Clete said.

"He call himself Mookie. He says he's from Miami. But he talks French and he know all about fishing in the bayous up I-10."

"Mookie what?" I said.

"I don't want to even be knowing his first name. I just want to get my li'l boy from my mother's house and go somewheres else."

"Why are they putting you out?"

She kneaded the top of her forearm and looked out at the shell road in the twilight.

"They said my urine was dirty when I come back to the house the other day. I say you can look at my arm, I ain't got no new tracks. The proctor, she says I'm skin popping in my thighs, the other women halfways seen it in the shower. I ain't skin popped, though, that's the troot, and I ain't smoked no rock in thirty-seven days."

"How'd you UA dirty, then?" Clete said.

She picked at her earlobe and raised her eyebrows. "Don't ax me," she said.

"Why'd Mookie kill your John?" I asked.

"He said he was doing it to hep out some friends. He said the guy didn't have no bidness messing around with black women anyway."

"You work for Dock Green, Brandy?" I asked.

"I got a street manager."

"You got a Murphy artist," Clete said.

Her jawbone flexed along one cheek.

"Why'd Mookie let you slide?" I asked.

"He said he liked me. He said I could have China white, all the rock, all the tar I want, all I gotta do is ax. He was smoking rock in his car. He got a look in his face that makes me real scared. Suh, I gotta get out of Lou'sana or he's gonna find me again."

"You've got to give me more information, Brandy," I said.

"You the po-liceman from New Iberia?"

"That's right."

"He know all about you. He know about this one wit' you, too."

Clete had started to light a cigarette. He took it out of his mouth and looked at her.

"He was saying, now this is what he say, this ain't my words, 'If the fat one come around again where he ain't suppose to be, I got permission to burn his kite.' "

"When was this?" I said.

"A week ago. Maybe two weeks ago. I don't remember."

"Is there a way I can get a message to this guy?" Clete asked.

"I don't know no more. I ain't axed for none of this. Y'all gonna give me train fare for me and my li'l boy?"

I pulled an envelope from my back pocket and handed it to her.

"This ain't but two hundred dollars," she said.

"My piggy bank's tapped out," I said.

"That means it's out of the man's pocket," Clete said.

"It don't seem very much for what I tole y'all."

"I think I'll take a walk, throw some rocks at the garfish. Blow the horn when you're ready to boogie. Don't you love being around the life?" Clete said.

THE NIGHT BEFORE the election I lay in the dark and tried to think my way through the case. Why had the gargantuan black man with the conked hair hung around New Orleans after the hit on the screenwriter? Unless it was to take out Mingo Bloomberg? Or even Clete?

But why expect reasonable behavior of a sociopath?

The bigger question was who did he work for? Brandy Grissum had said the black man had made a threat on Clete one or two weeks ago, which was before we visited Dock Green. But Dock had probably already heard we'd been bumping the furniture around, so the time frame was irrelevant.

Also, I was assuming that Brandy Grissum was not lying. The truth is, most people who talk with cops—perps, lowlifes of any stripe, traffic violators, crime victims, witnesses to crime, relatives of crime victims, or irritable cranks who despise their neighbors' dogs—feel at some point they have to lie, either to protect themselves, somebody else, or to ensure that someone is punished. The fact that they treat you as a credulous moron seems to elude them.

I was still convinced the center of the case lay on the LaRose plantation. The three avenues into it led through Jimmy Ray Dixon, Dock Green, and Jerry Joe Plumb. The motivation that characterized all the players was greed.

It wasn't a new scenario.

But the presence of power and celebrity gave it a glittering mask. The LaRoses were what other people wanted to be, and their sins seemed hardly worthy of recognition.

Except to one man, whose ankles were marbled with bruises from leg chains and whose thoughts flared without respite like dry boards being fed into a furnace.

Chapter
16

BUFORD WON.

The northern portion of the state was split by a third-party racist candidate, while the southern parishes voted as a bloc for one of their own, a Catholic bon vivant football hero who descended from Confederate cavalry officers but whose two Ph.D.'s and identification with the New South would never allow his constituency to be embarrassed.

The celebration that night in Baton Rouge received the kind of network coverage that one associates with Mardi Gras.

Wednesday night the celebration moved to the LaRose plantation in New Iberia. The moist air smelled of flowers and meat fires, and as if the season had wanted to cooperate with Buford's political ascendancy, a full yellow moon had risen above the bayou and the cleared fields and the thoroughbreds in the pasture, all that seemed to define the LaRose family's historical continuity. First a Dixieland, then a zydeco band played on top of a flatbed truck in the backyard. Hundreds of guests ate okra and sausage gumbo and barbecued chicken wings off of paper plates and lined up at the crystal bowls filled with whiskey-sour punches. They behaved with the cheerful abandon of people who knew their time had come; the crushed flower beds, the paper cups strewn on the grass, the red-faced momentary coarseness, were just part of the tribute they paid to their own validation.

Helen Soileau and I walked the treeline along the back fields, talked to two state policemen who carried cut-down pump shotguns, shined our flashlights in storage sheds and the barn and the stables, and then walked back down the drive toward our cruiser in front. It was going to be a long night.

Clay Mason was smoking a cheroot cigar between two parked automobiles, one booted foot propped on a bumper, looking wistfully at the cleared fields and the yellow moon that had filled the branches of a moss-hung oak.

"Ah, Mr. Robicheaux, how are you?" he asked.

"Are you visiting, sir?" I said.

"Just long enough to extend congratulations. By God, what an event! I'm surprised Buford's father didn't get up out of the grave for it."

"I hear he was quite a guy."

"If that's how you spell 'sonofabitch,' he was."

"How'd you know his father?"

"They owned the ranch next to my family's, out west of the Pecos."

"I see."

"My father used to say it takes sonsofbitches to build great countries. What do you think about a statement like that?" He puffed on his cigar.

"I wouldn't know." I saw Helen get in the cruiser and close the door in the dark.

"Son, there's nothing more odious than an intelligent man pretending to be obtuse."

"I'd better say good night, Dr. Mason."

"Stop acting like a nincompoop. Let's go over here and get a drink."

"No, thanks."

He seemed to study the silhouette of the oak branches against the moon.

"I understand y'all matched the fingerprints of that Klansman, Crown, is that his name, to some tin cans or cigarette papers you found in the woods," he said.

"That's right."

He flipped his cigar sparking into a rosebed. "You catch that racist bastard, Mr. Robicheaux."

"I don't think Aaron Crown's a racist."

He placed his hand, which had the contours of a claw, on my arm. An incisor tooth glinted in his mouth when he grinned.

"A Ku Klux Klansman? Don't deceive yourself. A man like that will rip your throat out and eat it like a pomegranate," he said.

The breeze blew his fine, white cornsilk hair against his scalp.

FIFTEEN MINUTES LATER I had to use the rest room.

"Go inside," Helen said.

"I'd like to avoid it."

"You want to take the cruiser down the road?"

"Bad form."

"I guess you get to go inside," she said.

I walked through the crowds of revelers in the yard, past the zydeco musicians on the flatbed truck, who were belting out "La Valse Negress" with accordion and fiddle and electric guitars, and with one man raking thimbles up and down a replicated aluminum washboard that was molded like soft body armor to his chest. The inside of the house was filled with people, too, and I had to go up the winding stairs to the second floor to find an empty bathroom.

Or one that was almost empty.

The door was ajar. I saw a bare male thigh, the trousers dropped below the knee, a gold watch on a hairy wrist. Decency should have caused me to step back and wait by the top of the stairs. But I had seen something else, too—the glassy cylindrical shape between two fingers, the thumb resting on the plunger, the bright squirt of fluid at the tip of the needle.

I pushed open the door the rest of the way.

When Buford connected with the vein, his eyes closed and opened and then glazed over, his lips parted indolently, and a muted sound rose from his throat, as though he were sliding onto the edge of orgasm.

Then he heard me.

"Oh . . . Dave," he said. He put the needle on the edge of the lavatory and swallowed dryly, his eyes flattening, the pupils constricting with the hit.

"Bad shit, Buford," I said.

He buttoned his trousers and tried to fix his belt.

"Goat glands and vitamins. Not what you think, Dave," he said.

"So that's why you shoot it up in your thighs?"

"John Kennedy did it." He smiled wanly. "Are you going to cuff the governor-elect in his home?"

"It wouldn't stick. Why not talk to somebody you trust about this, before you flame out?"

"It might make an interesting fire."

"I never met a hype who was any different from a drunk. I'm talking about myself, Buford. We're all smart-asses."

"You missed your historical period. You should have sat at the elbow of St. Augustine. You were born for the confessional. Come on, a new day is at hand, sir, if you would just lend me yours for a moment."

I helped him sit down on top of the toilet seat lid, then I watched, almost as a voyeur would, as the color came back in his face, his breathing seemed to regulate itself, his shoulders straightened, his eyes lifted merrily into mine.

"We glide on gilded wings above the abyss," he said. "The revelers wait—"

I shattered his syringe in the toilet bowl.

"Mark one off to bad manners," I said.

EARLY THE NEXT morning the sheriff called me into his office.

"Lafayette PD wants us to help with security at the Hotel Acadiana on Pinhook Road," he said.

"Buford again?"

"The guy's turned the governor's office into a rolling party. We're probably going to be stuck with it a little while."

"I want off it, skipper."

"I want my old hairline back."

"He's a hype."

"You're telling me we just elected a junkie?"

I told him what had happened the night before. He blew out his breath.

"You're sure he's not diabetic or something like that?" he asked.

"I think it's speed."

"You didn't want to take him down?"

"Busting a guy in his bathroom with no warrant?"

He rubbed his temple.

"I hate to say this, but I'm still glad he won rather than one of those other shitheads," he said. He waited. "No comment?"

"He's bad news. We'll pay for it down the line."

"God, you're a source of comfort," he said.

I PICKED UP MY morning mail and went into my office just as my phone rang. Dock Green must have hit the floor running.

"You tell that Irish prick he wants to get in my face, I'll meet him in the street, in an alley, out on a sandbar in the middle of the Atchafalaya. Somebody should have busted his spokes a long time ago," he said.

"Which Irish prick?" I said.

"Duh," he answered. "He caused a big scene at my casino. Customers were going out the doors like it was a fire drill. He threw a pool ball into a guy's head at my restaurant."

"Tell him yourself."

"I would. Except I can't find him. He's too busy wiping his shit all over the city."

"Clete's a one-on-one type guy, Dock."

"Yeah? Well, I'm a civilized human being. Jimmy Ray Dixon ain't. Your friend's been down in Cannibal Town, saying they give up this black ape been making threats against him or he's going to staple somebody's dork to the furniture. I hope they cook him in a pot."

"The shooter we want is a guy named Mookie. He's telling people he has permission to take Purcel out. Who'd give him that kind of permission, Dock?"

"Try to fit this into your head, Robicheaux—"

Then I heard a woman's voice and hands scraping on the receiver, as though someone were pulling it from Dock's grasp.

"Mr. Robicheaux?"

"Yes."

"This is Persephone Green. I met you years ago when my name was Giacano."

"Yes, I remember," I said, although I didn't.

"Are you sure? Because you were drunk at the time."

I cleared my throat.

"My husband is trying to say, we don't have anything to do with problems in New Orleans' black community," she said. "You leave us alone. You tell your friend the same thing."

"Your husband's a pimp."

"And you're an idiot, far out of his depth," she said, and hung up the phone.

Either the feminists had reached into the mob or the New Orleans spaghetti heads had spawned a new generation.

I USED MY OVERTIME to take the afternoon off and went to Red Lerille's Health and Racquet Club in Lafayette. I did four sets of curls and military and bench presses with free weights, then went into the main workout room, which had a glass wall that gave onto a shady drive-way and the adjacent tennis courts and was lined with long rows of exercise machines. Because it was still early in the day, there were few people on the machines. A half dozen off-duty steroid-pumped La-fayette cops were gathered around a pull-down bar, seemingly talking among themselves.

But their eyes kept drifting to the end of the room, where Karyn LaRose lay on a bench at an inverted angle, her calves and ankles hooked inside two cylindrical vinyl cushions while she raised herself toward her knees, her fingers laced behind her head, her brown thighs shiny with sweat, her breasts as swollen as grapefruit against her Harley motorcycle T-shirt.

I sat down on a Nautilus leg-lift machine, set the pin at 140, and raised the bar with the tops of my feet until my ankles were straight out from my knees and I could feel a burn grow in my thighs.

I felt her on the corner of my vision. She flipped her sweat towel against my leg like a wet kiss.

"Our bodyguard isn't speaking these days?" she said.

"Hello, Karyn."

She wiped her neck and the back of her hair. Her black shorts were damp and molded to her body.

"You still mad?" she said.

"I never worry about yesterday's box score."

Her mouth fell open.

"Sorry, bad metaphor," I said.

"If you aren't a handful."

"How about requesting me off y'all's security?" I asked.

"You're stuck, baby love."

"Why?"

"Because you're a cutey, that's why." She propped her forearm on top of the machine. She let her thigh touch mine.

"Sounds like control to me," I said.

"That's what it's all about, sweetie." She bumped me again.

"Stop playing games with people, Karyn. Aaron Crown's out there. He doesn't care about clever rhetoric."

"Then go find him."

"I think he'll find us. It won't be a good moment, either."

She looked down the aisle through the machines. The off-duty Lafayette cops had turned their attention to a dead-lift bar stacked with one-hundred-pound plates. Karyn sucked on her index finger, her eyes fastened on mine, then touched it to my lips.

LATER, I DROVE TO Sabelle Crown's bar down by the Lafayette Underpass. Even though the day was bright, the bar's interior was as dark as the inside of a glove. Sabelle was in a back storage shed, her body crisscrossed with the sunlight that fell through the board walls, watching two black men load vinyl bags bursting with beer cans onto a salvage truck.

"I wondered when you'd be around," she said.

"Oh?"

"He wouldn't come here. I don't know where he is, either."

"I don't believe you."

"Suit yourself . . ." She turned to the black men. "Okay, you guys got it all? Next week I want you back here on time. No more 'My gran'mama been sick, Miz Sabelle' stuff. There're creatures with no eyes living under the garbage I got back here."

She watched the truck, its slatted sides held in place with baling wire, lumber down the alley. "God, what a life," she said. She sat down on a folding chair next to the brick wall and took a sandwich out of a paper bag. A crazy network of wood stairs and rusted fire escapes zigzagged to the upper stories of the building. She pushed another chair toward me with her foot. "Sit down, Dave, you're making me nervous."

I looked at a smear of something sticky on the seat and remained standing.

"There's only one person in the world he cares about. Don't tell me he hasn't tried to contact you," I said.

"You want a baloney sandwich?"

"We can still turn it around. But not if he hurts Buford."

"Buford was born with a mammy's pink finger up his butt. Let him get out of his own problems for a change."

"How about your father?"

"Nobody will ever change Daddy's mind about anything."

Her expression was turned inward, heated with an unrelieved anger.

"What did Buford do to you?" I asked.

"Who said he did? I love the business I run, fighting with colored can recyclers, mopping out the john after winos use it. Tell Buford to drop by. I'll buy him a short-dog."

"He said he didn't know you."

Her eyes climbed into my face. "He did? Wipe off the chair and sit down. I'll tell you a story about our new governor."

She started to rewrap her sandwich, then she simply threw it in an oil barrel filled with smoldering boards.

THAT EVENING IT was warm enough to eat supper in the backyard.

"You have to work in Lafayette tonight?" Bootsie said.

"Worse. Buford has a breakfast there in the morning. I'll probably have to stay over."

"They're really making their point, aren't they?"

"You'd better believe it."

"You mind if I come over?"

"I think it's a swell idea."

"Oh, I forgot. Somebody left a letter in the mailbox with no stamp on it."

"Who put it in there?"

"Batist said he saw a black man on a bicycle stop out on the road ... It's on the dining room table."

I went inside and came back out again. My name and address were printed in pencil, in broken letters, on the envelope. Bootsie watched my face while I read the note inside.

"It's from *him*, isn't it?"

I lay the sheet of Big Chief notebook paper on the picnic table so she could read it.

I killed the two blak boys in the tool bin cause they wuldnt let me be. But I still aint to blame for the first one. Tell that bucket of shit done me all this grief he aint going make Baton Rouge. You was good to me. So don't be standing betwix me and a man that is about to burn in hell wich is where he shud have been sent a long time ago.

Yours truly,
Aaron Jefferson Crown

"He uses a funny phrase. He says he 'aint to blame' rather than 'innocent,'" I said.

"He probably can't spell the word."

"No, I remember, he always said 'I ain't did it.' "

"Forget the linguistics, Dave. Pay attention to the last sentence. I'm not going to let you take one for Buford LaRose."

"It's not going to happen."

"You've got that right. I'm going to have a talk with our friend Karyn."

"Don't complicate it, Boots."

"She's a big girl. She can handle it."

"When the sheriff wants me off, he'll pull me off."

"Nice Freudian choice, Streak. Because that's what she's doing—fucking this whole family."

I STILL HAD A half hour before I had to drive to the Hotel Acadiana on the Vermilion River, where Buford and Karyn were being hosted by a builders' association. I sat at the picnic table and took apart my 1911 model U.S. Army .45 automatic that I had bought for twenty-five dollars in Saigon's Bring Cash Alley. It felt cool and heavy in my hand, and my fingers left delicate prints in the thin film of oil on the blueing. I ran the bore brush through the barrel, wiped the breech and the outside of the slide free of the burnt powder left from my last visit to the practice range, slid each hollow-point round out of the magazine, oiled the spring, then replaced them one at a time until the eighth round snugged tight under my thumb.

But guns and the sublimated fantasies that went along with cleaning them were facile alternatives for thinking through complexities. The main problem with this case lay in the fact that many of the players were not professional criminals.

Sabelle's story was not an unusual one. In small southern towns, since antebellum times, the haves and the have-nots may have either despised or feared one another in daylight, but at night both sexual need and the imperious urge had a way of dissolving the social differences that were so easily defined in the morning hours.

I say it wasn't an exceptional story. But that doesn't mean it is any less an indicator of the people we were. I just didn't know if it had a bearing on the case.

He had never really noticed her at New Iberia High. She had been one grade behind him, one of those girls who wore a homemade tattoo on her hand and clothes from the dry goods section of the five-and-dime and trailed rumors behind her that were too outrageous to be believed. She was arrested for shoplifting, then she left school in the eleventh grade and became a waitress in the drive-in and bowling alley at the end of East Main. The summer of his graduation he had gone to the drive-in for beers in his metallic green Ford convertible with three other ballplayers after an American Legion game. He was unshowered, his face flushed with victory and the pink magic of the evening, his uniform grass stained, his spikes clicking on the gravel when he walked to the service window and saw her wiping the moisture off a long-necked Jax with her cupped hand.

She leaned over the beer box and smiled and looked into his eyes and at the grin at the corner of his mouth and knew that he would be back later.

He drove his friends home and bathed and changed clothes and sat at one of the plank tables under the live oaks and drank beer and listened to the music that was piped from the jukebox into loudspeakers nailed in the tree limbs, until she finally walked out in the humid glare of the electric lights at midnight and got into his car and reached over and blew his horn to say good night to the other waitresses who stood giggling behind the drive-in's glass window. He took no notice of her presumption and seemingly proprietary display; he even grinned good-naturedly. No one else was in the lot except an elderly Negro picking up trash and stuffing it in a gunny sack.

They did it the first time on a back road by Lake Martin, in the way that she expected him to, on the backseat, the door open, his pants and belt around his ankles, his body trembling and awkward with his passion, his jaws already going slack and his voice a weak and hoarse whisper before he had fully penetrated her.

Three nights later he went by her home, the Montgomery Ward brick house on the coulee, and convinced her to call in sick at work.

This time they drove down the Teche toward Jeanerette and did it in the caretaker's cottage of a plantation built on the bayou by West Indies slaves in 1790, which Buford's father had bought not because of its iron-scrolled verandas or oak-canopied circular drive or wisteria-entwined gazebos or the minié balls drilled in its window frames by Yankee soldiers but simply as a transitory real estate investment for which he wrote a check.

As the summer passed, Buford and Sabelle's late-night routine became almost like that of an ordinary young couple who went steady or who were engaged or whose passion was so obviously pure in its heat and intensity that the discrepancy in their family backgrounds seemed irrelevant.

In her mind the summer had become a song that would have no end. She looked at calendar dates only as they indicated the span of her periods. The inept boy who had trembled on top of her that first night by Lake Martin, and who had sat ashamed in the dark later, his pants still unbuttoned over his undershorts while she held his hand and assured him that it had been a fine moment for her, had gradually transformed into a confident lover, realizing with the exhalation of her breath, the touch of her hands in certain places, the motion of her hips, what gave her the most pleasure, until finally he knew all the right things to do, without being told, and could make her come before he did and then a second time with him.

His triangular back was corded with muscle, his buttocks small and hard under her palms, his mouth always gentle on her body. From the bed in the caretaker's cottage she could look down the corridor of oaks that gave onto the Teche, the limbs and moss and leaves swelling in the wind, and through the dark trunks she could see the moon catch on the water like a spray of silver coins, and it made her think of a picture she had once seen in a children's book of biblical stories.

The picture was titled *The Gates of Eden.* As a child she had thought of it as a place of exodus and exclusion. Now, as she held Buford between her legs and pressed him deeper inside, she knew those gates were opening for her.

But in August he began to make excuses. He had to begin early training for the football season, to be asleep early, to go to Baton Rouge for his physical, to meet with coaches from Tulane and Ole Miss and the University of Texas who were still trying to lure him away from LSU.

On the last Saturday of the month, a day that he had told her he would be in New Orleans, she saw his convertible parked outside Slick's Club in St. Martinville, with three girls in it, sitting up on the sides, drinking vodka Collinses that a Negro waiter brought them from inside.

She was in her father's car. One headlight was broken and the passenger window was taped over with cardboard and the body leaked rust at every seam. She drove around the block twice, her hands sweating on the wheel, her heart beating, then she pulled up at an angle to the convertible and got out, her words like broken Popsicle sticks in her throat.

"What?" one of the girls said.

"Where is Buford? You're with Buford, aren't you? This is his car," Sabelle said. But her voice was weak, apart from her, outside of her skin, somehow shameful.

The girls looked at one another.

"Buford the Beautiful?" one of them said. The three of them started to laugh, then looked back at her and fluttered their eyes and blew their cigarette smoke at upward angles into the warm air.

Then a huge, redheaded crewcut boy, his hair stiff as metal with butch wax, with whiskey-flushed cheeks, in a gold and purple LSU T-shirt, erupted out the door of the club with someone behind him.

The crewcut boy, who had been an All-State center at New Iberia High, took one look at Sabelle and turned, his grin as wide and obscene as a jack-o'-lantern's, and held up his palms to the person behind him, saying, "Whoa, buddy! Not the time to go outside. Not unless you want the family jewels on her car aerial."

She saw Buford's face in the neon light, then it was gone.

She couldn't remember driving home that night. She lay in the dark in her bedroom and listened to the frogs in the woods, to her father getting up to urinate, to her neighbor, a trash hauler, crushing tin cans in the bed of his truck. She watched an evangelist preacher on the black-and-white television set in her tiny living room, then a movie about nuclear war. The movie made use of U.S. Army footage that showed the effects of radiation burns on living animals that had been left in pens five hundred yards from an atomic explosion.

As she listened to the bleating of the animals, she wanted everyone in the movie to die. No, that wasn't it. She believed for the first time she understood something about men that she had never understood before, and she wanted to see a brilliant white light ripple across the sky outside her window, burn it away like black cellophane, yes, a perfect white flame that could superheat the air, eat the water out of the bayou, and instantly wither a corridor of oaks that in the moonlight had become biblical gates in a children's book.

But her anger and the relief it gave her melted away to fatigue, and when the dawn finally came it was gray and wet and the rain ran down inside the walls of the house, and when she heard the trash hauler's wife yelling at her children next door, then striking one of them with a belt, viciously, the voice rising with each blow, Sabelle knew that her future was as linear and as well defined as the nailheads protruding from the buckled linoleum at her feet.

I HADN'T WATCHED THE time. I went to get in my truck and head for Lafayette, but Bootsie's Toyota was parked behind me. I heard her open Alafair's bedroom window behind me.

"Take my car," she said. "I can use the truck."

"See you in Lafayette," I said.

"What's your room number?"

"I don't know. Ask at the desk."

I backed out into the dirt road and looked once again at my truck parked in the opening of the old barn that we used as a garage. I almost went back and got it, but it had been running fine since I had gotten it out of the shop.

And I was running late.

What a bitter line to remember.

Chapter
17

Years ago Pinhook Road in Lafayette had been a tree-lined two-lane road that led out of town over the Vermilion River into miles of sugarcane acreage. Just before the steel drawbridge that spanned the river was an antebellum home with arbors of pecan trees in the yard. The river was yellow and high in the spring, and the banks were green and heavily wooded. Feral hogs foraged among the trees. The only businesses along the river were a drive-in restaurant called the Skunk, where college and high school kids hung out, and the American Legion Club on the far side of the bridge, where you could eat bluepoint crabs and drink pitcher beer on a screened porch that hung on stilts above the water.

But progress and the developers had their way. The oaks were sawed down, the root systems ground into pulp by road graders, the banks of the river covered with cement for parking lots. Overlooking all this new urban environment was the Hotel Acadiana, where builders and developers and union officials from all over the state had come to pay a three-hundred-dollar-a-plate homage to their new governor.

"Do you hear little piggy feet running toward the trough?" Helen Soileau said. We were standing like posts by one side of the banquet room entrance. A jazz combo was playing inside. Helen kept stoking her own mood.

"What a bunch . . . Did you see Karyn in the bar? I think she's half in the bag," she said.

"I don't think she's entirely comfortable with her new constituency."

"Not in the daylight, anyway . . . Check out who just came in the door."

Persephone Green wore a black see-through evening dress and a sapphire and diamond necklace around her throat. Her shoulders were as white and smooth as moonstone.

"How do you know Dock Green's wife?" I said.

"I was in uniform with NOPD when she shot a prowler at her home in the Garden District. She shot him five times."

Persephone Green paused by the banquet room door, her black sequined bag dangling from her wrist by a spidery cord.

"You get around," she said to me. Her hair was pulled straight back and threaded with a string of tiny diamonds.

"Looking after the common good, that sort of thing," I said.

"We'll all sleep more secure, I'm sure." Her gaze roved indolently over Helen's face. "You have a reason for staring at me, madam?"

"No, ma'am."

"I know you?"

"I was the first officer at the scene when you popped that black guy by your swimming pool. I pulled his head out of the water," Helen said.

"Oh yes, how could I forget? You're the charm school graduate who made some accusations."

"Not really. I probably have poor night vision. I was the only one who saw a powder burn by the guy's eyebrow," Helen said.

"That's right, you made quite a little squeaking noise, didn't you?"

"The scene investigator probably had better eyesight. He's the one took early retirement the same year and bought a liquor store out in Metairie," Helen said.

"My, what a clever sack of potatoes."

Persephone Green walked on inside the banquet room. The back of her evening dress was an open V that extended to the lower tip of her vertebrae.

"I'm going up on the roof," Helen said.

"Don't let her bother you."

"Tomorrow I'm off this shit. The old man doesn't like it, he can have my shield."

I watched her walk through the crowd toward the service elevator, her back flexed, her arms pumped, her expression one that dissipated smiles and caused people to glance away from her face.

I walked through the meeting rooms and the restaurant and bar area. Karyn LaRose was dancing by the bandstand with Jerry Joe Plumb. Her evening dress looked like frozen pink champagne poured on her body. She pulled away from him and came up to me, her face flushed and hot, her breath heavy with the smell of cherries and bourbon.

"Dance with me," she said.

"Can't do it on the job."

"Yes you will." She slipped her hand into mine and held it tightly between us. She tilted her chin up—a private thought, like a self-indulgent memory, seemed to light her eyes.

"It looks like you're enjoying yourself," I said.

"I know of only one moment that feels as good as winning," she said. She smiled at the corners of her mouth.

"Better have some coffee, Karyn."

"You're a pill. But you're going to end up in Baton Rouge just the same, honey bunny."

"*Adios,*" I said, and pulled loose from her and went out the side door and into the parking lot.

It was warm and muggy outside, and the moon was yellow and veiled inside a rain ring. There were Lafayette city cops in the parking lot and state police with rifles on the roof. I walked all the way around the hotel and talked with a state policeman and a black security guard at the back door, then checked the opposite side of a hedge that bordered the parking lot, and, finally, for want of anything else to do, walked down toward the river.

Where would Aaron Crown be, I asked myself.

Not in a town or city, I thought. Even before he had been a hunted man, Aaron was one of those who sought out woods and bogs not only as a refuge of shadow and invisibility but as a place where no concrete slab would separate the whirrings in his chest from the power that he instinctively knew lay inside rotted logs and layers of moldy leaves and caves that were as dark as a womb.

Maybe in the Atchafalaya Basin, I thought, holed up in a shack on stilts, smearing his skin with mud to protect it from mosquitoes, eating nutria or coon or gar or whatever bird he could knock from a tree with a club, his ankles lesioned with sores from the leg chains he had run in.

If he tried to get Buford tonight, in all probability it would have to be from a distance, I thought. He could come down the Vermilion, hide his boat under a dock, perhaps circle the hotel, and hunch down in the shrubbery behind the parking lot. With luck Buford would appear under a canvas walkway, or between parked automobiles, and Aaron would wind the leather sling as tightly as a tourniquet around his left forearm, sight the scope's crosshairs on the man who had not only sent him to prison but had used and discarded his daughter as a white overseer would a field woman, then grind his back teeth with an almost sexual pleasure while he squeezed off the round and watched the world try to deal with Aaron Crown's handiwork.

But he had to get inside the perimeter to do it.

I used the pay phone in a restaurant on the riverbank to call Bootsie. While I listened to my own voice on the answering machine, I gazed out the window at the parking lot and the four-lane flow of headlights on Pinhook. A catering truck turned into the hotel, a rug cleaning van driven by a woman, a white stretch limo filled with revelers, a half dozen taxicabs.

I hung up the phone and went back outside. It was almost 9 P.M. Where was Bootsie?

I went back inside the hotel and rode the service elevator up to the roof. The wind was warm and smelled of rain, and there were yellow slicks of moonlight, like patches of oil paint, floating on the river's surface.

Down below, at the service entrance, the caterers were carrying in stainless steel containers of food, and a blonde woman in a baggy gray dress was pulling a hamper loaded with rug cleaning equipment from her van. A drunk man in a hat and a raincoat wandered through the parked cars, then decided to work his way into the hedge at the back of the lot, simultaneously unzipping his fly. The state policeman at the service door walked out into the lot and paused under a light, his hands on his hips, then stepped close in to the hedge, raised on his toes, and tried to see the man in the raincoat. The state policeman disappeared into the shadows.

"What is it?" Helen said.

"A state trooper went after a drunk in the hedge. I don't see either one of them now . . . Get on the portable, will you?"

"What y'all got down there?" she said into her radio.

"Ain't got nothing," the voice of a black man said.

"Who is this?"

"The security guard."

"Put an officer on."

"They ain't one."

"What's going on with the guy in the hedge?"

"What guy?"

"The drunk the state trooper went after. Look, find an officer and give him the radio."

"I done tried to tell you, they ain't nothing going on. Except somebody down here don't have no bidness working in a hotel."

"What are you talking about?" Helen said.

"Somebody down here got BO could make your nose fall off, that's what I'm talking about. That clear enough?" There was a pause. The security guard was still transmitting but he was speaking to someone else now: "I told you, you got to have some ID . . . You ain't suppose to be inside here . . . Hey, don't you be coming at me like that . . ."

The portable radio struck the floor.

Helen and I ran for the service elevator.

* * *

BY THE TIME we got down to the first floor a Lafayette city cop and a state policeman were running down the hallway ahead of us toward the service entrance. Through the glass I could see the catering truck and the rug cleaning van in the parking lot.

"There ain't anybody here," the city cop said, looking at the empty hallway, then outside. He wore sideburns and his hat was too large for his head. He sniffed the air and made a face. "Man, what's that smell? It's like somebody rubbed shit on the walls."

The hallway made a left angle toward the kitchen. Halfway down it were two ventilated wood doors that were closed on a loud humming sound inside. A clothes hamper loaded with squeegee mops and a rug cleaning machine and bottles of chemicals rested at an angle against the wall. I opened one of the doors and saw, next to the boilers, a thin black man, with a mustache, in the uniform of a security guard, sitting against a pile of crumpled cardboard cartons, his knees drawn up before him, his hands gripping his loins, his face dilated with shock.

"What happened to you, partner?" I said.

"The woman done it," he answered.

"The woman?"

"I mean, she was dressed like a woman. She come at me. I ain't wanted to do it, but I hit her with my baton. It didn't even slow her up. That's when she grabbed me. Down here. She twisted real hard. She kept saying, 'Tell me where LaRose at or I tear it out.'" He swallowed and widened his eyes.

"We'll get the paramedics. You're going to be all right," I said. I heard Helen go back out the door.

"I ain't never had nothing like this happen," he said. His face flinched when he tried to change the position of his legs. "It was when I seen her socks. That's what started it, see. I wouldn't have paid her no mind."

"Her socks?" I said.

"The catering guys went in the kitchen with all the food. I thought it was one of them stinking up the place. Then I looked at the woman's feet 'cause she was tracking the rug. She had on brogans and socks with blood on them. I axed her to show me some ID. She say it's in the van, then y'all called me on the radio."

"Where'd this person go?" I said.

"I don't know. Back outside, maybe. She was kicking around in these cartons, looking for something. I think she dropped it when I hit her. It was metal-looking. Maybe a knife."

Helen came back through the door.

"Check this. It was out in the lot," she said, and held up a fright wig by one ropy blonde strand.

"You did fine," I said to the security guard. "Maybe you saved the governor's life tonight."

"Yeah? I done that?"

"You bet," I said. Then I saw a piece of black electrician's tape and a glint of metal under a flattened carton. I knelt on one knee and lifted up the carton and inserted my ballpoint pen through the trigger guard of a revolver whose broken wood grips were taped to the steel frame.

"It looks like a thirty-two," Helen said.

"It sure does."

"What, that means something?" she asked.

"I've seen it before. In a shoebox full of military decorations at Sabelle Crown's bar," I said.

AN HOUR LATER, a half mile away, somebody reported a grate pried off a storm drain. A Lafayette city cop used his flashlight and crawled down through a huge slime-encrusted pipe that led under the streets to a bluff above the Vermilion River. The bottom of the pipe was trenched with the heavy imprints of a man's brogans or work boots. The prints angled off the end of the pipe through the brush and meandered along the mudbank, below the bluff and an apartment building where people watched the late news behind their sliding glass doors, oblivious to the passage of a man who could have stepped out of a cave at the dawn of time.

He found a powerboat locked with a chain to a dock, tore the chain and the steel bolt out of the post, then discovered a hundred yards downstream that he had no gas. He climbed up the bank with a can, hung the dress in the brush, and followed a coulee to a lighted boulevard, climbed through a corrugated pipe, and walked into a filling station, wearing only his trousers and brogans, his hairy, mud-streaked torso glowing with an odor that made the attendant blanch.

Aaron opened his callused palm on a bone-handle pocketknife.

"How much you give me for this?" he asked.

"I don't need one," the attendant replied, and tried to smile. He was young, his black hair combed straight back; he wore a tie that attached to the collar of his white shirt with a cardboard hook.

"I'll take six dollars for it. You can sell it for ten."

"No, sir, I really don't need no knife."

"I just want five dollars' gas and a bag of them pork rinds. That's an honest deal."

The attendant's eyes searched the empty pavilion outside. The rain was slanting across the fluorescent lights above the gas pumps.

"You're trying to make me steal from the man I work for," he said.

"I ain't got a shirt on my back. I ain't got food to eat. I come in out of the rain and ask for hep and you call me a thief. I won't take that shit."

"I'll call my boss and ax him. Maybe you can talk to him."

The attendant lifted the telephone receiver off the hook under the counter. But Aaron's huge hand closed on his and squeezed, then squeezed harder, splaying the fingers, mashing the knuckles like bits of bone against the plastic, his eyes bulging with energy and power an inch from the attendant's face, his grip compressing the attendant's hand into a ball of pain until a cry broke from the attendant's throat and his free hand flipped at the power switch to an unleaded pump.

Aaron left the pocketknife on top of the counter.

"My name's Aaron Crown. I killed two niggers in Angola kept messing with me. You tell anybody I robbed you, I'll be back," he said.

BUT THE PARTY at the Acadiana never slowed down. The very fact that Aaron had failed so miserably in attempting to penetrate the governor-elect's security, like an insect trying to fight its way out of a glass bell, was almost a metaphorical confirmation that a new era had begun, one in which a charismatic southern leader and his beautiful wife danced like college sweethearts to a Dixieland band and shared their own aura with such a generosity of spirit that even the most hardbitten self-made contractor felt humbled and ennobled to be in their presence.

But I was worn out when I got back from the search for Aaron Crown and didn't care anymore about the fortunes of the LaRose family and just wanted to go to sleep. There was a message from Bootsie at the desk when I picked up my room key: *The truck broke down by Spanish Lake and I had to wait for the wrecker. I'm borrowing my sister's car but will be there quite late.*

I left a note for Bootsie with the room number on it and started toward the elevator.

"Mr. Robicheaux, you have another message," the clerk said.

I took the piece of paper from his hand and read it.

Streak, I got the gen on our man Mookie. We're talking about your mainline subhuman here. I'll fill you in later. Let's ROA at the bar. Dangle easy, big mon—Clete.

"I'm a little confused. This is my friend's handwriting. He's here at the hotel?" I said.

The clerk took the slip of paper out of my hand and looked at it.

"Oh yes, he's here. He is certainly here, sir."

"Excuse me?"

"I think there was a problem about his invitation. He didn't seem to have it with him. Someone tried to put his hand on your friend's arm and walk him to the door."

"That must have made an interesting show."

"Oh it was, sir. Definitely." The clerk was laughing to himself now.

I went into the bar and restaurant, looked on the dance floor and in the banquet and meeting rooms. Normally tracking Clete Purcel's progress through a given area was like following the path of a wrecking ball, but I saw no sign of him and I rode the elevator up to the top floor, where I had been given a room at the end of the hall from

Buford and Karyn's, unlocked the door, undressed, and lay down on the bed in the dark.

It was storming outside now, and through the wide glass window I could see the flow of traffic across the bridge and the rain falling out of the electric light into the water. At one time this area had been called Vermilionville, and in 1863 Louisiana's boys in butternut had retreated up the Teche, exhausted, malnourished, their uniforms in rags, often barefoot, and had fought General Banks' federal troops, right here, on the banks of the river, to keep open the flow of supplies from Texas to the rest of the Confederacy.

As I fell onto the edges of sleep I saw sugarcane fields and houses burning and skies that were plum-colored with smoke and heard the popping of small-arms fire and the clatter of muskets and bayonets as a column of infantry ran down the dirt road toward an irrigation ditch, and I had no doubt which direction my sleep was about to take.

This time the sniper was not Victor Charles.

I was trapped in the middle of the dirt road, my feet unable to run. I saw a musket extend itself from a clump of violent green brush, saw the stiffness of its barrel rear in the sunlight, and in my mind, as though I had formed a contract between the condemned and the executioner, the sniper and I became one, joined irrevocably together as co-participants in my death, and just before the .58 caliber round exploded from the barrel I could feel him squeeze the musket in his hands, as though it were really I who cupped its wet hardness in my palms.

In my sleep I heard the door to the hotel room open, then close, heard someone set down a key on the nightstand and close the curtains, felt a woman's weight on the side of the bed and then her hand on my hip, and I knew Bootsie had arrived at the hotel safely.

I lay on my back, with the pillow across my face, and heard her undressing in the dark. She lay beside me, touched my stomach, then moved across my loins, her thighs spread, and put my sex between her legs. Then she leaned close to me, pushed the pillow from my face, and kissed my cheek and put her tongue inside my mouth and placed my sex inside her.

Her tongue tasted like candy, like cherries that had been soaked in bourbon. She raised herself on her arms, the tops of her swollen breasts half-mooned with tan.

I stared upward into the face of Karyn LaRose, who smiled lazily and said, "Tell me you don't like it, Dave. Tell me. See if you can tell me that . . . Tell me . . . tell me . . . tell me . . ."

Chapter
18

I FOUND CLETE PURCEL at the bar. He was drinking a shot of tequila, with a Corona and a saucer of salted limes on the side, his porkpie hat cocked over one eye. The band was putting away its instruments and the bar was almost empty.

"Where you been, noble mon? You look a couple of quarts down," he said.

"A long day." I sat next to him and rubbed my face. My skin felt cold, dead to the touch.

"I thought I saw Boots go out the lobby."

"You did."

"What's going on?"

"Don't worry about it. What'd you find out about this guy Mookie?"

His eyes seemed to go inside mine, then he tipped back the shot and drank from the bottle of Corona.

"The black broad, Brandy Grissum, came into Nig's office hysterical today. Dig this, she used the two yards you gave her to score a shitload of rock and get wiped out. So while she was on the nod at her mother's house in St. John the Baptist, our man Mookie tools on up for some more R&R. Guess what? Mookie decided he wasn't interested in a stoned-out twenty-buck street whore. So he sodomized her little sister."

He put a Lucky Strike in his mouth and fiddled with his Zippo, as though he were trying to remove an image from his mind, then dropped the Zippo on the bar without lighting the cigarette.

"His last name is Zerrang," he said. "He used to be a leg breaker for a couple of shylocks on the Mississippi coast, then he made the big score as a hit man for the greaseballs in Miami. He must be pretty slick, though. I had a friend at NOPD punch on the computer. He's never been down."

"Who's he working for now?"

"Brandy doesn't know. This time I think she's telling the truth . . . You don't look good, Streak. What's troubling you, mon?"

I told him. We were the only people at the bar now. Clete listened, his face empty of expression. He rubbed his thumb against his cheekbone, and I could see white lines inside the crow's-feet at the corner of his eye.

He made a coughing sound in his throat.

"That's quite a story," he said.

I picked up one of the salted limes from his saucer, then set it down again.

"Bootsie walked in on it?" he asked.

"When Karyn was dressing."

"How did the LaRose broad get in?"

"She got a passkey from the maid."

"Dave, you were throwing her out. Bootsie doesn't know that?"

"I didn't have a chance to tell her. I'll call her when she's back home."

"Man." He breathed through his nose, his lips crimped together. "You told Karyn LaRose to peddle her bread somewhere else, though?"

"Something like that." A scrolled green and red Dixie beer sign was lit over the row of whiskey bottles behind the bar. I felt tired all over and my palms were stiff and dry when I closed and opened them.

"You didn't do anything wrong. You just got to make Boots see that. Right? This isn't a big deal," he said. He watched me rub the salt in the saucer with the tip of my finger. "Let's find a late-night joint and get a steak."

"I'm going to take a shower and go to bed," I said.

"I'm going up with you."

"The hell you are."

"I *know* you, Streak. You're going to get inside your own head and build a case against yourself. The slop chute is closing. For you it's closed permanently. You got that, big mon?"

"There's no problem here, Clete."

"Yeah, I bet. That broad couldn't buy you, so she decided to fuck your head." He stood up from the barstool, then grimaced slightly. "I feel like an upended bottle. Come on, let's get out of here. Remind me in the future to drink in low-class dumps that aren't full of the right people."

"You're the best, Cletus."

He put his arm on my shoulder, and we walked together toward the elevator like two impaired Siamese twins trying to get in sync with each other.

THE NEXT MORNING I was part of the caravan that escorted Karyn and Buford back to their home on the Teche. It was balmy and gray after the rain, and you could smell the wet earth in the fields and hear the clanging of the sugarcane refinery down the bayou. It was a fine, late-fall morning, disjointed from the events of last night, as though I had experienced them only in a drunken dream.

From my car I watched Karyn and her husband enter their front door, their faces opaque, perhaps still numb from the alcohol of the night before, or perhaps masking the secrets they waited to share or the buried anger they would vent on each other once inside.

Bootsie was in the backyard, at the redwood picnic table, with a cup of coffee and a cigarette when I parked in the drive. She wore sandals and a terrycloth red shirt and a pair of khakis high on her hips.

"Hi," I said.

Her legs were crossed, and she tipped her ashes in an inverted preserve jar cap and looked at the ducks skittering across our pond.

"You don't smoke," I said.

"I'm starting."

I sat down across from her. Her eyes moved up to meet mine.

"I told you the truth last night," I said.

"For some reason that doesn't make it any easier."

"Why?"

"How'd she come to have this obsession with you? What's your end of it?"

"I didn't want to go out to their house when we were first invited there. I tried to avoid her."

"Who are you putting on?"

I felt my throat close. My eyes burned, as though I were looking into a watery glare.

She threw her cigarette in a flower bed full of dead leaves by the back wall of the house. Her cheeks were hot and streaked with color. Before I went into the house, I removed the burning cigarette from the leaves and mashed it out in the jar cap in front of her, my gesture as foolish as my words were self-serving.

THE WALL PHONE was ringing in the kitchen. I picked it up, my eyes fixed on Bootsie's back through the window. Her hair was thick and woven with gold in the gray light.

"Aaron Crown dumped the boat down by Maurice," the sheriff said.

"Did anybody see him?"

"No, just the boat."

"He'll be back."

"You say that almost with admiration."

"Like an old gunbull said, Aaron's a traveling shit storm."

"Anyway, you got your wish. You're off it."

When I didn't reply, he said, "You're not going to ask me why?"

"Go ahead, Sheriff."

"Buford called and said you're resentful about the assignment. He said you don't need to come around his house again."

"He did, did he?"

"That's not all. He said you made a pass at his wife last night."

"He's a liar."

"I believe you. But why did he decide to make up a story about you now?"

"Ask him."

"I will . . . Dave, you still there?"

"I'll talk to you later, Sheriff. I have to go somewhere."

"I always knew this job would bring me humility . . . Say, you're not going out to get in Buford LaRose's face, are you?"

I DROVE BOOTSIE'S TOYOTA to the mechanic's garage, exchanged it for my truck, and asked the mechanic to drive the Toyota back to my house, then I headed out to the LaRose plantation.

But I was not the only person who had a grievance with Buford that day. Jerry Joe Plumb's blue Buick was pulled at an angle to the old LaRose company store, and Jerry Joe stood on the gallery between the two wooden pecan barrels that framed the double front doors, his hands on his hips, speaking heatedly into Buford's face.

I crunched across the shell parking lot and cut my engine. They both looked at me, then stepped inside the double doors with the oxidized and cracked windows and continued their argument, Jerry Joe jabbing his finger in the air, his cheeks pooling with color.

But I could still hear part of it.

"You're shorting me. Your old man wouldn't do this, Buford."

"You'll get your due."

"Three of the jobs you promised are already let to Dock Green."

"I gave you my word. You stop trying to cadge favors because you knew my family."

"Persephone let you put your head up her dress?"

Jerry Joe's back was to me. His shoulders looked stiff, rectangular, his triceps swollen with tubes of muscle, like a prizefighter's while he waits for the referee to finish giving instructions before the bell.

But Buford turned away from the insult and lit a cigar, cupping and puffing it in the gloom as though Jerry Joe were not there.

Jerry Joe's leather-soled oxblood loafers were loud on the gallery when he came out the double doors.

"What's the haps, Jerry?" I said.

He balanced on his soles, his face still glowing.

"He asks me the haps? Here's a lesson. You take up with piranha fish, don't expect them to go on a diet."

"Buford stiffed you?"

"That guy don't have the lead in his Eversharp to stiff anybody. Hey, keep your hammer in your pants or get you a full-body condom," he said, and got into his Buick and started the engine.

I got out of my truck and put my hand on his door window. He rolled it down with the electric motor.

"Spell it out," I said.

"You're in the way. She knows how to combine business and pleasure. Don't pretend you're a dumb shit." He pushed the window button again and scorched two lines in the shell parking lot out to the state highway.

I picked a handful of pecans out of one of the barrels by the door and went inside the store.

"You again. Like bubble gum under the shoe," Buford said.

The store was dark, the cypress floor worn as smooth as wood inside a feed bin, the half-filled shelves filmed with cobwebs. I put a half dollar for the pecans next to the brass cash register on the counter and cracked two of them together in my palm.

"Why are you telling lies about me to the sheriff?" I said.

"You propositioned Karyn at the Acadiana. What do you expect?"

"Who told you this?"

"Karyn, of course."

"Bad source. Your wife's a pathological liar."

"Your job's finished here. Go back to doing whatever you do, Dave. Just stay off my property."

"Wrong. As long as Aaron Crown is running loose, I'll come here anytime I want, Buford."

He combed his thick, curly hair back with his fingernails, a dark knowledge forming in his face.

"You want to bring me down, don't you?" he said.

"You're a fraud."

"What did I ever do to you? Can you answer that simple question for me?"

"You and your wife use each other to injure other people . . . You know what a *bugarron* is?"

The skin trembled along the lower rim of his right eye.

"Are you calling me a—" he began.

"You serve a perversity of some kind. I just don't know what it is."

"The next time you come here, I'll break your jaw. That's a promise."

He turned and walked down the length of the counter, past the display shelves that were covered with dust, and out the back screen door into the light. The screen slammed behind him like the crack of a rifle.

I TOOK THE REST of the day off and raked piles of wet leaves and pecan husks out of the lawn. The wind was still warm out of the south and the tops of the trees in the swamp were a soft green against the sky, and the only sound louder than my own thoughts was Tripod, Alafair's three-legged coon, running up and down on his chain in the side yard. I burned the leaves in the coulee, then I showered, took a nap, and didn't wake until after sunset. While I was dressing, the phone rang in the kitchen. Bootsie answered it and walked to the bedroom door.

"It's Batist," she said.

"What's he want?"

"He didn't say." She went into the living room, then out on the gallery and sat on the swing.

"That movie fella get a hold of you?" Batist asked.

"No. What's up?"

"He was down here wit' a truck and some people wit' cameras. I tole him he ought to talk to you about what he was doing. I seen him talking on one of them cordless phones. He ain't called you?"

"This man's not a friend, Batist. Is he there now?"

"No. He ain't the reason I called you. It's that big black man. He ain't up to no good."

"Which black man?"

"The biggest one I ever seen around here."

"I'll be down in a minute."

I went out on the gallery. Bootsie still sat in the swing, pushing it back and forth with one foot.

"I need to go down to the dock for a few minutes," I said.

"Right."

"Boots, you've got to cut me some slack."

"You don't see it."

"What?"

"You hate the LaRoses and what they stand for. That's the power they have over you."

"I'm a police officer. They're corrupt."

"You say they are. Nobody else does." She went inside. The swing twisted emptily on its chains under the bug light.

I walked down the slope through the trees to the dock. The string of lights was turned on over the dock, and you could see bream night-feeding off the insects that fell into the water. Batist was cleaning out the coffee urn inside the bait shop.

"Tell me about the black guy," I said.

Batist looked up from his work and studied my face. His head was tilted, one eyebrow arched.

"What you mad about?" he asked.

"Nothing."

"I can see that, all right . . . That movie fella rented a boat and took pictures up and down the bayou. That's when I first seen this black man up the road in a pickup truck, watching the bayou out the window. Later he come on in and axed if a movie's getting made here.

"I say that's what it looks like. He axed me if it's a movie about this white man broke out of Angola, the one killed that black civil rights man in Baton Rouge a long time ago. When I tole him I don't know, he said he's got a story he can give this movie fella, if he gets any money for it, he's gonna give me some, but he's got to find out where the movie man's staying at first.

"I said, 'What you want here?'

"He had on this straw hat, with a colored band around it. He took it off and the side of his head was shaved down to the scalp. He goes, 'I'm so strong I got muscles in my shit, old man. I'd watch what I say.' All the time smiling with gold all over his teet'.

"I go, 'I'm fixing to clean up. You want to buy somet'ing?'

"Dave, this man's arms was big as my thigh. His shoulders touched both sides of that do' when he come in. He goes, 'You sure that movie fella ain't tole you where he stay at?'

"I go, 'It ain't my bidness. Ain't nobody else's here, either.'

"He kept looking at me, grinning, messing with the salt shaker on top of the counter, like he was fixing to do somet'ing.

"So I said, 'Nigger, don't prove your mama raised a fool.'

"He laughed and picked up a ham sandwich and crumpled up a five-dollar bill and t'rew it on the counter and walked out. Just like that. Man didn't no more care if I insulted him than a mosquito was flying round his head."

"Call me if you see him again. Don't mess with him."

"Who he is, Dave?"

"He sounds like a guy named Mookie Zerrang. He's a killer, Batist."

He started to wipe down the counter, then flipped his rag into the bucket.

"They ain't nothing for it, is they?" he said.

"Beg your pardon?"

"They out there, they in here. Don't nobody listen to me," he said, and waved his arm toward the screened windows, the floodlighted bayou, the black wall of shadows on the far bank. "It ain't never gonna be like it use to. What for we brought all this here, Dave?"

He turned his back to me and began dropping the board shutters on the windows and latching them from the inside.

Chapter
19

Early Saturday morning I made coffee and fixed a bowl of Grape-Nuts and blueberries in the bait shop and ate breakfast by myself at the counter and watched the sun rise over the swamp. It had rained, then cleared during the night, and the bayou was yellow with mud and the dock slick with rainwater. A week ago Jerry Joe's vending machine company had delivered a working replica of a 1950s Wurlitzer jukebox while I wasn't in the shop; it sat squat and heavy in the corner, its plastic casing marbled with orange and red and purple light, the rows of 45 rpm records arrayed in a shiny black semicircle inside the viewing glass. I had resolved to have Jerry Joe's people remove it.

I still hadn't made the phone call.

I punched Jimmy Clanton's "Just a Dream," Harry Choates's 1946 recording of "La Jolie Blon," Nathan Abshire's "Pine Grove Blues."

Their voices and music were out of another era, one that we thought would never end. But it did, incrementally, in ways that seemed inconsequential at the time, like the unexpected arrival at the front gate of a sun-browned oil lease man in khaki work clothes who seemed little different from the rest of us.

I unplugged the jukebox from the wall. The plastic went dead and crackled like burning cellophane in the silence of the room.

Then I drove to the University of Southwestern Louisiana library in Lafayette.

*   *   *

BUFORD'S BIBLIOGRAPHY WAS impressive. He had published historical essays on the Knights of the White Camellia and the White League and the violent insurrection they had led against the federal occupation after the War Between the States. The articles were written in the neutral and abstruse language of academic journals, but his sentiments were not well disguised: the night riders who had lynched and burned had their roles forced upon them.

His other articles were in psychological and medical journals. They seemed to be diverse, with no common thread, dealing with various kinds of phobias and depression as well as hate groups that could not tolerate a pluralistic society.

But in the last five years he seemed to have changed his professional focus and begun writing about the science of psychopharmacology and its use in the cure of alcoholics.

I returned the magazines and journals to the reference desk and was about to leave. But it wasn't quite yet noon, and telling myself I had nothing else to do, I asked the librarian for the student yearbooks from the early 1970s, the approximate span when Karyn LaRose attended USL.

She hadn't been born into Buford LaRose's world. Her father had been a hard-working and likable man who supplied gumballs and novelties, such as plastic monster teeth and vampire fingernails, for dimestore vending machines. The family lived in a small frame house on the old St. Martinville road, and the paintless and desiccated garage that fronted the property was rimmed along the base with a rainbow of color from the gumballs that had rotted inside and leaked through the floor. If you asked Karyn what her father did for a living, she always replied that he was in the retail supply business.

Most of us who attended USL came from blue-collar, French-speaking families or could not afford to attend LSU or Tulane. Most of us commuted from outlying parishes, and as a result the campus was empty and quiet and devoid of most social life on the weekends.

But not for Karyn. She made the best of her situation, and her name and photograph appeared again and again in the yearbooks that covered her four years at USL. She made the women's tennis team and belonged to a sorority and the honor society; she was a maid of honor to the homecoming queen one year, and homecoming queen the next. In her photographs her face looked modest and radiant, like that of a person who saw only goodness and promise in the world.

I was almost ready to close the last yearbook and return the stack to the reference desk when I looked again at a group photograph taken in front of Karyn's sorority house, then scanned the names in the cutline.

The coed on the end of the row, standing next to Karyn, was Persephone Giacano. Both of them were smiling, their shoulders and the backs of their wrists touching.

I began to look for Persephone's name in other yearbooks. I didn't find it. It was as though she had appeared for one group photograph in front of the sorority house, then disappeared from campus life.

The administration building was still open. I used the librarian's phone and called the registrar's office.

"We have a Privacy Act, you know?" the woman who answered said.

"I just want to know which years she was here," I said.

"You're a police officer?"

"That's correct."

I heard her tapping on some computer keys.

"Nineteen seventy-two to nineteen seventy-three," she said.

"She dropped out or she transferred to another school?" I asked.

She was quiet a moment. Then she said, "If I were you, I'd look through some of the campus newspapers for that period. Who knows what you might find?"

It took a while. The story was brief, no more than four column inches with a thin caption on page three of a late spring 1973 issue of the *Vermilion*, written in the laconic style of an administrative press handout that does not want to dwell overly long on a university scandal.

A half dozen students had been expelled for stealing tests from the science building. The article stated the tests had been taken from a file cabinet, but the theft had been discovered before the examinations had been given, and the professors whose exams would have been compromised had all been notified.

At the very bottom of the article was the line, *A seventh U.S.L. student, Persephone Giacano, voluntarily withdrew from the university before charges were filed against her.*

I called the registrar's office again, and the same woman answered. "Can I look at an old transcript?" I asked. "You send those out upon request anyway, don't you?"

"Why don't you come over here and introduce yourself? You sound like such an interesting person," she answered.

I walked across the lawn and through the brick archways to the registrar's office and stood at the counter until an elderly, robin-breasted lady with blue hair waited on me. I opened my badge.

"My, you're exactly what you say you are," she said.

"Does everyone get this treatment?"

"We save it for just a special few."

I wrote Karyn's maiden name on a scratch pad and slid it across the counter to the woman. She looked at it a long time. The front office area was empty.

"It's important in ways that are probably better left unsaid," I said.

"Why don't you walk back here?" she answered.

I stood behind her chair while she tapped on the computer's keyboard. Then I saw Karyn's transcript pop up on the blue screen. "She was here four years and graduated in 1974. See," the woman said, and slowly rolled Karyn's academic credits down the screen, shifting in her chair so I could have a clear view.

Karyn had been a liberal arts major and had made almost straight A's in the humanities. But when an accounting class, or a zoology or algebra class, rolled across the screen, the grades dropped to C's, or W's for "Withdrew."

"Could you drop it back to the spring of 1973?" I asked.

The woman in the chair hesitated, then tapped the "page up" button. She waited only a few seconds before shutting down the screen. But it was long enough.

Karyn had made A's in biology and chemistry the same semester that Persephone Giacano had been forced to leave the university.

Karyn was nobody's fall partner.

I PARKED MY TRUCK in the alley behind Sabelle Crown's bar and entered it through the back door. The only light came from the neon beer signs on the wall and the television set that was tuned to the LSU–Georgia Tech game. The air was thick with a smell like unwashed hair and old shoes and sweat and synthetic wine.

Sabelle was mopping out her tiny office in back.

"I need Lonnie Felton's address," I said.

She stuck her mop in the pail and took a business card out of her desk drawer.

"He rented a condo over the river. Good life, huh?" she said. She resumed her work, her back to me, the exposed muscles in her waist rolling with each motion of her arms.

"Aaron was here, wasn't he?" I said.

"What makes you think that?" she answered, her voice flat.

"He was carrying the thirty-two I saw in that shoebox full of medals you keep behind the bar."

She stopped mopping and straightened up. Her head was tilted to one side.

"You didn't know that?" I said.

She went out to the bar and returned with the shoebox, slipped the rubber band off the top, and poured the collection of rings and watches and pocketknives and military decorations onto the desk.

Her gaze was turned inward, as though she were reviewing a filmstrip. I could hear her breathing through her nose in the silence. Her fingernails were curled into the heels of her hands.

"I guess I majored in being anybody's fuck," she said.

"You don't have to be."

She took a roll of breath mints out of her blue jeans and put one in her mouth with her thumb. "Lonnie was here. In the middle of the night," she said. "He interviewed Daddy right out there at the bar. I went out to get food. When I came back, only Lonnie was here."

"Felton knew your father had the gun?"

"You tell me," she said. The skin of her face was shiny and tight against the bone, her eyes swimming with an old knowledge about the nature of susceptibility and betrayal.

I found Lonnie Felton by the swimming pool, in the courtyard of the white brick condominium he had rented above the Vermilion River. The surface of the water was glazed with a slick of suntan lotion and the sunlight that filtered through the moss in the trees overhead. Lonnie Felton lay on a bright yellow double-size plastic lounge chair, with a redheaded girl of eighteen or nineteen beside him. They both wore dark glasses and wet swimsuits, and their bodies looked hard and brown and prickled with cold. Lonnie Felton took a sip from a Collins glass and smiled at me, his eyes hidden behind his glasses, his lips spreading back from his teeth. His girlfriend snuggled closer to his side, her knees and elbows drawn up tightly against him.

"You know what aiding and abetting is?" I asked.

"You bet."

"I can hang it on you."

He smiled again. His lips were flat and thin against his teeth, his sex sculpted against his swimsuit. "The Napoleonic Code supersedes the First Amendment?" he said.

"I think Mookie Zerrang was at my bait shop yesterday. He wanted to know where you lived."

"Who?"

"The black guy who murdered your scriptwriter."

"Oh yeah. Well, keep me informed, will you?"

"It's cold, Lonnie. I want to go inside," the girl next to him said. She teased the elastic band on his trunks with the tips of her fingers.

"I've got to admire your Kool-Aid. I'd be worried if a guy like that was looking for me," I said.

"Let me lay it out for you. Dwayne Parsons, that's the great writer we're talking about here, was an over-the-hill degenerate who factored himself into the deal because he filmed some friends doing some nasty things between the sheets. What I'm saying here is, he had a sick karma and it caught up with him. Look, if this black guy comes here to do me, you know what I'm going to tell him? 'Thanks for not coming sooner. Thanks for letting me have the life I've lived.' I don't argue with my fate, Jack. It's that simple."

"I have a feeling he won't be listening."

A cascade of tiny yellow and scarlet leaves tumbled out of the trees into the swimming pool. The redheaded girl rubbed her face against Lonnie Felton's chest and lay her forearm across his loins.

"You don't like us very much, do you?" he said.

"Us?"

"What you probably call movie people."

"Have a good day, Mr. Felton. Don't let them get behind you."

"What?"

"Go to more movies. Watch a rerun of *Platoon* sometime."

I drove along the river and caught the four-lane into Broussard, then took the old highway toward Cade and Spanish Lake into New Iberia. The highway was littered with crushed stalks of sugarcane that had fallen off the wagons on their way to the mill, and dust devils spun out of the bare and harrowed fields and in the distance I could see egrets rise like a scattering of white rose petals above a windbreak of poplar trees.

I had lied to Lonnie Felton. It was doubtful that I could make an aiding and abetting charge against him stick. But that might turn out to be the best luck he could have ever had, I thought.

I turned on the radio and listened to the LSU–Georgia Tech game the rest of the way home.

* * *

Bootsie was washing dishes when I walked into the kitchen. She wore a pair of straw sandals and white slacks and a purple shirt with green and red flowers printed on it. The tips of her hair were gold in the light through the screen.

"What's going on, boss man?" she said, without turning around.

I put my hand on her back.

"There's an all-you-can-eat crawfish buffet in Lafayette for six-ninety-five," I said.

"I already started something."

"I used all the wrong words the last couple of days," I said.

She rinsed a plate and set it in the rack. She gazed at a solitary mockingbird that stood on the redwood table.

"There're some things a woman has a hard time accepting. It doesn't matter what caused them to happen," she said.

She picked up another plate and rinsed it. I felt her weight lean forward, away from the touch of my hand.

"You want to go to afternoon Mass?" I said.

"I don't think I have time to change," she answered.

That night I took Alafair and a friend of hers to a movie in New Iberia and for ice cream afterward. Later, I found things to do in the bait shop, even though the fishing season was almost over and few customers would be there in the morning. Through the black silhouette of trees up the slope, I could see the lighted gallery of our house, the darkened living room, Bootsie's shadow moving on the drawn shades in our bedroom.

I called my AA sponsor, an ex-roughneck and barroom owner named Tee Neg, who'd had seven years' sobriety when he walked into a bait and liquor store owned by a black man and had asked for a bucketful of shiners, then on an impulse, with no forethought other than his ongoing resentment over the fingers he'd pinched off on a drill pipe, had changed his order to a quart of whiskey and stayed drunk for the next five years. His next AA meeting was at Angola Prison.

I told him about what had happened between me and Bootsie. I knew what was coming.

"You took a drink over it?" he said.

"No."

"Hey, you ever get drunk while you was asleep?"

"No."

"Then go to bed. I'll talk to you in the morning, you." He hung up.

After all the lights in the house went out, I walked up the slope and went inside and lay down on the living room couch in the dark.

Wally, the dispatcher, called at one in the morning.

"The St. Martin Parish sheriff's office is interviewing some hysterical kids at Henderson Swamp. I can't make sense out of it. You want to go up there?" he said.

"Not really."

"It sounds like Aaron Crown. That's where you think he's hid out at, right?"

"What sounds like Aaron Crown?"

"The one tore up these two people. They say the walls of the houseboat is painted with blood. The guy held the girl while he done the man, then he done it to the girl."

"You're not making sense, Wally."

"That's what I said. The deputy called it in didn't make no sense. So how about hauling your ass up there?"

Chapter
20

SOMETIMES THE LEAST reliable source in reconstructing a violent crime is the eyewitness to it. The blood veins dilate in the brain, the emotions short-circuit, memory shuts down and dulls the images that wish to disfigure the face of the human family.

Seven emergency vehicles were parked along the Henderson levee when I got there. The moon was up and the water and the moss in the cypress were stained the color of pewter. A wood gangplank led from the levee through a stand of flooded willows to a large, motorized houseboat whose decks burned with the floodlights from a sheriff's boat moored next to it.

The witnesses were an elderly man and his partially blind wife, who had been spending the weekend on their own houseboat, and a group of stoned high school kids who stunk of reefer and keg beer and were trembling at the prospect of what they had stepped into.

Earlier, they had all seen the victims having drinks at a restaurant farther up the levee. Everyone agreed they were a handsome couple, tourists perhaps, pleasant and certainly polite, although the woman seemed a little young for the man; but he was charming, just the same, athletic-looking, friendly toward the kids, a decent sort, obviously in control of things (one of the stoned-out high school students said he "was kind of like a modern business-type guy, like you see on TV");

the man had wanted to rent fishing gear and hire a guide to take him out in the morning.

The intruder came just before midnight, in a flat-bottomed aluminum outboard, the throttle turned low, the engine muttering softly along the main channel that rimmed the swamp, past the islands of dead hyacinths and the gray cypress that rose wedge-shaped out of the water at the entrance to the bays.

But he knew his destination. In midchannel he angled his outboard toward the houseboat rented by the couple, then cut the gas and let his boat glide on its own wake through a screen of hanging willows and bump softly against the rubber tires that hung from the houseboat's gunnels.

The people inside were still up, eating a late supper on a small table in the galley, a bottle of white wine and a fondue pan set between them. They either didn't hear the intruder, or never had time to react, before he pulled himself by one hand over the rail, lighting on the balls of his feet, his body alive with a sinewy grace that belied his dimensions.

Then he tore the locked hatch out of the jamb with such violence that one hinge came with it.

At first the kids, who were gathered around the tailgate of a pickup truck on the levee, thought the intruder was a black man, then they realized when he burst into the lighted cabin that he wore dark gloves and a knitted ski mask.

But they had no doubt about what took place next.

When the man they had seen in the restaurant tried to rise from his chair in the galley, the intruder swung a wide-bladed fold-out game dressing knife into the side of his throat and raked it at a downward angle into his rib cage, then struck him about the neck and head again and again, gathering the young woman into one arm, never missing a stroke, whipping the wounded man down lower and lower from the chair to the floor, flinging ropes of blood across the windows.

He paused, as though he was aware he had an audience, stared out of the holes in his mask toward the levee, then opened his mouth, which rang with gold, licked the neck of the screaming young woman he held pinioned against his body with one muscle-swollen arm, and drew the knife across her throat.

I stood just inside the torn hatch with a St. Martin Parish homicide detective and the medical examiner. The two bodies lay curled on the floor, their foreheads almost touching.

"You ever see a blood loss like that?" the plainclothes said. He was dressed in a brown suit and a fedora, with a plain blue necktie, and he had clipped the tie inside his shirt. He bit into a candy bar. "I got a sugar deficiency," he said.

Two paramedics began lifting the dead man into a body bag. His ponytail had been splayed by someone's shoe and was stuck to the linoleum.

"You okay, Dave?" the plainclothes said.

"Sure."

"The perp cleaned out their ID."

"His name was Lonnie Felton. I don't know who the girl was. He was a film director."

"You know him?"

I nodded and looked at the stare in Felton's eyes.

"I make Aaron Crown for this," the plainclothes said. "What do you think? How many we got around here could do something like this? . . . You listening, Dave?"

"What?" I said. The paramedic worked the zipper on the vinyl bag over Felton's face. "Oh, sorry . . ." I said to the plainclothes. "The kids were right the first time. It's a black guy. Mookie Zerrang's his name. It's funny what you said, that's all."

"Come again?"

"About listening. I told Felton the guy who'd do him wouldn't be a good listener. It seemed like a clever thing to say at the time."

The plainclothes looked at me strangely, a smear of chocolate on his mouth.

Chapter
21

AFTER I WAS DISCHARGED from the army, a friend from my outfit and I drove across the country for a fishing vacation in Montana. On July 4 we stopped at a small town in western Kansas that Norman Rockwell could have painted. The streets were brick, lined with Chinese elm trees, and the limestone courthouse on the square rose out of the hardware and feed and farm equipment stores like a medieval castle against a hard blue porcelain sky. Next to our motel was a stucco 3.2 beer tavern that looked like a wedding cake, shaded by an enormous willow that crowned over the eaves. At the end of the street you could see an ocean of green wheat that rippled in the wind as far as the eye could see. The rain that fell that afternoon on the hot sidewalks was the sweetest smell I ever experienced.

What's the point?

For years I thought of this place as an island untouched by the war in Indochina and disconnected from the cities burning at home. When I was a patrolman in uniform in the New Orleans welfare projects, I used to remember the hot, clean, airy smell of the rain falling on those sidewalks in 1965.

Then an ex–Kansas cop we picked up drunk on an interstate fugitive warrant told me the town that existed in my fond recollection was the site of Truman Capote's novel *In Cold Blood*, the story of two pathological killers who murdered a whole family for thirty-nine dollars and a radio.

You learn soon or you learn late: There are no islands.

IT WAS MONDAY morning and no one was in custody for the double homicide in St. Martin Parish.

"I'm afraid they're not buying your theory about a black hit man," the sheriff said.

"Why not?"

"There's no evidence the man was black."

"He had a mouthful of gold teeth, just like the guy who did the scriptwriter."

"So what? Maybe Aaron Crown has gold fillings, too."

"I doubt if Aaron ever bought a toothbrush, much less saw a dentist."

"You believe somebody was trying to stop Felton from exposing our governor-elect as a moral troglodyte. Maybe you're right. But for a lot of people it's a big reach."

"Crown didn't do this, Sheriff."

"Look, the St. Martin ME says both victims had been smoking heroin before they got it. Felton's condo had a half kee of China white in it. St. Martin thinks maybe the killings are drug related. Robbery's a possible motive, too."

"Robbery?"

"The killer took the girl's purse and Felton's wallet. Felton was flashing a lot of money around earlier in the evening . . ." He stopped and returned my stare. "I haven't convinced you?"

"Where are you trying to go with this, skipper?"

"Nowhere. I don't have to. It's out of our jurisdiction. End of discussion, Dave."

I OPENED THE MORNING mail in my office, escorted a deranged woman from the men's room, picked up a parole violator in the state betting parlor out by the highway, helped recover a stolen farm tractor, spent my lunch hour and two additional hours waiting to testify at the courthouse, only to learn the defendant had been granted a continuance, and got back to the office with a headache and the feeling I had devoted most of the day to snipping hangnails in a season of plague.

The state police now had primary responsibility for protecting Buford, and Aaron Crown and my problems with the LaRose family were becoming less and less a subject of interest to anybody else.

But one person, besides Clete, had tried to help me, I thought. The tattooed carnival worker named Araña.

I inserted the cassette Helen and I had made of his deathbed statement in a tape player and listened to it again in its entirety. But only one brief part of it pointed a finger: "The *bugarron* ride a saddle with flowers cut in it. I seen him at the ranch. You messing everything up for them. They gonna kill you, man . . ."

"Who's this guy?" my voice asked.

And the man called Araña responded, "He ain't got no name. He got a red horse and a silver saddle. He like Indian boys."

I clicked off the tape player and laid the cassette on my desk blotter and looked at it. Puzzle through that, I thought.

Then, just as chance and accident are wont to have their way, I glanced out the window and saw a man blowing his horn at other drivers, forcing his way across two lanes to park in an area designated for the handicapped. His face was as stiff as plaster when he walked across the grass to the front entrance, oblivious to the sprinkler that cut a dark swath across his slacks.

A moment later Wally called me on my extension.

"Dave, we got a real zomboid out here in the waiting room says he wants to see you," he said.

"Yeah, I know. Send him back."

"Who is he?"

"Dock Green."

"That pimp from New Orleans suppose to got clap of the brain?"

"The one and only."

"Dave, we don't got enough local sick ones? You got to import these guys in here?"

Dock Green wore a beige turtleneck polo shirt tucked tightly into his belt so that the movements of his neck and head seemed even more stark and elliptical, like moving images in a filmstrip that's been abbreviated. He sat down in front of my desk without being asked, his eyes focusing past me out the window, then back on my face again. The skin between his lip and the corner of his nose twitched.

"I got to use your phone," he said, and picked up the receiver and started punching numbers.

"That's a private . . . Don't worry about it, go ahead," I said.

"I'll pick you up at six sharp . . . No, out front, Persephone . . ." he said into the receiver. "No, I ain't wanted there, I don't like it there, I ain't coming in there . . . Good-bye."

He hung up and blew his breath up into his face. "I got a charge to file," he said.

"What might that be, Dock?"

"I can see you're on top of things. There's another side to Jerry the Glide."

"Yeah?"

"He went out to my construction site with some of his asswipes and busted up my foreman. He held him down on the ground by his ears and spit in his face."

"Spit in his face?"

"There's an echo in here?"

I wrote a note on my scratch pad, reminding myself to pick up a half gallon of milk on the way home.

"We'll get right on this, Dock."

"That's it?"

"Yep."

"You didn't ask me where."

"Why don't you let me have that?"

He gave me directions. I fingered the tape cassette containing the deathbed statement of the Mexican carnival worker.

"Let's take a ride and see what Jerry Joe has to say for himself," I said.

"Right now?"

"You bet."

The concentration in his eyes made me think of sweat bees pressed against glass.

We drove in a cruiser through the corridor of live oaks on East Main to the site on Bayou Teche where Jerry Joe was building his new home. The equipment was shut down, the construction crew gone.

"I guess we struck out," I said, and turned across the drawbridge and headed out of town toward the LaRose plantation.

"This ain't the way."

"It's a nice day for a drive."

I saw the recognition come together in Dock's face.

"You're trying to piss on my shoes. You know my wife's out at Karyn LaRose's," he said.

"I've got to check something out, Dock. It doesn't have anything to do with you."

"Fuck that and fuck you. I don't like them people. I ain't going on their property."

I pulled off on the shoulder of the road by the LaRoses' drive. Dust was billowing out of the fields in back, and the house looked pillared and white and massive against the gray sky.

"Why not?" I asked.

"I got to do business with hypocrites, it don't mean we got to use the same toilet. Hey, you don't think they got shit stripes in their underwear? They got dead people in the ground here."

"You're talking about the cemetery in back?"

"I ain't got to see a headstone to smell a grave. There's one by that tree over there. There's another one down by the water. A kid's in it."

"You know about a murder?"

But he didn't get to answer. A shudder went through him and he sank back into the seat and began to speak unintelligibly, his lips wrinkling back on his teeth as though all of his motors were misfiring, obscenity and spittle rolling off his tongue.

I put the transmission in gear and turned into the drive.

"You going to make it, Dock?" I said.

His breath was as dense as sewer gas. He pressed his palm wetly against his mouth.

"Hang loose, babe," I said, and walked through the drive and the porte cochere into the backyard, where a state trooper in sunglasses was eating a bowl of ice cream in a canvas lawn chair.

I opened my badge.

"I'd like to check the stables," I said.

"What for?"

I averted my gaze, stuck my badge holder in my back pocket.

"It's just a funny feeling I have about Crown," I answered.

"Help yourself."

I climbed through the rails of the horse lot and entered the open end of the old brick smithy that had been converted into a stable. The iron shutters on the arched windows were closed, and motes of dust floated in the pale bands of light as thickly as lint in a textile mill. The air was warm and sour-sweet with the smells of leather, blankets stiff with horse sweat, chickens that wandered in from outside, the dampness under the plank floors, fresh hay scattered in the stalls, a wheelbarrow stacked with manure, a barrel of dried molasses-and-grain balls.

I went inside the tack room at the far end of the building. Buford's saddles were hung on collapsible two-by-fours that extended outward on screwhooks from the wall. The English saddles were plain, utilitarian, the leather unmarked by the maker's knife. But on the western saddles, with pommels as wide as bulls' snouts, the cantles and flaps and skirts were carved with roses and birds and snakes, and in the back of each cantle was a mother-of-pearl inlay of an opened camellia.

But the man named Araña had said the *bugarron* rode a silver saddle, and there was none here.

"What you looking for in the tack room, Detective Robicheaux?" the trooper said behind me. He leaned against the doorjamb, his arms folded, his expression masked behind his shades. He wore a campaign hat tilted over his eyes, like a DI's, with the leather strap on the back of his head.

"You never can tell what you might trip across."

"Somehow that don't ring right."

"I know you?"

"You do now. Ms. LaRose says she'd prefer you wasn't on her place."

"She'll prefer it less if Aaron's her next visitor . . . Have a nice day."

I walked down the wood floor between the stalls toward the open end of the building.

"Don't be back in the stable without a warrant, sir," the trooper said behind me.

I climbed through the rails in the horse lot and walked under the trees in the backyard toward the porte cochere. Karyn LaRose came out the side screen door, a drink in her hand, with Persephone Green behind her. Karyn turned around and lifted her fingers in the air.

"Let me talk to Dave a minute, Seph," she said.

There was a pinched, black light in Persephone Green's face as she glared at me. But she did as she was asked and closed the door and disappeared behind the glass.

"I'm going to drain the blood out of your veins for what you did to me," Karyn said.

"What I did to you?"

"In front of your wife, in the hotel. You rotten motherfucker."

"Your problem is with yourself, Karyn. You just don't know it."

"Save the cheap psychology for your AA meetings. Your life's going to be miserable. I promise."

"Dock Green says there're dead people under the tree in your side yard."

"That's marvelous detective work. They were lynched and buried there over a century ago."

"How about the kid in the unmarked grave by the water?"

Her skin under her makeup turned as pale and dry as paper.

Chapter 22

T<small>HE NEXT MORNING</small> I walked up to Jerry Joe Plumb on his plot of tree-dotted land in the middle of the historical district on East Main. He was watching two cement mixers pour the foundation for his home on the bayou, one half-topped engineering boot propped on a felled tree. He wore khakis and his leather flyer's jacket, and the sunlight through the oaks looked like yellow blades of grass on his face.

"Dock Green says you knocked around his construction foreman," I said.

"It got a little out of hand."

"You held him down and spit in his face?"

"I apologized."

"I bet he appreciated that."

"I went on a tab for three hundred large to back Buford's campaign. You know what the vig is on three hundred large? Now Dock's wheeling and dealing with Buford while I got building suppliers looking at me with knives and forks."

"Then quit protecting Buford."

"You got it wrong . . . But . . . Never mind, come in my trailer and I'll show you something."

Inside, he spread a roll of architect's plans across a drafting table and weighted down the ends, then combed his hair while he looked admiringly at the sketch of the finished house. "See, it's turn-of-the-century. It'll fit right in. The brick's purple and comes out of a hundred-year-old house I found over in Mississippi," he said.

The building was three stories high, a medieval fortress rather than a house, with balconies and widow's walks and windbreaks that were redundant inside a city, and I thought of Jerry Joe's description of the LaRose home out west of the Pecos, where he had fled at age seventeen.

"You're going to let Buford burn you because of the old man, what was his name, Jude?" I said.

"If it wasn't for Jude, I'd a been majoring in cotton picking on a prison farm."

"I took Dock out to the LaRose plantation yesterday. He says there's a kid's grave down by the water."

"Better listen to him, then."

"Oh?"

"The guy hears voices. It's like he knows stuff people aren't supposed to know. He puts dead things in jars. Maybe he's a ghoul."

I started to leave. "Stay away from his construction site, okay?" I said.

"I'm not the problem, Dave. Neither is Dock. You got a disease in this town. The whole state does, and it's right up the bayou."

"Then stop letting Buford use you for his regular punch," I said.

Jerry Joe clipped his comb inside his shirt pocket and stepped close to my face, his open hands curved simianlike by his sides, the white scar at the corner of his eye bunching into a knot.

"We're friends, but don't you ever in your life say anything like that to me again," he said.

AFTER I GOT BACK to the department, the sheriff buzzed my extension and asked me to come into his office. He sat humped behind his desk, scraping the bowl of his pipe with a penknife.

"Our health carrier called this morning. They've developed a problem with your coverage," he said.

"What problem?"

"Your drinking history."

"Why call about it now?"

"That's the question. You were in therapy a few years back?"

"That's right."

"After your wife was killed?"

I nodded, my eyes shifting off his.

"The psychologist's file on you went through their fax this morning," he said. "It came through ours, too. It also went to the *Daily Iberian*." Before I could speak, he said, "I tore it up. But the guy from Blue Cross was a little strung out."

"Too bad."

"Dave, you're sober now, but you had two slips before you made it. I guess there was a lot of Vietnam stuff in that file, too. Civilians don't handle that stuff well." He set the pipe down and looked at the tops of his hands. "Who sent the fax?"

"The therapist died two years ago."

"So?"

"I'm not omniscient."

"We both know what I'm talking about."

"He had an office in the Oil Center. In the same suite as Buford LaRose's."

"It wasn't Buford, though, was it?"

"I don't know if Buford's potential has ever been plumbed."

"Dave, tell me you haven't been out to see Karyn."

"Yesterday . . . I took Dock Green out there."

His swivel chair creaked when he leaned back in it. His teeth made a clicking sound on the stem of his dead pipe.

AT DAWN THE next morning I cut the gas on my outboard engine north of the LaRose plantation and let the aluminum boat float sideways in the current, past the barbed wire fence line that extended into the water and marked the edge of Buford's property. The sun was an orange smudge through the hardwood trees, and I could hear horses nickering beyond the mist that rose out of the coulee. I used a paddle to bring the boat out of the current and into the backwater, the cattails sliding off the bow and the sides, then I felt the metal bottom bite into silt.

I could see the black marble crypt and the piked iron fence that surrounded it at the top of the slope, the silhouette of a state trooper who was looking in the opposite direction, a roan gelding tossing its head and backing out of spiderwebs that were spread between two persimmon trunks.

Part of the coulee had caved in, and the runoff had washed over the side and eroded a clutch of wide rivulets in the shape of a splayed hand, down the embankment to the bayou's edge. I pushed the paddle hard into the silt and watched the trees, the palmettos, a dock and boat-house, and the pine-needle-covered, hoof-scarred floor of the woods drift past me.

Then I saw it, in the same way your eye recognizes mortality in a rain forest when birds lift suddenly off the canopy or the wind shifts and you smell an odor that has always lived like a dark thought on the edge of your consciousness.

But in truth it wasn't much—a series of dimples on the slope, grass that was greener than it should have been, a spray of mushrooms with poisonous skirts. Maybe my contention with the LaRoses had breached the confines of obsession. I slipped one of the oar locks, tied a handkerchief through it, and tossed it up on the bank.

Then I drifted sideways with the current into the silence of the next bend, yanked the starter rope, and felt the engine's roar reverberate through my palm like an earache.

At sunset I put on my gym shorts and running shoes and did a mile and a half to the drawbridge, waved at the bridge tender, and turned back toward home, the air like a cool flame on my skin. Ahead of me I saw a Buick pull to the side of the road and park, the front window roll down, then the door open halfway. Jerry Joe remained seated, his arms propped in the window as though he were leaning on a bar, a can of Budweiser in one hand, a pint of whiskey in the other. He looked showered and fresh, and he wore a white suit with an open-collar lavender shirt. A flat cardboard box lay on the leather seat next to him.

"You gonna bust me for an open container?" he said.

"It's a possibility."

"I'm sorry about getting in your face yesterday."

"Forget it."

"You remember my mother?"

"Sure."

"She used to make me go to confession all the time. I hated it. She was a real coonass, you know, and she'd say, 'You feel guilty about you done something to somebody, Jerry Joe, you gonna try to pretend you don't know that person no more 'cause he gonna make you remember who you are and the bad thing you done, or maybe you're gonna try to hurt him, you. So that's why you gotta go to confess, you.' "

He tilted the bottle and threaded a thin stream of bourbon into the opening of his beer can. Then he drank from the can, the color in his eyes deepening.

"Yes?" I said.

"People like Karyn and Buford reinvent themselves. It's like my mother said. They don't want mirrors around to remind them of what they used to be."

"What can I do for you, partner?"

"I ain't lily white. I've been mixed up with the LaRose family a long time. But the deal going down now . . . I don't know . . . It ain't just the money . . . It bothers me."

"Tell somebody about it, Jerry Joe. Like your mom said." I tried to smile.

He reached around behind him and picked up the cardboard box from the seat. "I brought you something belongs to you. It was still buried behind the old house."

I rested the box on the window and lifted the top. The hand crank to our old phonograph lay in the middle of a crinkled sheet of white wrapping paper. The metal was deformed and bulbous with rust, and the wood handle had been eaten by groundwater.

"So I returned your property and I got no reason to be mad at you," he said. He was smiling now. He closed his car door and started his engine.

"Stay on that old-time R&B," I said.

"I never been off it."

I walked the rest of the way home. The sun was gone now and the air was damp and cold, and the last fireflies of the season traced their smoky red patterns in the shadows.

Chapter
23

WHEN YOUR STITCHES are popping loose and your elevator has already plummeted past any reasonable bottom and the best your day offers is seeds and stems at sunrise to flatten the kinks on a street dealer's speedball that can turn your heart into a firecracker, you might end up in a piece of geography as follows:

A few blocks off Canal, the building was once a bordello that housed both mulatto and white women; then in a more moral era, when the downtown brothels were closed by the authorities and the girls started working out of taxicabs instead, the building was partitioned into apartments and studios for artists, and finally it became simply a "hotel," with no name other than that, the neon letters emblazoned vertically on a tin sign above a picture glass window that looked in upon a row of attached theater seats. Old people seemingly numbed by the calamity that had placed them in these surroundings stared vacantly through the glass at the sidewalk.

The Mexican man had climbed the fire escape onto the peaked roof, then had glided out among the stars. He hit the courtyard with such an impact that he split a flagstone like it was slate.

The corridor was dark and smelled of the stained paper bags filled with garbage that stood by each door like sentinels. Clete opened the dead man's room with a passkey.

"A Vietnamese boat lady owns the place. She found the guy's pay stub and thought I could get his back rent from the state," he said.

Most of the plaster was gone from the walls. A mattress was rolled on an iron bed frame, and a pile of trash paper, green wine bottles, and frozen TV dinner containers was swept neatly into one corner. A flattened plastic wallet and a cardboard suitcase and a guitar with twelve tuning pegs and no strings lay on top of a plank table. The sound hole on the guitar was inlaid with green and pink mollusk shell, and the wood below the hole had been cut with scratches that looked like cat's whiskers.

"What was he on?" I said.

"A couple of the wet-brains say he was cooking brown skag with ups. The speed is supposed to give it legs. The mamasan found the wallet under the bed."

It contained no money, only a detached stub from a pay voucher for ninety-six dollars, with Buford LaRose's name and New Iberia address printed in the upper left-hand corner, and a Catholic holy card depicting a small statue of Christ's mother, with rays of gold and blue light emanating from it. Underneath the statue was the caption *La Virgin de Zapopan*.

I unsnapped the suitcase. His shirts and trousers and underwear were all rolled into tight balls. A pair of boots were folded at the tops in one corner. The toes were pointed and threadbare around the welt, the heels almost flat, the leather worn as smooth and soft as felt in a slipper. Under the boots, wrapped in a towel, was a solitary roweled spur, the cusp scrolled with winged serpents.

"It looks like the guy had another kind of life at one time," Clete said.

"Does NOPD know he worked for Buford LaRose?"

"The mamasan called them and got the big yawn. They've got New Orleans cops pulling armed robberies. Who's got time for a roof flyer down here in Shitsville?"

"Dock Green says a kid's buried on the LaRose property."

"You try for a warrant?"

"The judge said insufficient grounds. He seemed to think I had personal motivations as well."

"You're going about it the wrong way, Streak. Squeeze somebody close to LaRose."

"Who?"

"That old guy, the poet, the fuckhead left over from the sixties, he was working his scam out at Tulane last night. He's doing a repeat performance up on St. Charles this afternoon."

He drummed the square tips of his fingers on the face of the guitar.

"No grand displays, Clete," I said.

"Me?"

CLAY MASON'S POETRY reading was in a reception hall above a restaurant in the Garden District. From the second-story French doors you could look down upon a sidewalk cafe, the oaks along the avenue, the iron streetcars out on the neutral ground, a K&B drugstore on the corner whose green and purple neon hung like colored smoke in the rain.

Clete and I sat on folding chairs in the back of the hall. We were lucky to get seats at all. College kids dressed in Seattle grunge lined the walls.

"Can you believe anybody going for this guy's shuck today?" Clete said.

"It's in."

"Why?"

"They missed all the fun."

In reality, I probably knew a better answer. But it sounded like a weary one, even to myself, and I left it unsaid. Presidents who had never heard a shot fired in anger vicariously revised the inadequacy of their own lives by precipitating suffering in the lives of others, and they were lauded for it. Clay Mason well understood the nature of public memory and had simply waited for his time and a new generation of intellectual cannon fodder to come round again.

His pretentiousness, his feigned old man's humility and irreverence toward the totems, were almost embarrassing. He had been an academic for years, but he denigrated universities and academics. He spoke of his own career in self-effacing terms but gave the impression he had known the most famous writers of his time. In his eccentric western clothes, a Stetson hat cocked on his white head, a burning cigarette cupped in his small hand, he became the egalitarian spokesman for the Wobblies, the railroad hobos of Woody Guthrie and Hart Crane, the miners killed at Ludlow, Colorado, the girls whose bodies were incinerated like bolts of cloth in the Triangle Shirtwaist Factory fire.

His poems were full of southwestern mesas and peyote cactus, ponies that drank out of blood-red rivers, fields blown with bluebonnets and poppies, hot winds that smelled of burning hemp.

His words seemed to challenge all convention and caution, even his own death, which one poem described in terms of a chemical rainbow rising from the ashes of his soul.

The audience loved it.

Clete craned forward in his seat.

"Check it out by the door, big mon," he said.

Karyn LaRose was dressed in a pale blue suit and white hose, with a white scarf about her neck, her legs crossed, listening attentively to Clay Mason. The horn-rimmed glasses she wore only added to her look of composure and feminine confidence. Two state troopers stood within five feet of her, their hands folded behind them, as though they were at parade rest.

"Why do I feel like a starving man looking at a plate of baked Alaska?" Clete said. "You think I could interest her in some private security?"

A middle-aged woman in front of us turned and said, "Would you kindly be quiet?"

"Sorry," Clete said, his face suddenly blank.

After Clay Mason finished reading his last poem, the audience rose to its feet and applauded and then applauded some more. Clete and I worked our way to the front of the hall, where a cash drink bar was open and a buffet was being set up.

"Watch out for the Smokies. It looks like they're working on their new chevrons," Clete said.

Clay Mason stood with a group by Karyn's chair, his weight resting on his cane. When he saw me, the parchment lines in his pixie face seemed to deepen, then he smiled quickly and extended his hand out of the crowd. It felt like a twig in mine.

"I'm flattered by your presence, sir," he said.

"It's more business than pleasure. A Mexican kid who worked for Buford took a dive off a flophouse roof," I said.

"Yeah, definitely bad shit. They had to put the guy's brains back in his head with a trowel," Clete said.

I gave Clete a hard stare, but it didn't register.

"I'm sorry to hear about this," Clay Mason said.

On the edge of my vision I could see Karyn LaRose seated not more than two feet from us.

"What's happening, Karyn?" I said, without looking at her.

"You gentlemen wouldn't contrive to turn a skunk loose at a church social, would you?" Clay Mason said, a smile wrinkling at the corner of his mouth.

I took the pay stub from my shirt pocket and looked at it. "The guy's name was Fernando Spinoza. You know him?" I asked.

"No, can't say that I do," Clay Mason said.

"How about you, Karyn?" I asked.

The redness in her cheeks looked like arrow-points. But her eyes were clear with purpose and she didn't hesitate in her response.

"This man is a detective with the Iberia Parish Sheriff's Department," she said to the two troopers. "He's annoyed me and my husband in every way he can. It's my belief he has no other reason for being here."

"Is that right, sir?" one of the troopers said, his eyes slightly askance, rising slightly on the balls of his feet, his hands still folded behind him.

"I'm here because of a kid who had to be blotted off a flagstone," I said.

"You have some kind of jurisdiction in New Orleans? How about y'all get something to eat over at the buffet table?" the trooper said.

His face was lumpy, not unpleasant or hostile or dumb, just lumpy and obsequious.

"Here's today's flash, buddy," Clete said. "This old guy you're a doorman for, he popped his own wife. Shot an apple off her head at a party with a forty-four Magnum down in Taco Ticoville. Except he was stinking drunk and left her hair all over the wallpaper. Maybe we should be telling that to these dumb kids who listen to his bullshit."

The conversation around us died as though someone had pulled the plug on a record player. I looked over at Clete and was never prouder of him.

BUT OUR MOMENT with Clay Mason wasn't over. Outside, we saw him walk from under the blue canvas awning at the front entrance of the restaurant toward a waiting limo, Karyn LaRose at his side, leaning on his cane, negotiating the peaked sidewalk where the roots of oak trees had wedged up the concrete. A small misshaped black and brown mongrel dog, with raised hair like pig bristles, came out of nowhere and began barking at Mason, its teeth bared and its nails clicking on the pavement, advancing and retreating as fear and hostility moved it. Mason continued toward the limo, his gaze fixed ahead of him. Then, without missing a step, he suddenly raised his cane in the air and whipped it across the dog's back with such force that the animal ran yipping in pain through the traffic as though its spine had been broken.

THE NEXT EVENING, at sunset, I drove my truck up the state road that paralleled Bayou Teche and parked in a grove across the water from Buford's plantation. Through my Japanese field glasses I could see the current flowing under his dock and boathouse, the arched iron shutters on the smithy, the horses in his fields, the poplars that flattened in the wind against the side of his house. Then I moved the field glasses along the bank, where I had thrown the oar lock tied with my handkerchief. The oar lock was gone, and someone had beveled out a plateau on the slope and had poured a concrete pad and begun construction of a gazebo there.

I propped my elbows on the hood of my truck and moved the glasses through the trees, and in the sun's afterglow, which was like firelight on the trunks, I saw first one state trooper, then a second, then a third, all of them with scoped and leather-slung bolt-action rifles. Each trooper sat on a chair in the shadows, much like hunters positioning themselves in a deer stand.

I heard a boot crack a twig behind me.

"Hep you with something?" a trooper asked.

He was big and gray, close to retirement age, his stomach protruding like a sack of gravel over his belt.

I opened my badge holder.

"On the job," I said.

"Still ain't too good to be here. Know what I mean?" he said.

"I don't."

"This morning they found work boot prints on the mudbank. Like boots a convict might wear."

"I see."

"If he comes in, they don't want him spooked out," the trooper said. We looked at each other in the silence. There was a smile in his eyes.

"It looks like they know their work," I said.

"Put it like you want. Crown comes here, he's gonna have to kill his next nigger down in hell."

THE BACKYARD WAS dim with mist when I fixed breakfast in the kitchen the next morning. I heard Bootsie walk into the kitchen behind me. The window over the sink was open halfway and the radio was playing on the windowsill.

"Are you listening to the radio?" she said.

"Yeah, I just clicked it on."

"Alafair's still asleep."

"I wasn't thinking. I'll turn it off."

"No, just turn it down."

"All right," I said. I walked to the sink and turned down the volume knob. I looked out the window at the yard until I was sure my face was empty of expression, then I sat down again and we ate in silence.

We were both happy when the phone rang on the wall.

"You have the news on?" the sheriff asked.

"No."

"I wouldn't call so early but I thought it'd be better if you heard it from me . . ."

"What is it, skipper?"

"Short Boy Jerry. NOPD found his car by the Desire welfare project a half hour ago . . . He was beaten to death . . ."

I felt a tick jump in my throat. I pressed my thumb hard under my ear to clear a fluttering sound, like a wounded butterfly, out of my hearing. I saw Bootsie looking at me, saw her put down her coffee cup gently and her face grow small.

"You there, podna?" the sheriff said.

"Who did it?"

"NOPD thinks a gang of black pukes. I'll tell you up front, Dave, he went out hard."

"I need the plane," I said.

Chapter
24

THE SUN WAS pale, almost white, like a sliver of ice hidden behind clouds above Lake Pontchartrain, when Clete Purcel met me at the New Orleans airport and drove us back down I-10 toward the city.

"You really want to go to the meat locker, Streak?" he asked.

"You know another place to start?"

"It was just a question."

Morgues deny all the colors the mind wishes to associate with death. The surfaces are cool to the touch, made of aluminum and stainless steel, made even more sterile in appearance by the dull reflection of the fluorescent lighting overhead. The trough and the drains where an autopsy was just conducted are spotless; the water that wells across and cleanses the trough's bottom could have issued from a spring.

But somehow, in the mind, you hear sounds behind all those gleaming lockers, like fluids dripping, a tendon constricting, a lip that tightens into a sneer across the teeth.

The assistant wore a full-length white lab coat that looked like a nineteenth-century duster. He paused with his hand on the locker door. He had a cold and kept brushing at his nose with the back of his wrist.

"The guy's hands are bagged. Otherwise, he's like they found him," he said.

"This place is an igloo in here. Let's see it, all right?" Clete said.

The assistant looked at Clete oddly and then pulled out the drawer. Clete glanced down at Jerry Joe, let out his breath, then lifted his eyes to mine.

"When it's this bad, it usually means a tire iron or maybe a curb button. The uniforms found him on the pavement, so it's hard to tell right now," the assistant said. "You knew the guy?"

"Yeah, he knew the guy," Clete answered.

"I was just wondering what he was doing in that neighborhood at night, that's all," the assistant said. "If a white guy's down there at night, it's usually for cooze or rock. We on the same side here?"

Most of Jerry Joe's teeth had been broken off. One of his eyes looked like a tea-stained egg. The other was no longer an eye. I lifted his left hand. It felt like a heavy piece of old fruit inside the plastic bag.

"Both of them are broken. I don't know anything about this guy, but my bet is, he went the whole fifteen before they clicked off his switch," the attendant said.

"Thank you, sir, for your time," I said, and turned and walked outside.

I TALKED WITH THE scene investigator at the District from a filling station pay phone. He had a heavy New Orleans blue-collar accent, which is far closer to the speech of Brooklyn than to the Deep South; he told me he had to go to a meeting and couldn't talk to me right now.

"When can you talk?" I asked.

"When I get out of the meeting."

"When is that?"

"Leave your number."

We pulled back into the traffic. Clete's window was down and the wind whipped the hair on his head. He kept looking across the seat at me.

"Streak, you're making me tense," he said.

"You buy kids did this?" I asked.

"I think that's how it's going to go down."

"You didn't answer my question."

He took a swizzle stick off his dashboard and put it in his mouth. A neutral ground with palm trees on it streamed past his window. "I can't see Jerry Ace getting taken down by pukes. Not like this, anyway. Maybe if he got capped—"

"Why would he be down by the Desire?"

"He dug R&B. He was a paratrooper. He thought he had magic painted on him . . . Dave, don't try to make sense out of it. This city's in flames. You just can't see them."

Jerry Joe's blue Buick had already been towed to the pound. A uniformed cop opened the iron gate for us and walked with us past a row of impounded cars to the back of the lot. The Buick was parked against a brick wall, its trunk sprung, its dashboard ripped out, the glove box rifled, the leather door panels pried loose, the stereo speakers gouged with screwdrivers out of the headliner. A strip of torn yellow crime scene tape was tangled around one wheel, flapping in the wind.

"Another half hour and they would have had the engine off the mounts," Clete said.

"How do you read it?" I said.

"A gang of street rats got to it after he was dead."

"It looks like they had him made for a mule."

"The side panels? Yeah. Which means they didn't know who he was."

"But they wouldn't have hung around to strip the car if they'd killed him, would they?" I said.

"No, their consciences were clean. You hook them up, that's what they'll tell you. Just a harmless night out, looting a dead man's car. I think I'm going to move to East Los Angeles," he said.

We went to the District and caught the scene investigator at his desk. He was a blond, tall, blade-faced man named Cramer who wore a sky blue sports coat and white shirt and dark tie with a tiny gold pistol and chain fastened to it. The erectness of his posture in the chair distracted the eye from his paunch and concave chest and the patina of nicotine on his fingers.

"Do we have anybody in custody? No. Do we have any suspects? Yeah. Every gangbanger in that neighborhood," he said.

"I think it was a hit," I said.

"You think a hit?" he said.

"Maybe Jerry Joe was going to dime some people, contractors lining up at the trough in Baton Rouge," I said.

"You used to be at the First District, right?"

"Right."

"Tell me when I say something that sounds wrong—a white guy down by the Desire at night isn't looking to be shark meat."

"Come on, Cramer. Kids aren't going to kill a guy and peel the car with the body lying on the street," I said.

"Maybe they didn't know they'd killed him. You think of that?"

"I think you're shit-canning the investigation," I said.

"I punched in at four this morning. A black kid took a shot at another kid in the Desire. He missed. He killed a three-month-old baby instead. Short Boy Jerry was a mutt. You asking me I got priorities? Fucking 'A' I do."

His phone rang. He picked it up, then hit the "hold" button.

"Y'all get a cup of coffee, give me ten minutes," he said.

Clete and I walked down the street and ate hot dogs at a counter where we had to stand, then went back to the District headquarters. Cramer scratched his forehead and looked at a yellow legal pad on his blotter.

"That was the ME called," he said. "Short Boy Jerry had gravel and grains of concrete in his scalp, but it was from a fall, not a blow. There were pieces of leather in the wounds around his eyes, probably from gloves the hitter was wearing or a blackjack. Death was caused by a broken rib getting shoved into the heart."

He lit a cigarette and put the paper match carefully in the ashtray with two fingers, his eyes veiled.

"What's the rest of it?" I asked.

"The ME thinks the assailant or assailants propped Short Boy Jerry up to prolong the beating. The bruises on the throat show a single hand held him up straight while he was getting it in the stomach. The brain was already hemorrhaging when the rib went into the heart . . ."

"What's that numeral at the bottom of the page?" I asked.

"The blows in the ribs were from a fist maybe six inches across."

"You got a sheet on a gangbanger that big?" I said.

"That doesn't mean there's not one."

"Start looking for a black mechanic named Mookie Zerrang," I said.

"Who?" he said.

"He looks like a stack of gorilla shit with gold teeth in it. Feel flattered. He gets ten large a whack in Miami. I'm surprised he'd be seen in a neighborhood like this. No kidding, they say the guy's got rigid standards," Clete said, fixing his eyes earnestly on Cramer's face.

THAT EVENING I LET Batist go home early and cleaned the bait shop and the tables on the dock by myself. The air was cool, the sky purple and dense with birds, the dying sun as bright as an acetylene flame on the horizon. I could see flights of ducks in V formations come in low over the swamp, then circle away and drop beyond the tips of the cypress into the darkness on the other side.

I plugged in Jerry Joe's jukebox and watched the colored lights drift through the plastic casing like smoke from marker grenades. There were two recordings of "La Jolie Blon" in the half-moon rack, one by Harry Choates and the other by Iry LeJeune. I had never thought about it before, but both men's lives seemed to be always associated with that haunting, beautiful song, one that was so pure in its sense of loss you didn't have to understand French to comprehend what the singer felt. "La Jolie Blon" wasn't about a lost love. It was about the end of an era.

Iry LeJeune was killed on the highway, changing a tire, and Harry Choates died in alcoholic madness in the Austin city jail, either after beating his head bloody against the bars or being beaten unmercifully by his jailers.

Maybe their tragic denouements had nothing to do with a song that had the power to break the heart. Maybe such a conclusion was a product of my own alcoholic mentality. But I had to grieve just a moment on their passing, just as I did for Jerry Joe, and maybe for all of us who tried to hold on to a time that was quickly passing away.

Jerry the Glide had believed in Wurlitzer jukeboxes and had secretly worshipped the man who had helped burn Dresden. What a surrogate, I thought, then wondered what mine was.

A car came down the road in the dusk, then slowed, as though the driver might want to stop, perhaps for a beer on the way home. I turned off the outside flood lamps, then the string of lights over the dock, then the lights inside the shop, and the car went past the boat ramp and down the road and around the curve. I leaned with my forearm against the jukebox's casing and started to punch a selection. But you can't recover the past with a recording that's forty years old, nor revise all the moments when you might have made life a little better for the dead.

I could feel the blood beating in my wrists. I jerked the plug from the wall, sliced the cord in half with my pocketknife, and wheeled the jukebox to the back and left it in a square of moonlight, face to the wall.

Chapter
25

Early Sunday morning I parked my pickup in the alley behind Sabelle Crown's bar in Lafayette. The alley was littered with bottles and beer cans, and a man and woman were arguing on the landing above the back entrance to the bar. The woman wore an embroidered Japanese robe that exposed her thick calves, and her chestnut hair was unbrushed and her face without makeup. The man glanced down at me uncertainly, then turned back to the woman.

"You t'ink you wort' more, go check the mirror, you," he said. He walked down the wood stairs and on down the alley, stepping over a rain puddle, without looking at me. The woman went back inside.

I climbed the stairs to the third story, where Sabelle lived by herself at the end of a dark hallway that smelled of insecticide and mold.

"It's seven in the morning. You on a drunk or something?" she said when she opened the door. She wore only a T-shirt without a bra and a pair of blue jeans that barely buttoned under her navel.

"You still have working girls here, Sabelle?" I said.

"We're all working girls, honey. Y'all just haven't caught on." She left the door open for me and walked barefoot across the linoleum and took a coffee pot off her two-burner stove.

"I want you to put me with your father."

"Like meet with him, you're saying?"

223

"However you want to do it."

"So you can have him executed?"

"I believe Buford LaRose is setting him up to be killed."

She set the coffee pot back on the stove without pouring from it.

"How do you know this?" she said.

"I was out to his place. Those state troopers aren't planning to take prisoners."

She sucked in her bottom lip.

"What are you offering?" she asked.

"Maybe transfer to a federal facility."

"Daddy hates the federal government."

"That's a dumb attitude."

"Thanks for the remark. I'll think about it."

"There're only a few people who've stood in Buford's way, Sabelle. The scriptwriter and Lonnie Felton were two of them. Jerry Joe Plumb was another. He was killed yesterday morning. That leaves your dad."

"Jerry Joe?" she said. Her face was blank, like that of someone who has been caught unawares by a photographer's flash.

"He was methodically beaten to death. My guess is by the same black guy who killed Felton and his girlfriend and the scriptwriter."

She sat down at her small kitchen table and looked out the window across the rooftops.

"The black guy again?" she said.

"That means something to you?"

"What do I know about black guys? They pick up the trash. They don't drink in my bar."

"Get a hold of your old man, Sabelle."

"Say, you're wrong about one thing."

"Oh?"

"Daddy's not the only guy in Buford's way. Take it from a girl who's been there. When he decides to fuck somebody, he doesn't care if it's male or female. Keep your legs crossed, sweetie."

I looked at the glint in her eye, and at the anger and injury it represented, and I knew that her friendship with me had always been a presumption and vanity on my part and that in reality Sabelle Crown had long ago consigned me, unfairly or not, to that army of male violators and users who took and never gave.

MONDAY AN OVERWEIGHT man in a navy blue suit with hair as black as patent leather tapped on my office glass. There was a deep dimple in his chin.

"Can I help you?" I said.

"Yeah, I just kind of walked myself back here. This is a nice building y'all got." His right hand was folded on a paper bag. I waited. "Oh, excuse me," he said. "I'm Ciro Tauzin, state police, Baton Rouge. You got a minute, suh?"

His thighs splayed on the chair when he sat down. His starched dress shirt was too small for him and the collar button had popped loose under the knot in his necktie.

"You know what I got here?" he asked, putting his hand in the paper bag. "An oar lock with a handkerchief tied through it. That's a strange thing for somebody to find on their back lawn, ain't it?"

"Depends on who the person is."

"In this case, it was one of my men found it on Buford LaRose's place. So since an escaped convict is trying to assassinate the governor-elect, we didn't want to take nothing for granted and we took some prints off it and ran them through AFIS, you know, the Automatic Fingerprint Identification System. I tell you, podna, what a surprise when we found out who those prints belonged to. Somebody steal an oar lock off one of your boats, suh?"

"Not to my knowledge."

"You just out throwing your oar locks on people's lawn?"

"It was just an idle speculation on my part. About a body that might have been buried there."

"Is that right? I declare. Y'all do some fascinating investigative work in Iberia Parish."

"You're welcome to join us."

"Ms. LaRose says you got an obsession, that you're carrying out a vendetta of some kind. She thinks maybe you marked the back of the property for Aaron Crown."

"Karyn has a creative mind."

"Well, you know how people are, suh. They get inside their heads and think too much. But one of my troopers told me you were knocking around in the stables, where you didn't have no bidness. What you up to, Mr. Robicheaux?"

"I think Aaron's a dead man if he gets near your men."

"Really? Well, suh, I won't bother you any more today. Here's your oar lock back. You're not going to be throwing nothing else up in their yard, are you?"

"I'm not planning on it. Tell me something."

"Yes, suh?"

"Why would the LaRoses decide to put in a gazebo right where I thought there might be an unmarked burial?"

"You know, I thought about that myself. So I checked with the contractor. Mr. LaRose put in the order for that gazebo two months ago."

He rose and extended his hand.

I didn't take it.

"You're fronting points for a guy who's got no bottom, Mr. Tauzin. No offense meant," I said.

THAT NIGHT I WENT to bed early, before Bootsie, and was almost asleep when I heard her enter the room and begin undressing. She brushed her teeth and stayed in the bathroom a long time, then clicked off the bathroom light and lay down on her side of the bed with her head turned toward the wall. I placed my palm on her back. Her skin was warm through her nightgown.

She looked up into the darkness.

"You all right?" she said.

"Sure."

"About Jerry Joe, I mean?"

"I was okay today."

"Dave?"

"Yes?"

"No . . . I'm sorry. I'm too tired to talk about it tonight."

"About what?"

She didn't reply at first, then she said, "That woman . . . I hate her."

"Come on, Boots. See her for what she is."

"You're playing her game. It's a rush for both of you. I'm not going to say any more . . ." She sat on the side of the bed and pushed her feet in her slippers. "I can't take this, Dave," she said, and picked up her pillow and a blanket and went into the living room.

THE MOON WAS down, the sky dark, when I was awakened at five the next morning by a sound out in the swamp, wood knocking against wood, echoing across the water. I sat on the edge of the bed, my head still full of sleep, and heard it again through the half-opened window, an oar striking a log perhaps, the bow sliding off a cypress stump. Then I saw the light in the mist, deep in the flooded trees, like a small halo of white phosphorous burning against the dampness, moving horizontally four feet above the waterline.

I put on my khakis and loafers and flannel shirt, took a flashlight out of the nightstand and my .45 automatic out of the dresser drawer, and walked to the end of the dock.

The light out in the trees was gone. The air was gray with mist, the bayou dimpled by the rolling backs of gars.

"Who are you?" I called.

It was quiet, as though the person in the trees were considering my question, then I heard a paddle or an oar dipping into water, raking alongside a wood gunnel.

"Tell me who you are!" I called. I waited. Nothing. My words sounded like those of a fool trapped by his own fears.

I unlocked the bait shop and turned on the flood lamps, then unchained an outboard by the end of the concrete ramp, set one knee on the seat, and shoved out into the bayou. I cranked the engine and went thirty yards downstream and turned into a cut that led back into a dead bay surrounded by cypress and willows. The air was cold and thick with fog, and when I shut off the engine I heard a bass flop its tail in the shallows. Nutrias perched on every exposed surface, their eyes as red as sapphires in the glow of my flashlight.

Then, at the edge of the bay, I saw the path a boat had cut in the layer of algae floating between two stumps. I shined my light deep into the trees and saw a moving shape, the shadow of a hunched man, a flash of dirty gold water flicked backward as a pirogue disappeared beyond a mudbank that was overgrown with palmettos.

"Aaron?" I asked the darkness.

But no one responded.

I tried to remember the images in my mind's eye—the breadth of the shoulders, a hand pulling aside a limb, a neck that seemed to go from the jaws into the collarbones without taper. But the reality was I had seen nothing clearly except a man seated low in a pirogue and—

A glistening, thin object in the stern. It was metal, I thought. A chain perhaps. The barrel of a rifle.

My flannel shirt was sour with sweat. I could hear my heart beating in the silence of the trees.

I CAME HOME FOR lunch that day. Alafair was at school and Bootsie was gone. There was no note on the corkboard where we left messages for one another. I fixed a ham and onion sandwich and a glass of iced tea and heated a bowl of dirty rice and ate at the kitchen table. Batist called from the bait shop.

"Dave, there's a bunch of black mens here drinking beer and using bad language out on the dock," he said.

"Who are they?" I asked.

"One's got a knife instead of a hook on his hand."

"A what?"

"Come see, 'cause I'm fixing to run 'em down the road."

I walked down the slope through the trees. A new Dodge Caravan was parked by the concrete boat ramp, and five black men stood on the end of the dock, their shirtsleeves rolled in the warm air, drinking can beer while Jimmy Ray Dixon gutted a two-foot yellow catfish he had gill-hung from a nail on a light post.

A curved and fine-pointed knife blade, honed to the blue thinness of a barber's razor, was screwed into a metal and leather cup that fitted over the stump of Jimmy Ray's left wrist. He drew the blade's edge around the catfish's gills, then cut a neat line down both sides of the dorsal fin and stripped the skin back with a pair of pliers in his right hand. He sliced the belly from the apex of the V where the gills met to the anus and let the guts fall out of the cavity like a sack of blue and red jelly.

The tops of his canvas shoes were speckled with blood. He was grinning.

"I bought it from a man caught it in a hoop net at Henderson," he said.

"Y'all want to rent a boat?"

"I hear the fishing here ain't any good."

"It's not good anywhere now. The water's too cool."

"I got a problem with a couple of people bothering me. I think you behind it," he said.

"You want to lose the audience?" I said.

"Y'all give me a minute," he said to the other men. They were dressed in tropical shirts, old slacks, shoes they didn't care about. But they weren't men who fished. Their hands squeezed their own sex, almost with fondness; their eyes followed a black woman walking on the road; they whispered to one another, even though their conversation was devoid of content.

They started to go inside the shop.

"It's closed," I said.

"Hey, Jim, we ain't here to steal your watermelons," Jimmy Ray said.

"I'd appreciate it if you didn't call me a racial name," I said.

"Y'all open the cooler. I'll be along," he said to his friends. He watched them drift in a cluster down the dock toward the van.

"Here's what it is," he said. "That cracker Cramer, yeah, you got it, white dude from Homicide, smells like deodorant, is down at my pool hall, axing if I know why Jerry the Glide was in the neighborhood when somebody broke all his sticks."

Not bad, Cramer, I thought.

"Then your friend, Purcel, hears from this pipehead street chicken Mookie Zerrang's got permission to burn his kite, so he blames me. I ain't got time for this, Jack."

"Why *was* Jerry Joe in your neighborhood?"

"It ain't my neighborhood, I got a bidness there. I don't go in there at night, either." He brushed the sack of fish guts off the dock with his shoe and watched it float away in the current. "Why you got to put your hand in this shit, man?"

"You know how it is, a guy's got to do something for kicks."

"I hear it's 'cause you was fucking some prime cut married to the wrong dude. That's your choice, man, but I don't like you using my brother to do whatever you doing. Give my fish to the old man in there," he said, and started to walk away.

I walked after him and touched his back with the ball of my finger. I could feel his wingbone through the cloth of his shirt, see the dark grain of his whiskers along the edge of his jaw, smell the faint odor of sweat and talcum in his skin.

"Don't use profanity around my home, please," I said.

"You worried about language round your home? Man put a bullet in mine and killed my brother. That's the difference between us. Don't let it be lost on you, Chuck."

He got in the front passenger's seat of the van, slid a metal sheath over the knife blade attached to his stump, then unscrewed the blade and drank from a bottle of Carta Blanca, his throat working smoothly until the bottle was empty. The bottle made a dull, tinkling sound when it landed in the weeds by the roadside.

THE NEXT DAY I got the warrant to search the grounds of the LaRose plantation. Helen Soileau parked the cruiser in the driveway, and I got out and knocked on the front door.

Karyn was barefoot and wore only a pair of shorts and a halter, with a thick towel around her neck, when she opened the door. In the soft afternoon light her tan took on the dark tint of burnt honey. The momentary surprise went out of her face, and she leaned an arm against the doorjamb and brushed back her hair with her fingers.

"What are we here for today?" she said.

"Here's the warrant. We'll be looking at some things back on the bayou."

"How did you—" she began, then stopped.

"All I had to do was tell the judge the state police warned me off y'all's property. He seemed upset about people intruding on his jurisdiction."

"Then you should scurry on with your little errand, whatever in God's name it is."

"Does Jerry Joe's death bother you at all?"

Her mouth grew small with anger.

"There're days when I wish I was a man, Dave. I'd honestly love to beat the living shit out of you." The door clicked shut.

Helen and I walked through the coolness of the porte cochere into the backyard. The camellias were in bloom and the backyard was filled with a smoky gold light. I could see Karyn inside the glassed-in rear corner of the house, touching her toes in a crisscross motion, her thighs spread, the back of her neck slick with a necklace of sweat.

"You ever read anything about the Roman Coliseum? When gladiators fought on lakes of burning oil, that kind of stuff?" Helen said.

"Yeah, I guess."

"I have a feeling Karyn LaRose was in the audience."

We walked past the stables and through the hardwoods to the sloping bank of the Teche. A heavyset black state trooper sat in a folding chair, back among the trees, eating cracklings from a jar. His scoped rifle was propped against a pine trunk. He glanced at my badge holder hanging from my coat pocket and nodded.

"Crown hasn't tried to get through your perimeter, huh?" I said, and smiled.

"You ax me, he's been spooked out," he answered.

"How's that?" I asked.

"Man's smart. See the mosquitoes I been swatting all day?"

"They're bad after a rain," I said.

"They're bad in these trees anytime. Man don't see nobody out yonder on the bank, he knows what's waiting for him inside the woods. *That*, or somebody done tole him."

"You take it easy," I said.

Helen and I walked along the bank toward the spot where I had thrown the oar lock. I could feel her eyes on me, watching.

"You're damn quiet," she said.

"Sorry, I didn't mean to be."

"Dave?"

"What's up?"

"I'm getting a bad sense here."

"What's that?" I said, my eyes focused on the gazebo that two carpenters were hammering and sawing on around the bayou's bend.

"What that trooper said. Did you warn Crown?"

"We don't execute people in Iberia Parish. We want the man in custody, not in a box."

"We didn't have this conversation, Streak."

The carpenters were on all fours atop the gazebo's round, peaked roof, their nail bags swinging from their stomachs.

"That's quite a foundation. Y'all always pour a concrete pad under a gazebo?" I said.

"High water will rot it out if you don't," one man answered.

"What did y'all do with the dirt you excavated?"

"Some guy hauled it off for topsoil."

"Which guy?"

"Some guy work for Mr. LaRose, I guess."

"Y'all did the excavation?"

"No, sir. Mr. LaRose done that hisself. He got his own backhoe."

"I see. Y'all doin' all right?"

"Yes, sir. Anyt'ing wrong?"

"Not a thing," I said.

I walked down on the grassy bank, which was crisscrossed with the deep prints of cleated tires and dozer tracks. A fan of mud and torn divots of grass lay humped among the cattails at the bayou's edge. I poked at it with a stick and watched it cloud and drift away in the current.

"You want to bag some of it?" Helen said.

"It's a waste of time. Buford beat us to it."

"It was a long shot," Helen said. "You've got to consider the source, too, Dave. Dock Green's nuts."

"No, he's not. He's just different."

"That's a new word for it."

I didn't say anything. We walked up the slope and through the trees toward the house. The air was filled with gold shafts of light inside the trees, and you could smell the water in the coulee and the fecund odor of wet fern and the exposed root systems that trailed in the current like torn cobweb.

"Can I get out of line a minute?" Helen said.

I looked at her and waited. She kept walking up the incline, her face straight ahead, her shoulders slightly bent, her masculine arms taut-looking with muscle.

"The homicides you're worried about took place out of our jurisdiction. The Indian guy who tried to mess you over with the machete is dead. We don't have a crime connected with the LaRoses to investigate in Iberia Parish, Dave," she said.

"They're both dirty."

"So is the planet," she said.

We took a shorter route back and exited the woods by a cleared field and passed the brick stables and an adjacent railed lot where a solitary bay gelding stood like a piece of stained redwood in a column of dust-laden sunlight. The brand on his flank was shaped in the form of a rose, burned deep into the hair like calcified ringworm.

"They sure leave their mark on everything, don't they?" I said.

"What should they use, spray cans? Give it a break," Helen said.

"I'll tell them we're leaving now," I said.

"Don't do it, Dave."

"I'll see you in the car, Helen."

She continued on through the field toward the driveway. I walked through the backyard toward the porte cochere, then glanced through a screen of bamboo into the glassed-in rear of the house where Karyn had been doing her aerobic exercises. We stared into each other's face with a look of mutual and surprised intimacy that went beyond the moment, beyond my ability to define or guard against, that went back into a deliberately forgotten image of two people looking nakedly upon each other's faces during intercourse.

I had caught her unawares in front of a small marble-topped bar with a champagne glass and a silver ice bucket containing a green bottle of Cold Duck on it. But Karyn was not one to be undone by an unexpected encounter with an adversary. With her eyes fastened on my face, a pout on her mouth like an adolescent girl, she unhooked her halter and let it drop from her breasts and unbuttoned her shorts and pushed them and her panties down over her thighs and knees and stepped out of them. Then she pulled the pins from her platinum hair and shook it out on her shoulders and put the glass of Cold Duck to her mouth, her eyes fixed on mine, as empty as death.

Chapter
26

JIMMY RAY DIXON was one of those in-your-face people who insult and demean others with such confidence that you always assume they have nothing to hide themselves.

It's a good ruse. Just like offering a lie when no one has challenged your integrity. For example, lying about how you lost a hand in Vietnam.

After Jimmy Ray and his entourage had left the dock, I'd called a friend at the Veterans Administration in New Orleans.

The following day, when I got back to the department from the LaRose plantation, my friend called and read me everything he had pulled out of the computer on Jimmy Ray Dixon.

He didn't lose a hand clearing toe-poppers from a rice paddy outside Pinkville. A gang of Chinese thieves, his business partners in selling stolen PX liquor on the Saigon black market, cut it off.

A cross-referenced CID report also indicated Jimmy Ray may have been involved in smuggling heroin home in GI coffins.

So he lied about his war record, I thought. But who wouldn't, with a file like that?

That was not what had bothered me.

At the dock Jimmy Ray had said somebody had shot into his home and had killed his brother.

His home.

I went to the public library and the morgue at the *Daily Iberian* and began searching every piece of microfilm I could find on the assassination of Ely Dixon.

Only one story, in *Newsweek* magazine, mentioned the fact that Ely was killed in a two-bedroom house he rented for fifty dollars a month from his brother, Jimmy Ray, to whom the article referred as a disabled Vietnam war veteran.

I drove back to the department and went into the sheriff's office.

"What if the wrong man was killed?" I said.

"I have a feeling my interest is about to wane quickly," he said.

"It was the sixties. Church bombings in Birmingham and Bogalusa, civil rights workers lynched in Mississippi. Everybody assumed Ely Dixon was the target."

"You're trying to figure out the motivation on a homicide that's twenty-eight years old? Who cares? The victim doesn't. He's dead just the same."

He could barely contain the impatience and annoyance in his voice. He turned his swivel chair sideways so he wouldn't have to look directly at me when he spoke.

"I like you a lot, Dave, but, damn it, you don't listen. Leave the LaRoses alone. Let Aaron Crown fall in his own shit."

"I told Helen we don't execute people in Iberia Parish."

"Don't be deluded. That's because the electric chair doesn't travel anymore."

He began fiddling with a file folder, then he put it in his desk drawer and rose from his chair and looked out the window until he heard me close the door behind me.

BATIST WENT HOME sick with a cold that evening, and before supper Alafair and I drove down to his house with a pot of soup. His wife had died the previous year, and he lived with his three bird dogs and eight cats on a dirt road in an unpainted wood house with a sagging gallery and a peaked corrugated roof, a truck garden in a side lot and a smokehouse in back. The sparse grass in his yard was raked clean, his compost pile snugged in by chicken wire, his crab traps stacked next to a huge iron pot in the backyard where he cooked cracklings in the fall.

Over the years, in early spring, when he broke the thatched hardpan on his garden, his single-tree plow had furrowed back bits of square nails, the rusted shell of a wagon spring, .58 caliber minié balls, a corroded tin of percussion caps, a molded boot, a brass buckle embossed with the letters *CSA*, the remains from a Confederate encampment that had probably been overrun by federals in 1863.

I first met Batist when I was a little boy and he was a teenager, a blacksmith's helper in a rambling, red barnlike structure on a green lot out on West Main. Batist worked for a frail, very elderly man named Mr. Antoine, one of the last surviving Confederate veterans in the state of Louisiana. Every day Mr. Antoine sat in the wide doors of his smithy, to catch the breeze, in red suspenders and straw hat, the skin under his throat distended like an inverted cock's comb.

Anyone who wished could drop by and listen to his stories about what he called "the War."

Few did.

But I'll never forget one he told me and Batist.

It was during Jubal Early's last assault on the federals before the surrender at Appomattox. A fourteen-year-old drummer boy from Alabama was the only unwounded survivor of his outfit. Rather than surrender or run, he tied a Confederate battle flag to an empty musket and mounted a horse and charged the union line. He rode two hundred yards through a bullet-cropped cornfield littered with Southern dead, his colors raised above his head all the while, his eyes fixed on the stone wall ahead of him where five thousand federals waited and looked at him in disbelief.

Not one of them fired his weapon.

Instead, when the boy's horse labored up the slope and surged through a gap in the wall, three federal soldiers pulled him from the saddle and took his colors and pinioned him to the ground. The boy flailed and kicked until one soldier in blue said, "Son, you ain't got to study on it no more. You're over on the Lord's side now."

Mr. Antoine slapped his thigh and howled at the implications of his story, whatever they were.

Later, I would read a similar account about Cemetery Ridge. Maybe it was all apocryphal. But if you ever doubted Mr. Antoine's authority as a veteran of the Civil War, he would ask you to feel the cyst-encrusted pistol ball that protruded like a sparrow's egg below his right elbow.

The irony was the fact that the man who probably knew more first-hand accounts of Mr. Antoine's War, and the man who grew food in the detritus of a Confederate encampment, was a descendant of slaves and did not know how to read and write and consequently was never consulted as a source of information by anyone.

He sat down with the soup at the kitchen table in a pair of slippers and surplus navy dungarees and a denim shirt buttoned at the throat. The sun glimmered off the bayou through the trees behind his house.

"Fat Daddy Babineau brought me some poke chops, but they ain't good for you when you got a stomach upsetness. I didn't want to hurt his feelings, though," he said.

"You going to be all right by yourself?" I said.

"I'm gonna be fine." He looked at Alafair, who was examining some minié balls on his kitchen shelf. Then he looked back at me.

"What is it?" I asked.

"Fat Daddy just left. I was fixing to call you." He kept his eyes on my face.

"Alf, you want to take the truck to the four corners and get a half gallon of milk?" I said.

"Pretty slick way of getting rid of me. But . . . okay," she said, one palm extended for the keys, the other on her hip.

"Fat Daddy seen this man bring his pirogue out of the swamp," Batist said after Alafair had gone out the door. "Him and his wife was fishing on the bank, and this big nigger wit' one side of his head shaved paddled out of the trees. It was the same morning you seen that man wit' a light out past our dock, Dave.

"Fat Daddy said this big nigger had gold teet' and arms thick as telephone poles. There was a gun up in the bow, and when Fat Daddy seen it, the nigger give him such a mean look Fat Daddy's wife wanted to get in the car. It's the same man come to our shop, ain't it?"

"It sounds like him."

"That ain't all of it, no. Fat Daddy and his wife was walking down the levee when they seen the same nigger again, this time busting out the bottom of the pirogue with his foot. He smashed big holes all over it and sunk it right in the canal. Why he want to do somet'ing like that?"

"Who knows? Maybe he didn't want to leave his fingerprints around."

"That ain't all of it. He seen them watching him and he walked up on the levee and got between Fat Daddy and Fat Daddy's car and says, 'Why you following me around?'

"Fat Daddy says, 'We come here to fish, not to mind nobody else's bidness.'

"The nigger says, 'You gonna tell somebody you seen a man poaching gators? Because if you do, you a goddamn liar.'

"Fat Daddy goes, 'We don't know nothing about no gators. So you leave us alone. We ain't give you no truck.'

"The nigger smiles then. He says, 'You a nice fat man. You know why I bust up my pirogue? 'Cause it got leaks in it.' All the time he was squeezing his hand on his privates, like he got an itch, like he didn't care there was a woman there. Fat Daddy said when you looked into that nigger's face, you didn't have no doubt what was on his mind. He wanted you to say just one t'ing wrong so he could let out all his meanness on you.

"Fat Daddy's wife got in the car, not moving an inch, not hardly breathing she was so scared, praying all the time Fat Daddy would just come on and get them out of there.

"Then the nigger takes Fat Daddy's pole and his bucket out of his hand and puts them in the backseat and opens the front door and heps Fat Daddy get behind the wheel. He says, 'I'm gonna show y'all somet'ing I ain't sure I can still do. Y'all watch, now.'

"He hooked his hands under the front bumper and started straining, like all the veins in his face was gonna pop out of his skin, grinning with them gold teet', snuff running out of his mout'. Then the car come up in the air, and the back wheels started rolling off the levee, just befo' he let it crash on the ground again.

"He come around to the window, still grinning, like he done somet'ing great, and let spit drip out of his mout' on his finger. He took Fat Daddy's sun helmet off his head and put his finger in Fat Daddy's ear and then dropped his hat back on his head again. Didn't say one word. Just rubbed spit in po' Fat Daddy's ear and walked off.

"What kind of man do t'ings like that, Dave? It makes me feel real bad. I wish I'd done somet'ing to stop that man when he come in our shop. Lawd God, I do."

Batist shook his head, his spoon forgotten by the side of his soup bowl.

A THERAPIST ONCE TOLD me that dreams are not a mystery. They simply represent our hopes and fears, he said. But unfortunately I was never good at distinguishing between the two.

I see an arbor atop the grassy slope of Bayou Teche. The tree trunks look hard and white under the moon, stonelike yet filled with power, as though the coldness in the light has trapped a trembling energy inside the bark. Inside the arbor is a wicker picnic basket filled with grapes and bananas, a corked green bottle of burgundy, a bottle of black label Jack Daniel's wrapped in a soft towel, a bucket of shaved ice with two chrome cups chilling inside it.

I can taste the charcoal and the oak in the whiskey, as weightless as liquid smoke on the back of the tongue. I can feel its heat spread from my stomach into my chest and my loins. But my system is dry, as though my glands have become dust, and the real rush doesn't come until the second hit, a long deep swallow of sugar and shaved ice and mint leaves and bourbon, then it reaches every nerve in my body, just as if someone had struck a sulfurous match across the base of the brain.

But this time the dream is not just about the charcoal-filtered product of Lynchburg, Tennessee. She's on her knees inside the arbor, her bottom resting on her heels, eating a sandwich with both hands, somehow vulnerable and reminiscent of a wartime photo of a frightened and starving child. She smiles when she sees me, as she would greet an old friend, and she gathers her dress in her hands and works it over her head. Her tan body seems glazed with moonglow, her breasts swollen and hard, her face innocent of any agenda except the welcoming press of her thighs around mine. In the dream I know it's wrong, that I've reached a place where I can't turn it around, just like the whiskey that lights old fires and once again claims a landscape inside me I'd long forgotten. Her mouth is on mine, her fingers on my hips, then kneading the small of my back, and I feel something break inside me, like water bursting through the bottom of a paper bag, and when I look into her face, my body trembling with the moment, I see a tangle of platinum hair and eyes like black glass and a self-indulgent lazy smile that ends in a kiss of contempt upon the cheek.

I WOKE AND SAT on the side of the bed, my fingers clenched on my knees, my loins aching like those of an adolescent boy trapped inside the unrelieved fantasies of his masturbation.

Outside, I heard Tripod running on his chain and wind coursing through the trees and dead leaves swirling across the yard. When the wind dropped, the night was silent for only a moment, then I heard leaves again, this time breaking under someone's foot.

I looked out the window and saw Tripod sitting on top of his hutch, motionless, his face pointed toward the backyard.

I slipped on a pair of blue jeans and my tennis shoes, took my .45 out of the dresser and the flashlight from the nightstand, and checked the lock on the front door. Bootsie was asleep on the couch, her arm across her eyes, a magazine splayed on the floor by her. I turned on the flood lamp in the mimosa tree and stepped out into the yard.

The wind blew plumes of ash out of my neighbor's field and ruffled the starlight's reflection on the duck pond by my fence line. I searched the side yard, the horse lot and stable, the aluminum toolshed where we still kept my father's old tractor, then I walked along the edge of the coulee toward the duck pond.

The batteries in my flashlight grew weaker and I turned them off and started back toward the house. I heard the shrill, hysterical-like cry of a nutria out in the swamp.

A man with the sinewy proportions of an atavistic throwback moved out quickly from behind a stand of banana trees and shoved the blunt, round end of a hard object into the center of my back.

"I could have used a telephone. I come here in trust. Don't mess it up," he said.

"What do you want, Aaron?"

"Give me your pistol . . . I'll give it back. I promise. I ain't gonna harm nobody, either."

His hand moved down my arm and slipped the .45 free from my fingers. He smelled like humus and wool clothes full of wood smoke and dried sweat.

"I got you! Sonofabitch if I didn't! Slickered you good!" he said. He squatted and roared at his own humor, slapped his thigh with one hand. "Didn't have nothing but this old corncob pipe I got out of a garbage can! How you like that!"

"Why don't you act your age?"

"Did y'all use the same kind of smarts against them Viet Cong?" He danced like an ape under the overhang of withered banana leaves.

"You going to give me my piece back?" I said.

"Cain't do *that*." Then his face went as blank and stark as a sheet of tin under the starlight. "I want you to set up my surrender to Buford LaRose."

When I didn't reply, he said, "You deaf? Just set it up. Out in the country somewheres. He'll go for it. It'll make him a big man."

"I don't know if I trust what you've got in mind, partner."

"They sent a little pisspot Eye-talian after me. Man I was in jail with and knowed where my camp was at. Some people is cursed by their knowledge."

"What are you saying?"

His eyes were wide, lidless, burning with certainty about the adversarial nature of the world.

"You might say I talked to his conscience. He said me and you are the shit on somebody's nose and it's suppose to get wiped off before a certain governor gets sworn in. He was at a point in his life he didn't want to keep no secrets."

"I don't like what you're telling me, Aaron."

"They treated me worsen they would a nigger rapist. You think I give a fuck about what you don't like? . . . We got a mutual interest here."

"No, we don't."

He put the .45 under my jaw. "Then you walk to the shed."

"You're starting to seriously piss me off, Aaron."

He pushed the barrel harder into my throat. "LaRose used my daughter and throwed her away. Then he sent me to the penitentiary. You side with them, then you're my enemy."

His face was bloodless, his dilated nostrils radiating gray hair. He wasn't a bizarre old man anymore, or even a pitiful and ignorant victim. For some reason, as I stared into the vacuity of his eyes, I was absolutely convinced he would have found reason to wage war against Buford LaRose's world even if Buford LaRose had never existed.

"I'm not going in that shed, Aaron. It ends here," I said.

He breathed loudly in the darkness. His tongue looked like a gray biscuit inside his mouth.

"I done cut your phone line already. I'll give you back this later. But don't come after me," he said.

"You're a foolish man, sir."

"No, I'm a dead one. That's what they call people in the Death House, the Dead Men. Wait till you feel that big nigger's hand on you. Or one of yourn up at the house. See how goddamn liberal you are then."

"What did you say?"

But he was gone, running like a crab through the trees, his prison work boots crashing in the leaves.

I SAT ON THE floor by the couch where Bootsie slept. Her eyes opened into mine.

"What is it?" she said.

"Aaron Crown was outside . . ." I placed my hand on her arm before she could get up. "It's all right. He's gone now. But he cut the phone line."

"Crown was—"

"I'm giving it up, Boots. Aaron, the LaRose family, whatever they're into, it's somebody else's responsibility now."

She raised herself on one elbow.

"What happened out there?" she asked.

"Nothing. That's the point. Nothing I do will ever change the forces these people represent."

Her eyes steadied on mine and seemed to look inside me.

"You want to fix something to eat?" she said.

"That'd be swell. I'll use the phone in the bait shop to call the department."

When I locked the front door behind me, I could see her in the kitchen, shredding a raw potato on a grater to make hash browns, her robe cinched around her hips, just as though we were waking to an ordinary dawn and the life we'd had before I'd allowed the fortunes of Aaron Crown and the LaRose family to grow like a tentacle into our own.

In the morning Batist found my .45 wrapped in a Kentucky Fried Chicken bag under the doormat on his gallery.

Chapter
27

"WE'VE GOT A real prize in the holding cell," Helen said.

I followed her down the corridor to the lockup area and waited for the deputy to open the cell. The biker inside had a gold beard and a head of hair like a lion's mane. His eyes reminded me of red Lifesavers, pushed deep into folds of skin that were raw from windburn or alcohol or blood pressure that could probably blow an automobile gasket.

His name was Jody Hatcher. A year and a half ago the court had released him to the Marine Corps, in hopes, perhaps, that the whole Hatcher family would simply disappear from Iberia Parish. His twin sister achieved a brief national notoriety when she was arrested for murdering seven men who picked her up hitchhiking on the Florida Turnpike. The mother, an obese, choleric woman with heavy facial hair, was interviewed by CBS on the porch of the shack where the Hatcher children were raised. I'll never forget her words: "It ain't my fault. She was born that way. I whipped her every day when she was little. It didn't do no good."

"They treating you all right, Jody?" I said after the deputy locked me and Helen inside.

"I don't like the echoes, man. I can't tell what's out in the hall and what's inside," he said, grinning, pointing at his head. He wore skin-tight black jeans and a black leather vest with no shirt. His face seemed filled with a merry, self-ironic glow, like a man who's become an amused spectator at the dissolution of his own life.

Helen and I sat down on the wood bench against the far wall. In the center of the cell was a urine-streaked drain hole.

"They say your saddlebags were full of crystal meth," I said.

"Yeah, dude I lent my Harley to probably really messed me over. Wow, I hate it when they do that to you."

I nodded, as though we were all listening to a sad truth.

"I thought you were in Haiti," I said.

"Got cut loose, man. You saw that on TV about the firefight at the police station? That was my squad. See, this native woman was cheering us up on a balcony and an attaché busted her upside the head with a baton. That's why we was down at the police station. We camied-up and set up a perimeter 'cause we didn't want these guys hurting the people no more. The Corps is peace makers, not peace keepers, a lot of civilians don't understand that. We got the word these guys was gonna light us up, so this one dude comes outside and starts to turn toward us with an Uzi in his hand, and *pow*, man, I see the tracer come out of the lieutenant's gun, and then a shit storm is flying through the air and before I knew it I burned a whole magazine on just one guy, like chickens was pecking him to death against the wall. I wasn't up for it, man. That's some real cruel shit to watch."

He was seated on a wood bench, his wrists crossed on his knees, his fists clenched, his face staring disjointedly into space.

"Tell Detective Robicheaux about the Mexican cowboy," Helen said.

"We already covered that, ain't we? I don't like remembering stuff like that." He puckered his mouth like a fish's.

"You got to work with us, Jody, you want some slack on the meth," Helen said.

"It was right before I went in the Crotch. I met the Mexican guys in a bar in Loreauville. I was doing dust and rainbows and drinking vodka on top of it, and we all ended up out in a woods somewhere. It was a real weirded-out hot night, with fireflies crawling all over the trees and bullfrogs croaking and nutrias screaming out on the water.

These guys had some beautiful meth, high-grade clean stuff that don't foul your blood. But this one cowboy tied off and slapped a vein till it was purple as a turnip, then he spikes into it and *whop*, he doubles over and crumples on the ground, with the rubber tourniquet flopping in his teeth like a snake with its head cut off.

"It's not like skag. You don't drop the guy in cold water or a snowbank. The guy's eyes rolled, all kind of stuff came out of his mouth, his knees started jerking against his chest. What are you gonna do, man? I was wasted. Jesus, it was like watching a guy drown when you can't do nothing about it."

"Is that all of it, Jody?" I asked.

"Tell him," Helen said.

"They dug a hole and buried him," he said.

"Who?" I asked.

"Everybody. I run off in the trees. I couldn't watch it . . . Maybe he wasn't dead . . . That's what keeps going through my head . . . They didn't get a doctor or nothing . . . They should have put a mirror in front of his nose or something . . ."

"Who was there, Jody?" I asked.

"The guy who just got elected governor."

"You're sure?" I said.

"He was strung out, crying like a little kid. There was some other Americans there had to take care of him."

"Who?" I asked.

"I don't know, man. I blacked out. I couldn't take it. I can't even tell you where I was at. I woke up behind a colored bar in St. Martinville with dogs peeing on me."

His face was swollen, glazed like the red surfaces on a lollipop, decades older than his years. He wiped his eyes with the heel of his hand.

BACK IN MY office, Helen said, "What do you think?"

"Take his statement. Put it in the file," I answered.

"That's it?"

"Somebody snipped Jody's brainstem a long time ago."

"You don't believe him?"

"Yeah, I do. But it won't stand up. Buford LaRose won't go down until he gets caught in bed with a dead underage male prostitute."

"Too much," she said, and walked out the door.

SATURDAY MORNING CLETE Purcel drove in from New Orleans, fished for two hours in a light mist, then gave it up and drank beer in the bait shop while I added up my receipts and tried to figure my quarterly income tax payment. He spoke little, gazing out the window at the rain, as though he was concentrating on a conversation inside his head.

"Say it," I said.

"After I got to Vietnam, I wished I hadn't joined the Corps," he said.

"So?"

"You already rolled the dice, big mon. You can't just tell these cocksuckers you don't want to play anymore."

"Why not?"

"Because I keep seeing Jerry Joe's face in my dreams, that's why . . . That's his jukebox back there?"

"Yeah."

"What's on it?"

"Forties and fifties stuff. Every one of them is a Cadillac."

"Give me some quarters."

"I sliced the cord in half."

"That's a great way to deal with the problem, Streak."

A half hour later the phone rang. It was Buford LaRose. I walked with the phone into the back of the shop.

"Meet me at the Patio restaurant in Loreauville," he said.

"No, thanks," I said.

"Goddamn it, Dave, I want to get this mess behind us."

"Good. Resign your office."

"Crown's a killing machine," he said.

"If he is, you helped make him that way."

"You don't know, do you?"

"What?"

"About the guy who was just fished out of Henderson Swamp."

"That's St. Martin Parish. It's not my business. Good-bye, Buford."
I hung up the phone.

"That was dickhead?" Clete said.

"Yep."

"What did he want?"

I told him.

"You're just going to let it slide down the bowl?"

"That about sums it up."

"Mistake. Stay in their faces, Streak. Don't let them blindside you.
I'll back your play, mon."

He turned toward me on the counter stool, his scarred face as flat
and round as a pie tin, his eyes a deep green under his combed, sandy
hair.

"Listen to me for once," he said. "That was Mookie Zerrang you
saw in the pirogue. You want the button man out of your life, you
got to find his juice."

The bayou seemed to dance with yellow light in the rain. I wiped
down the counter, carried out the trash, stocked the cooler in back,
then finally quit a foolish dialogue inside myself and dialed Buford's
answering service in Lafayette so I wouldn't have to call him at home.

"This is Dave Robicheaux. Tell Mr. LaRose I'll be in my office at
eight Monday morning."

HE WAS IN at ten, with Ciro Tauzin from the state police at his side.
The St. Martin Parish sheriff's report on a body recovered from Henderson Swamp lay on my desk.

"You starting to get a better picture of Aaron Crown now?" Buford said.

"Not really," I said.

"Not really? The victim's stomach was slit open and filled with
rocks. What kind of human being would do something like that?"
Buford said.

"I have a better question, Buford. What was a New Orleans gumball, a hit man for the Giacano family, doing at Henderson Swamp?" I said.

"He celled with Crown," Buford said.

"So why would Crown want to kill his cell partner?" I asked.

"Maybe he was gonna turn Aaron in. The guy had some weapons charges against him. Criminals ain't big on loyalty, no," Tauzin said, and smiled.

"I think he was there to whack Crown and lost. What's your opinion on that, Mr. Tauzin?" I asked.

The coat of his blue suit looked like it was buttoned crookedly on his body. There were flecks of dandruff inside the oil on his black hair. He rubbed the cleft in his chin with his thumb.

"Men like Crown will kill you for the shoes on your feet, the food in your plate. I don't believe they're a hard study, suh," he said.

"You get in touch with him through his daughter," Buford said. "If he'll surrender to me, I'll guarantee his safety and I promise he won't be tried for a capital offense . . ." He paused a moment, then raised his hands off the arms of the chair. "Maybe down the road, two or three years maximum, he can be released because of his age."

"Pretty generous," I said.

Buford and Ciro Tauzin both waited. I picked up a paper clip and dropped it on my blotter.

"Dave?" Buford said.

"He bears you great enmity," I answered.

"You've talked with him." He said it as a statement, not as a question. I could almost hear the analytical wheels turning in his head. I saw a thought come together in his eyes. There was no denying Buford's level of intelligence. "He wants a meet? He's told you he'll try to kill me?"

"Make peace with his daughter. Then he might listen to you."

Buford's eyes wrinkled at the corners as he tried to peel the meaning out of my words.

"A short high school romance? That's what you're talking about now?" he said.

But before I could speak, Ciro Tauzin said, "Here's the deal, Mr. Robicheaux. You can hep us if you want, or you can tell everybody else what their job is. But if Aaron Crown don't come in, I'm gonna blow his liver out. Is that clear enough, suh?"

I held his stare.

"Should I pass on your remarks, Mr. Tauzin?" I answered.

"I'd appreciate it if you would. It's quite an experience doing bidness with you, suh. Your reputation doesn't do you justice."

I made curlicues with a ballpoint pen on a yellow legal pad until they had left the room.

Two minutes later, Buford came back alone and opened the door, his seersucker coat over his shoulder, his plaid shirt rolled on his veined forearms. His curly hair hung on his forehead, and his cheeks were as bright as apples.

"You'll never like me, Dave. Maybe I can't blame you. But I give you my solemn word, I'll protect Aaron Crown and I'll do everything I can to see him die a free man," he said.

For just a moment I saw the handsome, young LSU quarterback of years ago who could be surrounded by tacklers, about to be destroyed, his bones crushed into the turf, his very vulnerability bringing the crowd to its feet, and then rocket an eighty-yard pass over his tacklers' heads and charm it into the fingers of a forgotten receiver racing across the goal line.

Some Saturday-afternoon heroes will never go gently into that good night. At least not this one, I thought.

PROBABLY OVER 90 percent of criminal investigations are solved by accident or through informants. I didn't have an informant within Buford's circle, but I did have access to a genuine psychotic whose dials never failed to entertain if not to inform:

I called his restaurant in New Orleans and two of his construction offices and through all the innuendo and subterfuge concluded that Dock Green was at his camp on the Atchafalaya River.

The sky was gray and the wide expanse of the river dimpled with rain when I pulled onto the service road and headed toward the cattle guard at the front of his property. I could see Dock, in a straw hat and black slicker, burning what looked like a pile of dead trees by the side of the house. But that was not what caught my eye. Persephone Green had just gotten into her Chrysler and was roaring down the gravel drive toward me, dirt clods splintering like flint from under the tires. I had to pull onto the grass to avoid being hit.

A moment later, when I walked up to the trash fire, I saw the source of Persephone's discontent. Two stoned-out women, oblivious to the weather, floated on air mattresses in a tall, cylindrical plastic pool, fed by a garden hose, in the backyard.

"Unexpected visit from the wife, Dock?" I asked.

"I don't know why she's got her head up her hole. She's filing for divorce anyway."

He poked at the fire with a blackened rake. The wind shifted and suddenly the smell hit me. In the center of burning tree limbs and a bed of white ash was the long, charred shape of an alligator.

"It got stuck in my culvert and drowned. A gator don't know how to back up," he said.

"Why don't you bury it?"

"Animals would dig it up. What d' you want here?"

"You've been out in front of me all the time, Dock. I respect that," I said.

"What?"

"About the body on the LaRose plantation and any number of other things. It's hard to float one by you, partner."

His face was smeared by charcoal, warm with the heat of the fire. He watched me as he would a historical enemy crossing field and moat into his enclave.

"I spent some time in the courthouse this afternoon. You've got state contracts to build hospitals," I said.

"So?"

"The contracts are already let. You're going to be a rich man. Eventually Buford's going to take a fall. Why go down with him?"

"Good try, no cigar."

"Tell me, Dock, you think he'll have Crown popped if I set up Crown's surrender?"

"Who gives a shit?"

"A grand jury."

He brushed at his nose with one knuckle, huffed air out a nostril, flicked his eyes off my face to the women in the pool, then looked at nothing, all with the same degree of thought or its absence.

"You're dumb," he said.

"I see."

"You're worried about a worthless geezer and nigger-trouble that's thirty years old. LaRose'll put a two-by-four up your ass."

"How?"

"He wants company."

"Sorry, Dock, I don't follow your drift."

His thick palm squeezed dryly on the hoe handle.

"Why don't people want to step on graves? Because they care about the stiffs that's down there? If he gets his hand on your ankle, he'll pull you in the box with him," he said.

My lips, the skin around my mouth, moved wordlessly in the wind.

BOOTSIE AND I DID the dishes together after supper. It had stopped raining, and the sky outside was a translucent blue and ribbed with purple and red clouds.

"You're going to set it up?" she asked.

"Yes."

"Why?"

"I want to cut the umbilical cord."

"What's the sheriff say?"

"'Do it.'"

"What's the problem, then?"

"I don't trust Buford LaRose."

"Oh, Dave," she said, her breath exhaling, her eyes closing then opening. She put her hands on my arms and lay her forehead awkwardly on my shoulder, her body not quite touching mine, like someone who fears her embrace will violate propriety.

IN THE MORNING I called Sabelle Crown and told her of Buford's offer. Two hours later the phone on my desk rang.

"I can be out in two or three years?" the voice said.

"Aaron?"

"Is that the deal?" he asked.

"I'm not involved. Use an attorney."

"It's lawyers sold my ass down the river."

"Don't call here again. Understand? I've got nothing more to do with your life."

"You goddamn better hope you don't," he said, and hung up.

THE REST OF the workweek passed, and I heard nothing more about Aaron Crown. Friday had been a beautiful December day, and the evening was just as fair. The wind was off the Gulf, and you could smell salt and distant rain and night-blooming flowers and ozone in the trees, and you had to remind yourself it was winter and not spring. Bootsie and I decided to go Christmas shopping in Lafayette, and I asked Batist to close the bait shop and stay up at the house with Alafair until we returned.

It wasn't even necessary. She was playing at the neighbor's house next door. When we drove away, Batist was standing in our front yard, his overalls straps notched into his T-shirt, the smooth, saddle-gold texture of his palm raised to say good-bye.

Chapter
28

THE MAN IN the floppy hat and black rubber big-button raincoat
came at sunset, from a great distance, where at first he was just a
speck on the horizon, walking across my neighbor's burned sugarcane
acreage, ash powdering around his boots, the treeline etched with
fire behind him. He could have been a fieldhand looking for a calf
stuck in the coulee, a tenant farmer shortcutting home from his rental
acreage, or perhaps a hobo who had swung down from an S.P. freight,
except for the purpose in his gait, the set of his jaw, the switch in his
gloved hand that he whipped against his leg. When clouds covered
the sun and lightning struck in the field, the man in the raincoat never
broke stride. My neighbor's cows swirled like water out of his path.

Batist had been watching television in the living room. He went
back into the kitchen to refill his coffee cup, burned his lips with the
first sip, then poured it into the saucer and blew on it while he looked
out the kitchen window at the ash lifting in the fields, the rain slanting like glass across the sun's last spark in the west.

The window was open and he heard horses running on the sod and
cattle lowing in the coulee, and only when he squinted his eyes did he
see the hatted and coated shape of the man who whipped the switch
methodically against his leg.

Batist rubbed his eyes, went back into the living room for his glasses,
returned to the window, and saw a milky cloud of rain and dust rising

out of the field and no hatted man in a black coat but a solitary Angus heifer standing in our yard.

Batist stepped out into the yard, into the sulfurous smell blowing out of the fields, then walked to the duck pond and down the fence line until he saw the fence post that had been wedged sideways in the hole and the three strands of barbed wire that had been stomped out of the staples into the ground.

"Somebody out here?" he called.

The wind was like a watery insect in his ears.

He latched the screen door behind him, walked to the front of the house and stepped out on the gallery, looked into the yard and the leaves spinning in vortexes between the tree trunks, the shadows of overhead limbs thrashing on the ground. Down by the bayou, one of our rental boats clanked against its chain, thumping against the pilings on the dock.

He thought about his dogleg twenty gauge down in the bait shop. The bait shop looked small and distant and empty in the rain, and he wished he had turned on the string of electric lights over the dock, then felt foolish and embarrassed at his own thoughts.

He stood in the center of the living room, the wind seeming to breathe through the front and back screens, filling the house with a cool dampness that he couldn't distinguish from the sheen of sweat on his skin.

He pulled aside a curtain and looked across the driveway at the neighbor's house. The gallery was lighted and a green wreath and pinecones wrapped with scarlet ribbon hung on the front door; a Christmas tree, a blue spruce shimmering with tinsel, stood in a window. A sprinkler fanned back and forth in the rain, fountaining off the tree trunks in the yard.

He picked up the phone and started to dial a number, then realized he wasn't even certain about whom he was dialing. He set the receiver back in the cradle, ashamed of the feeling in his chest, the way his hands felt stiff and useless at his sides.

He wiped his face on his sleeve, smelled a sour odor rising from his armpit, then stood hesitantly at the front door again. In his mind's eye he saw himself walking down to the bait shop and returning up the slope with a shotgun like a man who finally concedes that his fears have always been larger than his courage. He unlatched the screen and pushed it open with the flat of his hand and breathed the coolness of the mist blowing under the gallery eaves, then stepped back inside and blew out his breath.

Batist never heard the intruder in the black rubber raincoat, not until he cinched his arm under Batist's throat and squeezed as though he were about to burst a walnut. He wrenched Batist's head back into his own, drawing Batist's body into his loins, a belt buckle that was as hard-edged as a stove grate, impaling him against his chest, his unshaved jaw biting like emery paper into the back of Batist's neck.

The intruder's floppy hat fell to the floor. He seemed to pause and look at it, as he would at a distraction from the linear and familiar course of things and the foregone conclusion that had already been decided for him and his victim.

From the corner of his eye Batist saw a gold-tipped canine tooth that the intruder licked with the bottom of his tongue. Then the arm snapped tight under Batist's chin again, and through the front screen Batist saw the world as a place where trees torn from their roots floated upside down in the rain.

"I'm fixing to pinch off your pipe for good, old man. That mean you don't get no more air. You'll just gurgle on the floor like a dog been run over across the t'roat . . . Where Robicheaux at?" the intruder said.

WHEN BATIST WOKE up, he was on his side, in the middle of the living room floor, his knees drawn up before him. The house was quiet, and he could see rain blowing through the screen, wetting the cypress planks in the floor, and he thought the hatted man in the rubber coat was gone.

Then he felt the intruder's gloved hand close on the bottom of his chin and tilt his face toward him, as though the intruder were arranging the anatomical parts on a store dummy.

"You went to sleep on me, old man. That's 'cause I shut off the big vein that goes up to your brain," the intruder said. He was squatted on his haunches, sipping from a half-pint bottle of apricot brandy. His eyes were turquoise, the scalp above his ears shaved bare, the color of putty.

"You best get out of here, nigger, while you still can," Batist said.

The intruder drank from the bottle, let the brandy roll on his tongue, settle in his teeth, as though he were trying to kill an abscess in his gum.

Batist raised himself into a sitting position, waiting for the intruder to react. But he didn't. He sipped again from the brandy, nestled one buttock more comfortably against the heel of his boot. His shirt and the top of his coat were unbuttoned, and a necklace of blue shark's teeth was tattooed across his collarbones and around his upper chest. Cupped in his right hand was a banana knife, hooked at the tip, the edge filed into a long silver thread.

"Fishing any good here?" he asked.

He reached out with one finger and touched Batist on the end of his nose, then tilted the brandy again, his eyes closing with the pleasure the liquor gave him.

Batist drove the bottle into the intruder's mouth with the flat of his hand, shattering the glass against the teeth, bursting the lips into a torn purple flower.

The intruder's face stiffened with shock, glistened with droplets of brandy and saliva and blood. But instead of reeling from the room in pain and rage, he rose to his feet and his right foot exploded against the side of Batist's head. He cleaned bits of glass out of his mouth with his fingers, spitting, as though there were peanut brittle on his tongue, his gashed lips finally re-forming into a smile.

He bent over, the hooked point of the banana knife an inch from Batist's eye. He started to speak, then paused, pressed his mouth against his palm, looked at it, and wiped his hand on his raincoat.

"Now you made me work for free. You ain't got nowhere to go for a while, do you?" he said, and thumbed the buttons loose on his coat.

Chapter
29

Forty miles away, in the Atchafalaya Basin, the same night the intruder came to my house, Aaron Crown threaded an outboard through a nest of canals until he reached a shallow inlet off the river, where a steel-bottomed oyster boat lay half-sunk in the silt. The decks and hull were the color of a scab, the cabin eaten to the density of aged cork by termites and worms. The entrance to the inlet was narrow, the willows on each side as thick as hedges, the river beyond it running hard and fast and yellow with foam.

He sat on a wood stool inside the cabin, his skin slathered with mud, the stolen Enfield rifle propped between his legs, his eyes fixed on the river, which they would have to cross. The light was perfect. He could see far into the distance, like a creature staring out of a cave, but they in turn could not see him. He had told them no helicopters, not even for the news people. If he heard helicopters, he would be gone deep into the canopy of the swamp before anyone could reach the entrance to the inlet.

The state police administrator had said it was all a simple matter. Aaron only had to wade into the sunlight, his rifle over his head. No one would harm him. Television cameras would record the moment, and that night millions of people would be forced to acknowledge the struggle of one man against an entire state.

He remembered his original arrest for the murder of the NAACP leader and the national attention it brought him. How many men were allowed to step into history twice?

The state policeman had confirmed the arrangement, two or three years in a federal old folks facility, no heavy work, no lockdown, good food, a miniature golf course, a television and card room, long-distance access to news reporters whenever he wanted.

But what if it went down wrong tonight? Even that could be an acceptable trade-off. Buford LaRose would be out there somewhere. Aaron squeezed the stock of the Enfield a little tighter in his palms, the dried mud on his palms scraping softly on the wood, his loins stirring at the thought.

He opened a can of potted meat and dipped a saltine cracker into it and chewed the cracker and meat slowly and then drank from a hot can of Coca-Cola. When the potted meat was almost gone, he split a cracker in half and furrowed out the meat from the seams at the bottom of the can, not missing a morsel, and lay the cracker on his tongue and drank the last of his Coca-Cola. He started to roll a cigarette, then saw a curtain of rain moving across the river's surface toward him, and inside the rain he saw three large powerboats with canvas tarps behind the cabins and the faces of uniformed men behind the water-beaded windows.

But where was the boat with the news people on it?

He rose to his feet and let the tobacco roll off his cupped cigarette paper and stick to his pants legs and prison work boots. The wind was blowing harder now, whipping the willow and cypress trees, capping the river's surface. The uniformed men in the boats hadn't seen him yet and had cut back their throttles and were drifting in the chop, the canvas tarps flapping atop the decks.

South of the squall, the sky was filled with purple and yellow clouds, like smoke ballooning out of an industrial fire. He squinted into the rain to see more clearly. What were they doing? The state police administrator, what was his name, Tauzin, should have been out on the deck with a bullhorn, to tell him what to do, to take control, to make sure the news people filmed Aaron wading out of the swamp, his rifle held high above his head, a defiant hill-country man whose surrender had been personally negotiated by the governor of the state.

Something was wrong. One, two, three, then a total of four men had come out the cabin doors onto the decks of their boats, cautious not to expose themselves, the bills of their caps turned backward on their heads.

It couldn't be what he thought. The offer had come through a man he trusted in the Iberia Parish Sheriff's Department. The state policeman had given his word, also. And where was that damn Buford LaRose? Aaron knew Buford would never miss an opportunity like this one, to stand before the cameras, with a wetlands background, his aristocratic face softened by the lights of humanity and conscience.

Then a terrible thought appeared in a bright, clear space in the center of his mind with such vividness that his face burned once again with a memory that was sixty years out of his past, a little boy in rent overalls being shoved into a school yard puddle by a boy whose father owned the cotton gin, the words hurled down at him, *Aaron, you're dumber than a nigger trying to hide in a snowbank.* It was the old recognition that his best efforts always turned out the same: he was the natural-born victim of his betters. In this case the simple fact was that Buford LaRose had already been elected. He didn't have to prove anything to anybody. Aaron Crown was nothing more than a minor nuisance of whom the world had finally tired and was about to dispose of as you would an insect with a Flit can.

Aaron saw this thought as clearly as he saw the face of the man with the inverted cap working his way forward on the lead boat, between the gunnel and cabin. They were like two bookends facing each other now. But Aaron refused to wince or cower, to let them see the fear that made his bowels turn to water. *You'd like to do it, yessiree Bob, blow hair and bone all over the trees, but you're one of them kind won't drop his britches and take a country squat till somebody tells you it's all right.* Aaron's hand crushed the aluminum soda can in his palm, the bottom glinting like a heliograph.

He was wrong.

The muzzle of the M-16 rifle flashed in the rain just as the boat's bow rose in the chop, and the .223 round thropped past Aaron's ear, punching a neat hole in the wall behind him, its trajectory fading deep in the swamp. A second later the other uniformed men cut loose in unison, firing tear gas and M-16's on full automatic and twelve-gauge pump Remingtons loaded with double-ought buckshot.

But Aaron was running now, and not where they thought he would. While gas shells hissed on the deck and buckshot and .223 rounds perforated the oyster boat's cabin, crisscrossing the gloomy interior with tubular rays of light, he slid down the ladder inside the ship's steel hull, his rifle inverted on its sling, then exited the boat through the far side, where the plates had been stripped from a spar by a salvager. As he ran through a chain of sandbars and stagnant pools of water, he could hear the steady dissection of the cabin, glass breaking, bullets whanging off metal surfaces, shattered boards spinning out into the trees like sticks blown from a forest fire.

He glanced once over his shoulder after he kicked over the outboard. *Fire.* He hadn't imagined it. Their magazines had been loaded with tracers, and the oyster boat's cabin was liquid with flames.

Inside the caked patina of mud on Aaron's face, his eyes were as pink as Mercurochrome, filmed with the reflected glow of what he knew now had been the final demonstrable evidence of the lifetime conspiracy directed at him and his family. Somehow that gave him a satisfaction and feeling of confirmation that was like being submerged and bathed in warm water. He bit down on his molars with an almost sexual pleasure but could not tell himself why.

Late that same night, a voice with a peckerwood accent that did not identify itself left a message on my recording machine: "Buford got to you. I don't know how. But I'd just as lief cut the equipment off two shithogs as one."

Chapter
30

THE ACCOUNT OF Aaron Crown's escape from the state police is my
re-creation of the story as it was related to me by a St. Martin Parish
deputy in the waiting room down the hall from Batist's room at Iberia
General. Clete Purcel and I watched the deputy get into the elevator
and look back at us blank-faced while the doors closed behind him.

"What are you thinking?" Clete asked.

"It's no accident Mookie Zerrang came to my house the same night
Crown was set up for a whack."

Clete leaned forward in his chair and rubbed one hand on the
other, picked at a callus, his green eyes filled with thought. He had
driven from New Orleans in two and a half hours, steam rising from
the hood of his Cadillac like vapor off dry ice when he pulled under
the electric arc lamps in the hospital parking lot.

"Zerrang's got to go off-planet, Streak," he said.

"He will."

"It won't happen. Not unless you or I do it. This guy's juice is
heavy-voltage, mon."

I didn't answer.

"You know I'm right. When they deal it down and dirty, we take it
back to them under a black flag," he said.

"Wrong discussion, wrong place."

"There's a geek in Jefferson Parish. A real sicko. Even the wiseguys cross the street when they see him coming. But he owes five large to Nig. I can square the debt. Mookie Zerrang will be walking on stumps . . . Are you listening?"

I went to the cold drink machine, then put my change back in my pocket and kept on walking to the nurses' station.

"I have to talk to my friend," I said.

"Sorry, not until the doctor comes back," the nurse said. She smiled and did not mean to be impolite.

"I apologize, then," I said, and went past her and into Batist's room.

He was turned on his side, facing the opposite wall, his back layered with bandages. The intruder had used a type of ASP, a steel bludgeon, sold in police supply stores, that telescopes out of a handle. The one used by the intruder was modified with an extension that operated like a spring or whip, with a steel ball the size of a small marble attached to the tip. The paramedics had to cut away Batist's overalls and T-shirt with scissors and peel the cloth off his skin like cobweb.

His head jerked on the pillow when he heard me behind him.

"It's okay, partner," I said, and walked around the foot of the bed.

His right eye was swollen shut, his nose broken and X-ed with tape.

"I ain't felt a lot of it, Dave. He hit me upside the head first, 'cause I raised up and caught him another one in the mout'," he said.

I sat down on a chair by his bedside.

"I promise we'll get this guy," I said.

"It ain't your fault, no."

"I helped set up Aaron Crown, Batist. I didn't know it, but I was giving somebody permission to wipe me off the slate, too."

"Who been doing all this, Dave? What we done to them?"

"They're right up there on the Teche. Buford and Karyn LaRose."

His left eye closed and opened as though he were on the edge of sleep or looking at a thought inside his mind.

"It ain't their way," he said.

"Why?"

"Their kind don't never see bad t'ings, Dave. Any black folk on a plantation tell you that. The white folk up in the big house don't ever want to know what happen out in the field or down in the quarters. They got people to take care of that for them."

The nurse and the doctor came through the door and looked at us silently.

"You going to be all right for a while?" I said.

"Sure. They been treating me good," Batist said.

"I'm sorry for this," I said.

He moved his fingers slightly on the sheet and patted the top of my hand as my father might have done.

CLETE FOLLOWED ME home and went to sleep in our guest room. I lay in the dark next to Bootsie, with my arm over my eyes, and heard rainwater ticking out of the trees into the beds of leaves that tapered away from the tree trunks. I tried to organize my thoughts, then gave it up and fell asleep when the stars were still out. I didn't wake until after sunrise. The room, the morning itself, seemed empty and stark, devoid of memory, as it used to be when I'd wake from alcoholic blackouts. Then the events of the previous night came back like a slap.

Batist's first reaction when he had seen me in the hospital had been to prevent me from worrying about his pain. He'd had no thought of himself, no desire for revenge, no sense of recrimination toward me or the circumstances that placed him in the path of a sadist like Mookie Zerrang.

I spent ten months in Vietnam and never saw a deliberate atrocity, at least not one committed by Americans. Maybe that was because most of my tour was over before the war really warmed up. I saw a ville after the local chieftain had called in the 105's on his own people, and I saw some Kit Carsons bind the wrists of captured Viet Cong and wrap towels around their faces and pour water onto the cloth a canteen at a time until they were willing to trade their own families for a teaspoon of air. Someone always had an explanation for these moments, one that allowed you to push the images out of your mind temporarily. It was the unnecessary cruelty, the kind that was not even recognized as such, that hung in the mind like an unhealed lesion.

A mental picture postcard that I could never find a proper postage stamp for: The mamasan is probably over seventy. Her dugs are withered, her skin as shriveled as a dried apple's. She and her granddaughter clean hooches for a bunch of marines, wash their clothes, burn the shit barrels at the latrine. Two enlisted men fashion a sign from cardboard and hang it around her neck and pose sweaty and barechested with her while a third marine snaps their photo with a Polaroid camera. The sign says MISS NORTH DAKOTA. If the mamasan comprehends the nature of the insult, it does not show in the cracked parchment of her face. The marines are grinning broadly in the photo.

Voltaire wrote about the cruelty he saw in his neighbor who was the torturer at the Bastille. He described the impulse as insatiable, possessing all the characteristics of both lust and addiction to a drug. Had he not been hired by the state, the neighbor would have paid to continue his tasks in those stone rooms beneath the streets of Paris.

Mookie Zerrang was not simply a hit man on somebody's payroll. He was one of those who operated on the edges of the human family, waiting for the halt and the lame or those who had no voice, his eyes smiling with anticipation when he knew his moment was at hand.

I couldn't swallow my food at breakfast. I went into the living room and finished cleaning the spot on the floor where we had found Batist. I stuffed the throw rug he had lain on and the paper towels I had used to scrub the cypress planks into a vinyl garbage bag.

"I'm going down to the bait shop," I said to Bootsie.

"Close it up for today," she replied.

"It's Saturday. There might be a few customers by."

"No, you want to make a private phone call. Do it here. I'll leave," she said.

"We didn't get much sleep, Boots. It's not a day to hurt each other."

"Tell it to yourself."

There was nothing for it. I unlocked the bait shop and dialed Buford LaRose's home number.

"Hello?" Karyn said.

"Where's Buford?"

"In the shower."

"Put him on the phone."

"Leave him alone, Dave. Go away from us."

"Maybe I should catch him another time. Would the inauguration ball be okay?"

"It's by invitation. You won't be attending . . ." She paused, as though she were enjoying a sliver of ice on her tongue. "By the way, since you're a conservationist, you'll enjoy this. I talked to someone about the swamp area around your bait shop being turned into a wilderness preserve. Of course, that will mean commercial property like yours will be acquired by the state or federal government. Oh, Buford's toweling off now. Have a nice day, Dave."

She set the phone down on a table and called out in a lilting voice, "Guess who?"

I heard Buford scrape the receiver up in his hand.

"Don't tell me," he said.

"Shut up, Buford—"

"No, this time you shut up, Dave. Aaron Crown didn't do what he was told. He was supposed to throw his rifle in the water. Instead, he flashed a soda can or something in a window and a trooper started shooting. I tried to stop it."

"You were there?"

"Yes, of course."

"I think you're lying," I said. But his explanation was disarming.

"It's what happened. Check it out."

"The black man who works for me was almost beaten to death last night."

"I'm sorry. But what does that have to do with me?"

I felt my anger and confidence wane. I rubbed at one eye with the heel of my hand and saw concentric circles of red light receding into my brain. My hands felt cold and thick and I could smell my own odor. I started to speak but the words wouldn't come.

"Dave, are you okay?" he said. His voice was odd, marked with sympathy.

I hung up and sat at the counter and rested my forearms on the counter, my head bent forward, and felt a wave of exhaustion and a sense of personal impotence wash through me like the first stages of amoebic dysentery. Through the window I heard Bootsie's car back into the road, then I saw her and Alafair drive away through the long corridor of oaks toward town. A small metallic mirror hung on a post behind the counter. The miniature face of the man reflected inside it did not look like someone I knew.

Chapter
31

CLETE AND I WENT back to Iberia General to visit Batist, then drove to Red Lerille's Gym in Lafayette. Clete ordered a baked potato smothered with cheese and sour cream and bacon strips and green onions at the cafe outside the weight room and ate it at a table by the glass wall and watched me while I worked out for a half hour on the machines. Then he put on a pair of trunks and swam outside in the heated pool and later met me in the steam room.

"How you feel?" he said.

"All right. It's just a touch of the mosquito."

A man sitting next to us folded the newspaper he was reading and laid it on the tile stoop and went out. Clete waited until the man closed the door behind him.

"You're beating up on yourself unfairly, big mon," he said.

"People are dead. No one's in custody. A man like Batist is attacked by a degenerate. Tell me what I've done right."

"You listen to me," he said, and raised his finger in my face. The skin of his massive shoulders and chest looked boiled and red in the steam. "You're a police officer. You can't ignore what you see happening around you. If you fuck up, that's the breaks. In a firefight you stomp ass and take names and let somebody else add up the arithmetic. Get off your own case."

"One day we're going to get your shield back," I said.

He cupped his hand around the back of my neck. I could feel the moisture and grease ooze out from under his palm and fingers. "If I had to play by the rules, I couldn't cover my old podjo's back," he said.

His smile was as gentle as a girl's.

I DROPPED HIM OFF at a motel by the four-lane in New Iberia and drove home alone. I waved at the deputy parked in a cruiser by the bait shop and turned into our dirt driveway and cut the engine and listened to it cool and tick while I looked at Bootsie's car and the doves that rose out of my neighbor's field against the late sun and then at Bootsie's face in the middle of a windy swirl of curtains at a window in the rear of the house before she turned away as though I were not there.

I started toward the back door, forming words in my mind to address problems I couldn't even define, then stopped, the way you do when thinking doesn't work anymore, and walked down the slope to the bait shop, into the green, gaslike odor of the evening, the pecan husks breaking under my shoes, as though I could walk beyond the box of space and time and loveless tension that my father's hand-hewn cypress house had become.

The string of electric lights was turned on over the dock and I could hear music through the screens.

"What are you doing, Alf?" I said.

"I got the key to the jukebox out of the cash register. Is that all right?"

"Yeah, that's fine."

She had wheeled Jerry Joe Plumb's jukebox away from the wall, where I had pushed it front end first, and unlocked the door and stacked the 45 rpm records on top of a soft towel on the counter.

"I'm playing each one of them on my portable and recording them on tape. I've already recorded fifteen of them," she said. "You like all these, don't you?"

I nodded, my eyes gazing out the window at the lighted gallery of the house. "That's great, Alf," I said.

"Who's the buttwipe who cut the electric cord on the box?"

"Beg your pardon?"

"The buttwipe who sliced off the cord. What kind of person would do that?"

"How about it on the language?"

"Big deal," she said. She slid a record off her machine and replaced it with another, her face pointed downward so that her hair hid her expression.

"Why are you so angry?" I asked.

"You and Bootsie, Dave. Why don't y'all stop it?"

I sat down on a stool next to her.

"I made some mistakes," I said.

"Then unmake them. You're my father. You're supposed to fix things. Not break the jukebox 'cause you're mad at it."

I crimped my lips and tried to find the right words. If there were any, I didn't know them.

"Everything's messed up in our house. I hate it," she said, her eyes shining, then brimming with tears.

"Let's see what we can do about it, then," I said, and walked up the slope, through the trees, across the gallery and into the stillness of the house.

Bootsie was at the kitchen table, drinking a cup of coffee. She wore a pair of straw sandals and white slacks and a stonewashed denim shirt. The surfaces of her face looked as cool and shiny as alabaster.

"The job's not worth it anymore. It's time to hang it up," I said.

"Is that what you want?"

"I can always do some PI stuff with Clete if we get jammed up."

"No."

"I thought you'd approve."

"I had to go to confession this afternoon," she said.

"What for?"

"I went to see Batist at the hospital. When I left I wanted to kill the man who did that to him. I wanted to see something even worse happen to Karyn and Buford. I told Father Pitre my feelings proba-bly won't go away, either. He said it was all right, it's natural to feel what I do . . . But it's not going to be all right, not until those people are punished. Nobody can be allowed to get away with what they've done."

Her neck bloomed with color. I stood behind her chair and put my hands on her shoulders and kneaded my thumbs on her spine, then leaned over and pressed my cheek against her hair. I felt her reach up over my head and touch the back of my neck, arching her head against mine, rubbing her hair against my skin. Then she rose from her chair and pressed herself against me, no holding back now, her breasts and flat stomach and thighs tight against me, her mouth like a cold burn on my throat.

Through the screen I could hear Alafair playing "La Jolie Blon" on her record player.

NO DUH DOLOWITZ was a Jersey transplant and old-time pete man who had been dented too many times in the head with a ball peen hammer, which didn't diminish his talents as a safecracker but for some reason did develop in him a tendency for bizarre humor, finally earning him the nickname among cops of the Mob's Merry Prankster. He backed up a truck to the home of a contractor in the Poconos and filled his wet bar and basement game room to the ceiling with bituminous coal, stole a human head from the Tulane medical school and put it in a government witness's bowling ball bag, and sabotaged the family-day promotion of a floating casino by smuggling a group of black transvestites on board to do the stage show.

Also, in terms of information about the underworld, he was the human equivalent of flypaper.

Sunday morning Clete and I found him in his brother-in-law's saloon and poolroom by the Industrial Canal in New Orleans. He wore a maroon shirt, white suspenders, knife-creased gray slacks, and a biscuit-colored derby hat. His face was tan and lean, his mustache as black as grease. He sat with us at a felt-covered card table, sipping black coffee from a demitasse with a tiny silver spoon in it. The poolroom had a stamped tin ceiling, a railed bar, wood floors, and big glass windows painted with green letters that gave a green cast to the inside of the room. It was still early, and the poolroom was closed.

"Give No Duh a beer and a shot. Put it on my tab," Clete called to the bartender, then said to Dolowitz, "You're looking very copacetic, No Duh."

"Shitcan the beer and the shot," Dolowitz said. "Why the squeeze?"

"We're looking for a guy named Mookie Zerrang," I said.

"A cannibal looks like King Kong?" he said.

"He hurt a friend of mine real bad. I think he killed Short Boy Jerry, too," I said.

His brown eyes looked without expression at a point on the far wall.

"I hear you're on the outs with the Giacanos," Clete said.

Dolowitz shook his head nonchalantly, his face composed.

"You and Stevie Gee got nailed on that pawnshop job. You made bond first and creeped Stevie's house," Clete said.

"He mentioned he boosted my mother's new car?" Dolowitz said.

"You've got bad markers all over town and you're four weeks back on the vig to Wee Willie Bimstine," Clete said.

"I'd tell you 'No duh,' Purcel, but I'm not interested in defending myself or having trouble with either one of yous. You want to play some nine ball? A dollar on the three, the six, and the nine."

"Dave can get you a few bucks from his department. I can get Wee Willie off your back. How about it?" Clete said.

"Zerrang's freelance," Dolowitz said. "Look, check my jacket. I burned a safe or two and did some creative favors for a few people. Zerrang blows heads. He's a sicko, too. He likes being cruel when he don't have to be."

"Three names I want you to think about, No Duh," I said. "Jimmy Ray Dixon, Dock Green, and his wife, Persephone."

He was motionless in his chair, the names registering in his eyes in ways you couldn't read. Then the skin at the side of his mouth ticked slightly. His eyes hardened and his upper lip filmed with moisture, as though the room had suddenly become close and warm.

"Here's the rest of it," Clete said. "You come up with the gen on these guys, I'll make you righteous with Wee Willie. But you shine us off and miss another week on the vig, you better get your skinny ass back up to the Jersey Shore, find a hole, and pull it in after you."

When we left him, his confidence had drained like water out of a sink and his face was filled with the conflict of a hunted animal.

Clete and I stood on the sidewalk under the dilapidated wood colonnade that shaded the front of the poolroom. It was cool in the shade, and the sunlight looked bright and hard on the neutral ground and the palm trees.

"I can't do this, Clete," I said.

"Don't screw it up, mon."

I tapped on the door glass for the bartender to open up.

"Do what you feel comfortable with, No Duh. Nobody's going to twist you," I said.

"Go play with your worms. Blimpo out there gets off on this. I hope in the next life both yous come back a guy like me, see how you like it," he replied.

Chapter
32

Aₛ A POLICE officer you accept the fact that, in all probability, you will become the instrument that delivers irreparable harm to a variety of individuals. Granted, they design their own destinies, are intractable in their attitudes, and live with the asp at their breasts; but the fact remains that it is you who will appear at some point in their lives, like the headsman with his broad ax on the medieval scaffold, and serve up a fate to them that has the same degree of mercy as that dealt out by your historical predecessor.

An image or two: A soft-nosed .45 round that skids off a brick wall and topples before it finds its mark; a baton swung too high that crushes the windpipe; or salting the shaft on a killer of children, a guy you could never nail legitimately, a guy who asks to see you on his last night, but instead of finding peace you watch him vomit his food into a stainless steel chemical toilet and weep uncontrollably on the side of his bunk while a warden reads his death warrant and two opaque-faced screws unlock the death cage.

So the job becomes easier if you think of them in either clinical or jailhouse language that effectively separates them from the rest of us: sociopaths, pukes, colostomy bags, lowlifes, miscreants, buckets of shit, street mutts, recidivists, greaseballs, meltdowns, maggots, gorillas in the mist. Any term will do as long as it indicates that the adversary is pathologically different from yourself.

Then your own single-minded view of the human family is disturbed by a chance occurrence that leads you back into the province of the theologian.

Early Monday morning three land surveyors in a state boat set up a transit instrument on a sandspit in the flooded woods across from the bait shop and began turning angles with it, measuring the bayou frontage with a surveyor's chain, and driving flagged laths at odd intervals into the mudbank.

"You mind telling me what y'all are doing?" I said from the end of the dock.

The transit operator, in folded-down hip waders and rain hat, swiped mosquitoes out of his face and replied, "The state don't have a recent plat."

"Who cares?"

"You got a problem with it, talk to my boss in Lafayette. You think we're putting a highway through your house?"

I thought about it. "Yeah, it's a possibility," I said.

I called his supervisor, a state civil engineer, and got nowhere. Then I called the sheriff's department, told Wally I'd be in late, and drove to Lafayette.

I was on Pinhook Road, down in the old section, which was still tree lined and unmarked by strip malls, when I saw Karyn LaRose three cars ahead of me, driving a waxed yellow Celica convertible. One lane was closed and the traffic was heavy at the red light, but no one honked, no one tried to cut off another driver.

Except Karyn.

She pulled onto the shoulder, drove around a construction barrier, a cloud of dust drifting off her wheels through the windows of the other cars, and then cut back into the line just before the intersection.

She changed the angle on her rearview mirror and looked at her reflection, tilted up her chin, removed something from the corner of her mouth with her fingernail, oblivious to everyone around her. The oak limbs above her flickered with a cool gold-green light. She threw back her hair and put on her sunglasses and tapped her ring impatiently on the steering wheel, as though she were sitting reluctantly on a stage before an audience that had not quite earned her presence.

An elderly black woman, bent in the spine like a knotted turnip, with glasses as thick as quartz, was laboring down a side street with a cane, working her way toward the bus stop, waving a handkerchief frantically at the bus that had just passed, her purse jiggling from her wrist. She wore a print cotton dress and untied, scuffed brown shoes that exposed the pale, callused smoothness of her lower foot each time she took a step.

Karyn stared at her from behind her sunglasses, then turned out of the traffic and got out of her convertible and listened without speaking while the old woman gestured at the air and vented her frustration with the Lafayette bus system. Then Karyn knelt on one knee and tied the woman's shoes and held her cocked elbow while the old woman got into the passenger seat of the convertible, and a moment later the two of them drove through the caution light and down the boulevard like old friends.

I'm sure she never saw me. Nor was her act of kindness a performance for passersby, as it was already obvious she didn't care what they thought of her. I only knew it was easier for me to think of Karyn LaRose in one-dimensional terms, and endowing her with redeeming qualities was a complexity I didn't need.

Twenty minutes later the state engineer told me an environmental assessment was being made of the swamp area around my dock and bait shop.

"What's that mean?" I said.

"Lyndon Johnson didn't like some of his old neighbors and had their property turned into a park . . . That's a joke, Mr. Robicheaux . . . Sir, I'd appreciate your not looking at me like that."

HELEN SOILEAU HAPPENED to glance up from the watercooler when I came through the back door of the department from the parking lot. She straightened her back and tucked her shirt into her gunbelt with her thumbs and grinned.

"What's funny?" I said.

"I've got a great story for you about Aaron."

"He's not my idea of George Burns, Helen. Let me get my mail first."

I picked up my messages and my mail from my pigeonhole and stopped by the cold drink machine for a Dr Pepper. On the top of the stack was an envelope addressed to me in pencil, postmarked in Lafayette, with no zip code. I had no doubt who had sent it.

I sat down in a chair by the cold drink machine and opened the envelope with one finger, like peeling away a bandage on a wound. The letter was printed on a paper towel.

Dear Mr. Roboshow,

I thought you was honest but you have shit on me just like them others. Thank God I am old and have got to the end of my row and cant be hurt by yall no more. But that dont mean I will abide your pity either, no sir, it dont, I have seen the likes of yall all my life and know how you think so dont try to act like you are better than me. Also tell that prissy pissant Buford LaRose I will settel some old bidness then finish with him too.

You have permision to pass this letter on to people in the press.

Sincerely yours,
a loyal democrat who voted for John Kennedy,
Aaron Jefferson Crown

Helen was waiting for me inside my office.

"Crown went after Jimmy Ray Dixon. Can you believe it?" she said.

I looked again at the letter in my hand. "What's his beef with Jimmy Ray?"

"If Jimmy Ray knows, he's not saying. He seems to have become an instant law-and-order man, though."

She repeated the story to me as it had been told to her by NOPD. You didn't have to be imaginative to re-create the scene. The images were like those drawn from a surreal landscape, where a primitive and half-formed creature rose from a prehistoric pool of genetic soup into a world that did not wish to recognize its origins.

JIMMY RAY HAD been at his fish camp with three of his employees and their women out by Bayou Lafourche. The night was humid, the dirt yard illuminated by an electric mechanic's lamp hung in a dead pecan tree, and Jimmy Ray was on a creeper under his jacked-up truck, working with a wrench on a brake drum, yelling at a second man to get him a beer from inside the shack. When the man didn't do it fast enough, Jimmy Ray went inside to get the beer himself, and another man, bored for something to do, took his place on the creeper.

Aaron Crown had been crouched on a cypress limb by the bayou's edge, listening to the voices inside the lighted center of the yard, unable to see past a shed at who was speaking but undoubtedly sure that it was Jimmy Ray yelling orders at people from under the truck.

He released his grasp on the limb and dropped silently into the yard, dressed in a seersucker suit two sizes too small for him that he had probably taken from a washline or a Salvation Army Dumpster, and brand-new white leather basketball shoes with layers of mud as thick as waffles caked around the soles.

One of Jimmy Ray's employees was smoking a cigarette, staring at the mist rising from the swamp, perhaps yawning, when he smelled an odor from behind him, a smell that was like excrement and sour milk and smoke from a meat fire. He started to turn, then a soiled hand clamped around his mouth, the calluses as hard as dried fish scale against his lips, and he felt himself pulled against the outline of Crown's body, into each curve and contour, molded against the phallus and thighs and whipcord stomach, suspended helplessly inside the rage and sexual passion of a man he couldn't see, until the blood flow to his brain stopped as if his jugular had been pinched shut with pliers.

The man under the truck saw the mud-encrusted basketball shoes, the shapeless seersucker pants that hung on ankles scarred by leg manacles, and knew his last night on earth had begun even before Aaron began to rock the truck back and forth on the jack.

The man on the creeper almost made it completely into the open when the truck toppled sideways and fell diagonally across his thighs. After the first red-black rush of pain that arched his head back in the dirt, that seemed to seal his mouth and eyes and steal the air from his lungs, he felt himself gradually float upward from darkness to the top of a warm pool, where two powerful hands released themselves from his face and allowed light into his brain and breath into his body. Then he saw Aaron bending over him, his hands propped on his knees, staring at him curiously.

"Damn if I can ever get the right nigger or white man, either one," Aaron said.

He looked up at a sound from the shack, shadows across a window shade, a car loaded with revelers bouncing down a rutted road through the trees toward the clearing. His face was glazed with sweat, glowing in the humidity, his eyes straining into the darkness, caught between an unsatisfied bloodlust that was within his grasp and the knowledge that his inability to think clearly had always been the weapon his enemies had used against him.

Then, as silently as he had come, he slunk away in the shadows, like a thick-bodied crab moving sideways on mechanical extensions.

"How do you figure it?" Helen said.

"It doesn't make sense. What was it he said to the man under the truck?"

She read from her notepad: "'Damn if I can ever get the right nigger or white man, either one.'"

"I think Aaron has an agenda that none of us has even guessed at," I said.

"Yeah, war with the human race."

"That's not it," I answered.

"What is?"

It's the daughter, I thought.

I visited Batist in the hospital that afternoon, then picked up three pounds of frozen peeled crawfish and a carton of potato salad in town, so Bootsie would not have to cook, and drove down the dirt road toward the house. The bayou was half in shadow and the sunlight looked like gold thread in the trees. Dust drifted out on the bayou's surface and coated the wild elephant ears that grew in dark clumps in the shallows. My neighbor was stringing Christmas lights on his gallery while his rotating hose sprinkler clattered a jet of water among the myrtle bushes and tree trunks in his yard. It was the kind of perfect evening that seemed outside of time, so gentle and removed from the present that you would not be surprised if a news carrier on a bike with balloon tires threw a rolled paper onto your lawn with a headline announcing victory over Japan.

But its perfection dissipated as soon as I pulled into the drive and saw a frail priest in a black suit and Roman collar step out of his parked car and glare at me as though I had just risen from the Pit.

"Could I help you, Father?" I said.

"I want to know why you've been tormenting Mr. Dolowitz," he said. His face called to mind a knotted, red cauliflower.

I stooped down so I could see the man in the passenger seat. He kept his face straight ahead, his biscuit-colored derby hat like a bowl on his head.

"No Duh?" I said.

"I understand you're a practicing Catholic," the priest said.

"That's correct."

"Then why have you forced this man to commit a crime? He's terrified. What the hell's the matter with you?"

"There's a misunderstanding here, Father."

"Then why don't you clear things up for me, sir?"

I took his hand and shook it, even though he hadn't offered it. It was as light as balsa sticks in my palm and didn't match the choleric heat in his face. His name was Father Timothy Mulcahy, from the Irish Channel in New Orleans, and he was the pastor of a small church off Magazine whose only parishioners were those too poor or elderly to move out of the neighborhood.

"I didn't threaten this man, Father. I told him he could do what was right for himself," I said. Then I leaned down to the driver's window. "No Duh, you tell Father Mulcahy the truth or I'm going to mop up the yard with you."

"Ah, it's clear you're not a violent man," the priest said.

"No Duh, now is not the time—" I began.

"It was the other guy, that animal Purcel, Father. But Robicheaux was with him," No Duh said.

The priest cocked one eyebrow, then tilted his head, made a self-deprecating smile.

"Well, I'm sorry for my rashness," he said. "Nonetheless, Mr. Dolowitz shouldn't have been forced to break into someone's home," he said.

"Would you give us a few minutes?" I said.

He nodded and started to walk away, then touched my arm and took me partway with him.

"Be easy with him. This man's had a terrible experience," he said.

I went back to the priest's car and leaned on the window jamb. Dolowitz took off his hat and set it on his knees. His face looked small, waxlike, devoid of identity. He touched nervously at his mustache.

"What happened?" I asked.

"I creeped Dock Green's house. Somebody left the key in the lock. I stuck a piece of newspaper under the door and knocked the key out and caught it on the paper and pulled it under the door. They got me going back out. They didn't know I'd been inside. If they had, I wouldn't be alive," he said.

"Who got you?"

"Persephone Green and a button guy works for the Giacanos and some other pervert gets off hurting people." For the first time his eyes lifted into mine. They possessed a detachment that reminded me of that strange, unearthly look we used to call in Vietnam the thousand-yard stare.

"What'd they do to you, partner?"

The fingers of one hand tightened on the soft felt of his hat. "Buried me alive . . ." he said. "What, you surprised? You think only Dock's got this thing about graves and talking with dead people under the ground? Him and Persephone are two of a kind. She thought it was funny. She laughed while they put a garden hose in my mouth and covered me over with a front-end loader. It was just like being locked in black concrete, with no sound, with just a little string of dirty air going into my throat. They didn't dig me up till this morning. I went to the bathroom inside my clothes."

"I'm sorry, No Duh. But I didn't tell you to creep Dock's house."

"My other choice is I miss the vig again with Wee Willie Bimstine and get fed into an airplane propeller? Thanks for your charitable attitudes."

"I've got a room behind the bait shop. You can stay here till we square you with Wee Willie."

"You'd do that?"

"Sure."

"It's full of snakes out here. You want the gen on Dock? Persephone eighty-sixed him after she caught him porking his broads."

"That's old news, No Duh."

"I got in his desk. It's full of building plans for hospitals. Treatment places for drunks and addicts. There was canceled checks from Jimmy Ray Dixon. Go figure."

"Figure what?"

"Dock supplies broads for every gash-hound in the mob. That's the only reason they let a crazy person like him come around. But he don't cut no deal he don't piece off to the spaghetti heads. When'd the mob start working with coloreds? You think it's a mystery how the city got splashed in the bowl?"

"Who set up Jerry Joe Plumb, No Duh?"

"*He* did."

"Jerry Joe set himself up?"

"He was always talking about you, how your mothers use to work together, how he use to listen to all your phonograph records over at your house. At the same time he was wheeling and dealing with the Giacanos, washing money for them, pretending he could walk on both sides of the line . . . You don't get it, do you? You know what will get you killed in New Orleans? When they look in your eyes and know you ain't like them, when they know you ain't willing to do things most people won't even think about. That's when they'll cut you from your package to your throat and eat a sandwich while they're doing it."

I took my grocery sack of frozen crawfish and potato salad out of the truck and glanced at the priest, who stood at the end of my dock, watching a flight of ducks winnow across the tops of the cypress trees. His hair was snow white, his face windburned in the fading light. I wondered if his dreams were troubled by the confessional tales that men like Dolowitz brought from the dark province in which they lived, or if sleep came to him only after he granted himself absolution, too, and rinsed their sins from his memory, undoing the treachery that had made him the repository of their evil.

I walked up the drive, through the deepening shadows, into the back door of my house.

Chapter
33

A<small>T SUNRISE</small> C<small>LETE</small> Purcel and I sat in my truck on the side street next to Persephone and Dock Green's home in the Garden District. The morning was cold, and clouds of mist almost completely blanketed the two-story antebellum house and the white brick wall that surrounded the backyard. Clete ate from a box of jelly-filled doughnuts and drank out of a large Styrofoam cup of coffee.

"I can't believe I got up this early just to pull No Duh's butt out of the fire," he said. When I didn't reply, he said, "If you think you're going to jam up Persephone Green, you're wrong. Didi Gee was her old man, and she's twice as smart as he was and just as ruthless."

"She'll go down just like he did."

"The Big C killed Didi. We never touched him."

"It doesn't matter how you get to the boneyard."

"What, we got an exemption?" he said, then got out of the truck and strolled across the street to the garden wall. The palms that extended above the bricks were dark green inside the mist. I heard a loud splash, then saw Clete lean down and squint through the thick grillwork on the gate. He walked back to the truck, picked up another doughnut and his coffee off the floor, and sat down in the seat. He shook an image out of his thoughts.

"What is it?" I said.

"It's forty-five degrees and she's swimming in the nude. She's got quite a stroke . . ." He drank out of his coffee cup and looked at the iron gate in the wall. He pursed his mouth, obviously not yet free from an image that hovered behind his eyes. "Damn, I'm not kidding you, Streak, you ought to see the gagongas on that broad."

"Look out front," I said.

A gray stretch limo with a rental U-Haul truck behind it pulled to the curb. Dock Green got out of the back of the limo and strode up the front walk.

"Show time," Clete said. He removed my Japanese field glasses from the glove box and focused them on the limo's chauffeur, who was wiping the water off the front windows. "Hey, it's Whitey Zeroski," Clete said. "Remember, the wet-brain used to own a little pizza joint in the Channel? He ran for city council and put megaphones and VOTE FOR WHITEY signs all over his car and drove into colored town on Saturday night. He couldn't figure out why he got all his windows broken."

A moment later we heard Dock and Persephone Green's voices on the other side of the garden wall.

"It don't have to shake out like this," he said.

"You milked through the fence too many times, hon. I hope they were worth it," she replied.

"It's over. You got my word . . . Come out of the water and talk. We can go have breakfast somewhere."

"Bye, Dock."

"We're a team, Seph. Ain't nothing going to separate us. Believe it when I say it."

"I hate to tell you this but you're a disappearing memory. I've got to practice my backstroke now . . . Keep your eyes somewhere else, Dock . . . You don't own the geography anymore."

We heard her body weight push off from the side of the pool and her arms dipping rhythmically into the water.

"Let's 'front both of them," Clete said, and started to get out of the truck.

"No, that'll just get No Duh into it deeper."

"Where's your head, Dave? That guy wouldn't piss on you if you were on fire. The object is to flush Mookie Zerrang out in the open and then take him off at the neck."

"We have to wait, Cletus."

I saw the frustration and anger in his face. I put my hand on his shoulder. It was as hard as a cured ham. When he didn't speak, I took my hand away.

"I appreciate your coming with me," I said.

"Oh hell yeah, this is great stuff. You know why I was a New Orleans cop? Because we could break all the rules and get away with it. This town's problems aren't going to end until we run all these fuckers back under the sewer grates where they belong."

"I think Persephone got to you, partner," I said.

"You're right. I should have been a criminal. It's a simpler life."

For a half hour Dock and two workmen carried out his office furniture, his computer, his files, and a huge glass bottle, the kind mounted on watercoolers, filled with an amber-tinted liquid and the embalmed body of a bobcat. The bobcat's paws were pressed against the glass, as though it were drowning.

Then the three of them drove away without the limo. Clete and I got out of the truck and walked to the gate. Through the grillwork and the banana fronds I could see steam rising off the turquoise surface of the pool and hear her feet kicking steadily with her long stroke.

"It's Dave Robicheaux. How about opening up, Persephone?" I said.

"Dream on," she replied from inside the steam.

"You stole a test for Karyn LaRose and got expelled from college. Why let her take you down again?"

"Excuse me?"

"Try this as a fantasy, Seph. You and all your friends are on an airliner with Karyn and Buford LaRose. Karyn and Buford are at the controls. The plane is on fire. There are only two parachutes on board . . . Who's going to end up with the parachutes?"

I could hear her treading water in the stillness, then rising from the pool at the far end.

She appeared at the gate in a white robe and sandals, a towel wrapped around her hair. She unlocked the gate and pulled it back on its hinges, then turned and walked to an iron table without speaking, the long, tapered lines of her body molded against the cloth of her robe.

She combed her hair back with her towel, her face regal, at an angle to us, seemingly indifferent to our presence.

"What's on your mind?" she said. Her voice was throaty, her cheeks pale and slightly sunken, her mouth the same shade as the red morning glories that cascaded down the wall behind her.

Clete kept staring at her.

"Has he been fed?" she asked.

"You got to pardon me. I was thinking you look like Cher, the movie actress. You even have a tattoo," he said.

"My, you have busy eyes," she said.

"Yeah, I was noticing, the hole over there by the compost pile. Is that where y'all buried No Duh Dolowitz?" he said.

"The little man with the grease mustache? That's what this is about?" she asked.

"He shouldn't have come here, Persephone. He thought he was doing something for me. It was a mistake," I said.

"I see. I'm going to have him hurt?"

"You're a tough lady," I said.

"I have no interest in your friends, *Dave*. You don't mind if I call you 'Dave,' do you, since you call me by my first name without asking?"

"Mookie Zerrang is a bad button man, Seph. He doesn't do it for money. That means you've got no dials on him."

"Did you ever have this kind of conversation with my father, or do you speak down to me just because I'm a woman?"

"In honesty, I guess I did."

"What Streak means is, he beat the shit out of Didi Gee with a canvas money bag filled with lug nuts. He did this because your old man had his half-brother shot. You might say y'all have a tight family history," Clete said.

Clete's mouth was hooked downward at the corners, his face heated, the scar tissue through his eyebrow and across his nose flexed tight against the skull. She tried to meet his gaze, then looked away at the tongues of vapor rising from her swimming pool.

"What was that about?" I asked him in the truck.

"I told you, I'm tired of being patient with lowlifes. You know what our finest hour was? The day we popped that drug dealer and his bodyguard in the back of their Caddy. The seats looked like somebody had thrown a cow through a tree shredder. Admit it, it was a grand afternoon."

"Bad way to think, Cletus."

"One day you're going to figure out you're no different from me, Dave."

"Yeah?"

"Then you're going to shoot yourself."

He tried to hold the seriousness in his face, but I saw his eyes start to smile.

"You'll never change, Streak," he said, his expression full of play again.

I turned the ignition, then looked through the front window and saw Whitey Zeroski, the limo driver, walking toward us. He wore a gray chauffeur's uniform, with brass buttons and a gray cap that sat low, military style, over his white eyebrows.

"What are you guys doing here?" he said through my window, his eyes focusing on the doughnut Clete was about to put in his mouth.

"You want a doughnut, Whitey?" Clete said.

"I don't mind . . . Thanks, Purcel . . . I'm stuck here . . . Dock says I should hang around in case his wife wants to meet him up at Copeland's for breakfast."

"Dock better do a reality check," Clete said.

"That fight, you mean? It goes on all the time. Dock might give up lots of things, but his wife ain't gonna be one of them."

"Oh yeah?" Clete said.

"Dock's nuts, but he ain't so nuts he forgot his wife's got the brains in the family."

"It's the stuff of great love affairs," Clete said.

"Who built the big casino downtown?" Whitey said. "Mobbed-up guys with real smarts from Chicago and Vegas, right? Where do they build it? Between Louis Armstrong Park and the Iberville welfare project, the two most dangerous areas in downtown New Orleans. If you win at the table, you just walk outside and hand your money over to the muggers. How's that for fucking smarts? You think the lesson is lost on the local schmucks?"

Clete and I looked at each other.

TWENTY MINUTES LATER we were on I-10, speeding past Lake Pontchartrain. Fog puffed out of the trees on the north shore of the lake, and the rain was falling on the lake's surface inside the fog.

"She's the funnel for the wiseguys and Jimmy Ray Dixon into LaRose's administration, isn't she?" Clete said.

"That's the way I'd read it."

"I don't think I'm going to survive having a wet-brain like Whitey Zeroski explain that to me," he said.

EARLY THE NEXT morning I went to Sabelle Crown's bar at the Underpass in Lafayette. The black bartender told me I'd find her at the city golf course on the northside.

"The golf course?" I said.

"That's where she go when she want to be alone," he said.

He was right. I found her sitting on a bench under a solitary oak tree by the first fairway, a scarf tied around her head, flipping bread crusts from a bag at the pigeons. The sky was gray, and leaves were blowing out of the trees in the distance.

"Your old man tried to drop a car frame on top of Jimmy Ray Dixon," I said.

"The things you learn," she said.

"Who got you started in the life, Sabelle?"

"You know, I have a total blackout about all that stuff."

"You left New Iberia for New Orleans, then disappeared up north."

"This is kind of a private place for me, Dave. Buford LaRose tried to have Daddy killed out on the Atchafalaya River. Haven't you done enough?"

"Were you in Chicago?" I asked.

She brushed the bread crumbs off her hands and walked to her parked automobile, the back of her scarf lifting in the wind.

AFTER I RETURNED TO the office, I got a telephone call from the sheriff.

"I'm in Vermilion Parish. Drop what you're doing and come over for a history lesson," he said.

"What's up?"

"You said this character Mookie Zerrang was a leg breaker on the Mississippi coast and a button man in Miami?"

"That's the word."

"Think closer to home."

I signed out of the office and met the sheriff on a dirt road that fed into a steel-and-wood bridge over the Vermilion River ten miles south of Lafayette. He was leaning against his cruiser, eating from a roll of red boudin wrapped in wax paper. The sky had cleared, and the sunlight on the water looked like hammered gold leaf. The sheriff wiped his mouth with his wrist.

"Man, I love this stuff," he said. "My doctor says my arteries probably look like the sewer lines under Paris. I wonder what he means by that."

"What are we doing here, skipper?" I said.

"That name, 'Zerrang,' it kept bouncing around in my head. Then I remembered the story of that Negro kid back during World War II. You remember the one? Same name."

"No."

"Yeah, you do. He was electrocuted. He was fourteen years old and probably retarded. He was too small for the chair, or the equipment didn't work right, I forget which. But evidently what happened to him was awful."

His face became solemn. He lay the wax paper and piece of boudin on the cruiser's hood and slipped his hands in his pockets and gazed at the river.

"I was a witness at only one execution. The guy who got it was depraved and it never bothered me. But whenever I think of that Zerrang kid back in '43, I wonder if the human race should be on the planet . . . Take a walk with me," he said.

We crossed an irrigation ditch on a board plank and entered a stand of hackberry and persimmon trees on the riverbank. Up ahead, through the foliage, I could see three spacious breezy homes on big green lots. But here, inside the tangle of trees and air vines and black-berry bushes, was Louisiana's more humble past—a cypress shack that was only a pile of boards now, some of them charred, a privy that had collapsed into the hole under it, a brick chimney that had toppled like broken teeth into the weeds.

"This is where the boy's family lived, at least until a bunch of drunks set their shack on fire. The boy had one brother, and the brother had a son named Mookie. What do you think of that?" he said.

"Where'd you get all this, Sheriff?" I asked.

"From my dad, just this morning. He's ninety-two years old now. However, his memory is remarkable. Sometimes it gives him no rest." The sheriff turned over a blackened board with the toe of his half-topped boot.

"Did your father grow up around here?"

The sheriff rubbed the calluses of one palm on the backs of his knuckles.

"Sir?" I said.

"He was one of the drunks who burned them out. We can't blame Mookie Zerrang on the greaseballs in Miami. He's of our own mak-ing, Dave."

Chapter
34

BATIST HAD BEEN released from the hospital that day, and after work I shopped for him at the grocery in town and then drove out to his house.

He was sitting in a soft, stuffed chair on the gallery, wearing a flannel shirt over the bandages that were taped on his shoulders. His daughter, a large, square woman who looked more Indian than black, was in the side yard, hammering the dust out of a quilt with an old tennis racquet.

I told Batist the story about the Zerrang family, the fourteen-year-old boy who was cooked alive in the electric chair, the drunks who burned his home.

Batist's face was impassive while I spoke. His broad hands were motionless on his thighs, the knuckles like carved wood.

"My daddy got killed by lightning working for twenty cents an hour," he said. "The white man owned the farm knowed mules draw lightning, but he sat on his gallery while it was storming all over the sky and tole my daddy to keep his plow turned in the field, not to come out till he'd cut the last row. That's what he done to my daddy. But I ain't growed up to hate other people for it, no."

"You need anything else, partner?"

"That nigger's out yonder in the swamp. Fat Daddy's wife had a dream about him. He was wading through the water, with a big fold-out knife in his hand, the kind you dress deer with."

"Don't believe in that stuff, Batist."

"Nigger like that come out of hell, Dave. Don't say he cain't go in your dreams."

I walked back out to my truck, trying not to think about his words, or the fact that Fat Daddy's wife had somehow seen in her dream the type of wide-bladed, foldout game dressing knife that Mookie Zerrang had used to murder Lonnie Felton and his girlfriend at Henderson Swamp.

EARLY THE NEXT morning I called an old friend of mine named Minos Dautrieve at the DEA in New Orleans. Then I called Buford at his house.

"Meet me in City Park," I said.

"Considering our track record, that seems inappropriate, Dave," he said.

"Persephone Green is destroying your life. Is that appropriate?"

A half hour later I was sitting at a picnic table when I saw him get out of his car by the old brick fire station in the park and walk through the oak trees toward me. He wore a windbreaker over an LSU T-shirt and white pleated slacks without a belt. His curly hair was damp and freshly combed and he had shaved so closely that his cheeks glowed with color. He sat down at the plank table and folded his hands. I pushed a Styrofoam cup of coffee toward him and opened the top of a take-out container.

"Sausage and eggs from Victor's," I said.

"No, thanks."

"Suit yourself," I said, and wrapped a piece of French bread around a sausage patty and dipped it in my coffee. Then I put it back in my plate without eating it. "Persephone Green is the bag lady for the Giacano family and Jimmy Ray Dixon and every other New Orleans lowlife who put money into your campaign. The payback is the chain of state hospitals for drunks and addicts," I said.

"The contracts are all going to legitimate corporations, Dave. I don't know all their stockholders. Why should I?"

"Stockholders? Dock tried to squeeze out Short Boy Jerry. When Jerry Joe wouldn't squeeze, they had him beaten to death. Is that what stockholders do?"

"Is this why you got me out here?"

"No. I couldn't figure why you kept this sixties character, Clay Mason, around. Then I remembered you'd published some papers on psychopharmacology, you know, curing drunks with drugs and all that jazz."

"You belong to AA. You know only one point of view. It's not your fault. But there're other roads to recovery."

"That's why you're on the spike yourself?"

I saw the hurt in his face, the stricture in his throat.

"I talked to a friend in the DEA this morning," I said. "His people think Mason's got money in your hospital chain. They also think he's involved with some crystal meth labs down in Mexico. That's mean shit, Buford. Bikers dig it for gangbangs, stomping people's ass, stuff like that."

"Do you get a pleasure out of this? Why do you have this obsession with me and my wife? Can't you leave us in peace?"

"Maybe I've been in the same place you are."

"You're going to save me? . . ." He shook his head, then his eyes grew close together and filmed over. He sat very still for a long time, like a man who imagined himself riding a bicycle along the rim of a precipice. "It's Karyn they own."

His face darkened with anger. He stared at the bayou, as though the reflected sunlight he saw there could transport him out of the moment he had just created for himself.

"How?" I asked. "The cheating back in college? Persephone has been blackmailing her over something that happened twenty years ago?"

"You know how many educational and honor societies she belongs to? She'd be disgraced. The irony is she didn't need to cheat. She was a good student on her own."

But not number one, I thought.

He studied my eyes and seemed to see the thought buried there.

"If you tell anybody this, I'll sue you for libel. Then I'll personally kick your ass," he said.

"I'm not your problem."

His face was puffed, naked, the eyes like brown marbles in a pan of water.

I picked up my coffee and the sausage patty I'd wrapped in a piece of French bread and walked to my truck. The sunlight looked like yellow smoke through the trees. Buford still sat at the plank table, his forehead on his palm, oblivious to the camellias that were in full bloom along the banks of Bayou Teche.

I DIDN'T TELL BUFORD all the content of my conversation with my friend Minos Dautrieve at the DEA in New Orleans. Minos and his colleagues were about to raid the ranch of Clay Mason seven hundred miles below the Texas border, in the state of Jalisco.

And Helen Soileau and I were invited.

Chapter 35

We flew into Guadalajara at noon with Minos and two other DEA agents. Minos was a tall, lean, cynical, good-natured man with blond close-cropped hair that was starting to whiten. When he had played forward for LSU years ago, sportswriters had nicknamed him "Dr. Dunkenstein" for the ferocious rim-jarring slam dunks that were his trademark. As we taxied toward the hangar, he pulled back the curtain on the charter plane's window and looked at the hills in the distance, then at a parked van with three wide backseats and, leaning against it, an unshaved man in blue jeans and a maroon football jersey with a holstered pistol and a gold shield clipped onto his belt.

"There's our ride," he said.

Helen stared out the window.

"I don't believe it. It's that smart-ass, what's-his-name, Heriberto, the one looks like his hair was cut with garden clippers," she said.

"You know that guy?" Minos asked.

"He's a Mexican drug agent. A priest up in the mountains told us he's dirty," I said.

"They all are. One of our guys got sold out here and tortured to death," Minos said. "This guy's fairly harmless."

"Great character reference," Helen said.

We drove out of the city and through the small village of Zapopan. In the center of the village square was a gazebo, surrounded by rain trees, where a band was playing and children were firing out of milk bottles rockets that popped high in the sky. On one side of the square was a grayish pink eighteenth-century cathedral whose stone steps had been worn smooth and cupped down the center by the knees of thousands of penitents who worked themselves painfully up the steps on their birthdays, simultaneously saying a rosary.

"That's a famous church. The statue of the Virgin of Zapopan's in there. There been a lot of miracles here, man," Heriberto said.

"This is the place," I said to Helen.

"What place?" she said.

"Mingo Bloomberg told me the guy named Araña was from a village in Jalisco that had a famous religious statue in it," I said.

Heriberto steered around a parked bus, on top of which sat two soldiers in camouflage fatigues and steel pots. A third soldier was urinating in the street. The street sign on the corner said EMILIANO ZAPATA.

"The guy the *rurales* shot by the mines? Yeah, he should have gone to church a lot more. But was *Indio*, you know. One day they're in church, the next day they're drunk, chasing *puta*, causing a lot of shit with the government. See, man, their real problem is they ain't big on work," he said.

Helen leaned forward from the seat behind us. "How about shutting the fuck up?" she said.

"*Gringuita*, I ain't got nothing against these people. But in the south they been killing our soldiers. You want to see what happens?" Heriberto said, lifting a shoebox of photographs from under the seat.

The photos were black-and-white, creased and hand-soiled around the edges, as though they had been passed around for viewing many times. In one photo three dead rebels lay by the side of a road, their bandannas still tied over the lower half of their faces. They had on U.S. Army web gear and bandoliers and looked like they had been killed while running. Several other photos showed another scene from different angles; a half dozen male corpses had been strung up by their feet from an adobe colonnade, their fingers inches above the dirt, their faces featureless with dried blood.

"The old guy we gonna see this afternoon? He encourages these guys, gives them money for guns, gets them killed. The guy comes from your country, *gringuita*," Heriberto said.

"If I were you, I wouldn't say any more," I said.

He opened his fingers in the air, as though he were releasing an invisible bird from them, and drove out of the village toward the mountains and a place that could have been sawed out of the revolutionary year of 1910.

WE DROVE ON a high switchback rock road through dead trees and a boulder-strewn landscape and rain that covered the windows like running plastic, then crested a ridge that was blackened by a forest fire, dancing with lightning, and dropped down out of the storm into sunlight again and a long cultivated valley with green hills in the distance and a volcano that was beveled across the top as though it had been sheared by tin snips. The road followed a river with wide, red clay alluvial banks that were scissored with the tracks of livestock, then we were inside another village, this one with cobblestone streets, buff-colored colonnades, a stone watering trough in front of the *cervecería*, a tiny open-air market where bees combs and uncured meat were sold off wood carts that were boxed with screens to keep out the blowflies.

The streets and walkways under the colonnades were filled with soldiers. They were all young and carried World War II M-1 rifles and M-16's. Some of the M-16's had a knob welded onto the bolt, which meant they were early Vietnam-era issue, notorious among grunts for the bolt that often jammed and had to be driven into the chamber with the heel of the hand.

We stood in the street while Minos talked with a collection of Mexican drug agents gathered around the tailgate of an army six-by. The air was shining and cool after the rain, and you could see for miles. Heriberto stared off in the distance at a rambling white ranch house with a blue tile roof on the slope of a hill. His legs were spread slightly, his expression contemplative.

"Big day for the *Tejano*. We gonna fuck him up good, man," he said.

"That's where he lives? You think maybe he's seen us coming?" I asked.

"We cut his phone. He ain't going nowhere."

I took Minos aside.

"What are they expecting to find up there, the Russian Army?" I said.

"A lot of these guys speak English, Dave."

"They've blown the operation."

"Not in their mind. This is how they say 'get out of town' to people they normally can't touch. Mason should be flattered."

"You don't like him?"

"My sister was a flowerchild back in the sixties. She thought this guy was a great man. She got loaded on hash and acid and floated out on the sunset from a ten-story window."

We followed a caravan of six army trucks down a winding dirt road to the walled compound that surrounded Clay Mason's ranch. The walls were topped with broken glass and spirals of razor wire, and the wood gates at the entrance were chain-locked and barred with a crossbeam inside. The lead truck, which was fronted with a plow-shaped dozer blade, gained speed, roaring across the potholes, the soldiers in back rocking back and forth, then crashed through the gates and blew them off their hinges.

The soldiers trashed the house, fanned out into the yards and out-buildings, kicked chickens out of their way like exploding sacks of feathers, and for no apparent reason shot a pig running from a barn and threw it down the well.

"Can you put a stop to this bullshit?" I said to Minos.

"You see that fat slob with the Sam Browne belt on? He's a grad-uate of the School of the Americas at Fort Benning. He also owns a whorehouse. He knocked the glass eye out of a girl for sassing him. No, thanks."

While his house was being torn apart, Clay Mason leaned against a cedar post on his front porch and smoked a hand-rolled cigarette, his pixie eyes fixed on me and Minos. His hair extended like white straw from under his domed Stetson hat.

"Karyn warned me you're a vindictive man," he said.

"I'm sorry about your place. It's not my doing," I said.

"Like hell it isn't." Then a yellow tooth glinted behind his lip and he added, "You little pisspot."

He flipped his cigarette away, walked to the corner of his house on his cane, and urinated in the yard, audibly passing gas with his back turned to us, shaking his penis, a small, hatted, booted man, in a narrow, ratty coat, whose power had touched thousands of young lives.

Helen and I walked behind the ranch house, where the soldiers had forced five field hands to lean spread-eagled against the stone wall of the barn. The field hands were young and frightened and kept turning their heads to see if guns were being pointed at their backs. The soldiers shook them down but kept them leaning on their arms against the wall.

"I don't like being in on this one, Dave," Helen said.

"Don't watch it. We'll be out of here soon," I said.

We walked inside the barn. The loft was filled with hay, the horse stalls slatted with light, the dirt floor soft as foam rubber with dried manure. Through the doors at the far end I could see horses belly-deep in grass against a blue mountain.

Hanging from pegs on a wood post, like a set used by only one man, were a pair of leather chaps, a bridle, a yellow rain slicker, a sleeveless knitted riding vest, flared gloves made from deer hide, and two heavy Mexican spurs with rowels as big as half dollars. I rotated one of the rowels with my thumb. The points were sticky and coated with tiny pieces of brown hair.

Behind the post, a silver saddle was splayed atop a sawhorse. I ran my hand across the leather, the cool ridges of metal, the seared brand of a Texas cattle company on one flap. The cantle was incised with roses, and in the back of the cantle was a mother-of-pearl inlay of an opened camellia.

"What is it?" Helen said.

"Remember, the guy named Araña said the *bugarron* rode a silver saddle carved with flowers? I think Clay Mason's our man."

"What can you do about it?"

"Nothing."

"That's it?"

"Who knows?" I said.

We walked back into the sun's glare and the freshness of the day and the wind that smelled of water and grass and horses in the fields.

But the young field hands spread-eagled against the stone wall of the barn were not having a good day at all. The shade was cool in the lee of the barn, but they were sweating heavily, their arms trembling with tension and exertion. One boy had a dark inverted V running down his pants legs, and the soldiers were grinning at his shame.

"School of the Americas?" I said to the fat man in the Sam Browne belt. I tried to smile.

He wore tinted prescription glasses and stood taller than I. His eyes looked at me indolently, then moved to Helen, studying her figure.

"What you want?" he said.

"How about cutting these guys some slack? They're not traffickers, they're just *campesinos*, right?" I said.

"We decide what they are. You go on with the woman . . . Is *guapa*, huh? Is maybe lesbian but *puta* is *puta*." He held out his palms and cupped them, as though he were holding a pair of cantaloupes.

"What'd you say?" Helen asked.

"He didn't say anything," I said.

"Yeah, he did. Say it again, you bucket of bean shit, and see what happens."

The officer turned away, a wry smile on his mouth, a light in the corner of his eye.

She started to step toward him, but I moved in front of her, my eyes fastened on hers. The anger in her gaze shifted to me, like a person breaking glassware indiscriminately, then I saw it die in her face. I walked with her toward the ranch house, the backs of my fingers touching her hand. She widened the space between us.

"Next time don't interfere," she said.

"Those kids would have taken our weight."

"Oh yeah? . . . Well . . . I'm sure you're right . . . You swinging dicks are always right . . . Let's close it down here. I've had my share of the tomato patch for today."

She walked ahead of me through the open front door of the house into the living room, where Clay Mason sat in a deep deer-hide chair amid a litter of shattered glass, antique firearms stripped from the walls, splayed books, and overturned furniture. On one stucco wall, pinned inside a broken viewing case, was a sun-faded flag of the Texas republic.

Mason's hands were folded on top of his cane, his eyes narrow and liquid with resentment.

"Don't get up . . . I just need to use your john . . . Such a gentleman . . ." she said, and continued on into the back of the house, without ever slowing her step.

"Looks like you're going to skate," I said.

"My family earned every goddamn inch of this place. We'll be here when the rest of you are dust."

An upper corner of the Texas flag had fallen loose from the blue felt backboard it was pinned to. I reached through the broken glass and smoothed the cloth flat and replaced the pin. Faded strips of butternut cloth, inscribed in almost illegible ink with the names of Civil War battles, were sewn around the flag's borders.

"This flag belonged to the Fourth Texas. Those were John Bell Hood's boys," I said.

"My great-grandfather carried that flag."

"It was your family who lived on the ranch next to the LaRoses', west of the Pecos, wasn't it? Jerry Joe Plumb told me how y'all slant drilled and ran wets across the river."

"Do you read newspapers? There's a revolution being fought here. Everything you're doing helps those men out there kill Mayan Indians."

"Men like you always have a banner, Dr. Mason. The truth is, you live vicariously through the suffering of other people."

"Get out . . ." He flicked at the air with the backs of his fingers, as though he were dispelling a bad odor.

I tried to think of a rejoinder, but I had none. Clay Mason had spent a lifetime floating above the wreckage he had precipitated, seemingly immune to all the Darwinian and moral laws that affected the rest of us, and my rhetoric sounded foolish compared to the invective he had weathered for decades.

I stepped across the broken glass on the oak floor toward the open doorway. Outside, the soldiers were loading up in the six-bys.

"Hold on, Streak," Helen said behind me. "It looks like our friend flushed the candy store down the commode. Except it backed up on him. Guess what got stuck under the rim?"

She dipped the tip of her little finger into a child's balloon and held the white powder up in a column of sunlight, then wiped her finger on a piece of tissue paper.

"It's a little wet. Can you call that fat guy in, see if he wants to do the taste test?" she said.

Chapter
36

I SHOULD HAVE SEEN it coming but I didn't.

The morning after our return from Guadalajara the sheriff opened the door to my office and leaned inside.

"That was Lafayette PD. You'd better get over there. Sabelle Crown's pinned inside a car on the Southern Pacific tracks."

"What happened?"

"She was abducted from the city golf course by this guy Zerrang. What was she doing on a golf course?"

"She feeds the pigeons there."

"Anyway, Zerrang must have taken her somewhere. Evidently it was pretty bad. When he was finished, he left her unconscious in her car on the train tracks. Why's Zerrang after Sabelle Crown?"

"He wants her father," I said.

"I don't get it."

"Mookie Zerrang works for Persephone Green and Jimmy Ray Dixon. Jimmy Ray knows sooner or later Aaron's going to kill him."

"What for?"

"I think it has to do with Sabelle."

"To tell you the truth, Dave, I really don't give a damn about any of these people's motivations. It's like figuring out why shit stinks. I just wish they'd stay the hell out of our parish. Get over there, will you?"

The sheriff brushed something out of his eye, then he said, "Except

305

why would this guy torture a woman, then leave her on the train tracks? Why didn't he just kill her and put her out of her misery?"

"Because he hurts a lot more people this way," I said.

Helen Soileau and I drove in a cruiser on the four-lane to Lafayette. Emergency flares burned inside the fog when we arrived at the railroad crossing where the freight locomotive had struck Sabelle's gas-guzzler broadside and pushed it fifty yards down the rails in a spray of sparks.

We parked on the shoulder of the road and walked through the weeds to the car's wreckage by the side of the tracks. It lay upside down, the engine block driven through the firewall, the roof mashed against the steering column. Lafayette firemen had covered the outside metal, the engine, and gas tank with foam and were trying to wedge open the driver's window with a hydraulic jack.

A paramedic had worked his way on his stomach through the inverted passenger's window, and I could hear him talking inside. A moment later he crawled back out. His shirt and both of his latex gloves were spotted with blood.

He sat in the grass, his hands on his thighs. A fireman put a plug of tobacco in the paramedic's mouth to bite off, then helped him up by one arm.

"How's it look?" I said.

"The car didn't burn. Otherwise, that lady don't have a whole lot of luck," he replied. He looked into my eyes and saw the unanswered question still there. He shook his head.

I took off my coat, slipped my clip-on holster off my belt, and squeezed through the passenger's window into the car's interior. I could smell gas and the odor of musty cushions and old grease and burnt electrical wires.

Sabelle's head and upper torso were layered with crumpled metal, so that she had virtually no mobility. I couldn't see the lower portion of her body at all. She coughed, and I felt the spray touch my face like a warm mist.

"What'd he do to you, kiddo?" I said.

"Everything."

"Those guys out there are the best. They'll have you out of here soon."

"When I close my eyes I can feel the world turning. If I don't open them quickly, I won't get back . . . I betrayed Daddy, Dave."

"It's not your fault."

"Mookie Zerrang knows where he is."

"There's still time to stop it. If you'll trust me."

Her eyes went out of focus, then settled on mine again. One cheek was marbled with broken veins. The rent metal around her head looked like an aura fashioned out of warped pewter.

She told me where to look.

"Jimmy Ray Dixon was your pimp in New Orleans, wasn't he? Then he took you north, to work for him in Chicago."

"I made my own choices. I got no kick coming."

"Your father murdered Ely Dixon, didn't he?"

"Wipe my nose, Streak. My hands are caught inside something."

I worked my handkerchief from my back pocket and touched at her upper lip with it. She coughed again, long and hard this time, gagging in her throat, and I tried to hold her chin so she wouldn't cut it on a strip of razored metal that was wrapped across her chest. The handkerchief came away with a bright red flower in the middle of it.

"I have to go now," I said.

"Tell Daddy I'm sorry," she said.

"You're the best daughter a father could have, Sabelle."

I thought her eyes wrinkled at the corners. But they didn't. Her eyes were haunted with fear, and my words meant nothing.

I backed out of the passenger window onto the grass. I could smell water in a ditch, the loamy odor of decayed pecan husks in an orchard, taste the fog on my tongue, hear the whirring sound of automobile tires out on the paved road. I walked away just as a team of firemen and uniformed Lafayette cops used the Jaws of Life to wrench open one side of the wrecked car. The sprung metal sounded just like a human scream.

* * *

HELEN AND I DROVE down I-10 toward the Atchafalaya River. It was misting, and the fields and oak and palm trees along the roadside were gray and wet-looking, and up ahead I could see the orange and blue glow of a filling station inside the fog that rolled off the river.

"What are you worrying about?" Helen said.

I touched the brake on the cruiser.

"I've got to do something," I said.

"What?"

"Maybe Zerrang didn't head right for the Basin. Maybe there's another way to pull his plug."

"You don't look too happy about it, whatever it is," she said.

"How would you like to save Buford LaRose's career for him?" I said.

I called his house from the filling station pay phone. Through the glass I could see the willows on the banks of the Atchafalaya, where we were to meet two powerboats from the St. Martin Parish Sheriff's Department.

"Buford?" I said.

"What is it?"

"Sabelle Crown's dead."

"Oh man, don't tell me that."

"She was tortured, then left on a train track in her car by Mookie Zerrang."

I could hear him take the receiver away from his ear, hear it scrape against a hard surface. Then I heard him breathing in the mouthpiece again.

"You were right about Aaron Crown," I said. "He killed Ely Dixon. But it was a mistake. He went to the house to kill Jimmy Ray. He didn't know that Jimmy Ray had moved out and rented it to his brother."

"Why would he want to kill Jimmy Ray Dixon?"

"Jimmy Ray got Sabelle started in the life . . . You're vindicated, Buford. That means you get word to Persephone Green to call Mookie Zerrang off."

"Are you insane? Do you think I control these people? What in God's name is the matter with you?"

"No, they control you."

"Listen, I just had that ghoul beating on my front door. I ran him off my property with a pistol."

"Which ghoul?"

"Who else, Dock Green. His wife dumped him. He accused me and Karyn of being involved in a ménage à trois with her. I guess that's her style."

"It seems late to be righteous," I said.

"What's that mean?"

"You treated Sabelle Crown like shit."

He was silent for what seemed a long time. Then he said, "Yeah, I didn't do right by her . . . I wish I could change it . . . Good-bye, Dave."

He quietly hung up the phone.

HELEN AND I SAT in the cabin of the St. Martin Parish sheriff's boat. The exhaust pipes idled at the water-line while a uniformed deputy smoked a cigarette in the open hatchway and waited for the boat skipper to return from his truck with a can of gasoline.

I could feel Helen's eyes on my face.

"What is it?" I said.

"I don't like the way you look."

"It hasn't been a good day."

"Maybe you shouldn't be in on this one," she said.

"Is that right?"

"Unless he deals it, Mookie Zerrang comes back alive, Streak."

"Well, you never know how things are going to work out," I said.

Her lips were chapped, and she rubbed them with the ball of her finger, her eyes glazed over with hidden thoughts.

WE WENT DOWN the Atchafalaya, with the spray blowing back across the bow, then we entered a side channel and a bay that was surrounded by flooded woods. Under the sealed sky, the water in the bay was an unnatural, luminous yellow, as though it were the only element in its environment that possessed color. Up ahead, in the mist, I could see the shiny silhouette of an abandoned oil platform, then a canal through the woods and inside the tangle of air vines and cypress and willow trees a shack built on wood pilings.

"That's it," I said to the boat pilot.

He cut back on the throttle, stared through the glass at the woods, then reversed the engine so we didn't drift into the shore.

"You want to go head-on in there?" he asked.

"You know another way to do it?" I said.

"Bring in some SWAT guys on a chopper and blow that shack into toothpicks," he replied.

A St. Martin Parish plainclothes homicide investigator who was on the other boat walked out on the bow and used a bullhorn, addressing the shack as though he did not know who its occupants were.

"We want to talk to y'all that's inside. You need to work your way down that ladder with one hand on your head. There won't nobody get hurt," he said.

But there was no sound, except the idling boat engines and the rain that had started falling in large drops on the bay's surface. The plainclothes wiped his face with his hand and tried again.

"Aaron, we know you in there. We afraid somebody's come out here to hurt you, podna. Ain't it time to give it up?" he said.

Again, there was silence. The plainclothes' coat was dark with rain and his tie was blown back across his shirt. He looked toward our boat, shrugged his shoulders, and went inside the cabin.

"Let's do it, skipper," I said to the pilot.

He pushed the throttle forward and took our boat into the canal. The wake from our boat receded back through the trees, gathering with it sticks and dead hyacinths, washing over logs and finally disappearing into the flooded undergrowth. The second boat eased into the shallows behind us until its hull scraped on the silt.

Helen and I dropped off the bow into the water and immediately sank to our thighs, clouds of gray mud ballooning around us. She carried a twelve-gauge Remington shotgun, with the barrel sawed off an inch above the pump. I pulled back the slide on my .45, chambered the top round in the magazine, and set the safety.

A flat-bottom aluminum boat with an outboard engine was tied to a piling under the shack. Helen and I waded through the water, ten yards apart, not speaking, our eyes fixed on the shack's shuttered windows and the ladder that extended upward to an open door with a gunny sack curtain blowing in the door frame.

On my left, the St. Martin plainclothes and three uniformed deputies were spread out in a line, breaking their way through a stand of willows.

Helen and I walked under the shack and listened. I cupped my hand on a piling to feel for movement above.

Nothing.

Helen held the twelve-gauge at port arms, her knuckles white on the stock and pump. Her faded blue jeans were drenched up to her rump. The air was cold and felt like damp flannel against the skin, and I could smell an odor like beached gars and gas from a sewer main.

Then I felt something tick against my face, like a mild irritant, a wet leaf, a blowfly. Unconsciously, I wiped at it with my hand, then I felt it again, harder this time, against my eyebrow, my forehead, in my hair, directly in my face as I stared upward at the plank floor of the shack.

Helen's mouth was parted wide, her face white.

I wiped my face on my coat sleeve and stared at the long red smear across the cloth.

I felt a revulsion go through my body as though I had been spat upon. I tore off my coat, soaked it in the water at my knees, and wiped my face and hair with it, my hand trembling.

Above me, strings of congealed blood hung from the planks and lifted and fell in the wind.

I moved out from under the shack, slipped the safety off the .45, and began climbing the ladder, which was set at a gradual angle, almost like stairs. Helen moved out into the water, away from the shack, and aimed the twelve gauge at the door above my head, then, just before I went inside, swung the barrel away and followed me.

I reached the top rung and paused, my hand on the doorjamb. The gunny sack curtain billowed back on the nails it hung from, exposing a rusted icebox without power, a table and chair, a solitary wood bunk, a coon hide that someone had been fleshing with a spoon.

I pulled myself up and went inside, tearing away the curtain, kicking back the door against the wall.

Except it did not fly back against the wall.

I felt the wood knock into meat and bone, a massive and dense weight that did not surrender space.

I clenched the .45 in both hands and pointed it at the enormous black shape behind the door, my finger slick with sweat inside the trigger guard.

My eyes wouldn't assimilate the naked man in front of me. Nor the fact that he was upside down. Nor what had been done to him.

The fence wire that had been looped around his ankles and notched into the roof beam was buried so deeply in his ankles that it was nearly invisible.

Helen lumbered into the room, her shotgun pointed in front of her. She lowered it to her side and looked at the hanging man.

"Oh boy," she said. She propped open the shutter on a window and cleared her throat and spit. She looked back at me, then blew out her breath. Her face was discolored, as though she had been staring into a cold wind. "I guess he got his," she said. Then she went to the window again, with the back of her wrist to her mouth. But this time she collected herself, and when she looked at me again her face was composed.

"Come on, we can still nail him," I said.

The plainclothes homicide investigator and two of the uniformed deputies were waiting for us at the bottom of the ladder.

"What's up there?" the plainclothes said. His eyes tried to peel meaning out of our faces. "*What*, it's some kind of company secret?"

"Go look for yourself. Be careful what you step in," Helen said.

"Crown killed Mookie Zerrang. He couldn't have gone far," I said.

"He ain't gone far at all," the third deputy said, sloshing toward us from the opposite side of the woods. "Look up yonder through that high spot."

We all stared through the evenly spaced tree trunks at a dry stretch of compacted silt that humped out of the water like the back of a black whale. It was covered with palmettos and crisscrossed with the webbed tracks of nutrias, and in the middle of the palmettos, squatting on his haunches, smoking a hand-rolled cigarette, was Aaron Crown.

We waded toward him, our guns still drawn. If he heard or saw us, or even cared if we were in his proximity, he showed no sign.

His body and clothes were painted with blood from his pate to the mud-encrusted basketball shoes he wore. His eyes, which were finally drained of all the heat and energy that had defined his life, seemed to look out of a scarlet mask. We stood in a circle around him, our weapons pointed at the ground. In the damp air, smoke hung at the corner of his mouth like wisps of cotton.

"You know about Sabelle?" I asked.

"That 'un in yonder couldn't talk about nothing else before he died," he replied.

"You're an evil man, Aaron Crown," I said.

"I reckon it otherwise." He rubbed the cigarette's hot ash between his fingers until it was dead. "If them TV people is out there, I need to wash up."

He looked up at our faces, his lidless eyes waiting for an answer.

Chapter
37

Oɴ Cʜʀɪsᴛᴍᴀs ᴍᴏʀɴɪɴɢ I sat at the kitchen table and looked at a photograph in the *Daily Iberian* of Buford and Karyn dancing together at the country club. They looked like people who would live forever.

Bootsie paused behind me, her palm resting on my shoulder.

"What are you thinking about?" she asked.

"Jerry Joe Plumb . . . No journalist will ever mention his name in association with theirs, but he paid their dues for them."

"He paid his own, too, Dave."

"Maybe."

The window was open and a balmy wind blew from my neighbor's pasture and swelled the curtains over the sink. I filled a cup with coffee and hot milk and walked outside in the sunshine. Alafair sat at the redwood picnic table, playing with Tripod in her lap and listening to the tape she had made of the records on Jerry Joe's jukebox. She flipped Tripod on his back and bounced him gently up and down by pulling his tail while he pushed at her forearm with his paws.

"Thanks for all the presents. It's a great Christmas," she said.

"Thanks for everything you gave me, too," I said.

"Can Tripod have some more eggnog ice cream?"

"Sure."

"Those creeps are gone, aren't they?"

"Yeah, the worst of the lot are. The rest get it somewhere down the road. We just don't see it."

I thought perhaps I might have to explain my remark, but I didn't. She had actually lived through more than I had in her young life, and her comprehension of the world was oftentimes far better than mine.

She went inside the house with Tripod under her arm, then came back out on the step.

"I forgot. We ate it all," she said.

"There's some in the freezer down at the shop. I'll get it," I said.

I walked down the slope through the leaves drifting out of the oak and pecan branches overhead. I had strung Christmas lights around the bait shop's windows and hung wreaths fashioned from pine boughs and holly and red ribbon on the weathered cypress walls, and Alafair had glued a Santa Claus made from satin wrapping paper to the door. The bayou was empty of boats, and the sound of my shoes was so loud on the dock that it echoed off the water and sent a cloud of robins clattering out of the trees.

I had gotten the ice cream from the game freezer and was about to lock up again when I saw Dock Green park a black Lincoln by the boat ramp and walk toward me.

"It's Christmas. We're closed," I said.

"LaRose has got my wife up at his house," he said.

"I don't believe that's true. Even if it is, she's a big girl and can make her own choices."

"I can give you that guy, diced and fried."

"Not interested."

"It ain't right."

He sat down at a spool table and stared out at the bayou. His neck was as stiff as a chunk of sewer pipe. A muscle jumped in his cheek.

"I think you were involved with Jerry Joe's death. I just can't prove it. But I don't have to talk with you, either. So how about getting out of here?" I said.

He rubbed the heel of his hand in one eye.

"I never killed nobody. I need Persephone back. It ain't right he can steal my wife, pull a gun on me, I can't do nothing about it . . . I told Seph this is how it'd be if we messed with people was born with money . . . They take, they don't give," he said.

Then I realized he was drunk.

"Get a motel room or go back to your camp, Dock. I'll get somebody to drive you," I said.

He rose to his feet, as though from a trance, and said, more to the wind than to me, "He controls things above the ground, but he don't hear the voices that's down in the earth . . . They can call me a geek, it don't matter, her and me are forever."

I went back into the shop and called for a cruiser. When I came outside again, he was gone.

THAT NIGHT ALAFAIR and Bootsie and I went out to eat, then drove down East Main, through the corridor of live oaks, looking at the lights and decorations on the nineteenth-century homes along Bayou Teche. We passed the city hall and library, the flood-lit grotto, which contained a statue of Christ's mother, where the home of George Washington Cable had once stood, the darkened grounds and bamboo border around the Shadows, and in the center of town the iron-and-wood drawbridge over the Teche.

I drove past the old Southern Pacific station and up the St. Martinville road, and, without thinking, like a backward glance at absolved guilt, I let my eyes linger on the abandoned frame house where Karyn LaRose had grown up. The garage that had contained her father's boxes of gumballs and plastic monster teeth and vampire fingernails still stood at the front of the property, the doors padlocked, and I wondered when she drove past it if she ever saw the little girl who used to play there in the yard, her hands sticky with the rainbow seepage from the gum that mildewed and ran through the cracks inside.

"Look, up the road, y'all, it's a fire," Alafair said.

Beyond the next curve you could see the reddish orange bloom in the sky, the smoke that trailed back across the moon. We pulled to the side of the road for a fire truck to pass.

"Dave, it's Buford and Karyn's house," Bootsie said.

We came around the curve, and across the cleared acreage the house looked like it was lit from within by molten metal. Only one pump truck had arrived, and the firemen were pulling a hose from the truck toward the front porch.

I stopped on the opposite side of the road and ran toward the truck. I could already feel the heat from the house against my skin.

"Is anybody in there?" I said. The faces of the firemen looked like yellow tallow in the light from the flames.

"Somebody was at the window upstairs but they couldn't make it out," a lieutenant said. "You're from the sheriff's department, aren't you?"

"Right."

"There's a trail of gasoline from the back of the house out to the stables. What the hell kind of security did y'all have out here?"

"Buford worried about Aaron Crown, not Dock Green," I said.

"Who?" he said.

Another pump truck came up the road, but the heat had punched holes in the roof now, the poplars against the side wall were wrapped with fire, and the glow through the collapsing shingles bloomed in an ever-widening circumference, defining everything in red-black shapes that was Buford's—the brick stables and tack rooms, the fields that had already been harrowed for next year's planting, the company store with the barrels of pecans on each side of the front doors, the stark and leafless tree that his ancestors in the Knights of the White Camellia had used to lynch members of the carpetbag government, the horses with Mexican brands that spooked and thudded through the rolling hardwoods as though they had never been bridled or broken.

Then I saw Buford come through the front door, a water-soaked blanket held in a cone over his head.

He tore the blanket away and flung it aside, as though the blanket itself contained the heat that had scalded his body. He smelled like ashes and charcoal and scorched hair, and smoke rose in dirty strings from his clothes.

"Where is she?" he said, staring wild-eyed at the firemen in his yard.

"Who? Who else is in there?" a fireman said.

"Where is she, Dave?"

"I don't know, Buford," I replied.

"She was on the stairs, right next to me . . ."

"She didn't make it out, partner," I said.

I reached out to take his arm in my hand. I felt the smooth hardness of his triceps brush my palm, then he was gone, running toward the rectangle of flame beyond the Greek pillars on the front porch. A fireman in a canvas coat and a big hat tried to tackle him and hit hard and empty-armed against the brick walkway.

Buford went up the steps, his arms in front of his face, wavering for just a moment in the heat that withered his skin and chewed apart the interior of his house, then he crossed his forearms over his eyes and went through the flames and disappeared inside.

I heard a fireman yell, "Pour it on him, pour it on him, pour it on him, goddamn it!"

The pressurized spray of water caromed off the doorway and dissected the vortex of fire that was dissolving the stairway, filling the chandeliers with music, eating the floor away, blowing windows out into the yard.

Then we saw them, just for a moment, like two featureless black silhouettes caught inside a furnace, joined at the hip, their hands stretched outward, as though they were offering a silent testimony about the meaning of their own lives before they stepped backward into the burning lake that had become their new province.

Epilogue

SPRING DIDN'T COME for a long time that year. The days were cold well into March, the swamp gray with winterkill. Batist would run his trotlines each morning at sunrise, his pirogue knocking against the swollen base of the cypress trunks. I would watch him from the bait shop window while he retrieved each empty hook and rebaited it and dropped it back in the water, wiping the coldness off his hand on his trousers, the mist rising about his bent shoulders. Then he would come back inside, shivering unduly inside his quilted jacket, and we would drink coffee together and prepare the chickens and sausage links for the few fishermen or tourists who might be in that day.

Persephone and Dock Green were never seen again; some say they fled the country, perhaps to South America. The irony was that even though a filling station attendant in St. Martinville identified Dock as the man who had bought gas in a can from him on the night Buford and Karyn died, the gas can found on the LaRose plantation had no fingerprints on it, and without an eyewitness to the arson Dock would have never been convicted.

The greater truth was that Dock Green's strain of madness had always served a function, just as Aaron Crown's had, and the new governor of Louisiana, a practical-minded businessman, was not given to brooding over past events and letting them encumber his vision of the future.

Jimmy Ray Dixon?

He has a late-hour radio talk show in New Orleans now, and with some regularity he tells his listeners that his brother's spirit has finally been laid to rest. Why now? He doesn't answer that question. He's not comfortable with the mention of Mookie Zerrang's name, and when he hears it, his rhetoric becomes more religious and abstruse.

Dock Green's girls still work the same bars and street corners, Jimmy Ray jerks his listeners around and they love him for it, and Aaron Crown sits in a maximum security unit at Angola, denying his guilt to European journalists who have done front-page features on him.

The players don't change, just the audience.

But maybe that's just a police officer's jaded interpretation of things, since few seem interested in the death of Short Boy Jerry, a man who everyone knew operated by choice on the edge of the New Orleans underworld and hence invited his fate.

No draconian sword fell into the life of Clay Mason, either. He was expelled from Mexico and his property seized, but in a short while he was visiting college campuses again, being interviewed on the Internet, selling his shuck on TV. A patron of the arts bought him a home in the hills outside Santa Fe, where his proselytes and fellow revelers from the 1960s gathered and a famous New York photographer caught him out on the terrace, his face as craggy and ageless as the blue ring of mountains behind him, a sweat-banded Stetson crimped on his head, his pixie eyes looking directly into the camera. The cutline under the photo read, "A Lion in Winter."

But I think I've learned not to grieve on the world's ways, at least not when spring is at hand.

It rained hard the third week in March, then the sky broke clear and one morning the new season was upon us and the swamp was green again, the new leaves on the flooded stands of trees rippling in the breeze off the Gulf, the trunks of the cypress painted with lichen.

Alafair and I rode her Appaloosa bareback down the road, like two wooden clothespins mounted on its spine, and put up a kite in the wind. The kite was a big one, the paper emblazoned with an American flag, and it rose quickly into the sky, higher and higher, until it was only a distant speck above the sugarcane fields to the north.

In my mind's eye I saw the LaRose plantation from the height of Alafair's kite, the rolling hardwoods and the squared fields where Confederate and federal cavalry had charged and killed one another and left their horses screaming and disemboweled among the cane stubble, and I wondered what Darwinian moment had to effect itself before we devolved from children flying paper flags in the sky to half-formed creatures thundering in a wail of horns down the road to Roncevaux.

That night we ate crawfish at Possum's in St. Martinville and went by the old church in the center of town and walked under the Evangeline Oaks next to the Teche where I first kissed Bootsie in the summer of 1957 and actually felt the tree limbs spin over my head. Alafair was out on the dock behind the church, dropping pieces of bread in a column of electric light onto the water's surface. Bootsie slipped her arm around my waist and bumped me with her hip.

"What are you thinking about, slick?" she said.

"You can't ever tell," I said.

That night she and I ate a piece of pecan pie on the picnic table in the backyard, then, like reaching your hand into the past, like giving yourself over to the world of play and nonreason that takes you outside of time, I punched on Alafair's stereo player that contained the taped recording of all the records on Jerry Joe's jukebox.

We danced to "Jolie Blon" and "Tes Yeux Bleu," then kicked it up into overdrive with "Bony Maronie," "Long Tall Sally," and "Short Fat Fanny." Out in the darkness, beyond the glow of the flood lamp in the mimosa tree, my neighbor's cattle were bunching in the coulee as an electric storm veined the sky with lightning in the south. The air was suddenly cool and thick with the sulfurous smell of ozone, the wind blowing dust out of the new cane, the wisteria on our garage flattening against the board walls while shadows and protean shapes formed and re-formed themselves, like Greek players on an outdoor stage beckoning to us, luring us from pastoral chores into an amphitheater by the sea, where we would witness once again the unfinished story of ourselves.

ABOUT THE AUTHOR

James Lee Burke, a rare winner of two Edgar Awards and named Grand Master by the Mystery Writers of America, is the author of thirty-seven novels and two short story collections, including numerous *New York Times* bestsellers, such as *Robicheaux*, *The Jealous Kind*, *Creole Belle*, and *Heaven's Prisoners*. He lives in Missoula, Montana.